PRAISE FOR JERUSHA AGEN

"You will love it."

DIANN MILLS, BESTSELLING AUTHOR OF *CONCRETE EVIDENCE*

"Jerusha Agen writes a gripping suspense filled with danger, romance, and K-9s complete with a strong faith thread. *Hidden Danger* kept me reading and on the edge of my seat from page one through the end."

SHAREE STOVER, BESTSELLING AUTHOR OF *FRAMING THE MARSHALL*

"Fast-paced, explosive thriller. I couldn't turn the pages fast enough."

CARRIE STUART PARKS, AWARD-WINNING, BESTSELLING AUTHOR OF *RELATIVE SILENCE* ON *RISING DANGER*

HIDDEN DANGER

HIDDEN DANGER

GUARDIANS UNLEASHED  BOOK ONE

JERUSHA AGEN

 SDG Words, LLC

ACKNOWLEDGMENTS

Every book I complete and publish seems nothing short of a miracle. God uses many people along the way to make that miracle happen, and I'd like to thank a few of those special people here.

To my readers and all passionate fans of Christian fiction—your enthusiasm for this book and Christian fiction has given this writer wings to fly.

Amanda Geaney, thanks for sharing your firsthand knowledge about FBOs.

Kristen Hogrefe Parnell and Stephanie M. Gammon, thank you for proving your friendship above and beyond by helping me polish this story to its finest sheen.

Jessica R. Patch, thanks for your friendship, encouragement, and for giving me some tough back cover copy love.

Sandra Ardoin and Emily Conrad, thanks for fielding my emergency questions along the path of this book's journey to publication.

The Quotidians, your support and friendship has been a special blessing. Thank you.

Mom, thank you for being the best brainstorming partner and first reader anyone could ever ask for.

To my "RA," you know who you are and that I couldn't do this without you. I thank God for you every day.

And to Him Who is able to do more than we can ask or imagine, I asked for You to make this book happen, but with the challenges before me, I didn't always imagine it could. Thank you for this miracle of another book—another story about You—in print.

To Mom, for loving imperfect me

Soli Deo Gloria

But he said to me, "My grace is sufficient for you, for my power is made perfect in weakness." Therefore I will boast all the more gladly of my weaknesses, so that the power of Christ may rest upon me. For the sake of Christ, then, I am content with weaknesses, insults, hardships, persecutions, and calamities. For when I am weak, then I am strong.

2 Corinthians 12:9-10

ONE

Cora Isaksson's pulse jerked with her arm when Jana tugged hard to the right. The golden retriever never pulled on her leash unless she caught scent of one of two things—narcotics or a human in need of rescue.

Jana tugged toward a black suitcase parked upright next to a man in the baggage claim of Minneapolis International Airport.

"Get that dog away from my luggage." The middle-aged, heavyset man had a smudge of dark hairs on his head and a long, sagging mustache that shaped his mouth into a severe frown.

Cora's mind raced. She and Jana were off the clock, finished logging in their hours searching for narcotics at Departures. The usual TSA officer who accompanied her had left, and Cora had handed in her radio for the day.

But Jana sat next to the man's suitcase and aimed her big brown eyes up at Cora.

She'd found drugs.

Cora swallowed. She glanced past the scattered crowds of people, her gaze finding the nearest glass exit doors.

A security guard, Frank O'Donnell, stood by the exit, talking to a woman with suitcases piled in a precarious stack.

Cora should be able to get help from Frank if the traveler didn't cooperate.

"I said, get it away from me." The man's voice lowered as he grabbed the long handle of his suitcase and started walking. Toward the exit.

"Sir, wait." Cora grabbed a handful of treats from her pocket on autopilot and gave them to Jana as she hurried after the escaping passenger.

A younger man stepped into the mustached man's path, halting him abruptly.

They appeared to exchange some words, then glared at Cora as she approached with Jana.

The golden smelled the suitcase, her feathered tail swishing with excitement.

"Sir, I'm afraid you're going to have to stay and allow your suitcase to be searched." Cora's voice trembled slightly as trepidation coursed through her veins. Confronting a suspect without backup from an officer was risky, but she couldn't let him go. "This is a narcotics detection K-9, and she has identified there may be illegal narcotics in your suitcase."

"I don't care what you or your dog think. You can't stop me from leaving." The man nodded to his companion, and they turned to leave again.

"No." Cora's heart thudded against her ribs, as if an instinctive warning of self-preservation. But she darted in front of the two men, using Jana's wagging body to help block them. "I'm sorry, but you can't leave." She started to turn toward Frank.

Someone grabbed her arm and yanked her backward.

Cora gasped.

"Don't you dare." The younger man leveled the threat in a low growl. He stood just behind her to one side, his body an uncomfortable inch or two away from hers. He squeezed her arm as he leaned in, an odor that suggested he hadn't bathed in a while assaulting her nostrils.

"Feel this?" He pressed something hard into her back through her jacket.

She held her breath. She'd never had a gun poking her before, but somehow, she knew without a doubt what it was. *Father, please help me.*

"You're gonna walk out of here with us like everything is normal. Got it?"

"Díaz, what are you doing?" The mustached man's gruff words returned a burst of oxygen to Cora's lungs. Would he help her?

"What does it look like?"

"We can't afford to kidnap someone right now."

"Maybe you can't." Díaz's grip on her arm cut tighter. "I can't go back to prison. We're getting out of here."

The older man cursed, making Cora wince.

Díaz dug the gun into her spine. "I'm gonna put this in my pocket, but my finger will be on the trigger the whole time. You talk or make a wrong move, and that security guard dies. And whatever other people I can take out before I go down. Got it?"

She moistened her lips as she darted her gaze around the baggage claim. There must be something she could do.

"Got it?" He jerked her arm. "Or I can start shooting right now."

"No." The word popped from her mouth with air she didn't know she had. "Don't hurt anyone. I'll go."

"Move." He released her arm, allowing blood and circulation to return with a surge of pain.

She walked toward the exit, Jana following at her side with her tail swishing as if it were the normal day it had been moments ago. *Please, Father. Don't let anyone get hurt. Show me what to do.*

If only she had made more headway with her proposal to the airport that metal detectors be installed at the baggage claim entrance. Most airports didn't have any such security measures in their arrivals area but Cora had been concerned about the vulnerability that created. And now a man had brought a gun in, just as she'd feared could happen someday.

Frank smiled as she neared.

The two men walked a few paces behind her.

Blood rushed in her ears. Should she run? Make a dash for the shuttle service counter near the doors and shout a warning to Frank?

Jana bumped lightly into Cora's leg as they walked.

No. Jana could get hurt. Frank could get shot. Anyone here could become a victim of her self-preservation.

She pasted on a smile and waved at Frank. "Have a good afternoon." Did her voice sound normal? It might have held a hint of the trembling that was now more constant than her breathing as fear took control of her body.

"You, too, Cora." Frank turned his head away as she passed through the doors.

Thank you, Lord. She must not have shown the growing terror that threatened to buckle her knees.

What would happen outside on the sidewalk? There were so many people. More than indoors but spread farther apart.

"Get in." Díaz cinched her arm in his grip again, standing too close. "Brown car."

She tried to swallow but coughed instead as frigid, January air broke into her lungs.

"Move." He pushed her forward, toward the empty brown four-door that waited by the curb. Waiting to take her. Where?

Jana nudged Cora's gloved hand with her nose.

Cora looked down at the beautiful golden's face, her hopeful gaze directed up at Cora. What would happen to Jana?

Never get in. Phoenix Gray's words blared through Cora's mind. How many times had Cora's employer told her this was where she was to draw the line? If anyone ever attempted to abduct her, she should do whatever it took to avoid getting into a vehicle. As the owner and founder of Phoenix K-9 Security and Detection Agency, Phoenix should know.

The mustached man opened the front passenger door and slipped inside as if he couldn't get away fast enough.

Díaz yanked open the back door. He started to push her inside.

She stiffened and pulled back.

Giggles.

She jerked her head to the left.

Three children hugged a suited man who kneeled on the

sidewalk. He was likely their father, probably returned from a business trip.

"They'll be the first I'll shoot. Get in."

She couldn't risk that Díaz meant what he said. She turned back to Jana and the kidnapper's car. "In."

The golden jumped in easily at the command, as calm and steady as always.

Cora sat beside Jana on the backseat, her fingers shaking as she stroked the dog's fur. Thank the Lord Jana didn't have an ounce of guardian instinct, as her co-worker Bristol liked to joke. If she did, the men might have hurt her in their effort to kidnap Cora.

Or maybe…perhaps, Jana knew something Cora didn't. That there was nothing to fear.

As Díaz jerked the car into gear and pulled away from the curb, Cora's pulse pounded in her ears.

The remainder of Phoenix's repeated warning about abductions seared her thoughts.

If you get in, you're dead.

TWO

Special Agent Kent Thomson lowered his coffee cup to the drink holder as he waited for another car, and then a shuttle, to pull out behind his suspects. He shifted into drive and slid into one of the lanes that would lead to the exit from the arrivals area of Minneapolis Airport.

He swore under his breath. What in the world were those two idiots thinking? Sure, the twenty-year-old lackey the cartel had sent for the pickup could probably be impulsive and dumb. But Marco Ramos, a regional manager for the Guajardo drug cartel's U.S. distribution network? Kent would've thought he'd do anything to stay under the radar.

Kidnapping wasn't the best way to manage that.

Assuming Kent read the signs right and this was a kidnapping.

When the suspects had exited the building with an attractive blonde, Kent was poised to add her to his mental list of suspects as an accomplice. Even when he saw the dog wearing a harness labeling it a working K-9, he couldn't be sure the woman wasn't cooperating with the cartel.

But she'd put on the brakes when the young perp pushed her toward the car.

And she'd stared at people on the sidewalk. Some kids with an adult male, it looked like from the angle of her head.

Kent had been ready to pop out and open fire on the kidnapper if he tried to shoot anyone. But it would've been messy, at best.

And not at all what he'd planned would be the outcome of this day.

The woman had gotten into the car with her dog, but with the limp posture of someone who'd lost a battle, not joined one by choice.

Kent pushed out a frustrated grunt. If this was a kidnapping, he'd have to apprehend both the suspects.

He slowed behind the vehicles as the drivers chose which path to take, either circling back into the airport maze or leaving to enter the freeway. As he'd expected, the brown sedan followed the curve to the freeway entrance ramp.

Maybe Kent would get lucky, and it'd turn out the woman was working with the cartel. Or maybe they'd take him to some location where he could catch bigger fish.

He'd let it play out. Just for a little bit. Stay close enough not to lose them but far enough back they wouldn't know they were being tailed. At least until he could figure out where they were headed or what they were up to.

After all, he couldn't be positive the willowy blonde wasn't working for them. He knew better than anyone what happened when people misjudged criminals. Looking at some kids didn't automatically make her a stand-up citizen.

He'd play it safe and assume she was as dirty as the drug dealers until he saw otherwise. He'd be more than happy to let her lead him up the chain of command in the cartel along with the other two suspects.

But if she was a hostage, this could turn ugly real fast.

The car that could be chauffeuring Cora to her death had been on the road for an hour and a half. Díaz had abandoned the freeway thirty minutes ago and now navigated snowy, half-plowed rural roads into countryside Cora didn't think she'd ever seen before.

Her training for search and rescue had taken her to forests and other wilderness areas outside the city, but not the farmland they drove through now. At a different time, the beauty of the snow-covered landscape would have been a joy to see.

But today, Cora's thoughts were too preoccupied, primarily with the smartphone in the rear pocket of her dress pants that dug uncomfortably into her lower back. She hadn't dared remove it.

The mustached man in the passenger seat had stopped pointing his gun at her some time ago to smoke his second cigarette, but both kidnappers still checked on her frequently. They might see the phone and take it from her if she removed it at the wrong moment. But the device was her only hope of rescue now.

Jana's warm body and even breathing as she lay nestled on Cora's feet on the floor were a lifeline of comfort. The golden's eyes pressed closed in sweet sleep.

If only Cora could find the same peace. She could barely breathe, thanks to fear and the cloud of cigarette smoke that filled the car.

Father, please give me an opportunity to get to my phone. She'd bathed nearly every moment of this nightmare in such prayers as she sat in the silence, hoping if she didn't talk or move, the men would forget about her.

But fear wouldn't loosen its grip.

She kept trying to think of what Phoenix would do. Not that it helped. Cora wasn't capable of half the skills Phoenix had or her quick, clever thinking and courage.

The digital clock between Cora's captors in the front flicked to another number: *1:04.* Five minutes since the mustached man had looked back to check on her. The second time he'd waited that long.

He turned his head to glance at her, cigarette dangling from his mouth between the ends of his limp mustache.

She sat still and tried to appear relaxed, though her heart rate sprang into a gallop.

He looked forward again.

Now was her chance. She slowly pulled the phone from her back pocket with as little movement as possible, glad she'd removed her gloves earlier for maximum feel and control.

Díaz flicked his gaze to the rearview mirror.

She froze, the device in her clammy palm behind her back. Hopefully, he couldn't see that low through the mirror.

His gaze returned to the road.

She released her pent-up oxygen, just a shallow bit through her nostrils, as if any more might catch their attention.

Keeping the phone alongside her cold thigh, she tilted the screen toward her. Thank the Lord for the daylight that streamed through the windows so the screen's illumination wouldn't call attention to her actions.

She navigated with her thumb to the text app and tapped the conversation with Phoenix.

A scraping sound jerked her head upward.

The mustached man brought a fist to his mouth as he coughed and cleared his throat.

It was now or never.

Cora dropped her gaze back to the phone and slid her thumb across the letters to form one word: *Firebird*.

"Hey!"

Cora jumped at the shout from the mustached man. But she touched the send button.

"She's got a phone. Give me that." The man held up his gun, aimed at Cora.

Her hand shook as she extended the phone to him.

He snatched it, glaring at the screen. "Who did you text?"

"She texted somebody?" Fear raised Díaz's voice an octave. "Oh, man."

"Who's Phoenix?" The older kidnapper flashed the screen at her. "What does this 'Firebird' mean?"

She cleared her throat, trying to find the voice she hadn't

used for what felt like a lifetime. "It's a play on words. Phoenix and Firebird."

"What is she talking about?" The driver's tone reminded Cora of her brother Bradley when he was six and becoming overtired. In fact, everything about Díaz conjured memories of Bradley.

"Shut up." The mustached man still aimed his gun at Cora. "I don't think you were texting someone for a word game at a time like this."

She moistened her lips. It shouldn't matter if she told him now. And it might make her seem more cooperative, perhaps even get him talking to her. "It's a code word. A friend of mine wanted to have a code word we could use if we were ever in trouble. She chose Firebird."

"She?" The shoulders of both men visibly relaxed. "Cute." The man lowered his gun and turned forward. "Why didn't you check her for a phone?" He shot the scolding question at the youngster beside him.

"Why didn't you?"

"Because I have people for kidnappings and…" he waved the back of his hand toward Cora, "cleanups like this."

"What do we do about the text?" Díaz slowed by a farmhouse and barn at a corner.

"I'll watch the phone to see if there's a response. But she didn't say anything besides 'Firebird.' There's no way anybody could find her based on that."

Thank you, Lord. Please, don't let them realize.

They might destroy her phone if they thought of the possibility that someone could track it. She prayed Phoenix was doing just that this very moment. Knowing Phoenix, she'd probably already begun tracking moments ago, the instant she received the text.

And she and the team of the Phoenix K-9 Security and Detection Agency would find Cora and rescue her from the men.

She only hoped they'd reach her before it was too late.

Because she had realized one fact about a half hour ago.

They hadn't blindfolded her. She had been relieved at first, thinking she could remember the route so she could know where to go if she escaped or be able to lead law enforcement back after she was free.

But then, she had remembered another lesson learned from Phoenix and this protection business they were in.

Kidnappers didn't bother concealing their identity and location in only one situation—when they intended to kill the victim.

THREE

The bumpy, ice-patched driveway jostled Cora and Jana as Díaz pulled past a dilapidated, two-story, white house and swung around behind a barn. It wasn't one of the newly painted, updated red and white barns pictured in magazines, but a precarious structure held up by faded, grayish brown boards that let light and most assuredly cold through the panels.

The car door to Cora's right swung open.

"Get out." Díaz pointed his gun at her.

She stepped onto the dirt that was frozen hard where it peeked through the snow. She shuddered, but not from the cold. "Jana, with me."

The golden immediately appeared at her side, landing on the ground and brushing against Cora's leg with support she desperately needed.

The barn loomed large and foreboding before them. The angle of the foot of snow on the slanted roof suggested it might collapse as soon as they entered.

Was this where they were going to hold her? Where she would...die?

The thought sent another shudder through her limbs.

"Move." Díaz gestured with the gun, indicating she should go to the open barn door.

The darkness within yawned at her like a large mouth waiting to swallow her whole.

Father, please rescue me somehow. Send the PK-9 team. Or anyone. Please.

"Who's in the house?" The mustached man's gruff question for Díaz came from behind her.

"Nobody. My uncle died years ago. My aunt never comes here."

No help possible from the house, then.

Mustiness and mold filled Cora's nostrils as she stepped into the darkness. She pressed her face into her arm as a sneeze built up and released.

Díaz laughed. "City girl, huh?"

It was true, she had been born and raised in the city, but this barn was hardly in normal condition for a working farm. The interior wasn't as dark as it had appeared from the outside. Light easily penetrated through the deteriorating structure and through the open entrance they'd used, illuminating countless dust particles that floated in the air.

Shadowed corners hid dismantled bales of straw and discarded pieces of equipment Cora couldn't identify. A beam, perhaps meant to support the barn in some way, had fallen and slashed at an angle across one quarter of the barn from ceiling to floor. Boxes, a child's wagon, a wheelbarrow, a rooster lawn ornament, and other forgotten items clustered along the walls —shadows of habitation that now cast an eerie pall of foreboding and…death.

Stop it. The Lord will save you. Think. Don't give up.

Phoenix and Amalia, and the other women on the PK-9 team, wouldn't helplessly await rescue. They'd try to get out, probably fight their way out. Cora almost wished she'd heeded Phoenix's counsel and taken more than a basic self-defense class. But even if she had, could she really hurt someone to save herself? Hopefully, she'd never have to find out.

"What's your plan now?" The mustached man crossed his arms over his thick chest, his gaze directed at the younger man.

Cora's breath hitched. What was to be her fate?

"I don't know. Hide her here, I guess."

The older man's mustache flitted away from his mouth as he smirked. "For how long?"

"She won't last past tonight."

"You're going to let her freeze to death here? That's your big plan?"

Cora shivered.

Jana leaned against her leg and whined softly. Poor girl was probably tired and thirsty. And likely hungry.

Cora squatted down and gave Jana some treats from her pocket, stroking the golden's soft fur. How much longer would she be able to enjoy being with Jana? Cora's throat swelled.

"And the dog?" The mustached man gestured to Jana. "What if it barks or goes for help?"

Cora's attention perked. The man must have read about dogs doing such heroic acts. Or watched animal movies?

"We can shoot it."

Cora abruptly stood, her hand covering Jana's head. *Father, no. Please don't let them hurt her.*

"You'd shoot the dog, but not the girl. What are the police going to think when they see the dog was shot? You'll still be suspected anyway." The mustached man swore. "It's your family's place. Didn't you think of that?"

Cora forced herself to breathe and consider. The facts, observations she'd been too panicked to catalog before, clicked into place in her mind. The older man hadn't wanted to kidnap her in the first place. He'd rarely met her gaze the whole drive, even when he had checked on her. He hadn't become violent when he had caught her using her phone. He knew about heroic dogs, as if he perhaps enjoyed feel-good stories.

And though he was clearly smarter than the younger man and held more authority, he hadn't used that against Cora. At least not yet.

"What are we going to do?" Díaz bounced a frightened glance from Cora to the older man.

"I'm not going to do anything." The man's mustache twitched with his mouth. "You got yourself into this mess.

You take care of it and meet me back at the car in one minute. You're driving me back to the city to where you were supposed to drop me off. And then if I ever see you again, I'll kill you." He turned on his heel and started for the bright opening.

Díaz threw a panicked look at Cora.

He would shoot her. And Jana.

Phoenix couldn't have reached this location yet. She needed more time.

"Wait, please." Cora moved to follow the older man.

"Hey, you're not going anywhere." Díaz grabbed her sore arm and yanked her back.

A yelp sprang from her lips.

The mustached man turned back. He didn't say a word, but he had stopped.

Jana pressed her nose into Cora's hand, probably concerned by her cry of pain.

But Cora focused on the man who looked back, her chance to keep a bullet at bay. "You have a daughter, don't you?"

He took one step toward her.

Her heart lifted. She'd guessed right.

"How did you know that?"

"It changes a person, doesn't it? Having a child? A girl."

He looked to the side, his stocky frame silhouetted in the bright light of the doorway behind him. His head turned to her again. "Not necessarily."

But it had changed him. His evasive answer confirmed her hunch. "Does she have blond hair?"

He paused. Then he opened his mouth. "Curls. Blond curls."

"My mom said I had curls when I was little."

"What are you trying to do?" Díaz squeezed her arm harder.

Cora winced.

"Stop it." The mustached man launched the sharp command.

"What?" Confusion wobbled the young kidnapper's response.

The older gentlemen walked closer and stopped a few feet away. "Stop hurting her."

"Why? I'm going to have to kill her or something. You just said so."

Cora had to intervene, before Díaz's line of reasoning prevailed. "But you wouldn't want someone to treat your little girl this way, would you?"

The mustached man looked at her. Conflicting emotions warred in his eyes.

"What's her name?" Cora asked the question with a soft tone.

"Sydney." The word floated from the father's lips, burgeoning with love he seemed to be trying to hide, to conquer.

Cora smiled. "That's a lovely name."

He met her gaze, softness melting the hardness she'd seen there before.

Hope rose in her chest. Would he free her?

"I can't save you. I'm sorry."

The hope crashed to the dirt at her feet.

"Do what you have to." He barely looked at Díaz as he delivered her death sentence and turned to leave.

They were going to kill her anyway.

"Wait!" The woman's shout pierced the cold air just as Kent reached the barn.

He'd parked on the road a distance away where a stand of trees hid his car from view. He had come in carefully, using the house and whatever he could as cover as he made his way to the barn. Wasn't about to get caught in an ambush.

The house looked empty, but he couldn't be sure. Had to keep an eye on it.

"I told you. I can't help you." A low, gruff voice. Maybe Ramos's? "This idiot got us in too deep."

Kent squatted and peered around the corner of the barn.

Sounded like Ramos was inside, somewhere through the massive open doorway.

"If you let him kill me, you'll be implicated, too." The woman. A hostage, not accomplice.

Wonderful. Months of work down the drain. And the best lead of his career blown to bits. So much for following these suspects up the chain of the cartel.

Kent hadn't called for backup. Couldn't risk it without first knowing if the woman was part of the drug operation. Now he'd have to get her out of here by himself. Alive.

He rounded the corner, kept his shoulder near the wall, weapon in his hands as he crept closer to the opening ahead.

"What happens when you're caught or killed?"

Kent paused next to the edge of the doorway as the hostage talked more.

"Think of your Sydney. Who would protect her?"

Kent lifted his Glock and pressed his back against the wall. For the first time in his tenure with the DEA, a wave of surprise made him hesitate. The woman was trying to reason with a member of the Guajardo drug cartel. And not just any member. A regional manager—the elite among a select handful of trusted and dirty-up-to-their-elbows gangsters. She had guts, he'd give her that. But she couldn't win.

Silence filled the air that chilled Kent's face.

Were they about to shoot her?

He couldn't risk sneaking a look and getting his head blown off. Couldn't risk her life either.

He stepped away from the wall, just far enough to see the southern portion of the dark barn. Clear.

He darted inside. "DEA! Lay down your weapons!" Kent moved to the right, so the interior wall stood at his back instead of the light of the doorway. He aimed his Glock at the young dealer.

"You can't come in here!" The kidnapper pressed the barrel of a 9mm to the hostage's head. Held her by the arm.

She loosely grasped a leash connected to the golden retriever that whined and panted as it fidgeted by her side.

Ramos, no weapon visible, shifted to stand mostly behind the young guy. Smart man. The lackey would take any bullets for his superior without knowing he'd volunteered to be a human shield.

"Put it down, and I'll let you live." Kent kept moving in a curve to the right, half-circling the gunman.

"Stop it!" Panic elevated the dealer's shout. "Don't move, or I'll kill her."

Kent paused. "Okay. I'm not moving." His Glock stayed fixed on the perp. "Now put down your weapon, and we can all walk out of here alive."

"No." He shook his head slowly, his mouth puckering. "You're not going to take me. I have the gun on her. I'll kill her. I will. Unless you put yours down right now."

The blonde's wide eyes caught Kent's gaze. She stared at him, her fear palpable. Fear and something else. Hope? Pleading?

A twinge of sympathy threatened to distract him.

He yanked his attention back to the kidnapper. "Okay." Kent took one hand off his weapon, angled it sideways in his grip and lowered it to the dirt floor. He straightened, leaving the Glock at his feet.

"Kick it away."

Kent slid the weapon with his foot, sending it four feet. "Look man, we can do this the easy way or the hard way. Your choice. Either way, I win."

The dealer laughed, confidence returning. "I got all the cards now, Fed."

"Then what's your play?" Kent smiled.

The kidnapper's grin wobbled, confusion creating an inch between his gun and the hostage's head.

"Let her go." The regional manager's words hit Kent's ears like an electric shock.

What?

The gunman tilted his head but didn't look away from Kent. "What are you talking about?"

Pretty much Kent's thoughts at the moment.

"The girl's right." Ramos watched Kent with a measured gaze. "We don't want to go away for this."

"I'm not going to!" The kidnapper spewed out the protest. "I'm leaving now. All I have to do is shoot the girl and the cop and go." He shoved the woman forward, lowering his gun to point at her torso.

Kent's gut told him what was happening before his brain knew. He snatched his secondary weapon from behind his back.

Ramos grabbed the gunman's shoulder.

Kent pulled the trigger. The shot exploded, struck the young dealer in the thigh.

He went down, screaming, weapon dropped in the dirt.

"Ma'am, are you okay?"

"Yes." Her voice was barely a whisper as she watched the writhing man on the floor.

"I need you to come over here by me. With your dog."

She didn't move. Like she was transfixed by her kidnapper instead of scared of him. "He needs help."

The woman had just been nearly killed by the pusher, and now she was worried about him? No wonder she'd gotten kidnapped. Way too soft, which made her a prime target. "I'll call for medical response as soon as you come over here." He didn't know what Ramos was up to, interfering with his cartel buddy's shot like that. But Kent wasn't going to let Ramos turn and grab the hostage again.

The blonde finally started toward him.

Kent kept his weapon trained on Ramos, but the guy's mustache didn't even twitch.

He just stared at the woman like he wasn't sure what to make of her. Or like she had some hold on him.

"Ramos, you've got a weapon on you." A guess, but one he'd bet on. "I want to see it now."

The dealer reached behind his back underneath his leather jacket.

"Slowly." Kent barely tracked the hostage as she stopped near his side, his attention trained on Ramos. "Set it down."

The man did as instructed.

"Back away, hands up."

Ramos took several steps back, tame as a pussycat. Weird. Was he setting Kent up for a trap?

A snarl came from the doorway.

Two silhouettes stood outlined in the backlit opening. A growling dog and a person with a gun in a lowered hand. A woman?

Kent swung his weapon to her.

"Looks like you have everything under control."

"Phoenix." The blonde let out the word like a sigh of relief.

"Who?" Kent didn't turn his head from the new arrivals.

"Phoenix Gray. Owner of Phoenix K-9 Security and Detection Agency. I work for her."

The agency that had made headlines last year when it took down the terrorist who was bombing Minneapolis river dams. "Anyone with you?" Kent swung his weapon back to cover Ramos, who still stood passively where Kent had left him.

"FBI and an ambulance. Phoenix K-9 backup on their way."

FBI? He'd heard this Phoenix Gray was well connected.

Before he could say another word, FBI agents poured in, ready to secure the scene he'd already handled. He lowered his weapon and stepped toward Ramos as an FBI agent cuffed him.

"Thank you." The soft voice behind him stopped his progress.

He turned to the hostage.

Her big eyes, blue as a summer sky, met his gaze. "'Thank you' can't say enough. But it's all I have. Thank you for saving me." She touched his forearm with the gentleness of a feather. "I'm so grateful the Lord sent you to rescue me."

He stared, thought of telling her his car brought him, not God. But the words stuck in his throat.

Kindness and sincerity filled her eyes, and a sweet smile lit her face.

"You're welcome," seemed to be the only words he could push out.

"Cora." A deeper female voice spoke from behind her, and she turned away.

Cora. He'd have to find out who she was and how she'd ended up a hostage. Only for the sake of his documentation.

But for now, he needed to make sure the FBI hadn't run off with the man he'd thought this morning would be his ticket to bringing down the most dangerous drug cartel in the nation.

And he'd have to start working on another means to bring about the justice he'd been waiting nineteen years to serve.

FOUR

He could have been Bradley. The thought had haunted Cora all afternoon and evening.

She stared somewhere beyond the coffee mug in her hands but saw only her brother's face as she remembered it.

The young man who'd held Cora at gunpoint could have once been a sweet boy, transformed by evil influences and addiction, just like Bradley. Was Bradley involved in something as awful as kidnapping and...murder? No, she couldn't believe it of her little brother. But his drug addiction had changed him before her eyes, torn him from her grasp, from her life.

You'll never see me again!

She flinched at the memory of his shout and the door slam that had followed.

She'd barely recognized the eighteen-year-old who had walked out the door of their family home. And that was seven years ago. Every one of those years had been marked by the pain of not being able to look for him, to know where he was and if he was okay. He wasn't a missing person in the eyes of the law. He'd left of his own volition, a legal adult, clearly wanting nothing more to do with her.

"Where are you, Bradley?" She whispered the question that squeezed her heart.

"Are you okay?" The kind voice beside Cora pulled her from her thoughts.

Jazz Lamont's eyebrows drew together as she watched Cora.

"Sorry, yes." Cora smiled. "I'm fine. Just lost in thought."

"I can't imagine what you're going through right now. After...what happened today. You must be tired." Jazz angled her green-eyed gaze at the Phoenix K-9 team members who occupied the chairs and sofa in the center of Cora's sitting room, chatting and laughing. "I hope you didn't feel like you still had to hold this party for me. I would have completely understood if you'd wanted to cancel."

"Oh, please don't feel badly about it. I wanted to still have the party tonight. I wouldn't want to miss welcoming you to PK-9. Besides, this is for me, too." Cora smiled at the women scattered in the coziest room of her home. "These ladies are my family."

"That's so cool." A touch of wistfulness feathered Jazz's tone.

"You're part of our family now, too."

A smile widened Jazz's mouth, brightening her lovely features. "I'd like that."

"You'll see. And Flash, of course." Cora squatted by the Belgian Malinois who stood next to his partner.

He stepped close to sniff her face, and Cora smiled at the tickle of his gentle breath. The retired military working dog had a fascinating aura of worldly wisdom, caution, and bridled power.

If Flash and Jazz had been at the airport today instead of Cora, they wouldn't have let things disintegrate to the point where a young man got shot.

"Okay, Cora." Nevaeh Williams tossed her contagious grin their way over the back of the sofa where she sat, beckoning them with a raised arm. "We need you over here."

Cora stood and gave Jazz's shoulder a reassuring squeeze before she headed for the sofa, trying to pause her incessant mental critique of her choices and actions during the kidnapping.

Jana didn't rise to follow Cora as she usually would have. The sweet golden stayed sleeping by the wall where Cora had been standing, exhausted from the day's events.

Regret pinched Cora's chest. She should have kept Jana from being put in danger today. She should have protected her.

Cora paused at the nearest end of the sofa where Amalia Pérez sat with the head of Gaston, her chocolate Newfoundland, stretched up to reach her lap. The rest of the huge dog's body sprawled on the floor in front of her. His lazy relaxation belied the energy he put into water rescue. Cora focused on the humorous sight and her friends, pushing aside her regrets for a moment. "How can I help?"

Amalia flashed her beaming smile up at Cora, her black, glossy waves of hair falling away from her warm-toned, sandy complexion. "Bris wants input on the color scheme for the wedding. I think you're the only one of us who can help her."

Nevaeh and Amalia broke into laughter.

Bristol Bachmann rolled her eyes from the chair she occupied across the room. Her black Labrador Toby lay at her feet, his head lifted as he panted and watched the laughing women like he wanted to join in. The explosives detection K-9 never wanted to miss out on anything fun.

Raksa, Amalia's German Shepherd protection K-9 had somehow ended up lying by the far side of Bris's chair, likely after playing with Toby.

Bris lifted her hands off the armrests of the chair. "I only said I was trying to decide between royal blue or red for the flowers and your maid of honor dress."

"Well, I would guess Nevaeh said red."

"You know it." Nevaeh grinned, wearing her favorite color in the form of a red blazer that complemented the bronze undertones of her smooth brown skin.

Even Cannenta, Nevaeh's corgi mix who sat on her lap, sported a red bandana around her neck.

"And Amalia probably said you should pick whatever you want to?"

Amalia's dark eyes twinkled with humor at Cora's deduction. "That's our girl. You know us well."

Phoenix, sitting to Cora's right in an armchair, likely hadn't said anything about it, just watched the women have the discussion. Though, Cora suspected she'd have more insight than any of them if she'd chosen to express it.

"What do you think, Jazz?" Cora turned to the tall redhead who hung back slightly.

She tucked her wavy hair behind one ear. "I'd think blue." She looked at Bris. "The color of the bouquet would bring out the blue in your eyes."

Cora beamed at her. "Exactly what I was going to say."

"Bam! Give it here, girl." Nevaeh reached behind the sofa, her fist stretched out toward Jazz.

Their new teammate fist-bumped Nevaeh's hand with a grin on her face.

"Thanks, ladies." Bris smiled at Jazz and Cora. "Blue it is. And now Rem will be eternally grateful to you all that he doesn't have to hear me agonizing over this decision anymore."

Cora was quite sure Remington Jones, Bris's fiancé, would gladly listen to her talk about anything for hours given how smitten he was, but she joined in the ladies' laughter.

The grandfather clock in the corner chimed the hour. Eight o'clock already?

"Oh, I'm sorry, ladies." Cora pressed her palms to her cheeks. "I should have brought out dessert earlier. I have cheesecake. Anyone hungry?"

"Oh, yeah." Nevaeh nodded, three black curls teasing her forehead like renegades from her gorgeous head of hair. "Girl, I'm always hungry."

Bris got to her feet. "I'll help you."

Toby popped up, too. The lab's nails clicked on the vinyl floor at a faster rhythm than Jana's usually did as he followed Bris and Cora into the kitchen.

"How are you doing?"

Cora sent Bris a grateful smile before turning away to retrieve dessert plates from the cabinet above the counter. "I'm tired and still feeling…anxious. A little nervous." She set the plates on the countertop by the raspberry cheesecake and faced Bris.

Concern clouded her friend's gray-blue eyes. "We were so worried when Phoenix told us you'd used the emergency code and tracking showed you were way out in the country somewhere. I prayed nonstop after that."

"Thank you." Tears pricked Cora's eyes. "God answered your prayers."

"I just wish we could've reached you faster."

Cora nodded, a tear escaping as the memories returned— Díaz's grip on her arm, the gun pressed to her head, the fear she couldn't protect Jana, that they both might die. "God sent someone who could."

"I heard a DEA agent followed you and helped, but I didn't see him by the time I was on scene."

"He was amazing." Cora didn't think she'd ever forget his handsome face, the dark, brooding countenance matched by his black hair. Or the intensity in his green eyes. Her Godsend in time of need.

"'Amazing,' huh?" Bris's lips tucked at the corners. "You better not let Nevaeh or Amalia hear you say that, or they'll never stop ribbing you."

"Oh, no. I didn't mean it like that." She cleared her throat and stepped to the silverware drawer to pull out dessert forks. "Just that he was very skilled and knew what he was doing. He could be on the PK-9 team. I mean, if he had a dog. He's good enough." She met Bris's watchful, amused gaze. Cora let the defensive lift of her shoulders drop as she smiled. "Yes, I'd appreciate you not repeating what I said to the other ladies. I know how much they teased you about Rem in the early days."

Heat rushed to Cora's cheeks as she realized the comparison she'd unintentionally made. "Not that this situation is anything like—"

"Cora, I get it. It's okay. Though I have to say, now I'm dying to meet this guy." Bris laughed. "But that's *all* I'll say."

She walked to the counter by Cora and reached for the cheese-cake. She stopped and looked down. "Toby, leave it."

The black lab was opening the cabinet door with his nose.

Bris chuckled and gently pulled Toby back as Cora closed the door. "He probably hoped you store dog food in there like I do."

"Sorry, buddy." Cora smiled at Toby as Bris turned on the faucet to wash her hands.

"Maybe Toby will be as laidback as Jana one day. But…"

"Probably not." Cora finished the sentence with Bris, and they both laughed.

Bris's smile faded as she dried her hands. "I'll keep praying for you. I know this has to be really hard, recovering from what happened today. But things will get better."

As a survivor of more than one trauma, Bris spoke from experience and a depth of understanding that gave sincerity to her words.

"Thank you." Cora's heart warmed as she met her friend's caring gaze. What a blessing to have a fellow Christian on the Phoenix K-9 team. Since Bris came to Christ nine months ago, she had become a special comfort and close friend for Cora in their shared faith. And with her blunt observations, Bris had challenged Cora more than once.

Bris glanced over her shoulder, her gaze seeming to catch on something.

Cora turned to look.

Phoenix stood in the doorway. Dagian, her sandy-colored dog with upright ears and piercing blue eyes stood at attention, glued to her side as usual.

"Bris, would you mind taking the plates to the sitting room?" Cora smiled at her. "I'll bring the cheesecake."

"Sure thing." Bris grabbed the plates with the forks stacked on top, and Phoenix stepped in the room to clear the path for Bris and Toby.

Phoenix met Cora's gaze with her steady blue one. "You won't do better next time if you fixate on the unknowns." Her firm voice halted the swirling questions in Cora's mind, the constant review of what she should have done differently.

She'd ask how Phoenix knew what she was thinking but there was no point. Phoenix always knew nearly everything, but seldom shared how. "I'm sorry. I know you've always told me never to get in the car. But they were going to shoot the children with their dad outside the airport. I couldn't let that happen."

"They preyed on your vulnerability. That's what predators do."

Cora's chest squeezed. "I could have prevented the whole thing. If I'd just approached it differently from the beginning."

"I doubt it." The blunt answer could have been offensive, but Cora knew what Phoenix meant.

"I should have been more aware of my surroundings like you're always telling me. You would have seen Díaz was armed. You would've contained them instead of walking right up to them and trying to talk."

Phoenix crossed her arms over her steel gray sweater. "I wasn't there. You were."

And Cora fell far from the skill and perfection Phoenix, Amalia, and all the other women of PK-9 seemed to possess. "I just..." Cora moistened her lips. "I could have kept Jana safer. I could have prevented Díaz from getting shot."

Cora's imagination instantly conjured the image of him on the floor of the barn, yelping and crying in pain. She shuddered.

"Drug dealing. Kidnapping. Attempted murder. He doesn't deserve your pity."

"Maybe so. But I don't deserve your kindness toward me right now, when you know I should have done what you've told me to do. When I should have done so much better."

Phoenix stared at her, silently for a moment. Processing.

At least, that's what Cora imagined Phoenix was doing when she went quiet. A great deal of thinking seemed to go on behind the nearly unreadable façade of Phoenix Gray.

"Focus on a plan for what you'll do next time and work hard

now to be ready. That's the best anyone can do. Regrets will hold you back."

The start of a smile found Cora's mouth and lightened some of the weight on her shoulders. Most people would never think of Phoenix as an optimist. But sometimes she was more of one than Cora. "You're right. I'll try."

"I'll help you do it."

Cora nodded. "I know. Thank you." Phoenix was so generous not to say more. Not to remind Cora of the opportunities she'd had with Phoenix and the agency to learn more about protection, weapons, and martial arts. But Cora hadn't been able to bring herself to embrace any of those pursuits. She wasn't gifted or comfortable with such things, much preferring to focus on detection and security technologies. The events of the day loomed in her mind like a challenge to her resolution.

She picked up the cheesecake. "The ladies will be wondering what happened to us. Would it be all right with you if we sing 'She's a Jolly Good Fellow' for Jazz?"

Phoenix stared at Cora, then one of her rare close-lipped smiles curved her mouth. "Go ahead."

"Oh, good." Excitement bubbled in place of the nerves from moments ago. "I really want to show Jazz how glad we are to have her on the th—"

Dagian rumbled a low-pitched growl.

Cora froze as the protection K-9 spun around to face the sitting room.

A bark burst from the sitting room, then more. Sounded like Raksa. And maybe Flash? Cora hadn't heard him bark before.

"Follow me." Phoenix marched with Dag through the short hallway to the sitting room at the front of the house.

"Car door shut in the driveway." Amalia spoke just loudly enough to be heard above Raksa's barking.

"Are you expecting someone?" Phoenix didn't look away from the front door and windows.

"No." Cora's stomach clenched. But she was at home with the PK-9 team. Surely, she was safe. "It's probably just Mrs.

Bates wanting to borrow some sugar." Cora's elderly neighbor enjoyed baking and visiting, both of which supplied her with excuses to stop by. Although not usually at this time of night.

Jazz emerged from the study with Flash. "Got a look." In the dark study where no indoor light would give her away if she pulled back the curtain.

Cora knew Phoenix had been right to hire Jazz.

The beautiful redhead didn't show a hint of the hesitation she'd had during the party as she continued. "Silver Honda Civic. One male, tall and slim, dark hair. Approaching the front door."

Phoenix turned from Jazz to Cora. "Check your camera."

"I would, but I didn't get my phone back from today." For all she knew, it could have been logged with other evidence in the drug dealer's car and ended up in FBI evidence holding somewhere. "I could get my computer."

Phoenix stared at the door. "Amalia, flank him."

"Raksa." The one word from Amalia silenced the shepherd's barking as Amalia darted away toward the back door of Cora's house, Raksa sprinting after her.

The sing-song ding of the doorbell rang out.

Cora jumped when Flash and even Gaston barked.

"Bristol, the door."

She moved forward at Phoenix's command, her hand going to the gun holster at her hip.

"No, wait." Cora stepped closer to Phoenix. "I appreciate all the effort, but I'm sure it's nothing dangerous. May I please just open the door and see who it is?" Poor Mrs. Bates would be terrified by an armed greeting.

Phoenix leveled her gaze at Cora, giving her a measured look.

Cora smiled slightly. "I just need to be normal again right now. I know you care, and I really appreciate it. But I can do this. Especially with all of you here."

Phoenix's jawline firmed. But she gave a nod.

Cora approached the front door, her stomach tense despite her bravado with Phoenix. It was so silly. There was nothing dangerous about someone ringing her doorbell at night. She simply wasn't recovered from the day's frightening events.

She took in a breath and opened the door a few inches.

A tall man stood with his back to her, as if he'd been about to leave.

There was something familiar about him.

He turned, the porch lamp bathing his face in light.

The air whooshed from her lungs and her hand shot to the doorframe to keep herself from falling.

Bradley.

FIVE

Kent scanned the darkness one final time before he would enter it.

Midnight and ten degrees Fahrenheit meant an abandoned park. Except for the desperate few who might try to survive the night in the public bathrooms or sheltered under picnic tables.

But from the vantage point of Kent's car, parked near the central building used for indoor events, all he could see was an empty parking lot and cleared, dark paths cutting through the snow. Shadows played tag with light from the parking lot lamps and scattered along the main path.

Not a great place for a meeting. But Navarro was taking a big risk as it was. Kent had to go where the confidential informant was willing to meet, especially if his intel was as good as his last tidbit. Navarro had been spot-on about the cartel's regional manager flying in within a few days. When Navarro contacted Kent to meet this time, all he'd said was he'd gotten wind of something big going down.

That was worth more than a little risk. Kent slid his secondary weapon into the waistband behind his back, covering it with his black leather jacket before he opened his car door.

A blast of frigid air whipped inside. The freezing weather deserved gloves, but he needed to be able to handle his weapon and feel the trigger.

He headed up the path that curved around the circular building.

The well-lit route made him too visible—a potential target if anyone invited themselves to this party. But with the foot of snow on either side of the path, Kent had little other choice. Should've worn boots.

He kept his gaze moving, darting from side to side and skipping ahead, around the edge of the building as he followed its curve.

Turning off at the first path that split away, he soon left the lampposts behind.

Snow and moonlight provided the only light here as leafless trees closed in on both sides of the narrower path. Harder to see, but harder to be seen—a tradeoff he'd take any day.

A sound—a crack—jerked his gaze to the left.

He stopped, crouched low as he pulled his weapon from the concealed holster.

Animal or human?

He watched. Listened. His breath puffed a white cloud in front of his face.

Nothing.

He slowly straightened. Walked a few steps. Paused.

Still no repeated sound. No movement between the dark trunks of trees.

He continued a few feet, turned onto another path, this one covered with snow that must have had the top layer shoveled off or plowed before the latest inches of accumulation. This lesser-used trail had sported gravel instead of pavement when Kent had met Navarro here once last summer.

Icy cold penetrated his fingers that held the Glock at his side. The darkness deepened as the bare trees grew thicker.

Only a little farther, and he should see the trail marker that Nav—

Pfoot. Pfoot.

The loud noise hit Kent's ears.

A suppressed gun. Two shots.

He jumped off the trail, plunged into the deep snow. He cut

behind trees, Glock gripped in his hands, ready as he moved parallel with the path.

The darkness shifted. A person?

The clip and snap of a gun's action gave Kent a split-second warning.

He ducked behind a tree just as the suppressed pop sounded.

The bullet thudded into a tree trunk behind him.

He aimed his weapon past the tree that concealed him.

Rapid footsteps crunched the snow. A dark figure fled on the path.

Kent darted out from behind the tree, scrambled to the path.

The shooter disappeared into the darkness.

He couldn't fire without knowing he had a clear shot or issuing a warning. And he didn't want to give away he was DEA until he knew what had happened to Navarro.

He turned around.

The answer lay on the path. Navarro. Dead?

Kent approached the CI, scanning the darkness beyond his still body, checking behind before he squatted. Felt his neck for a pulse.

None.

Two dark holes pierced the chest of Navarro's navy-blue jacket.

Kent let out a sigh, the resulting cloud blurring Navarro's face. What a waste. Navarro wasn't a bad guy. A pusher for years, but a guilty conscience or hero complex had eventually made him turn informant. And bringing down the Guajardo cartel became a real possibility.

Somebody in the cartel apparently figured that out.

And claimed another victim.

Kent would add Navarro's name to the list he kept hidden at his apartment. The innocent people murdered by the cartel.

The people he would vindicate the day he brought the whole organization to its knees.

"You know, I don't have to stay here. I could crash at a motel or something."

Cora looked up from the cups of tea she carried to the sofa where Bradley sat. "Of course not. I wouldn't dream of letting you stay anywhere else." She handed him one of the cups. Her heart squeezed at the sight of his face—so familiar, yet unfamiliar where time had changed it. "Unless...you want to."

"Your boss didn't look happy about the idea of me staying here." Bradley gave her one of his sideways grins, the one that appeared when he wanted her reassurance. The one she hadn't seen for a long time even before he had left.

Cora sat beside him, and Jana came close, sliding into a down position and laying her head on Cora's foot. "Phoenix is just concerned about my safety. She doesn't know you like I do. Only the facts she's learned."

"You mean like the drug addict part. And the stealing your money part?"

Cora took in her brother's more mature visage, the smooth, eighteen-year-old skin she had once known now aged with tiny lines beginning to show at the corners of his mouth. Not from laughter but from the tense way he held his lips when he was stressed, as he was now.

"Phoenix is one of my closest friends. No..." She leaned forward to set her mug of tea on the coffee table in front of them. "More than that. She's my mentor. And the most protective person I've ever known. She likes to take care of the people in her family."

"Family?"

"The Phoenix K-9 Agency is like a family. We take care of each other. But Phoenix does most of the protecting and guiding."

"She sounds like you."

Cora laughed. "Oh, no. She's much stronger and more knowledgeable than I am. It's different with her."

"So is your dog one of the K-9s at the agency?" He looked down at Jana, resting on Cora's feet. "Does she do something?"

"She does a lot." Cora smiled at her brother's wording. "Jana and I are part of the detection arm of the agency. Like several of the dogs at PK-9—that's what we call the Phoenix Agency—Jana is a dual-purpose K-9."

Bradley reached for a mug on the table. "What's that mean?"

"She does more than one job. She does search and rescue work whenever the need arises. But on a daily basis, she and I are busy with…" Her throat tightened as she hesitated. How would Bradley react? "Narcotics detection."

He lowered the mug that had almost reached his lips. "A drug-sniffing dog?"

She met his widened gaze. "Yes."

He clunked the cup onto the table and stared at it as if the tea had given him the shock.

Cora's pulse wavered. Did he think she had done that to get back at him or punish him somehow? "It's not what you might think. After you left, I wanted to do something…to help. I couldn't help you because I didn't know where you were." And because he'd made it painfully clear he hadn't wanted her help.

She kept the thought to herself and moistened her lips before continuing. "But I thought that perhaps by finding drugs, I could help other people—especially families and children. I want to find the drugs that users and dealers want to keep hidden, in time to stop or prevent addiction and the pain it causes. At least, that's my hope in what I try to do with Jana."

Bradley turned his face toward her. "That sounds like you."

From the tuck of the corner of his mouth and the softness in his hazel eyes, she hoped he meant that as a good thing. "I need to tell you something, Bradley." Her hand lifted to touch his shoulder, but she halted the movement. He had never appreciated physical touch before. "I want you to know that even though I made many mistakes that drove you away, I always loved you. And I've never stopped loving you. Even when I didn't know where you were."

He looked away, his gaze drifting to the wall across the room. His throat scraped. "I'm sorry...for how things went down when I left."

Her chest warmed. She had never expected an apology. Perhaps that meant he wanted to make amends and try again, too. But she'd been the one mostly to blame, and she needed to acknowledge that. "No, I'm sorry, Bradley. I should have handled things differently."

The scene she'd played and replayed a million times in the seven years since he had left started to unfold in her mind once again. But she knew, from years of analyzing, that the problems hadn't begun that night. "Not just that night. I should have prevented your situation from ever getting so bad. I'm so sorry, and I hope you'll forgive me."

Promise me you'll take care of your brother. He'll need a mother. Raise him to know Jesus.

Tears blurred Cora's vision with the echo of her mother's words, among the last she'd ever spoken.

Oh, Father. Cora's prayer was voiceless but rang out from her regretful heart. *I tried. But I fell so far short.*

Cora looked at her brother, sitting silently beside her, home with her at last. *Please, let this be my second chance. Help me to do it right this time. Show me how to help him, to point him to You.*

"I guess I just didn't know what to do when Mom died." Bradley's voice cracked on the last words. He shrugged and swiped his hand against his nose as if emotion had caused it to drip. "I was just a kid, you know? Kids do dumb things. And Dad sure wasn't any help." He glanced at her from the corner of his eye. "Is he still the same?"

Cora chose her words carefully. "He's very busy. I call him about once a month."

"And he talks to you?"

"I leave messages."

Bradley snorted. "Figures." He bounced his gaze around the room. "Did he pay for this place?"

"No, I saved for it through work."

"Why? You could've gotten one of those 300 mil jobs with your trust fund."

"I like to use that money for charity and ministries." Their father's obsession with his career and profit had irreparably damaged their parents' marriage and left Cora and Bradley to grow up in a single-parent environment. Profiting from that tragedy was unthinkable.

"If he'd let me access *my* trust fund, I'd be spending it like crazy."

Not on drugs, hopefully. She kept the thought to herself.

Bradley threw her a glance. "I don't mean I'd spend it on coke. That's what you were thinking, right?" The defensive note in his voice kept her from meeting his gaze, afraid he might see his accusation was correct.

He got to his feet and stalked across the room, running his hand over the short brown hair that had been more of a dark blond when he had left.

"I didn't mean to hurt you, Bradley." Cora's stomach tensed as she searched for the right words to say. She needed to be careful. She couldn't risk accidentally prompting him to leave again. "I don't know where you've been or what you've been doing. I probably don't know who you are anymore, but I'd really like to learn. I want to get to know you again, to be friends like we used to be when we were young. Remember?"

His back faced her as she forced herself to wait and not say more. To give him space.

He sighed, shoulders lowering, and his hands going to his denim-clad hips. He was still so thin. As if he didn't eat any more now than before he had left, when he was so sullen and depressed...and high on drugs.

"I remember." The words were rough, as if scraping against the pain mirrored in her own heart. He slowly turned and ran a hand down his face. "I went straight."

"What?" The word slipped out before she caught it.

But he didn't look offended this time. "A year after I left, I hit bottom." He paced to the right, then the left and paused, his profile to her. "I knew I was going to die. But then I remembered..." A sound, like a hiccup or sob escaped. He covered his mouth as Cora squeezed her hands together and forced herself not to go to him and comfort him as she had when he was a boy.

He had said she comforted too much, controlled him too much.

You're not Mom! Just leave me alone! The memory of his shout singed her ears with the same wounding power they'd wielded the day he'd flung the words and run out the front door of their father's mansion. The day he'd fled her and her pathetic attempts to keep her promise.

"I remembered something Mom said before she..." Bradley's unfinished sentence summoned her back to the present. "Something she asked me to do." He sniffed. "I knew I had to keep going. Had to survive, at least until I'd done it."

Their mother had asked him to do something? Possibilities cycled through Cora's mind, but it wasn't her place to ask. Bradley would tell her if he ever wanted her to know.

"That's when I quit."

"You quit drugs? Oh, Bradley." Cora pressed her fingers to her lips, hope rising to her throat and filling her eyes with new tears.

He nodded, a slight smile beginning to curve his lips. "I checked myself into rehab. Got clean." He walked back to the sofa and sat beside Cora. He hesitantly reached for her.

She put her hands in both of his.

"Cora, I haven't used since." He stared into her eyes, urgency in his hazel orbs. "No drugs at all. I swear."

Tears spilled onto Cora's cheeks as she smiled. "I believe you. Oh, Bradley, this is incredible news. Praise the Lord. I'm so, so thankful."

His fledgling smile widened. "You sound like Mom."

A laugh tumbled from Cora's lips. "That's the best compliment anyone has ever paid me."

Jana stood and squeezed between Cora's knees and the

coffee table. She stopped by Bradley and rested her head on his lap, staring up at him with her brown eyes.

He looked at the dog.

"She wants to congratulate you, too."

He stroked Jana's head with the awkwardness Cora would expect from the boy who'd never been allowed to have pets growing up. "Well, thanks."

"It's amazing, Bradley. You're free."

He lifted his gaze from Jana. "And I suppose you'd like to know what my plans are now."

"No." Cora smiled. "You can tell me all of that when you're ready. I'm just thankful you're home, and I want to bask in the wonder of that for a long time."

"Or at least until tomorrow morning?" The humor she hadn't seen in Bradley's eyes in at least eight years—well before he'd left home—twinkled for just a moment.

Tomorrow. Would she really get to spend more days in the company of her brother? He almost seemed like an illusion, a dream that would fade to reality when she awoke in the morning.

But she'd have to trust this was real, that the Lord was giving her another chance to help her brother and be everything he needed. "Yes." She smiled. "Tomorrow."

SIX

She couldn't mess up this time.

Jana walked ahead of Cora, her tail swishing rapidly back and forth as she smelled the row of lockers in the hallway of Lofland High School.

But Cora's mind was not on the search for narcotics. The memory of the argument with Bradley when he had left seven years ago consumed her focus.

Just back off, will you? You're not Mom!

"Are you okay, Miss Isaksson?"

Cora blinked at the sound of the deep voice beside her.

Julian Morris dipped his head, peering at her as if he thought she might be ill.

Cora's heart warmed at the concern in the security guard's eyes and the old-fashioned way he insisted on the formal term of address at school though they'd become close friends. "Yes, I'm sorry. I don't mean to be distracted."

"Hey, you can be distracted anytime you want. I'm just worried is all." Julian slid his big hand over the dark brown skin of his bald head. "But you got a reason to be preoccupied today. With your brother coming back."

Cora hiked her shoulders as she drew in a breath. "I'm worried I might not be what he needs again, and he'll..." She couldn't finish the sentence. She'd just gotten him back. What if he left again as abruptly as before?

"Nobody can be everything that boy needs. It's not up to you."

"I know. God is in control."

Julian nodded. "Amen."

"But I can still do things poorly. This weekend did not go as I'd planned. I made breakfast for him on Saturday, but I had to put it in the refrigerator because he didn't get up until one in the afternoon."

"Oh, man." Julian scrunched his features sympathetically.

"Then I hoped we could go out for dinner together, but he said he had other plans and disappeared until eleven at night. When he got back, I invited him to go with me to church in the morning." She glanced at her friend walking beside her. "You should have seen the look on his face. As if he was fifteen again, and I was trying to run his life."

Julian shook his head. "You only want what's best for him, whether he knows it or not. You gotta do what's right."

"Yes, but it seems like I always go about it the wrong way. I shouldn't have assumed he'd want to do things together. He's a grown man now. And I shouldn't have invited him to go to church only his second day at home. I should have given him more time to adjust and for me to see where he's at spiritually." She let out a heavy sigh. "I'm afraid in just one weekend I may have already done the wrong things like last time, and my mistakes will be the reason he leaves. Or the reason he doesn't get the help and support that he needs."

Jana knew the routine of this now-daily search so well that she automatically swerved when she reached the end of the hall and led the way across to the facing wall of lockers.

"You can point him to the help he needs, and he might still refuse it. But that ain't your fault." Emotion clenched Julian's voice.

"Oh, I'm so sorry." Cora looked at him, mortification flooding her face with heat. "I didn't think about what I was saying, how it might sound. You know I didn't mean Davey… that you could have—"

"I know that. Don't give that another thought. I worry about *you*, Miss Isaksson."

"You are the sweetest man I know." Cora smiled at the sixty-year-old gentleman she had bonded with over their similar situations. Few people knew of Bradley's history with drug addiction. Not because Cora kept it a secret, but because the topic didn't often come up. She had found a fellow sufferer in Julian when she learned he had lost his teenaged son to drug overdose sixteen years ago. "I hope Bradley coming home to me doesn't cause more grief or pain for you."

"Don't think that'd be possible. But I'm just happy for you that your boy could come home."

"Yes." Cora nodded. "And I'm so thankful. It was so special to have him at the house for breakfast this morning. He told me he's going to go out looking for a job today. He seems to be doing well, but…"

"You're worried about what might happen now. What you should do."

"Yes, I—" Her gaze caught on Jana.

The golden sat in front of a locker near the end of the wall. She drew her tongue into her mouth and lifted her ears as she tilted her head to stare at Cora.

"She's found drugs." Trusting Jana's foolproof nose and perfect record, Cora doled out the treats the golden would walk off a cliff to receive. "Good girl, such a good girl."

Jana popped up and munched the treats, her tail pumping.

"Oh, man." Julian stepped back from checking the locker number and shook his head.

"What is it?"

"This locker is Hayden Simpson's. Eighteen-year-old kid who thinks he runs the world and his daddy's money says so. He bought all-new equipment for the football team last season. Hayden's the quarterback. A real piece of work. I thought he might be connected to our drug problem but couldn't prove it."

Julian unclipped the radio from his belt. "This ain't gonna be pretty."

He radioed the head of security, and by the time the principal arrived with a teen boy who looked ready to explode, Cora knew what Julian meant.

"I have a right to privacy." Hayden Simpson stood head and shoulders above Julian and glowered down at the security guard. "You must think your job's pretty secure to accuse me of something like this."

"No one's accusing you of anything, Hayden." Principal McFadden stepped between Hayden and Julian, though shorter than them both. He gestured to Hayden's locker. "Would you open your locker?"

"Why? Just because some dog likes the smell of it?" He glared at Jana.

Cora rested her hand on Jana's head, the golden standing calmly at her side.

"Probably smelled my burger wrapper."

"Just open the locker, Hayden." The principal pointed at the gray door.

"Or what?"

"Or I will open it for you."

Good for Principal McFadden. The forty-something man with a small stature and wire-framed glasses didn't appear to be quite so tough, but she'd learned through his eagerness to crack down on the school's drug problem that his looks were deceiving.

"Go ahead. But you have no right to do this, and you can bet my dad is going to hear about it."

You have no right to be in here! This is my room!

The memory of Bradley's shout, full of hurt and fear, when she'd confronted him about the drugs when he was fifteen rang in Cora's ears. She blinked away the memory as Principal McFadden swung open the locker door.

A bag, books, and disgusting photos that would have shocked her in the years before she'd started searches at high schools littered the inside of the compartment.

No drugs were obvious at first glance, but Jana was never wrong.

"See?" Hayden smirked.

The principal glanced at Cora.

Jana wagged her whole body, probably from the stronger whiff of narcotics spewing from the locker. No one but Jana could smell the scent, but her body language confirmed she had a real find.

Cora gave the principal a nod.

"Allow me, Principal McFadden." Julian stepped toward the locker.

Hayden reached for the door, slamming it shut in front of Julian's face. "There's nothing in there, and you're not pawing through my property."

Principal McFadden sighed. "Hayden, do not make this situation worse for yourself. We could call in the police right now, if you like."

Hayden slowly backed up, his glare not weakening.

"Go ahead." The principal nodded to Julian, who opened the locker and reached inside, pulling things out.

The last item he lifted out was a paper bag from a fast-food restaurant.

The locker stood bare.

Julian looked back at Cora.

"Try feeling along the bottom."

He slid his fingers around the base, then paused. He grasped something in his fingers and pulled.

The floor of the locker lifted, revealing a hidden compartment underneath.

Julian leaned in. "Whew. Check this out, Principal."

Principal McFadden stepped closer. His milky cheeks changed to the shade of pink lemonade. "Call the police." He turned to Hayden.

The boy's fingers curled into fists at his side.

"I trust you won't try to run, Mr. Simpson." The principal gave the student a severe stare. "It would only make things worse for you."

Hayden snorted. "I'm not afraid of you or anyone else." He shifted his glare from the principal to Cora. "This is all your fault." He pointed a finger at her. "You and that stupid mutt. You better watch your back, lady. You have no idea who you're messing with."

Cora continued to stroke Jana, hoping to offset the hostility the golden might sense from the overwrought teen.

"That's enough of that, Mr. Simpson." Principal McFadden intervened as Julian stepped between Hayden and Cora, shielding her from the boy.

Bradley had been just as upset when she'd taken his drugs away, but he hadn't threatened her.

Hayden was just blurting things out in anger. He might not mean it. Though, he had the size and strength to do something about it.

Cora mentally pushed away the fear that started to speed her pulse. The events of yesterday must have made her more skittish than usual, not that she was very brave to begin with.

But she'd made a decision six years ago, when she had started working for Phoenix. Any risk to her was worth it if she could prevent one person from becoming as lost to drugs as Bradley.

The moment Julian shifted to the side, Hayden shot daggers at Cora with his glare.

She met his silent fury with what she hoped was a kind expression. She prayed that she and Jana had been on time to help Hayden.

"You want me to what?" The question popped from Kent's mouth with more irritation than he meant to show.

"Work with her." Camilla Velasquez, Special Agent in Charge of the Minneapolis Drug Enforcement Administration office grabbed a file from the stack on the desk in front of her and flipped it open.

"You can't be serious." He leaned forward in the chair facing her desk and braced his elbows on his knees. "Is this a way of putting me out of commission for a while? Because I will find another way into the cartel. You can count on that."

Velasquez raised her dark gaze and peered at him above her reading glasses. "And I do. But I also know you can handle more than one assignment at a time. Cora Isaksson proved she and her K-9 could be an asset."

"She got herself kidnapped."

Velasquez pressed her lips together as she stared at him. "She found narcotics and one of the cartel's big players. And, from what I heard, she nearly talked her way out of the hostage situation herself."

Kent got to his feet and moved to stand behind his chair. "I don't need anyone to help me bust dealers and find drugs. My record proves that."

"Thomson, no one is questioning your abilities. And no one is saying you need help." Velasquez sighed and pulled the glasses off her nose. "Will you please sit down? I'd like to explain this better."

Kent clenched his jaw but rounded the chair and sat.

"The find she made showed that arrivals may be a weakness in our efforts to prevent drug trafficking through the airport. Which is why I decided we would contract her through the Phoenix K-9 Agency to work for us on a limited basis. All I want you to do is spend one week with Ms. Isaksson to search arriving baggage and see how frequently we can catch narcotics that would otherwise slip through."

"One week?"

She nodded. "That's all. You can even put in the seven days at your own pace, as your time away from other cases allows. And while you're at the airport, you can also be in a prime location to watch for more of the cartel's distributors arriving. You don't know yet why their regional manager came, do you? Or the 'something big' your CI was going to tell you about?"

He leaned back, a muscle twitching in his jaw. "No."

"Then this is one way you can be in a good position to see anyone unusual coming in."

It was a good plan. Just ill-timed. Finding a new lead in the Guajardo cartel case had to be his priority. The last thing he wanted to do was spend his time with the woman whose interference had forced him to throw his best leads in jail.

Díaz had tried to cut a deal and talked a blue streak, but he didn't know anything useful. Ramos was being handled more carefully and his processing was slower. But though Kent would be able to talk to him soon, he didn't expect the guy to roll. The higher up the position in the cartel, the deeper the perp was involved and the less likely he would be to risk his own skin by talking.

"Agreed?" Velasquez watched him.

"You're only pairing me with her because of the K-9, right?"

The corner of Velasquez's lips tugged. "Of course. You can't smell the drugs in closed luggage yourself, can you?"

"Very funny." He narrowed his eyes at her as he got up. "I'll do it for a week."

"What a relief." Sarcasm flattened her tone. "One of these days, I might have to pull rank on you, Thomson."

"I'll look forward to that." He lifted a hand behind his back in a casual wave as he exited her office.

He made his way to the cubical and sat in front of his computer, tapping a key to wake up the screen. If he was going to be forced to work with someone, he wouldn't do it blind. He entered his login password and navigated to the database where he could begin a background check.

Cora Isaksson, he typed into the search function.

Thank you. The look in her blue eyes as she'd touched his arm clouded his vision. What was it about her that had made him feel so...

He shook his head. It was nothing. Just a weird effect she had. Or maybe he'd just been rattled that day because his plan had blown up so badly.

And now his best CI had been murdered. Velasquez was probably putting him on this new assignment because she knew his case had stalled.

He glanced away from the computer to look at the contents of the plastic bag on his desk.

The CI's personal effects, found in his pockets. Lighter, wallet with a few bucks inside, an old lottery ticket. Nothing to hint at anything Navarro might have been about to tell Kent last night. And little to give the man's family if anyone showed up to claim his belongings. Maybe the guy didn't even have any family.

Kent returned his gaze to the computer screen and caught sight of a notification. New email.

He checked the inbox. Froze.

Vince156700. A sender address Kent hadn't expected to see until next Christmas.

No subject line.

He clicked it open.

In your area. Meet for lunch?

Characteristically cryptic style for his brother. But nothing normal about the content. What was Vince doing here, and why in the world would he want to meet with Kent? The once-every-Christmas email or phone call had been their only contact for years.

Kent was supposed to meet the Isaksson woman at 1:00, and with all the files and intel he had to review and emails he had to answer, there was no way he'd fit in a lunch break today.

He typed a response: *Can't make lunch. Around tomorrow? Could do early breakfast.*

Vince was always up before the sun, so it might work. But that would leave Kent to spend all of today wondering why his brother had come to Minnesota from Oklahoma and wanted to see him in person.

Kent blew out a breath, trying to release the tension knotting in his belly. Probably wasn't anything. Maybe Vince had just gotten a truck load up north instead of the southern routes he usually drove. What bad news could be the cause behind the sudden visit anyway? They didn't have anyone left to get bad news about.

Whatever the reason, Kent had more important things to focus on.

Like the blonde whose driver's license ID photo illuminated his computer screen. She took an unusually good photo. Her hair had been pulled back in a bun the day of the kidnapping. In this photo, it hung a few inches past her chin, framing her face with gentle waves.

He pulled his gaze from her picture and turned his attention to the facts. It would take a while to be thorough, but he needed to know if he could trust her if she was going to be working by his side even for a short time.

No tickets, charges, or arrests on her record. But few people had nothing to hide.

He searched for relatives, next of kin who may not be so clean or who would at least give him a better picture of her background.

Francis Isaksson. Her father apparently was a massively successful CEO—making headlines at the helm of more than one Fortune 500 company. Maybe that's why his name was familiar.

Kent's skimming gaze stopped on something else.

Bradley Isaksson.

And a juvenile record. Sealed.

That was suspicious.

Isaksson. Francis and Bradley. Why did he know those names?

He pulled up the digitized version of the files he'd gotten from Special Agent Dean Wentworth when he'd retired. All the details of the investigation and progress Wentworth had made in crippling the Guajardo cartel.

Navigating to the file his memory told him could be connected, he opened it and scrolled through the pages on the screen.

His eyes caught on words that solidified his certainty he shouldn't work with this woman.

Bradley Isaksson. Guajardo dealer.

SEVEN

"You're doing it again, aren't you?"

Cora returned the carafe to the coffeemaker on the break-room table at Phoenix K-9 headquarters and turned to meet Bris's questioning gaze.

"You're reviewing what happened today and finding something you think you did wrong." A hint of a smile hovered at the corners of Bris's mouth.

"Not exactly. Would you like a cup? It's fresh."

Toby pushed his nose high to reach the top of the table, checking out the peanut butter cookies Cora had made for the lunch break.

"Toby, leave it." Bris shook her head with a smile. "Sometimes that nose of his is a definite disadvantage."

"But then other times, it saves lives." Cora returned the smile with a teasing shrug.

Bris laughed. "Yeah, there is that." She dropped her gaze to the cookies. "No, on the coffee, but yes to a cookie."

Guilt twinged Cora's conscience as she placed a cookie in a napkin and handed it to her friend. "I wasn't completely honest when I answered your question. Yes, I was reviewing what happened, but I'm mostly noticing things I should have done instead—what I should have done better."

"You caught a teenager with drugs. What could you have

51

possibly done better?" Bris bit off a mouthful of cookie as her brow furrowed.

"I wonder if I should have talked to Hayden, the teen. I could have tried to get through to him. Maybe I could have shared Bradley's story. But I just stayed quiet."

"Yeah," Nevaeh appeared between them at the table and reached for a mug. "As the dude threatened you." She poured coffee into the cup. "Am I right?"

"Yes."

"Thought so." Nevaeh nodded with a satisfied set of her lips and walked away, returning to Alvarez, her Rottweiler mix protection K-9, who relaxed by the sofa.

"So probably not the best time to try to talk to him?" Bris lifted her eyebrows.

"Maybe not." Or perhaps Cora could have calmed him down and found a soft place in his conscience still untouched by drugs and crime.

"Ladies." Phoenix marched into the room, Dag trotting at her side. "We have a lot to cover today, and we only have an hour."

With the protection K-9s hired for another overnight security gig, the noon hour was the only time they'd be able to gather all at once for now.

Cora and Bris headed to the center of the room where Phoenix rounded the sofa and chairs to stand at the far side, facing the door as she always preferred.

Cora sat in the armchair Jana had picked to lie beside when they'd entered the breakroom.

"First off, congratulations to Cora and Jana."

Cora looked at Phoenix with a start.

"For those of you who haven't heard, Jana detected narcotics in a teen's locker at Lofland High this morning. The drugs were recovered. Charges against the teen are pending." Phoenix started clapping, and the other PK-9 team members joined in.

Amalia let out a whoop from the sofa. Nevaeh whistled, which drew suspicious looks from protection dogs Raksa and

Dag. Alvarez stayed relaxed, apparently used to his partner's odd behavior.

But Flash, standing by the armchair where Jazz sat, stared intensely at Nevaeh until Jazz leaned forward and put her hand on his shoulders.

Cora's cheeks heated as she waved off their praise. "We were only doing our job."

"And you did it very well." The outright praise from Phoenix warmed Cora's heart as well as her face.

"Thank you."

"But Cora won't be able to stay for our meeting today. She has another assignment."

"I do?"

"The SAC at the DEA office here called me this morning and contracted us—you and Jana specifically—to search arrivals baggage at Minneapolis Airport. You have a meeting at the airport today with the agent you'll be working with."

"Oh." Cora blinked. She never seemed to fully adjust to how quickly things moved at PK-9. And she was the office manager. She'd have to figure out how to fit in more time to keep up with her office duties or she was going to end up out of the loop and behind. "Do you know the agent?"

"You do. Special Agent Kent Thomson."

Cora's pulse hiccupped. "The man who rescued me?"

"Yes."

"Oh, my."

"Is that a problem?" Phoenix watched her closely.

"No, not exactly." Cora searched for an explanation for her reaction when she didn't entirely understand it herself. "He just seemed very...intense when I met him." *Unfriendly* sounded too judgmental for her to say. "But I suppose the situation could account for that. He's probably much friendlier under normal circumstances."

A partially suppressed laugh drew her attention to Nevaeh, who moved her hand off her mouth to uncover a full-blown grin. The other women wore similar smiles as they watched her —all except Phoenix, of course.

"You got a picture of this guy?" Nevaeh looked like she'd soon burst if she didn't let her laughter release all the way.

"No, no." Bris's face was lit with similar humor as she intervened. "I won't let you put Cora through the torture you did me with Rem. You all are relentless." Bris meant well, but the comparison to her fiancé only encouraged the idea that Cora was romantically interested in Kent. And flamed Cora's cheeks even more.

Amalia let out her hearty laugh—contagious when Cora wasn't the target of the teasing. "You can't blame us, Bris. You and Cora have the best tells. Those lovely pink cheeks. Never try poker, ladies."

"Cora, you need to get going."

Cora could've hugged Phoenix for interrupting.

"Your meeting is at one."

Cora checked the clock on the wall. In forty-five minutes? She'd have a lot of traffic to navigate to get out of town and drive the distance to the airport. Hopefully, she could make it in time.

"Okay. Goodbye, ladies." Cora sent Phoenix a grateful glance as she got Jana up and made a quick exit. Not that she was running from inferences about Agent Thomson.

The memory of his face drifted to the front of her mind. He certainly was handsome, with his defined cheekbones, chiseled jawline, and black, tousled hair that looked like he ran his fingers through it in the morning and then let it do its own thing. Somehow, his careless style ended up looking very nice.

Cora pushed through the front door into the cold air. It was his green eyes that—

She stopped, her gaze locked on her parked Volkswagen Beetle.

Words streaked across the white doors in black spray paint.

BACK OFF.

EIGHT

Cora's nerves were still tied in knots as her PK-9 family worked hard to wash the spray paint off her car before it dried. The frigid air wasn't helping, nor the fact that the vandals had painted the same message on both sides of her vehicle.

The PK-9 ladies claimed they only had enough sponges and paper towels among the supplies they kept on hand for the cleaning service for three of them to work at a time. Meaning, Cora wasn't allowed to assist in the cleanup.

More than likely, they were taking pity on her since she'd probably appeared as rattled as she had felt when she'd told them about the scrawled message on her car. She never wanted to appear weak in front of these incredible women, but she just couldn't seem to develop the nerves of steel they all seemed to have when facing danger.

"I can't believe someone would do this right outside head-quarters in broad daylight." Jazz resoaked her blackened sponge in a bucket that splashed water onto the black pavement. "Didn't they see the cameras?"

"I hope not." Nevaeh discarded her handful of used paper towels and grabbed more off the roll. "'Cause then we'll have them on camera and..."

"...Busted!" Jazz said the word at the same time as Nevaeh, and they bumped fists.

"Oh, yeah. You know it, girl." Nevaeh's curls swirled as she spun in a dance move that Jazz mimicked, both ending in laughter.

Their antics brought a smile to Cora's face and loosened the tension in her stomach slightly. What a cute pair the two must have made when they were friends as schoolgirls. It seemed like a happily-ever-after tale that Phoenix had been able to not only hire Jazz at Nevaeh's recommendation but also to bring Flash back to the U. S. to reunite with his Army partner.

"Think it was the kid you busted today?" Amalia, squatting by the car to scrub at the paint, looked over her shoulder at Cora.

"I don't think so. His father might be able to get the charges dropped, since he sounds very influential and wealthy." Much like her own. Cora hugged her arms around herself over her jacket. "But even if Hayden were to get off, he'd still be in processing right now."

"Correct." Phoenix's strong voice came from behind Cora. Dag walked beside her as they exited PK-9 headquarters, and she led Jana at her other side on-leash. Cora had let Jana go back indoors earlier, since there wasn't much point in her standing out in the cold while they washed the car. "I checked. He's still at the police station."

"But other people aren't who should be." Bris carried the office laptop out into the parking lot. "See?"

Cora moved closer to see the screen, shielding it with her hand from the daylight that paled the image.

Two male figures approached her car. They wore ski masks above their dark jackets and jeans. One painted the message on her car while the other kept glancing at the front door of PK-9 headquarters. He patted the graffiti culprit on the back, and the two ran out of the camera's view.

"They must have parked on the street, or the dogs would've heard the car." Bris shut the laptop.

Phoenix handed Jana's leash to Cora. "We'll examine the recording closely and see if we can determine who they are. You need to get going."

The meeting. Cora had nearly forgotten. She checked the slim watch on her wrist. "Oh, my."

"I already informed him through his supervisor that you'd be late due to unforeseen car trouble."

"Thank you." Cora let out a sigh and looked at her Beetle. "At least most of the paint came off."

Amalia straightened and stepped back from the car as the other ladies did the same. "Sorry, that first part was already too dry. We might have to paint over it or something."

"Don't worry about it. It's only a few streaks." Cora smiled, a wave of gratitude washing over her for the kindness of these women. "You've all been so wonderful to pitch in and help."

"And don't forget the part about freezing our fingers off." Nevaeh dropped her sponge on the pavement and cupped her hands by her mouth, blowing warm air on them. "Remind me never to do another car wash in a Minnesota winter."

"Aww, and I was just going to put up our car wash sign along the road." Jazz beamed a teasing smile at Nevaeh.

"Yeah, we were planning on getting more customers today." Amalia squished her wet sponge in her bare fingers, flashing a devious grin.

"Hey, Mals." Nevaeh snatched up her sponge from the ground. "You missed a spot." She chucked the sopping sponge at Amalia, who dodged out of the way with a grin.

"You're asking for it now." She returned fire with her own sponge as Nevaeh darted away.

Cora laughed. "Okay, don't kill each other over my car wash, please. It's not worth it. And when did you switch to Mals?" Nevaeh, the team's resident nickname generator, used to call Amalia, *Mali*, for short.

Nevaeh shrugged, still wearing her grin as she kept an eye on Amalia. "Mals fits better."

"Keep trying, girl." Amalia laughed as she bent to pick up the bucket and sponge.

"Well, as fun as this is, I'd better get going. Thanks, again." Cora loaded Jana into the backseat and waved at her teammates as she left the lot.

Back off.

The memory of the aggressive message on her car made her grip the wheel more tightly. What did it mean? Back off of whom or what? And who would want to threaten her like that?

Other than Hayden that morning and the bomber Bris and the PK-9 team had apprehended last year, she'd never received any other threats.

And she didn't like the fear it sparked inside her.

Father, please protect me and show us who is behind this threat. And please help me with this meeting and working with Agent Thomson.

The prospect of meeting with the grim agent only tightened her nerves more. But perhaps he'd be warmer and friendlier now, in more relaxed circumstances.

And maybe the vandalism to her car was merely a prank, completely random.

But the twist of knots in her stomach belied the optimistic theory.

Someone could be targeting her, and she didn't even know why. If she didn't back off—whatever that referred to—what would they do next?

Kent watched Cora Isaksson enter the baggage claim and look around. She'd brought her dog with her, sporting the same black harness it had on before. Ms. Isaksson wore a long purple puffer jacket, pink gloves, and a matching scarf that peeked above the high neckline of the jacket.

The woman was so unsuited for this kind of work. Drug dealers, cartels, and his work as a DEA agent did not mix with pink accessories.

She had an aura of elegance that didn't belong in this line of business either. Not to mention the fragile quality that made her seem like a breakable china doll in need of protection.

She faced away and walked in the opposite direction from him.

As packed as the baggage claim was with people right now, he wasn't surprised she didn't spot him in the crowds.

He followed her, lengthening his stride to quickly catch up. "Ms. Isaksson."

She turned. Stepped into the path of a guy with a suitcase who ran toward her like he was on fire or late for a shuttle.

Kent grabbed her arms and spun her out of the man's path.

Her dog darted away just in time.

"Th—thank you." She blinked huge blue eyes at him, her hands lightly resting on the coat that covered his chest.

After looking at her ID photo a few too many times, he was still startled by her beauty in person. Her blond hair was swept up on her head, emphasizing her delicate features, the slimness of her neck where the scarf had fallen away, and her perfect, ivory skin. Her cheeks were highlighted at the cheekbones with a brush of natural pink color, likely brought on by the cold outside or the close call with suitcase dude. Or something else?

He brought his gaze to meet her eyes. "We have to stop meeting like this." The line was out of his mouth before he planned to say it. He dropped his hands away from her arms and took a step back, checking peripherals for any more oncoming traffic.

Confusion showed in her hesitant smile. "Yes. Thank you, again. You're very good at it."

He tilted his head slightly, fighting to beat back a smile that irrationally wanted to show itself.

"I mean, at rescuing me." More pink flushed her cheeks as her gaze skittered away. "That is, rescuing people in general. And your job. You're very good at your job."

There was something undeniably cute about her embarrassment.

Cute? Where had that come from? Vince would think Kent was going soft if he could hear his thoughts right now.

Giving himself a mental thrashing in his brother's absence, Kent resumed his game face and focused on the goal of this meeting: to see if the woman could handle this assignment. "I've secured a room for our meeting. Follow me." He turned and headed toward the staff-only doors along the back wall of the baggage claim.

She and her dog followed just behind his shoulder. "Will we do the searches out here in the baggage claim area?"

She was assuming the job was a sure thing. Probably the way Velasquez had presented it to her. But with the information Kent had uncovered, he was far from sure. He'd see what she had to say and then take his information to Velasquez. Hopefully, he'd be back to flying solo by late afternoon. The sooner he could stop wasting time and return to planning a new strategy to take down the Guajardo cartel, the better. Before more people got hurt.

NINE

"Care to tell me about your brother and his history with drugs?"

As soon as Agent Thomson had led her into a room used to hold flagged passengers until they could be questioned or handed over to the authorities, Cora had the feeling she was about to be interrogated. Given the personal question he'd just flung at her, her sense of foreboding was warranted.

She took a moment to think and try to calm her fidgeting pulse. Agent Thomson worked for the Drug Enforcement Administration. Of course, he would be concerned about her connection to any drug-related charges.

"My brother Bradley is two years younger than I. He suffered psychologically and emotionally from our mother's death when he was thirteen." She met Agent Thomson's gaze from the chair where he had told her to sit behind a table.

He stood on the opposite side. No sympathy registered in his gaze when she mentioned her mother's passing.

Jana slid her head onto Cora's lap, and Cora gratefully smoothed her hand over her comforter's soft fur.

"I tried the best I could to raise him and step into my mother's place, but I didn't do as well as I should have. One day, when he was at school—or so I thought—I discovered he had drugs hidden in his bedroom." She swallowed, her throat swelling with the memory. "I reported the drugs to the police."

Agent Thomson stepped closer to the table and crossed his arms over his black wool coat. "You reported your own brother." The question was more of a statement, made in a tone that suggested he was trying to process what she'd said, what she had done.

"Of course. The law exists for our protection, and I certainly wasn't going to shield my brother from the consequences of breaking it." She looked down at Jana's head on her lap. "As much as I wanted to."

"Very noble." Cynicism layered his voice.

What had happened to him that he couldn't understand someone wanting to follow the law even when it required sacrifice? Her silent question was immediately followed by the answer. Simply working with the DEA had likely created that skepticism. He must have seen some of the worst of fallen humanity in his career.

"I didn't want Bradley to keep going as he was, and I hoped tasting some consequences for his actions might stop him from falling any deeper into drug use."

"So he was charged with possession."

"Yes. But he didn't have to do any jail time thanks to... assistance from our father."

He lifted a dark eyebrow. "Money and lawyers, right?"

She nodded, meeting his gaze. She had nothing to hide and shouldn't act like she did. He'd only believe her if she was as honest and open as possible.

"And after that? What did your brother do?"

"He continued to have issues with drugs. He became addicted to them, to the point where I was afraid for his life. His character and personality completely changed." Cora stroked Jana's head, drawing comfort from her. "I was worried he might overdose or do something terrible while on drugs."

Agent Thomson turned away and walked to the end of the short table. He stood with his back to her. "Did he?"

"Praise the Lord, no. He left and disappeared for a while, but he just came back yesterday."

"Came back?" Agent Thomson faced her again, his features tightened as if he were holding something back. Or holding some emotion in?

"Yes. And he's free from his addiction." Joy brought a smile to her face as she remembered what Bradley had told her. "He went to a treatment center and was able to end his dependence on drugs."

"Really."

"Yes." At least, that was what he had told her. She had to give him the benefit of the doubt and believe him. Trust him.

"Okay, and what about you, Ms. Isaksson?"

"Me?"

"What is your history with illegal narcotics?"

"Well, my experience with my brother led me to want to help others affected by drugs. I found a way to do that with Phoenix Gray and her offer to give me Jana, my narcotics detection K-9."

He pulled out the chair on his side of the table and sat facing her. "Not what I meant. What is your history with illegal drugs, personally? Have you ever used them?"

Shock hit Cora like a blast of the cold air outside. "Of course not."

He stared at her, his eyes intense and hard.

She met his gaze, searching for some sign of softer emotion in the green irises, some explanation as to why he was questioning her instead of briefing her on the job they were to do.

Then she saw it. Not a pliability but the slight angle of his firmly set jaw. Defensiveness. He felt challenged by her somehow. Or, perhaps, threatened?

"Agent Thomson, do I make you feel uncomfortable for some reason?"

How could someone who looked so innocent—downright angelic—do exactly what she'd just surmised. Make him uncomfortable enough to want to shift in his seat. Or tell her outright that he wasn't going to work with her.

She was so open. So seemingly honest, yet far too idealistic or naïve to be on the level. Still, he couldn't believe she was lying when she denied having used illegal drugs. The stunned horror in her eyes was too genuine to be an act. The emotion in her voice when she spoke of her fear that her brother would OD was authentic enough to take him right back—to his tiny childhood house, huddled up on the sofa, the first dead body he'd ever seen lying in the next room.

"If you'd rather not work with me because of my family history, I understand. I won't be offended."

Was this woman for real? He stared at her but couldn't detect any farce or trace of inauthenticity in her soft gaze. She'd hit the nail on the head of the reason for his interrogation, and she did so without a hint of malice. She was practically unoffendable. And far more perceptive than her naïve demeanor had led him to believe.

Which meant she could already know the truth about her brother. One way to find out. "Did you know your brother was a drug dealer for the Guajardo cartel?"

Her cream complexion turned the shade of the white wall behind her. If she hadn't been sitting down already, he'd reach to catch her. "Ms. Isaksson?"

She swayed slightly.

He lurched to his feet, leaned across the table, reaching for her shoulders.

"I—" Her gaze jerked to his face, as if his movement had startled her. "That can't be true. He used drugs. He was addicted. But he didn't sell them."

Kent lowered himself to the chair again. "He did. One of the special agents investigating the Guajardo cartel back then recorded your brother's activities, among others, as a dealer for the organization."

"That's—" She leaned forward, bracing her head with a

hand against her forehead and her elbow propped on the table. "Isn't that the cartel Díaz and the other man were from? The two who tried to kidnap me yesterday?"

"Yes."

"I can't believe it. Bradley wouldn't have been involved with people like that. With organized crime?" Her big blue eyes turned on him as if he held the answers she was looking for.

But he only had information she didn't want to hear. "The facts don't lie, ma'am. People do all kinds of things you wouldn't expect when they're on drugs."

Her lashes dropped, but not before he caught sight of moisture glistening in her eyes. "Yes. I suppose I should know that."

His chest tightened. She wasn't going to cry, was she? Clearly, he didn't need to ask his follow-up questions about whether or not she had cartel connections.

"I'm sorry." She sniffed and lifted her head. No tear tracks marked her smooth skin. "I honestly didn't know he'd been involved with the cartel. I'll ask him about it. But I believe he's clean now, that he's given up the drugs. And he's been away for seven years."

"That wouldn't preclude him working for the cartel. Their U. S. distribution is nationwide."

"But they wouldn't be at a rehab center, and Bradley likely went where he knew they wouldn't bother him." She gazed at him with such urgency, like she was hoping he'd confirm her theory.

He couldn't look away. "I suppose it's possible." How she got him to admit that he'd never know.

"Thank you." She tucked some stray strands of fine hair behind her ear. "But you probably still don't want to work with me at the airport."

He cleared his throat again, something he seemed to do a lot around this woman. "It's nothing personal. I just prefer working alone. I don't need anyone to help me do my job, and I find others can just complicate things."

"That's understandable. If you'd like to tell your supervisor that we met and weren't a good fit, that would be fine."

He narrowed his eyes. Was she calling his bluff? Or did she not want to work with him for some reason? *As in, the charming way you've been treating her for the last twenty minutes.*

The sarcastic thought made him rethink his strategy. He knew what Velasquez would say if he showed her the intel on Cora's brother. She'd say Kent should know better than anyone that having a family member with a drug problem did not disqualify that person from working with the DEA. She wouldn't let him off this assignment on those grounds.

He was stuck. "No. We need your K-9's abilities to thoroughly scan the arrivals luggage."

Cora nodded. "I understand. Will you fill me in on what we'll be doing and show me where we'll search?"

He fought to keep from staring again. No one was that unoffendable. She didn't even mind his unintended slight about needing the dog, not her. Or if she did, she didn't show it on her highly readable face.

"Ms. Isaksson, there's one thing you should know. This could be a very dangerous job. You got a taste yesterday of the kind of people we might be dealing with. I'll try to keep you out of harm's way as much as possible, but there will still be some level of risk."

"I appreciate that, Agent Thomson." The firmness in her tone tightened her smooth jawline. "But stopping the sale and use of drugs however I can is worth any risk to my safety."

He watched her a moment.

She held his gaze. Didn't blink.

"Okay, then." He stood and led her out of the room to take her to the luggage sorting area behind the baggage claim where they would do most of their searching.

All the while, he hid his surprise at her gutsy response as he reassessed this delicate beauty. The china doll may not be as fragile as he'd thought.

Tension still unsettled Cora's stomach as she reached her car in the parking lot of the airport. What a nerve-wracking meeting. The conversation continually replayed in her mind. Had she responded to Agent Thomson's questions and defensiveness the way she should have?

And what about Bradley? *Father, is it true? Please show me how to help him. He was in even deeper than I knew. How could I have let that happen to my little brother?*

Jana bumped into Cora's leg as she pranced from foot to foot, eager to get in the car so she could receive her treat and water.

"I know, girl. I'm sorry." Cora pressed the button on her key fob twice to unlock all the doors. She reached for the handle of the back door and pulled.

The door didn't open.

She tugged harder.

It didn't budge.

Oh, no. Was it frozen?

She looked at the edges of the door. A film of clear ice covered the seams. She'd been in such a rush to get here, already late, that she hadn't thought of drying the car first.

She stepped to the driver's door and pulled. It was stuck, too. She set her purse on the hood of her car and tried yanking the door handle with both hands.

Her fingers slipped off. The door still wouldn't move.

Father, is there something you're trying to tell me today? She looked heavenward for a moment. Bad days happened to everyone. And bad days weren't really bad days. Just days God meant for special lessons to be learned and character to be formed. She closed her eyes and let out a calming breath.

Hot water. She'd go inside and wet some paper towels from the restroom with hot water. Perhaps applying them to the door would melt the ice and get it unstuck.

"Trouble?" The masculine voice popped Cora's eyes open, and she whirled to face the speaker.

Agent Thomson stood a few feet away, his hands in the pockets of the peacoat that skimmed his broad-shouldered, trim physique, and his dark hair askew in a decidedly flattering way. Even the coat collar he must have turned up for warmth framed his chiseled features to advantage.

Nevaeh and Amalia would never let her live it down if they saw this man's model looks and knew she'd noticed. But dark and brooding had never been her taste. And thankfully, it would take more than a handsome face to access her heart.

"Yes. Well, minor trouble." She gestured to the car. "The doors won't open. I think they may be frozen."

He stepped closer. "Frozen?"

"We had to wash my car before I came here. That's why I was late."

He gave her the perplexed look she'd seen on his face a couple times since their meeting. "An emergency car wash?"

Should she tell him about the vandals leaving a message on her car? No, it would likely only make her more suspicious in his mind. Phoenix always told her never to give someone unnecessary information. It was safer that way. "Something like that. I didn't think about drying it off, since I was running late."

"Ah." He brushed past her to the driver's door. "Let's see what we can do."

"I thought of getting warm water and seeing if I could melt it that way."

"Might not have to." He leaned hard against the door, pressing his body weight into it.

A slight cracking sound signaled the ice was breaking.

He straightened and gave the door a hard yank.

It opened.

"You did it!" Cora smiled, and Jana rushed up to him as if to say thank you. And possibly to try to get in the car from the front seat.

"No problem."

It hadn't seemed to be for him. She'd make a comment about his strength coming in handy but didn't want to risk sounding flirtatious. "Would you mind doing the same thing for the back door so I can let Jana in there?"

"Sure." He stepped to the other door and paused. He leaned over, looking at something.

Gray residue left from the black graffiti message.

"Is that spray paint?" The narrowed eyes made a repeat appearance as he turned to her.

She sighed. "Yes. Someone left a message for me when my car was parked at Phoenix K-9 headquarters today."

"What kind of message?" His voice pitched lower and took on an edge, as if it made him angry, though she didn't know why.

"It said to 'back off.'"

"Of what?"

She lifted her shoulders. "I'm not sure."

"Who left it?"

"I don't know that either."

"Doesn't your boss have security?"

A smile found Cora's lips despite the tension pinching her ribs. His question was like asking if birds had nests.

"Yes, she does. Very good security." Which Cora had helped install, but he didn't need to know that. "We caught the culprits on camera, but they wore ski masks. Phoenix was going to examine the footage more closely to see if we can identify them without facial recognition."

"I see." He watched her for a few more moments. Then he rotated back to the door and pushed hard, freeing it in short order. He took a step back and pushed his hands into his pockets. "Sounds like you have everything under control. Good luck finding out who did it."

"Thank you."

"And I guess I'll see you here tomorrow morning at eight."

She nodded. "See you then."

He turned and started to walk away.

"Agent Thomson."

He paused and angled halfway toward her.

"Thank you for coming to my rescue. Again." She gave him a smile.

His head tilted slightly as he watched her. "Anytime." He

lifted one hand in a still wave and left, walking up the row of parked cars until he veered to cut across the aisles between vehicles.

Jana bumped into Cora's leg.

"Sorry, girl. I need to get you in the car, don't I?" She let the eager golden jump onto the backseat and went through the habitual motions of giving Jana a dog biscuit and water from an insulated thermos she kept in the car.

But her mind was on the softening demeanor of Agent Thomson. It was certainly a blessing to have someone around who seemed to always show up when she needed help. Perhaps he wouldn't be so hard to work with, after all.

TEN

Energy buzzed through Kent's veins as he navigated the busy hallways of the precinct police station, headed for the interview room where drug distributor Marco Ramos waited for him. Kent could hardly believe what the Assistant District Attorney had told him when she'd phoned.

Ramos had said he'd talk for a deal. But he'd only talk to Kent.

Hadn't thought the guy had bonded with him so much at the site of the shooting and hostage rescue.

Fact was, Kent hadn't spoken to Ramos at all. Just made the arrest and sent him to be processed. Why he wanted to talk to Kent was beyond him. But the possibility that a regional manager of the Guajardo cartel might actually give them information was enough to pulse adrenaline through his body as if he were headed into a gunfight. He'd have to be at the top of his game to handle this perp right.

112.

Kent spotted the numbered plate on the door of the room that held Ramos.

He took in a breath and opened the door. Entered with a calm stride as he took in the officer standing in the corner and Ramos, seated at a table in the center of the room.

The rectangular table was empty except for a blank tablet.

Wishful thinking that Ramos might have something to write on it. Like a confession or everything Kent needed to know to bring down the Guajardo cartel.

"Hi, there." Kent pulled out the chair on the opposite side of the table from Ramos and sat, assuming a relaxed posture that should communicate Ramos could be at ease.

The drug dealer watched him, his head drooped slightly over his cuffed wrists, braced in line with his elbows on the table.

Kent glanced at the officer in the corner. "Can we get these cuffs off?"

Ramos's gaze went to Kent's face. The fifty-two-year-old man looked older than when Kent had last seen him. As if being held for twenty-four hours had already aged him another three years.

The officer moved in and used a key to remove the cuffs.

As he stepped away, Kent tried for a half-smile. "Better?"

"Thanks." Ramos's voice was rough, like it was dry from disuse.

"Could we get some water in here?" Another question for the officer.

He came out of the corner. "Sure." He opened the door and stepped from the room.

"I heard you want to talk to me." Kent gave Ramos a casual look.

"I guess so." He stared at his hands, which he flattened on the table like that was all they'd been freed to do.

Sounded like he might be backtracking. Having second thoughts. Kent kept his position relaxed, but inwardly his pulse picked up speed. "Let's start simple. What made you want to talk to me?"

Ramos slid his right hand in a partial circle, his gaze following its movement. "Do you know that girl?"

"What girl?"

"The one Díaz took. The one we rescued."

So, the guy fancied himself some knight in shining armor because he pulled the gunman away from Cora? Kent worked to repress the irritation that rose to the surface before it reached his expression. But he couldn't quite tamp down the heat that surged in his chest at the dealer's interest in Cora. What did he want with her?

Kent kept his tone even and unemotional as he responded. "I had never seen her before."

Ramos looked up, his gaze hitting Kent's. "I'd like to know who she is, but not for the reason you think." Ramos leaned back, letting his hands slide off the table and onto his lap. "The stuff she said, it…" He looked away. "I can't even…"

His hands came up to slide down the sides of his face. When they lowered to meet in front of him again, he faced Kent's scrutiny. "I don't get it, but what she said was so…right. She was right." He lifted his hands in the air and dropped them at his sides. "I don't want to be in prison for the rest of my little girl's childhood. I want to take care of her. And I don't want to work with the kind of people who might do to her what Díaz was going to do to the blonde."

Kent couldn't believe his ears. Nobody changed that fast after a life of crime. Not when they were fifty-two years old—a thirty-year veteran of the cartel's way of doing business.

"I've been thinking about it for a while. Since Sydney was born. The stuff I never gave a thought to before suddenly seemed different, you know? Like it didn't feel okay anymore. Maybe it's Sydney's mom. She keeps telling me to get out if I want to be a good dad."

He glanced away, then returned his attention to Kent. "But the way the blonde put it. I never thought of it like that. I'm all Sydney has to protect her. And I can't do that in the cartel or jail."

"So you want to talk?" Kent needed to throw down an obstacle, a test to see how legit this change of heart was. "You know we can't let you off with no time. Your record is too extensive for that."

"I know. But I could get a reduced sentence, right? Maybe community service or something? And I'll work off the rest with what I can give you. You won't be disappointed. I can get you all the way to the top."

"To Rodrigo Guajardo?"

Ramos met Kent's gaze without hesitation this time. Gave a nod.

The door opened, and Ramos jumped as if the kingpin himself was entering instead of the officer with water in a paper cup.

Kent waited until the officer set the cup down and returned to his stance in the corner. "You realize I can't just take your word for it, that you suddenly want to turn informant. You spent a lot of years working your way up in the cartel. Hands as dirty as yours don't get clean overnight."

Ramos took a drink of water, tucking the cup under his dangling mustache. "I'll prove it." His voice was just as scratchy even after the liquid. "A sample of what I can give you."

"I'm listening."

"A shipment of fentanyl just came to the Twin Cities. I can tell you where it's stashed right now. It's scheduled to be distributed on Friday."

Kent grabbed the tablet from the end of the table and slid it in front of Ramos. Kent glanced at the officer. "Can we get a pencil?"

Bringing his attention back to Ramos, he tapped the edge of the tablet. "You write down the address, and I'll look into it myself."

"And we'll have a deal?" His dark eyebrows, speckled with touches of gray, lifted.

"You'll get a second meeting with me. That's all I can promise right now." But if Ramos really was on the level, Kent would do whatever was necessary to get him a deal that would make him talk and lead Kent to the drug lord himself.

And Kent might want to say thanks to a certain lovely woman who'd had an odd effect on this career criminal. Whether she had dumb luck or a peculiar talent, he didn't know. But part of him wanted to find out.

They forgot all about me.

Cora halted the memory of her conversation with Bradley that was stuck on repeat in her head as she turned over to check the clock on her nightstand by the bed.

1:02 a.m.

She rolled back to face away from the illuminated numbers. Why couldn't she get back to sleep?

After dinner, she and Bradley had talked for two hours. About things he had seen when he'd traveled through most of the states in the eastern part of the U. S. About what she had done since he had left, her adventures with Phoenix K-9 as their communications and technology specialist, narcotics detection handler, and office manager.

They'd managed to keep their conversation confined to light topics. Nothing about their past in the Twin Cities, other than a few positive memories they shared from their childhood.

Until she brought up what Agent Thomson had told her about the Guajardo cartel.

"I didn't want you to know." Bradley hadn't been able to meet her gaze as he admitted the truth. As her heart broke into pieces like the day she'd found drugs in his bedroom. "I didn't mean to work for people like that. But..." Sitting in the armchair kitty-corner from where Cora sat, Bradley rubbed his hands across his thighs to his knees. "I could get supply for free. So long as I did them favors."

He glanced her way, then quickly darted his gaze elsewhere. "That's all it was supposed to be, at first. Just some favors. Trades for what I needed."

As if he had ever needed drugs. Concern trickled through Cora's bloodstream. Did he still think of drugs that way? As something he needed? She chose her words carefully as she responded. "Then they pulled you in deeper."

He nodded, still not looking at her. "Once you're in, you're in for good. I saw some stuff. Knew stuff. Enough that I thought I couldn't get out even if I ever wanted to."

She caught the implication in his words and his tone. He hadn't wanted to get out. It made logical sense since they were giving him free access to the substance he thought he couldn't do without. But the truth still stung. Not only had she missed her baby brother getting hooked on drugs, but she'd also had no idea he was working for a criminal organization that used his addiction to essentially hold him hostage. Did they still have that power over him?

She ventured the question sending fright through her body. "I need you to tell me the truth, Bradley. I won't be upset either way, but I need to know for your own safety. Are you still working for the cartel now?"

He straightened, shaking his head. "No. I told you, I'm clean."

"I know, and I believe you, but you said the cartel won't let anyone go."

"Yeah, but I realized when I wanted to get clean that if I checked into rehab in a different city from where I'd gotten my supply, the cartel wouldn't know me there. I shook them off. And I spent such a long time away, not buying from any street dealers, that they forgot all about me." He smiled, his gaze drifting to find hers at last. "I'm out, Sis. For good."

The tension coiling Cora's nerves released with a relieved exhale. The theory she'd proposed to Agent Thomson had been right. Bradley wasn't involved with the cartel or drugs any longer.

"Hey, remember that time you took me to the zoo and the llama spit at me?"

Cora had taken Bradley's hint and followed the lighter trajectory of conversation he'd introduced. They'd ended the night with upbeat reminiscing and laughter.

Reconnecting with her brother in such a warm and friendly manner had left Cora relaxed and ready to sleep when she turned in for the night. She'd fallen asleep as soon as her head touched the pillow.

But something had awakened her a few minutes after midnight. She didn't know what it had been. As soon as she was awake, her thoughts started to pile up in her head—reviewing her conversation with Bradley and her interaction with Agent Thomson that afternoon.

And, especially, the angry message painted on her car.

She needed to calm the anxiety pinching her chest or she would never get back to sleep.

A jingle of tags signaled that Jana had gotten up from her bed in the corner and was approaching Cora. A brown nose on the end of a snout appeared in front of Cora's face.

"Hey, girl." Cora pulled her hand out from under the covers to stroke the golden's soft head. "Are you here to help me calm down and go back to sleep?"

Cora pushed up on an elbow, catching sight of Jana's tail, wagging in response. Cora lowered her head and kissed Jana's soft forehead.

The golden's tail wag sped up as she seemed to grin.

Cora laughed. "You're such a sweetheart. You always know just what people need, don't you?" A trait that made her an excellent therapy dog when Cora took her to visit hospitals and the children's reading program at the public library.

A thud made them both start.

Had that come from downstairs?

Cora held still, her hand on Jana's head between the dropped ears she'd perked high as she stared at Cora's open bedroom doorway.

Bradley.

The realization released the air caught in Cora's lungs. He must be foraging in the kitchen for a late-night snack. He used to do that nearly every night as a teenager, despite Cora's efforts to train him to get his nourishment during the day.

Although, the thud had sounded a bit like the back door when she would let it swing shut.

A bark popped from Jana's mouth.

Cora started, her heart slamming her ribs. Jana never barked. Not since she'd grown into an adult and left puppy play-barking behind.

"Shh. It's okay, girl." Cora whispered the automatic comfort as she gave Jana a stroke, feeling a bit like a liar as her pulse sprinted with fear. Cora slid her feet out from under the covers and touched them to the floor. She lifted her cell phone from her nightstand and powered it on.

She should call Phoenix. Or the police.

The screen lit.

Wait, it played a jingle when it turned on.

She quickly stuffed the phone under her pillow and pressed it tight over the device. The plush down muffled the cheery tune, hopefully enough that no one else could hear.

If someone was in the house.

The thought sent a tremor through her body.

But reason followed on its heels. She didn't know there was an intruder. There had only been a noise, which was more likely Bradley wandering around downstairs than a home invader.

She wouldn't call for help only to learn she'd let her imagination run away with her. She was likely overreacting because of the stress of the day and lack of sleep.

She stood and picked up the fleece robe she kept on the bench at the end of her bed. Pulling it on over her cotton pajama shirt and pants, she slowly went to the doorway.

Jana stayed beside her, the golden's movements a soft brush on the carpeted floor. At least Jana seemed normal again, panting with a relaxed demeanor as she paused with Cora in the doorway. That was a good sign.

But why, then, did Cora's pulse still pound in her ears?

She shook her head. She was going to feel so silly when Bradley came up those stairs, carrying a snack.

The alarm.

How could she have forgotten her state-of-the-art security system? She'd installed it herself. She must be more tired than she realized. She had just shown Bradley the alarm system last night, so he wouldn't accidentally trigger it if he wanted to leave and could disarm it if he came home when she was gone during the day.

If any intruder tried to enter her house from the back door, front, or any of the windows, her security system would be triggered, and ear-deafening alarms would be sounding right now.

But the house was silent.

Not even another noise from downstairs.

Cora stepped out of her room, her bare feet sinking into the carpet as she moved toward the wall that hid the staircase from view.

Her heart rate still hadn't slowed, refusing to heed her logic.

She peered around the wall.

The gray-carpeted stairs were empty. The shadow of the railing cast an eerie outline on the wall.

A dark object darted past the stairs below.

She sucked in a breath, covering her mouth as she pulled back behind the wall.

A person. In dark clothing. In her house.

ELEVEN

Cora crept back into her room, Jana following with a cheery tail wag as if enjoying her partner's peculiar behavior.

How had the intruder entered without triggering the exterior alarm? It made no sense. The system was set to automatically arm at eleven o'clock.

Her fingers shook as she closed the door behind her, slowly turning the knob to shut it without a sound.

Breathe. Find a weapon.

She scanned her bedroom, the pink and blue floral décor accented with soft pillows and blankets—her den of comfort. Nothing she could use for self-defense.

A nail file? She had one in the upstairs bathroom if she dared risk going out into the hall to get it.

She pictured holding it in her hand as the dark figure approached her.

Her stomach lurched. She could never stab anyone.

She'd have to rely on her backup plan.

If he tried to come upstairs, it should work.

Father, please protect me. And Bradley.

She pressed her fingers to her lips. Bradley must still be sleeping in his room close to the top of the stairs. She needed to warn him.

She slowly opened the door.

A creak reached her ears. The first stair at the bottom always creaked when stepped on.

She froze. She told Jana to stay with a hand signal.

Whoop, whoop, whoop.

The security alarm blared, stinging her ears and startling poor Jana, who flattened her ears against her head. But Cora may never have heard any sound so welcome.

Emboldened by the alarm and the help she knew her system was calling, she went to the wall by the stairs and peeked around it.

The dark figure ran from the stairs.

She listened as rapid footsteps thudded through the rooms downstairs.

The back door slammed.

She dashed to Bradley's bedroom door and knocked rapidly. "Bradley? Are you okay?" She pressed her ear to the door to hear past the blaring alarm. "Bradley?"

Why hadn't he come out to see what was going on?

Hesitantly turning the knob, she opened the door just enough to lean her head inside.

His bed was empty, the covers tousled as if he'd lain in it.

She walked in, and Jana scurried in beside her, the golden's ears still flattened against her head in response to the uncomfortable noise. "I'm sorry, girl. I'll turn it off as soon as I make sure…" Her words trailed off as she went into the connecting bathroom and turned on the lights.

Empty.

Bradley was gone.

The nice thing about breaking into a holding location for the cartel was there was no alarm system to worry about. They wouldn't exactly want the police or a security firm showing up.

Kent crouched next to the chain-link fence that surrounded the lot where a warehouse stood. The warehouse Ramos had claimed stored drugs.

This hunting expedition would show if the regional manager was on the level. If he was, he might be able to lead Kent to the biggest bust of his career—the infamous drug lord, Rodrigo Guajardo.

Kent had cased the perimeter of the location, and only two men were posted outside, likely armed with concealed weapons. They each stood near entrances to the warehouse at the front and back, dressed like typical cartel thugs. No uniforms like security guards at a legit business. A good sign this place might be what Ramos had said.

Only two cars were parked at the far side of the building, likely belonging to the guards. Which meant no one should be in the warehouse.

If Kent climbed over the fence here, toward the side of the building, he wouldn't be seen by either of the guards.

The fence was probably ten feet high. Three strands of barbed wire taunted him at the top. As if they were enough to stop him.

He took off the leather jacket he wore over his black sweater and flung it over his shoulder. Stretching up both arms, he inserted his fingers around the chain links and started to climb. His grip was weaker than in his teen years, when he'd done this often for kicks with friends. But he hadn't forgotten how.

Reaching the top, he paused, held his weight with one hand and the toes of his shoes while he whipped the jacket off his shoulder. He swung it above his head, draping it over the barbed wires.

He pressed off with his feet and gripped the wires through his jacket. The leather would never be the same. But it was worth it if this paid off.

Swinging his body over the barbed wires, he held on, letting his legs dangle as low as possible on the other side. He dropped, squatted as he landed and leaned forward to let his hands soften the fall.

He scanned the darkness inside the fence. The side of the building, about fifty feet ahead, wasn't lit like the front and back. Another advantage to this approach. But he'd still have to get in past the guards somehow.

One problem at a time.

He hurried across the open area. Lucky somebody had plowed the blacktop of the lot, or the snow would've made staying concealed impossible.

He hit the concrete wall of the warehouse and pressed against it, checking his peripherals. At least here, crates were stacked along the wall, so he had some cover.

Now to get inside without being seen.

Velasquez would have his hide if she knew he was doing this without a search warrant. But he wasn't going to arrest anyone or take anything. No one would know he was here. He only needed to get a glimpse of the goods to verify Ramos's story. And to show the SAC he was making progress and needed to focus on this case, alone. Not partner with a narcotics K-9 handler to search baggage.

He rounded a set of crates.

Someone appeared at the corner of the building.

Kent ducked behind more crates. Only fifteen feet from the guard.

The black shoulder of the guy's jacket was all Kent could see when he peered past the wooden crate in front of him.

The guard moved again, heading back the way he had come. Disappeared behind the building.

If the thug at the front was starting to patrol and move around more, Kent wouldn't try to get by him. More lamps lit the front anyway.

He turned and headed for the back of the warehouse instead, darting in between crate stacks. He checked behind him frequently, in case the front guard got curious again.

On one glance back, his gaze caught on something—a window above a stack of three crates he'd just passed. The window was short but wide. Wide enough to let a person through.

He went back to the crates, each standing about six feet high. Whoever had stacked them wasn't a perfectionist. They were twisted at imperfect angles on top of each other. Ideal for climbing.

He looked toward the front of the building. Then the back.

No guards.

He hefted himself up onto the first crate, then made the easy climb up the next two.

The window was nearly level with the top crate.

Kent reached for the bottom of the grimy, paned glass and pushed.

It angled inward, away from the sill.

Kent's pulse tripped. His lucky day.

Flattening his body, he lifted the window with one hand until he crawled through far enough to let his back prop it open.

He stopped, his head and shoulders through the window, legs still behind on the crate outside.

Nothing stood below him. No object he could use to safely get down from the fifteen-foot height. Not a good scenario when he was headfirst.

He grunted. Maybe he could—

"Hey!"

He jerked his head toward the shout.

Two men appeared from around a massive row of shelves. Pulled their guns.

Kent swore and scrambled backward.

Pop, pop.

Fiery pain tore through his shoulder. He'd been hit.

TWELVE

Bris leaned close to hand Cora a steaming mug of coffee. "I'll bring you some cream and sugar, too."

Cora looked up at her friend from the sofa, mustering a shaky smile. "Bless you."

Bris gently rubbed Cora's shoulder before leaving to return to the kitchen where she'd brewed the strengthening beverage. It was only one of the many wonderful things Cora's PK-9 family had done for her since they'd swept in, police squads at their heels.

Phoenix had immediately sent Amalia and Nevaeh to check the grounds with Raksa and Alvarez. Meanwhile, Jazz and Phoenix had cleared the house itself, searching it with Flash and Dagian ready to defend against anyone foolish enough to have lingered when the alarm went off.

No one was found, nor much evidence of a break-in. Phoenix had sent the police on their way, letting them know she'd give them pertinent information if she found any.

About ten minutes ago, Jazz had joined Amalia and Nevaeh outside to continue patrol while Bris had assumed Cora's usual role—the mothering, as the ladies teasingly called it. Cora couldn't be more grateful for each and every one of them right now.

And for Jana, who hadn't left her side since the incident began and now laid her warm head on Cora's feet.

Still, Cora had only just begun to stop trembling, covered in her favorite fleece blanket Bris had retrieved from Cora's bedroom. She shuddered again. Would she ever feel safe here? Enough to sleep in her own home?

A clatter made her jump.

"Sorry." Bris sent her a glance as she set the creamer and sugar on the coffee table in front of Cora. "Didn't mean to startle you."

Cora shook her head. "It's not you." She lowered the mug and went through the motions of adding enhancements to the coffee, hoping the normalcy of the movement would help her calm down.

"Your cameras caught him." Phoenix looked up from Cora's notebook computer, perched on her lap in the armchair. She'd been sitting there for the last fifteen minutes, at least. She was so quiet, Cora could almost forget she was there if not for the slow and steady improvement in her edginess since Phoenix had stayed with her. There was something so calming and reassuring about being near Phoenix. Nothing would happen with her here.

"He covered his face, of course. Ski mask. Nondescript black clothing. Gloves." Phoenix closed the computer, drawing a glance from Dag, who rested on the floor beside her. "I doubt we're going to find much evidence we can use other than the pick job he did on the back door. There are tire treads in the snow by the curb on the street where he may have parked. But there's no way to be certain they came from his vehicle."

"Some of us parked there last night for the party." Bris shoved her hands into the kangaroo pocket of her brown hooded sweatshirt.

"We found footprints in the snow at the back door." Phoenix's strong, comforting voice continued without a hint of the worry or tension that Cora was battling. "We were careful not to damage them. The sneaker print looks undistinctive, but we'll get a cast and see what we can find."

Cora took a sip of the coffee and closed her eyes as the hot liquid slid down her throat, sending warmth to her belly.

"Did you check the security system to be sure it was armed before you went to bed?" Phoenix watched Cora, gentleness in her dark blue eyes.

"No." Cora set down the mug on the table. "I suppose I should have. But my system has been so reliable. It always activates according to how I've programmed it. I'll have to look at it and see what went wrong."

Bris glanced at Phoenix, who kept her gaze on Cora.

"What is it?" Cora glanced from Bris to Phoenix.

"I already checked the activity of the system on your computer. A person deactivated it."

Cora sucked in a breath. "The intruder?"

"It was deactivated at 12:03 a.m."

"But I didn't hear someone break in until after 1:00."

Phoenix stared, letting her non-response do her communicating as she so often did.

"You mean someone else deactivated it. Bradley?" He never would have purposely let someone into Cora's house. And he hadn't even been home when the intruder entered. Praise the Lord for that. "Perhaps he deactivated the alarm because he needed to go somewhere and then forgot to reactivate it." Cora looked at Phoenix, whose expression didn't convey an opinion on the theory. "Or maybe he intended to come right back in, so he didn't bother to turn it on again."

"Seems plausible to me." Bris glanced at Phoenix before bringing her gaze to Cora. "But why would he leave in the middle of the night? Would he have a good reason to do that?"

Cora pulled the blanket tighter around her shoulders. "I don't know." She didn't know her own brother anymore. The brother she'd promised her mom she'd take care of, the boy she would raise to love and serve the Lord. How could she have failed so badly?

But she did know he would never harm her or intentionally cooperate with anyone who would put her in danger. She swallowed and looked up. "I'm certain, though, that he had nothing to do with the intruder."

"Then who do you think broke in?" Phoenix had a knack for prodding Cora to face realities she didn't want to. In this case, the identity of someone who would want to invade her home.

Someone who wanted to go upstairs to…do what? Attack her? Kidnap her? Or kill.

But why? She didn't know of anyone who disliked her that much. Unless…

Hayden's face, twisted with resentment and anger, filled her vision.

"He's a likely suspect." Phoenix watched Cora, giving voice to the accusation Cora didn't want to think let alone speak.

"But he's just a boy. A hurting boy."

"Who?" Bris looked back and forth between Phoenix and Cora.

Cora moistened her lips. "Hayden."

"Oh. I wondered if it could be him. Hayden's tall and skinny, right? Did you see if his build could be a match?"

"I couldn't tell. I only caught a glimpse of the intruder in the dark." Cora reached for her coffee mug and took another sip. Perhaps it would bolster her courage. And the caffeine wouldn't matter since she didn't expect to sleep anymore tonight regardless.

"I'll see if we can find out where he was at the time of the invasion." Phoenix leaned forward and stood. Dag got to his feet beside her. "If we can't, I'll get the police to question him as a suspect."

Cora wrapped her fingers around the mug to warm them. "It could have been a random burglary, I suppose."

"The intruder didn't go for the electronics—computer, TV— on the first floor." Phoenix stepped to the coffee table and set the computer down. "The target seems to have been something or someone upstairs."

The target. Was that what she was to someone?

Or had they been after Bradley? The thought made her shudder.

"What is it?" Concern colored Bris's voice as she watched Cora.

"I learned something today. About Bradley." Cora leaned forward to set the mug on the table before her quivering fingers dropped it. "Agent Thomson said Bradley was involved with the cartel. That he was…a drug dealer for them."

"Oh, wow." Bris stepped closer and rested her hand on Cora's shoulder. "I'm sorry, Cora."

"I talked to Bradley about it, and he admitted the truth. But he also assured me he hasn't had anything to do with the cartel in years. He's happy they've forgotten about him." Cora locked her eyes on Phoenix, watching for any sign of agreement, of affirmation that the cartel would have forgotten her brother.

"You'll stay with me tonight." The statement came from Phoenix's deep voice, but shock stopped Cora from believing it.

She glanced at Bris instinctively for confirmation that she'd heard Phoenix correctly.

Bris's eyes were as wide as Cora guessed her own were.

"Me?" An unnecessary question, probably, but the only reply Cora could think of to confirm Phoenix meant what she had said.

She directed her firm gaze at Cora. "Yes. You'll be safe at my house."

Cora had anticipated she'd have to resist Phoenix's insistence on leaving her protection Doberman, Apollo, with Cora to guard her at home. Or that Phoenix would post the PK-9 women in her yard overnight to patrol. She'd never expected an invitation to stay with Phoenix at her home. In the six years that she'd known and worked for Phoenix, she didn't think Phoenix had ever let anyone visit her home. Not even for a meal, let alone an overnight stay.

And right now, *safe* sounded like the most wonderful word in the world.

"Okay." Cora looked up at Phoenix. "Thank you."

Phoenix jerked a nod and turned away, heading for the front door. "I'm going to check with Amalia. See what they found." She paused. "I'll have Jazz and Flash watch your place tonight as a precaution in case the intruder returns." She opened the door. "Pack what you need, and we'll leave in ten minutes." She exited without glancing back.

"Wow." Bris turned to Cora. "You'll have to tell me what her place is like. I didn't think she ever invited anyone over."

"I don't think she does."

"She really likes to take care of you."

Cora stood, her movement prompting Jana to push up to a sitting position. "She takes care of everyone on the team."

"True."

But what Bris meant—what they both knew—was true. Phoenix did take special care of Cora. She always had, since they first met when Cora was a senior in college, doing an internship at a computer technologies company.

As Cora folded the fleece blanket and excused herself to pack, her mind drifted back six years to that first encounter. Phoenix had been hired to consult on the company's security system. Cora was assigned to help her and implement the changes Phoenix recommended. By the end of the job, Phoenix had recruited Cora to work for her, first as a technology specialist and office manager, and soon after as Jana's handler for narcotics detection, as well.

From early on, Cora had noticed Phoenix treated her differently than she treated other people. Cora still didn't know the reason for the difference, but she thought Phoenix might trust her enough someday to tell her. For now, she had only to be grateful for Phoenix's protection and care, especially tonight.

The dark night when the security of her home had been shattered, her brother went missing again, and her life was in danger without her even knowing why.

THIRTEEN

Blood dripped into the sink. The same red liquid soaked the paper towels heaped in the wastebasket in the corner.

The bathroom of Kent's apartment looked like a homicide crime scene. Reminded him of the search warrant he'd been part of as a rookie that had exploded into a shooting that left several dead. Three dealers, one agent.

Wasn't the first time he'd witnessed death. But it was the first time the dead hadn't been his family.

He turned on the faucet, watched the water swirl red, then clear as the blood was washed down the drain. He grabbed a large bandage from the first aid kit he kept on hand.

Despite the pain, the bullet had only cut through a bit of flesh. He should be able to avoid a hospital visit—with all the paperwork and chastising from Velasquez that would involve—so long as he kept the wound clean.

He winced as he pressed the bandage onto his shoulder.

How he'd love to have returned fire on the thug who'd plugged him. But he'd had to hightail it out of there as if he were running scared. At least he'd made it over the fence and back to his car with enough distance between him and the thugs that he was sure they couldn't ID him.

He'd take more time to case the warehouse before going in

again. But he would go back. And soon. He'd figure out when they had fewer guards or find a way to get past them all without being seen. He had to know if Ramos could be trusted. Because if he could, Kent had big plans for the cartel's regional manager.

Kent's cell phone buzzed on the shelf above the sink.

He picked it up, checked the screen. Text message.

From Vince. *Okay. Breakfast at 6.*

Just like Vince to pick the time and state it like a command.

Kent typed a response in kind. *Mackinaws.* He set the phone back on the shelf. There wouldn't be a response unless Vince disagreed with the restaurant choice for some reason.

Kent's gut tightened as he picked up his blood-soaked T-shirt and sweater from the floor and dropped them in the bathtub.

He turned on the shower head, ran cold water on the clothes, ridding them of the evidence that would stain if not eliminated right away.

Is that what Charlie had done when he'd gone home that night? Had he stood in his bathroom, washing away the evidence that he'd murdered the man who'd tried to help him? The father of two boys who were waiting for him to come home.

Kent jerked back, shut down the thoughts. He twisted the knob to turn off the water. Turned, stalked out of the bathroom.

Vince wouldn't have come to talk about that. They never talked about it.

But why had he shown up now? Kent grabbed a bottle from the fridge and sat in the chair in the corner of his dimly-lit living room. No point in going to bed. The wondering and the pain—in his arm and much deeper inside him—would keep him awake for the few hours that remained of the night.

The steel door slid shut behind them with a clang that made Cora jump.

She looked back at the shiny silver barrier that had emerged from a pocket in one wall to seal tightly against the other, completely blocking the front door that had appeared so normal from the outside.

Cora had expected Phoenix would have tight security, but this was a level beyond anything she had imagined. And why had Phoenix taken her out of the attached garage to enter through the front door instead of through the connecting entrance?

Phoenix paused at the door and typed something into her smartphone while Dag waited by her side.

A light blinking on a screen fixed to the wall beside the vault-like door changed from red to green.

Perhaps she had used her phone to arm or disarm an alarm system. They had set up something similar for the Phoenix K-9 headquarters, but no steel doors were involved. And they also had a keypad option at the headquarters so all team members could control the system if needed without private account access.

"No one will be able to hurt you here." Phoenix's reassuring voice reached through the tangle of nerves clogging Cora's chest as she passed Cora and her small suitcase to lead the way through the narrow hallway to another door. This one was heavy steel with a normal knob but a fingerprint-activated lock.

With security this extreme at her home, some might think Phoenix was afraid of something. But Phoenix wasn't afraid of anything. At least, nothing that had to do with physical danger.

There had to be more to it than that, but it wasn't Cora's place to ask. Especially when she knew how much this meant that Phoenix had invited her here and was letting her into the privacy of her home. Cora wouldn't do anything to make her regret that.

Muffled sounds, like barking, came from the other side of the door.

Probably Apollo and Birger.

Dag let out a bark himself as Phoenix opened the door.

"Stand down, guys. Just Cora."

Good thing Cora already knew the big Doberman Pinscher and Great Pyrenees who surged toward her. And that she knew enough about dogs to recognize when their body language switched to friendly before the barking had stopped.

Phoenix let the heavy door slam shut behind them, but Cora didn't startle this time. She was too busy with the dogs that greeted her.

Apollo, the tall, muscled Doberman, gave her a few sniffs and accepted a pet on the head before he walked away, apparently satisfied she wasn't a threat.

But the white, fluffy Great Pyrenees, Birger, stayed for petting from Cora and an enthusiastic greeting with Jana. Cora laughed as Birger bumped into her in his eagerness to reach Jana. His gorgeous, bushy tail swished against Cora, leaving long, white hair on her olive-green slacks.

She pointed to the fur on her clothes and looked at Phoenix. "Proof I've been loved by a Great Pyrenees."

A small smile curved Phoenix's closed lips.

"Will I get to meet Azami?"

"You might get to see her." Phoenix bent to remove Dag's harness and leash. "We can try a greeting in a bit. I'll have you sit at the dining table and let her come out and approach if she wants to."

"That would be great." Such precautions were understandable, though Cora had long wanted to meet Phoenix's only non-working dog. The small, mixed-breed dog was a rescue from a situation where she'd been abused and, as a result, she was terrified of strangers.

"She's better with women, so she might come close, but she probably won't want you to pet her."

"That's fine. It would just be lovely to see her."

"Let's get you settled first."

Dag walked away from Phoenix and went to drink water in an elevated stand by an island in the kitchen.

Cora hadn't observed the kitchen before amid the doggy greeting, but it now captivated her attention. It was gorgeous, sporting state-of-the-art appliances in stainless steel and equipped with pots and pans that hung from hooks on the walls, gleaming under the overhead lights. The kitchen reminded her of the professional ones she'd seen on TV. Did Phoenix cook?

"Your bedroom is this way."

"Okay. Come on, Jana." Cora grabbed the long handle of her suitcase and wheeled it behind her as she and Jana followed Phoenix past the kitchen and into a series of hallways. Though the short hallways turned frequently, they still led deeper and deeper back. The house must be larger than Cora had thought from the outside. They passed closed doors a few times, but many of the hallways had no doors at all.

In some of the halls, Cora noticed tracks that crossed the floor and ceiling in line with the edge of a door—or perhaps a gate—that was recessed into the wall.

"Here." Phoenix stopped at a closed door, another made of heavy steel but with a knob like the second entry door at the front of her house. "This is secured with a numbered code." She pulled a small slip of paper from her pocket and handed it to Cora. "This is the code you can use tonight and tomorrow."

Cora looked at the numbers written in Phoenix's hand. Then looked up to see Phoenix watching her.

"Go ahead and make sure it works."

"Oh. Of course." Cora released the handle of her suitcase, sitting it upright on the wheels as she went to the keypad and entered the code.

It beeped and blinked a green light.

Cora reached for the knob and turned. It didn't open.

"Push harder."

"Sorry." She tossed an embarrassed glance at Phoenix as she realized her mistake. The door was simply heavier than a normal one. She leaned her body against it and pushed it inward.

Jana, the only dog who still followed them at the moment, brushed past Cora into the room that looked surprisingly normal once the automatic sensor lights switched on.

Cora followed Jana inside as she scanned the space.

It was sparsely furnished, but neat and clean with a charcoal-colored bedspread that matched the light gray walls of the room. A black nightstand with modern lines held a small lamp and an alarm clock. Recessed lighting in the ceiling accounted for the brightness of the room that had no windows.

"Your bathroom is connected." Phoenix went to the open door opposite the bed and reached inside to turn on the light. She disappeared for a second, then emerged. "It's clear."

Cora's chest tightened. In her fascination with Phoenix's house, she'd forgotten about the danger for a moment. Whatever that danger really was.

"I installed your system in the hall outside this room, as well." Phoenix's blue eyes fixed on Cora, as if reading her fear. "If anyone were to bypass external security and reach this room —which would be extremely unlikely—the alarm in the hall would trigger before they got to your door. There are no windows and no other point of entry. But if you need a way out, you'll find an escape hatch under the bed. Apollo and Birger will patrol the grounds outside. And you've seen some of my other security on the way in. You'll be safe here."

Cora stared at Phoenix, her pulse rate surging from the scenarios that seized her imagination with each security measure Phoenix listed. She'd had a feeling Phoenix's home would be as unique and impressive as the woman herself. But right now, the idea that Cora needed such extreme security was too frightening to leave room for fascination.

And what about Bradley? The reminder that he could be in danger sent another spark of fear through her system. "Phoenix, do you think the intruder could have been from the cartel?"

"It's possible."

"They could have been looking for Bradley?"

"Or you."

Cora stared at Phoenix. "What do you mean?"

"I learned from my sources at the precinct that one of the men who kidnapped you is a top distributor for the Guajardo cartel. He's now in custody, thanks to you."

"Oh, my. You think they may want revenge? To…kill me?"

"They've killed for less."

Cora's hand went to her throat as her body turned cold all over. But she couldn't let fear for herself make her forget her most important priority, the only thing that mattered. "What about Bradley? If they could have been after him, it's even worse that I don't know where he is." Cora stepped closer to the woman she knew could do almost anything. "Phoenix, could you find him somehow and make sure he's safe?"

Phoenix folded her arms over her open black jacket. "He is safe. For now."

Relief flooded Cora's limbs. "You know where he is?"

"I hired Remington Jones to follow him."

Bris's fiancé? Cora knew Rem had opened a private investigations agency of his own earlier in the year. But she hadn't thought Phoenix would be one of his clients.

"We don't have the staff to tail your brother and keep up with our contracts, so I brought in Jones."

Cora's mind raced to fill in the blanks, why and when Phoenix would have hired Rem to follow Bradley. Most likely, she had hired Rem the night Bradley returned. "You thought Bradley might put me in danger."

"It appears he's done just that."

"But we don't know that this has anything to do with him." The defensive response surprised Cora the moment she said the words. Where did she suddenly get the impetus to challenge Phoenix? She never did that. Yet, an odd spark of indignation made her keep going. "Perhaps it wasn't even the cartel, but Hayden, the high schooler."

Phoenix gave Cora a searching look—not quite the intense, interrogation stare she'd seen Phoenix give others, but something similar. "The invasion could also have been attempted burglary. Or attempted attack or abduction for no rational motive." If Phoenix had been the type to let her voice carry emotion, Cora was sure there would be an edge to her tone right now.

Cora sighed. "I'm sorry. I just have a hard time believing

Bradley could have caused any of this. I know he wouldn't have put me at risk purposely. I know that. Did Rem see when he left the house?"

"12:04, just after the security system was disarmed according to the log. Jones followed him to a park. He didn't appear to meet anyone there. Bradley drove back to your house, slowed, then continued past. Jones believes the emergency vehicles spooked him. He went to a motel and checked in for the night."

"Oh." Cora crossed her arms in front of her chest, her heart sinking. Why wouldn't Bradley have come in to check on her when he saw the police there?

She drew in a shaky breath. He was probably frightened, perhaps by the cartel or the police since he had a difficult history with them. Now he was alone at a motel. "Will Rem stay with him tonight? To watch him, I mean?"

"He'll keep tabs on him one way or another."

Probably by using a tracking device when Rem couldn't have eyes on Bradley.

Cora nodded. "Thank you for asking Rem to do this. It helps to know where Bradley is." It was also comforting to know Phoenix cared so much, even if she didn't share everything with Cora.

Phoenix's reasoning was sound, as always. The intruder hadn't behaved like a burglar since he hadn't taken the easy-access electronics and other valuables downstairs. He had wanted to go upstairs for some reason. Hayden might have done so for some kind of revenge and been easily scared off by the alarm.

But if the cartel had sent someone, would he have run? Perhaps, since he wouldn't have anticipated an internal alarm activated on the stairs. Yet, the idea of someone trying to hurt her or Bradley so intentionally was almost too terrifying for her mind to grasp.

"Phoenix," Cora moistened her lips, "do you think someone really wants to harm Bradley or...me?"

Phoenix's expression didn't reveal a hint of an answer, despite Cora searching for one there. But, then, she spoke. "I'm not going to let that happen."

Cora had her answer. But not the one she'd hoped for.

FOURTEEN

A silence as thick as the scent of bacon in the air hung between Vince and Kent as they ate their spicy sausages and eggs.

They sat at the end of the Mackinaws Diner counter where they could both see the front entrance and had the rear exit close by. They hadn't talked about where to sit. Just naturally chosen it. Same way they'd always locked their doors, parked Kent's bicycle inside their apartment, and kept their eyes moving whenever they walked on the street. Survival tactics born of the neighborhood they'd grown up in and the unnatural deaths of two parents.

They'd been at the diner for twenty minutes, and Vince still hadn't said anything beyond a "Hello," and, "Pass the salt."

Not that he'd ever said very much.

The silence should have felt normal. Comfortable. They'd always gotten along well, except for the minute when Kent's teenage rebellion had nearly gotten out of hand. And they'd never said many words, especially Vince.

But there was nothing normal about Vince's sudden urge to come to Minnesota and see Kent.

Stuffing another bite of over-hard eggs into his mouth, Kent snuck a glance at his brother's profile.

He'd grown a full beard since Kent had seen him. The black, bushy hairs were flecked with silver strands. As if Vince could get old someday. Always a burly and naturally muscled guy, he'd put on some extra pounds but still looked like he could whip any challenger with one thick arm pinned behind his back.

When Kent was a teen, he had wanted Vince to use that toughness to scare away the gang members Kent had crossed when he'd stopped them from harassing a girl from his high school on her way home.

You can take care of yourself, little man.

A smile tugged Kent's lips at the memory of Vince's response when he'd asked for his help. He'd been right.

"What's wrong with your shoulder?" Vince's voice was rougher than Kent had remembered from Christmastime last month when they'd talked on the phone.

"What do you mean?"

Vince set down his fork on the plate, now cleared of food, and angled his head toward Kent. His mouth quirked sideways and split into a grin. "You been favoring it since you came in. If you don't want people to notice, you gotta stop babying it."

Kent shook his head with a chuckle. "So is that why you came here and suddenly wanted to see me? To tell me to sit up straight?"

Vince pointed at Kent's injured shoulder. "You're not gonna tell me, are you?"

"Maybe. If you tell me why you're here."

"Got a load up here. Figured it'd be stupid to come and not stop by. Save the money for a phone call at Christmas, right?" He let out a one-note laugh and grabbed the mug of coffee in front of him.

"Hey, if you need a cheaper plan, I can set you up. Unlimited long-distance calls. It's a thing." Something Kent was pretty sure Vince knew about and probably used. Even if he was a dinosaur at thirty-seven and carried a flip phone. But Vince was clearly avoiding any explanation for his weird behavior. Kent would have to dig. "How's work?"

Vince took a drink of the coffee and lowered his mug. "Good. With a different company now. Hauling water tanks."

"Is that what you brought on this trip?"

Vince cocked his head at Kent. "You're sounding suspicious."

"You're sounding evasive." Kent smiled, meeting the challenge in his brother's gaze.

Vince's brown eyes squinted with the laugh before Kent heard it. The single-tone, short laugh that used to make Kent think that was all the happiness Vince could find in the empty well inside them both. "I sure raised you right."

"Thought I raised myself." The quip popped out naturally, the banter they'd developed in recent years. But they both knew Vince had been behind Kent's self-reliance and independence. Had equipped Kent to survive.

"I'm older than either of them."

Kent froze, fingers on his fork. Was Vince bringing them up? He never did that. Kent dropped the utensil and reached for his coffee.

He took a sip. Another.

Vince cleared his throat, a scrape Kent hoped would clear away this topic and return his brother to normal.

"The shoulder...you do that on the job?"

Kent lowered the mug, set it back in the ring of coffee on the counter. "Maybe."

Vince grunted and shifted to reach in his back pocket. Pulled out his wallet.

"No, I got this." Kent didn't know why he felt obligated to pay. Such courtesies weren't something he and Vince did. But this was his city, after all.

Vince laid enough money on the counter to cover his breakfast. He picked up his baseball cap from where he'd set it next to his plate. Pulled it on, tugging the bill down near his eyes.

He stuck out his hand.

Kent stood and shook his brother's hand with the firm grip Vince had made him practice as a kid.

Vince held on just as tight. His mouth angled in a smile that didn't part his lips. "The work you do...it's dangerous, but it's important. Dad would be proud."

The oxygen vanished from Kent's lungs as if Vince had socked him in the stomach. He couldn't say a word past the foreign emotion welling up inside him. Before he knew what was happening, moisture burned at the back of his eyes.

He dropped Vince's hand and jerked away, pretended to grab his own wallet to pay the bill.

No way could he let his brother see a reaction like that.

No weakness. Be strong, little man.

Kent drew himself up straighter and mentally shook off the crazy feeling that had come over him. Enough with Vince's weird behavior. Kent couldn't afford to have anybody distract him right now.

He turned back to ask his brother straight out what was going on.

But he was too late.

Vince was gone.

"Then what made you decide to take geology?" Cora glanced at Venetia Savoy, the airport employee who lifted a suitcase off the huge conveyer belt hidden from the public in this room behind the walls of the baggage claim.

"Heard the prof was super easy." Venetia laughed as she leaned over the suitcase's handle to check the damaged tag.

"Ah. Very smart." Cora smiled at the young woman she'd gotten to know when Venetia had worked in different areas of the airport where Cora searched with Jana.

"It's just a Gen Ed. I don't want to waste my time, you know?" Venetia tossed her glossy black braid over her shoulder. A thick streak of neon purple hair twisted through the braid. "The other classes are hard enough, plus I gotta work here, and then there's the kids."

"You can't do it all. My mom always said you have to keep important the things that are important."

"You got a smart mama." Venetia typed the numbers from the tag into the computer on the workstation next to her.

A lump swelled in Cora's throat. She'd never told Venetia her mother was gone, so she couldn't know. "You're right about that." Cora threw a glance across the expansive width of the conveyer belt to see if Agent Thomson had heard anything they'd said.

He still stood at the other workstation, his brow furrowed as he hovered over the computer screen that showed passengers' ID photos as the luggage was scanned.

The man gave new meaning to the strong, silent type. She'd attempted small talk several times without any success. She couldn't even raise a smile from him this morning.

He seemed to wear intensity like a second skin, but there was something different today. His eyes, in the few glimpses she'd had of them, were shadowed and distracted, as if he carried an additional burden that was preoccupying his mind. One shoulder began to slump the longer they searched, perhaps in disappointment because they hadn't found any narcotics yet.

Cora transferred her attention to Jana between them. The golden swished her tail as she scampered around the luggage on the wide conveyer belt elevated about three feet off the floor where Cora stood. Jana sniffed all items that passed by, quickly clearing them and moving to the next items that slid through the large, square opening shrouded by heavy strips of leather that hung from the top.

Then again, perhaps Cora was only interpreting Agent Thomson's body language and silence in light of her own feelings today. She couldn't stop thinking about Bradley. After a night in the safety of Phoenix's fortress of a home, Cora's fear from the invasion had lessened while her worry about Bradley increased.

Why had he left last night? Had she behaved too distantly? She had tried to show how pleased she was that he had come home, but perhaps she hadn't demonstrated or said enough. Or maybe she'd been too effusive and that had scared him away. Why could she never find the right balance or learn what Bradley needed her to do and to be? She couldn't bear it if she made another mistake that led to his harm.

Several packages came through the opening from the outside at once, and Jana stayed with them as they traveled farther past Cora. She walked along the conveyer belt, moving closer to where Venetia monitored the computer at her workstation.

Venetia shifted closer to the computer when Cora came near.

"Sorry. I didn't mean to crowd you."

"No problem." Venetia shot a glance over her shoulder at Cora, then jerked her head forward again and peered at the screen that was abnormally close to her face.

Cora had once chatted with Venetia when the younger woman had been replacing paper towels in a restroom while Cora washed her hands. The space between them then had been far less than the four feet that separated them now, but Venetia hadn't shown an ounce of discomfort. Why did she want to have so much personal space now?

Cora kept her attention on Jana for a minute. "Good girl." She took a step back and to the side as if moving with Jana's progress. Glancing from the corner of her eye without rotating her head much, Cora caught sight of Venetia, again pressing away.

Or was she pushing closer to the workstation? Was Venetia hiding something?

Cora's mind raced as her pulse hurried to catch up. She didn't want to believe fun-loving Venetia would have anything to hide. Perhaps Cora was simply misreading the situation or there was a different explanation than the one her imagination grabbed hold of.

There was one way to find out.

"Agent Thomson?"

He instantly looked away from the computer, giving Cora his attention across the distance between them. Had he not been as lost in his work as she had thought?

She moistened her lips, her mouth starting to feel clammy. She really hoped she was wrong about this. "I think we should call it quits pretty soon. Jana will go all day, if I let her, but I need her to have something left for searching the high school yet."

"Sure." He turned back to the computer and punched something on the keyboard.

How could she warn him without making Venetia suspicious? An idea lit her mind. "Will you please grab something for me?"

He stepped away from the workstation and watched her over the conveyer belt.

"I left Jana's special toy in the car. She would love that as a reward for her hard work here today." All true words, though Cora didn't give Jana her toy as a reward in this context. The golden loved food much more than toys.

Agent Thomson's gaze didn't shift away from Cora, and not even his eyebrows moved. But Cora felt it—the connection, the sense that he had understood she was giving him a signal. Goosebumps raised on her arms, hidden under the sleeves of her sweater.

"You got it." He walked along the conveyer belt in the direction of the exit door.

Now for the next phase of Cora's hastily crafted plan.

"Okay, Jana."

The golden popped up her head to stare at Cora.

"Let's go."

Jana jogged toward Cora and jumped down from the conveyer belt with ease.

"Good girl, such a good girl." Cora petted Jana vigorously and lavished verbal praise. "Okay, time to go."

Cora straightened and turned to see Venetia watching her with a frown instead of her normal, friendly expression. Cora managed to muster a smile of her own. "Have a good afternoon."

"You, too."

Cora's chest squeezed as she intentionally walked Jana past the workstation, pretending they were going to swing around it and head back toward the door.

Jana veered to the right, shoving between Venetia and the workstation to bury her nose in a lower shelf.

"Hey!" Venetia reached for Jana's harness, but it was too late.

Jana sat and looked at Cora.

Cora's heart pounded and hurt at the same time. "Venetia, what are you hiding?"

Venetia stared at Cora, her big eyes glistening with moisture.

She lurched toward the workstation and grabbed something off the shelf. The drugs?

No. A gun.

And it was aimed at Cora.

FIFTEEN

Kent crouched behind the rounded end of the conveyer belt that carried luggage out to the baggage claim. He gripped his weapon. Good thing he'd caught on to the warning Cora had given him.

He hadn't much idea why she wanted him to pretend to leave, but he'd figured it had something to do with the employee who was starting to look nervous and fidgety.

The one who now held a gun on Cora.

Once he had understood Cora's hint, he'd gone to the door they'd entered through and opened it. A glance had assured him the girl's attention was on Cora, so he had closed the door without leaving and ducked down. Peering above the conveyer belt had enabled him to watch Cora and the girl, right up to the moment she'd pulled her pistol.

Wasn't too hard to get a weapon through to this part of the airport. Even if she'd had to go through an employee security check, she'd probably been screened by a buddy who'd laughed and chatted with her too much to be thorough.

Cora's K-9 was signaling the girl had narcotics at her workstation. Maybe taken out of luggage that had come through in a pre-planned smuggling attempt.

He could find out the details in questioning. But for now, he had to get Cora out of a sticky situation. Again.

He tucked his Glock behind his back and crawled on all fours to stay concealed behind the conveyer belt.

"Oh, Venetia." Cora's voice, heavy with sadness, carried to Kent over the noise of the conveyer belt. "You don't want to hurt me, do you?"

Not the first question he'd ask if the gun were aimed at him, but at least Cora was keeping her busy.

"We're friends. I know you. Your favorite color is the shade of purple you dyed your hair. You love your nieces and nephew. You're helping support them. You went back to school because you have goals and plans for your life."

Kent rounded the curve of the foundation supporting the baggage belt and paused.

The girl had her back mostly to Kent. And the pistol still pointed at Cora.

"Your secret favorite song is 'Amazing Grace.'" Cora just wouldn't give up.

Kent crouched as he moved closer, pulled his weapon out.

"Do you know my favorite line from that song?"

Kent couldn't see the girl's reaction to Cora's words.

Her pistol remained level, her hands wrapped around the grip.

"'I once was lost, but now I'm found.' We're never so lost that God can't find us, Venetia." Cora took a step closer to the pistol.

What was she doing?

Kent darted away from the conveyer belt, quietly moving to an angle that would clear Cora if he had to shoot.

"He can help you. Whatever you're mixed up in, He can show you the way out."

"It's too late for that." The employee's voice shook, like she might be crying. She took one hand off the gun and reached toward a shelf in the workstation. She pulled out a small bag—a makeup bag? Probably concealing the merchandise.

"I have to get out of here. I don't want to hurt you, but it's either me or you."

"It doesn't have to be that way, Venetia. You have options. You have a choice."

"No." The girl's braid swished against her back as she shook her head. "I don't have any choice. I can't let you tell anyone about this."

She was going to shoot.

"Hold it!" Kent braced his Glock in his hands, aimed at the employee.

She spun to face him.

Good. Her pistol aimed at him instead of Cora now.

"Set your weapon gently on the floor, and you won't get hurt."

"Agent Thomson, wait." Cora stepped closer to Venetia.

Tension clenched Kent's chest. Did the woman want to get shot?

"Please." Cora held up an open hand toward Kent. "Venetia…"

The girl swung the gun to Cora again, her head rotating back and forth between the apparently suicidal blonde and Kent.

"Venetia, I don't want to see you get hurt." Cora was going to be the one getting hurt if she didn't keep quiet and let Kent handle this. "I've seen Agent Thomson work, and he's very good at his job. He won't let you leave here."

"What if I shoot you?" The girl swung her head to Kent. "I could shoot her. I…will if you don't let me walk." Her hesitation showed in her voice, but even people who didn't intend to kill often did.

"Venetia, will you please look at me?"

The girl gradually turned her head back to Cora, the pistol inches from Cora's chest.

"You do not want to live with the guilt of having shot me. You want to be able to see your niece and nephew. You want to have a future outside of prison. I know you. This isn't what you want. And I want you to have the future you dreamed of someday." Cora held her gaze intently on the girl's face. "Please, give me the gun." She extended her hand toward the girl, palm up as if she actually thought the employee would hand over her weapon.

Kent aimed carefully, ready on the trigger to blast the gun from the girl's hand if she so much as twitched a finger.

Her wrist moved. Not the trigger finger.

Kent stared. No way.

She twisted the pistol sideways and laid it in Cora's hand.

Cora closed her fingers around the weapon as a smile illuminated her face. "Thank you."

Kent hurried toward them, weapon trained on the girl to discourage escape attempts and protect against more surprises.

Cora handed him the pistol with barely a glance.

As soon as he took the weapon from her hand, she reached for the girl and pulled her into an embrace.

"'I was lost, but now I'm found.' It'll be okay, Venetia. Praise the Lord, it'll be okay."

Tears tracked down Venetia's dark brown cheeks as she closed her eyes, her head resting on Cora's shoulder in the hug. "I'm sorry. I'm so sorry."

"I know. I forgive you. I'm sorry this happened." Cora pulled back, her gaze going to the handcuffs Kent pulled out. "I don't think we'll need those. Venetia won't run, will you?" She looked at the employee, who sniffed and shook her head.

"It's standard procedure." And the only smart thing to do under the circumstances. The girl had just nearly shot Cora. He cuffed her and got out his phone to call for transport.

But a half hour later, watching the police squad leave with the perp in the back, Kent still wasn't sure what had happened.

Cora had to be the luckiest woman alive to have talked her way out of another attempted shooting. And this time, she'd done it so well that no shots needed to be fired by him either. But the result could have been the reverse.

"Well, I guess I had better get going. I'm late for our search at the high school." Cora stepped down from the sidewalk of the baggage claim drop off lane and crossed in front of parked shuttles and taxis to head for the parking lot.

"Ms. Isaksson." Kent took a few quick strides to catch up to her, falling into pace beside her with the dog between them. "You need to know that what you did back there was extremely dangerous." And stupid, but he'd keep his uncensored thoughts to himself.

"I was in danger already, Agent Thomson."

He cut a glance at her. There it was again. Either a hidden wit that had unexpected bite or a skill for debate he never would've predicted from her angelic demeanor. "You weren't in much danger. I was there."

"And I can't tell you how much I appreciate that." She sent a smile his way as they stepped onto the sidewalk and turned to follow the curve that would lead them to the parking area. "I'm so thankful you caught my hint. How did you know I didn't want you to go to my car?"

Was she intentionally changing the subject? He'd let her do it for a bit. "I didn't have your keys, and you didn't offer them. Plus, you seem pretty prepared for your work. You wouldn't forget something your dog needed."

"Well, thank you." Her smile broadened. "Somehow, I knew you'd understand."

"Sure, but we need to work on the part that comes after the warning." The implication of his words—that they were partners and would be working together more—flared alarm in his brain. But he pushed on, hoping she wouldn't notice. "You can't talk your way out of everything, especially when people are trying to shoot you. You need to let me do my job and just try to stay out of the way."

Cora stopped abruptly and faced him. "I'm sorry, Agent Thomson. I didn't mean to interfere with your job. I didn't think of it like that." Small furrows crimped her forehead. "You do your job very well, and I'm so grateful for your protection. I would never want to make your job harder."

He blinked at the sincerity in her blue eyes. She wasn't going to argue? Launch the obvious comeback that her way worked today?

He cleared his throat. "Call me Kent."

"Thank you." Her forehead smoothed as she smiled. "And I hope you'll call me Cora."

He'd better not call her anything. With the weird softening effect she was having on him, he'd be better off making a dash to his car, telling Velasquez he couldn't work with this woman anymore, and never seeing her again.

"Agent...I mean, Kent, I did want to talk to you about something."

His feet stayed rooted to the sidewalk, unable to leave like he should.

"I'm worried that my brother may not be done with the cartel. Or, rather, that they may not be done with him."

"What makes you think that?"

She pulled back the cuff of her jacket to check her watch. "It's a long story, and I really do have to run. But suffice it to say I think they might be after Bradley." She met his gaze, her mouth set in a line. "I can't let him get hurt again. I know you're working on breaking up the organization and bringing the cartel to justice, and I want you to know I'll do anything to help you do that."

Amusement softened the spark of irritation that flared at the insinuation he needed her help. "I don't think I'll be needing help."

"I'm sure you don't. But Jana is very good at finding narcotics humans can't find." She glanced down at the golden retriever who sat patiently by her side.

She had a point.

"Well, I'm off. I'll see you tomorrow." Cora smiled and gave a wave as she walked away, the dog popping up to trot alongside her.

"Cora," Kent paused at the feel of her name on his tongue. Smooth, easy, natural.

"Yes?"

She's waiting, Thomson. He walked closer to where she had stopped and turned back. "I could use a narcotics K-9, actually."

"You could?"

"Yeah. I got a tip that the cartel is storing merchandise at a warehouse, but I need to confirm it's true without disturbing any of the scene. They can't know I've found it. Can your dog manage that?"

That smile brightened Cora's face again. "She certainly can."

"Great. Can you come today?"

"I'll have to go to the high school first, but we could join you later this afternoon."

Afternoon. He'd check with the DEA agent he had watching the warehouse, but he was pretty sure the building would be vacant at that time. "Perfect. Call me when you're done, and we'll meet there."

At least the last part made it sound less like he was planning a date. He hid a cringe as she agreed and headed off. He wasn't asking for help, and he didn't need it.

And the surge of anticipation when he thought of searching the warehouse had nothing to do with a lovely blonde with the sweetest smile he'd ever seen.

"Good girl, Jana." Cora petted the golden's back as they took a mini break after completing their search of the lockers at Lofland High. "At least there weren't any drugs today, huh, girl?" Although, that was probably a disappointment from Jana's point of view.

"I'll go make my rounds." Julian gave Cora a smile. "Good to see you, Miss Isaksson. And you, Jana." He gave Jana a quick stroke on her head with his big hand.

"Take care, my friend."

Julian nodded and trudged up the hallway.

"Finishing up?"

Cora startled at the voice behind her. Quite silly, given that it was Phoenix. Cora turned to see Phoenix and Dag standing in the hall, the sandy dog sporting his black PK-9 harness. "Yes, we're done with the usual search."

"Did you get my message?" Phoenix's dark blue eyes watched Cora from beneath the brim of her gray PK-9 cap.

Cora nodded, thinking back to the voicemail she'd found on her phone when she'd left the airport—a heads-up that Phoenix would be coming by the school today. "You said something happened here last night. Julian told me they had a break-in and vandalism?"

"Apparently. I'm here for a meeting with the principal. They want to contract us for overnight security."

"Can we handle that along with the other overnight job?"

"We'll make it work. Good timing for Jazz and Flash to have joined us."

"Yes, praise the Lord for that."

Phoenix didn't show even a flicker of response to Cora's reference to God's providence. But Cora would keep trying and praying. Bris had come to Christ, which fueled Cora's hope and determination to keep witnessing to her PK-9 family until they were all saved.

"You're going to headquarters now?"

"Actually..." Cora briefly told Phoenix about Kent's request to search the warehouse.

Phoenix's silence indicated she wasn't too thrilled, but she agreed Cora could go since it was a DEA mission. "I need to get to my meeting." Phoenix started to pass Cora and Jana.

"Okay. Is anyone else from PK-9 here?"

"Jazz and Flash are sweeping the grounds to get the layout."

"Oh, good." Cora smiled. "Maybe we'll see them as we leave. Do you know where Principal McFadden's office is?"

"We'll find it." Phoenix and Dag headed in the correct direction.

"See you later." Cora watched Phoenix leave, her long blond braid swishing against the back of her charcoal parka. "Come on, girl."

Jana happily trotted alongside Cora as they left via the glass exit doors.

Bright sunlight made Cora squint and softened the cold air's bite.

She scanned the parking lot and the sidewalk that bordered it as she walked, hoping to catch sight of Jazz and Flash. It would be nice to say hello.

No sight of the K-9 security team. Cora pointed her gaze ahead to where her Volkswagen was parked next to a red SUV that blocked the little Beetle from view.

Next up, the narcotics search with Agent Kent Thomson. She'd call him from the car once she was sure she wouldn't be delayed talking to Jazz last minute.

Cora smiled as she remembered the way he had suddenly said she should call him Kent. He'd looked as if the words surprised him as much as they surprised her. The warmth the gesture infused into her heart surprised her, too. They'd gotten along so much better today, as if they could be friends. She did feel terrible about interfering with him doing his job, though. She'd only wanted to help Venetia and try to persuade her to do the right thing on her own. If Venetia had gotten shot because of Cora, she couldn't have lived with herself.

"Hey, drug lady."

Cora pulled up short behind the SUV.

The source of the masculine voice stepped out from between the SUV and Cora's Beetle. A very tall, thickly built young man. He looked to be Hayden's age, a high school senior. His green sweatshirt boasted the football team's logo—a bobcat baring its teeth.

The teen smiled as he walked toward Cora, but the expression looked more like a sneer than friendliness.

Jana pulled toward the teen, wagging her tail, eager to greet him.

But the young man stopped as soon as his gaze moved to the golden.

Thank you, Lord, that he doesn't know dogs very well. He seemed to think Jana might be aggressive, which worked to Cora's advantage right now.

"Me and my buddies thought we'd watch your car for you. You really shouldn't leave it parked here, you know. Anybody could mess with it."

Alarm spiked Cora's pulse. "Mess with it?"

"Sure. Hayden's got friends here, you know?"

Movement on the other side of her car caught Cora's gaze.

Two more exceptionally large teenagers walked out, stopping by their friend at the back of her little Beetle. One of them also wore the football team's sweatshirt, and the other was so big, she knew he had to be a linebacker even though he didn't wear team paraphernalia.

They all sported the same sneering grin and cocky demeanor.

She swallowed, searching for her voice. They were only children. Teens, as Bradley had once been. "I don't think we've met before. I'm Cora. What are your names?"

"Aww," the first young man guffawed and grinned at his teammates, "ain't that sweet, boys? She wants to be friends."

The others joined in the laughter as Cora's pulse raced faster. What had they done to her car? And what might they do to her if she tried to reach it or return to the building?

"What's so funny, boys?"

Jazz.

Cora closed her eyes with relief at the sound of her new friend's voice behind her.

And the low, warning rumble that must be coming from Flash.

The look on the boys' faces as they stared past Cora would have made her laugh if not for the fright still quivering through her system. Their eyes bulged like saucers as Flash continued to growl.

"Nothing." The ringleader moved sideways, past the SUV. "We've gotta get to class."

Cora looked over her shoulder at Jazz in time to catch her hard stare at the teens as they scurried away. Looked like Jazz would be another fierce PK-9 warrior for the team, especially with the intense Belgian Malinois at her side whose stare was even more intimidating.

"Okay, Flash. Good boy." Jazz leaned down and scratched the dog on his chest.

"Thank you both for showing up when you did."

Jazz straightened with a smile. "No problem. I wonder what those creeps were doing by your car."

Cora let Jana walk over to Flash, and the two dogs smelled each other, their tails wagging in friendly body language. "He claimed they were watching it so no one would vandalize it."

"That's rich." Jazz turned and Flash followed her as she went to the far side of the Beetle.

Cora walked to the near side, scanning for more spray paint.

"Oh, man. Cora…"

"I see it." Her gaze locked on her tires.

Garish slashes gouged the rubber in a message as loud as the spray paint. Hayden Simpson had friends here all right. And they clearly had a score to settle.

SIXTEEN

A soft, flowery scent teased Kent's nostrils as Cora settled in the passenger seat of his car and buckled her seat belt.

"Thanks for picking us up." She looked over her shoulder, probably checking on Jana in the backseat.

"No problem." Kent shifted the car into reverse and glanced in the rearview mirror. So far, it looked like the dog was staying on the towel Cora had laid down to protect the upholstery. "You said you had car trouble at the high school?" He backed away from the Phoenix K-9 Agency headquarters.

"Of a sort." Cora turned her head toward the passenger window as Kent directed the car toward the street. "My tires were slashed."

"What?" Kent braked, shifted into park, his muscles tensing as he looked at Cora.

She aimed her bright blue eyes at him. "While I was searching with Jana at the school."

"Who did it?" He heard the hard edge in his own voice as he fired the question.

"Some students, I believe. Friends of the teenager who had drugs Jana and I found."

"Are they being charged?"

She looked ahead, out the windshield. "No."

Kent's fingers clenched the wheel as anger rose in his chest. "Why not?"

"I saw them by my car, but I didn't see them slash the tires. They claim they were trying to protect my car."

"Of course, they do." Kent clenched his jaw. "No security footage?"

"Nothing conclusive. They can be seen approaching my car, but a large SUV blocked them from view of the school's camera after that."

Kent swore and shoved the car into drive again. "You shouldn't go to that school anymore until they get the situation under control." He pulled onto the street and regripped the wheel as if it were the punks' necks. "I could look into it. Sounds like a gang might be forming, or at least organization around drug retail. I don't want you anywhere near there until I break it up." He shot a glare at the rearview mirror.

A gray Malibu drove behind him with several more cars following.

He dropped his gaze to the traffic and road in front of him.

And realized she hadn't said a word.

His last statement—more like a command—seemed to echo in the silence, allowing him to hear himself. Where had that come from?

His hands were clenched on the wheel, muscles ready for action. Just because she'd told him her tires were slashed? That barely registered as a crime on the scale he dealt with most days. So why did he feel so mad? So...protective?

Cora watched him with her amazing eyes, her delicate mouth slightly upturned. At least she wasn't glaring at him.

"I didn't mean that the way it sounded." He hopped his gaze back to the road and focused on driving. "Just wanted you to be aware it's dangerous there." He flexed his fingers, loosening his death grip on the wheel. "You can do whatever you want."

"I appreciate your concern."

"I'm not concerned. Well, not about you." He glanced her way in time to see her delicate eyebrows lift.

His mouth turned dry as sandpaper. "I'm concerned about the drug problem."

"Of course. I understand." Did she mean she understood more than he wanted her to? "I'm concerned, as well. It's tragic when children are exposed to drugs."

He shot her a glance, but her profile as she looked out the windshield didn't betray any suspicion.

He didn't know where his overreaction had come from, but the last thing he needed was to send the wrong signals. She could think he liked her or something. That he cared about her safety. That he wanted a relationship. None of which would ever cross his mind. He didn't need that kind of crutch in his life.

"This warehouse we're going to, then. You must consider it safe?"

He angled a glance at her. Was she calling his bluff again?

But she looked at him with no challenge or amusement on her lovely face.

He squelched the urge to shift his injured shoulder. "Should be. A fellow agent was watching the place today, and she reported that everyone left the building about a half hour ago. This type of storage facility doesn't get much traffic or business, and what they do get would be mostly at night."

Cora nodded. "Because they don't want to be seen, I suppose."

Kent checked the rearview mirror again. His gaze caught on the Malibu. The same one that had been behind him since they left Phoenix K-9 headquarters. "Do you know what kind of car those teenagers drive?"

"No. Why?"

"Someone may be following us."

"Oh." She faced the windshield, her posture going rigid. "I don't think it would be the teens. They were still at the school when we left, and I rode with Amalia. No one could possibly tail her without her knowing."

That was doubtful. None of those women were federal

agents. They were just dog handlers. But no use making a thing of it.

Kent checked for tails frequently enough and kept a low profile—no one would be tailing him. "Anyone else you can think of who would want to follow you?"

"I don't believe so."

Kent couldn't believe it either. Who, beyond some angry kids, could possibly have anything against this woman?

"Although, there was the incident last night."

"Last night?" He tossed her a glance before checking on the tail again.

"Yes. Someone invaded my home."

The dramatic phrasing—or maybe sheer disbelief—left him uncertain of what she meant. "Like an unexpected guest or a burglary?"

"More like a burglary, though nothing was stolen."

Alarm cinched his chest. Someone broke into her house? "Were you home?"

"Yes." She sounded so calm.

But he detected a quiver in her fingers before she tucked them under the arms she wrapped around herself.

She was scared.

Heat surged through his veins. "Were you hurt?" His heartbeat thumped loudly in his ears as he stared ahead, waiting for her answer.

"No."

A breath expelled from his nose as if he'd been holding it. "You should've called me." As soon as the words escaped, he wanted to snatch them back. What was he doing? She wasn't his to protect or help.

He felt without looking that she was watching him.

He checked the rearview mirror.

The Malibu was gone. Must have pulled off somewhere while he was losing his cool and his mind.

He cleared his throat before sending her an even glance. "It could've been related to your kidnapping. By the cartel." He doubted there was any relationship at all, but he had to come up with some excuse to cover his protective reaction.

Her widened eyes blinked. "Oh, yes. We thought of that. A vendetta killing attempt."

"Killing? No, that's not likely. Too much risk for the gain in your case. You wouldn't be that important to them."

"I hadn't thought of that. I suppose that's true."

Man, he sure had a way with words. One of the many reasons he worked alone. "It's nothing personal. You were just a bystander not associated with the cartel—a hostage of convenience. They know you're a nobody who didn't try to get their guys arrested. They'd blame me for that, if anyone."

"Agent Thomson, I understand." Her smile seemed to brighten the black interior of his car. "I'm not offended. You're honest, and I appreciate that."

Good. Not that he was apologizing for telling it like it was. If she couldn't take it, she was getting involved in the wrong kind of work.

"Is the car still following us?"

"What?" He blinked at the road, then registered her question. "Oh." He checked the rearview mirror again. "No. Peeled off a while ago."

"Praise the Lord." Sincerity lifted her tone.

Didn't hear that every day. "You seem pretty religious."

"In some ways, I am. I said, 'Praise the Lord,' because I know He's the one Who prevented us from being followed or harmed."

He threw her a glance. "I'm the one who kept driving, and the other driver decided to go somewhere else. Probably wasn't tailing us at all."

"And your actions and those of the other driver were governed by the Providence of God."

"I guess believing that gives you somebody to blame when you mess up, huh?"

Silence thickened between them. Had he finally managed to offend her? A lump settled in his throat, as if he didn't like the idea.

"No. My mistakes are entirely my own fault." A heaviness clung to her words like she carried a burden attached to them.

But she still had the crutch of a God she thought would help her. Someone to depend on. Kent didn't need any make-believe hero. He could handle anything life could throw at him on his own.

"We thought the break-in could be related to my brother."

"Is he still involved with the cartel?"

"No, he told me he wasn't."

And she believed him, of course.

"Do you think the cartel could want to kidnap him or hurt him?" Concern clouded her voice.

"Sure. If they thought he was a threat to them or they wanted him back. How deep was he into the cartel?"

"I don't know, exactly. Enough to hide from them when he left."

Which meant deep enough that the cartel might want him either working for them or dead. And that meant Cora could get caught in their net.

His gut clenched. He shouldn't care a bit. Caring would make him vulnerable. Weak.

But the warning bells clanging in his mind weren't enough to stop the urge he had to never let this woman out of his sight until he made sure she was safe.

Cora trusted Kent when he said the warehouse would be safe for their search this afternoon. In which case, she shouldn't still have jitters and the instinct to hide behind the rows of stacked crates they encountered inside.

Thankfully, Jana was unaffected by Cora's nervousness. When the golden had a job to do, she was one-hundred-percent focused and having the time of her life. Jana scampered from crate to crate, smelling for any scent of narcotics. Packaging the drugs with innocuous items may fool a customs inspector or shipping company but would never dupe Jana and her nose.

Kent walked behind Cora and Jana as they moved down each long row. Cora followed his example of keeping quiet, and she noticed he kept checking the front doors and the back entrance where he had picked the lock to get in.

"Nothing?" He asked the question in a whisper.

Cora glanced back as Jana reached the end of the first row of crates. "No, not yet."

Kent's brow furrowed in a way that squeezed Cora's chest. She hoped he wouldn't be disappointed if they didn't find narcotics here.

She followed Jana's eager turn around the end of the row to the second one. "Bringing down this cartel seems to mean a lot to you."

"It's my job."

Cora watched Jana sniff the bottom edges of a large crate and then lift her nose higher. "Of course." But she couldn't help feeling it was more than that to him. She had worked with other DEA agents and narcotics officers, but she hadn't seen them pick locks to search buildings without a warrant. He was taking a lot of risk, as if he had a great deal at stake. As if it was personal.

Jana stopped beside a crate. She sat and turned her gaze to Cora.

Cora's heart lifted. "There it is."

"Drugs?"

"Yes." She stepped to Jana and took out treats from her pocket to hand the always-hungry golden. "Good girl. Such a good girl."

"Are you sure? Is it positive?"

Cora turned to see an expression she hadn't before on his usually serious face.

His green eyes were slightly widened, and his lips parted as he awaited her answer. Hope. Yes, this was definitely personal for him.

"I'm positive. Jana has never been wrong yet."

He nodded, looking away as if he didn't care.

But she caught the upturn of his lips that told a different

story.

A slam banged through the air, jolting Cora's body with surprise.

Kent jerked toward the sound that reverberated on an echo from the front of the building.

"You sure no one followed you here?" A male voice.

The illusion of safety vanished.

Someone was here.

SEVENTEEN

Kent grabbed Cora's arm and pulled her with him around the nearest crate, his Glock gripped in his other hand. He squatted behind the concealment, let go of her when she did the same.

She tapped Jana's shoulder.

The dog looked at her as if she knew what a tap meant.

Cora put her hand out flat, palm-down, and lowered it.

Jana instantly slid into a lying position on the floor.

Impressive. Hopefully, Cora would understand hand signals, too.

The men who had entered were harder to hear now. Just murmurings of male voices. He had to get closer to ID them. But without putting Cora in danger.

He touched her shoulder.

She jerked toward him, startled.

He stuck a finger in his chest, then turned it to point toward the voices. He directed his finger at her, then held up a flat hand facing toward her, indicating she should stay put.

She nodded.

He started to raise up, just enough to see over the crate they hid behind.

"I left it back here." The voice was closer.

Movement crossed between crates in the next row over,

glimpses of clothes, skin, and hair Kent tried to piece together. Two men?

He dropped back down.

"I don't know about this." The man's gruff voice signaled they were even nearer. "I usually deal directly with Trent."

Footsteps clopped on the floor, moving into this row.

Where Cora was. She huddled behind the crate, her face white as a sheet. Probably afraid for her life.

Kent held back the grunt of frustration he wanted to let out. Why did they have to randomly show up when he'd brought Cora along?

But there was no way he'd let anything happen to her. Whatever it took, she'd be safe.

"He said I should pick it up." Another male voice. Sounded younger. "I'm meeting him tomorrow night. He wanted me to bring the sample."

"All right, but if I hear he didn't get it, you're the one I'll come after. Got it?"

"Yeah, I get it." The young guy sounded more bored than intimidated. "Just show me the stuff."

A loud creak, like a lid being pried off a crate, split the cavernous silence of the warehouse.

Cora flinched at the sound.

Kent reached to put his hand on her shoulder to comfort her but drew back before contact. He'd probably just startle her more.

Jana turned her head toward Cora, and she lifted her hand in the signal Kent assumed meant the dog should stay. Good thing Jana didn't seem to bark or growl.

"High grade." The deeper voice again. "Maybe too good for your market. You'd have to charge more."

"Yeah. I'll see what Trent thinks. This all?"

"All you need for now." A smack indicated the guy closed the crate lid. "If Trent wants more, he can come himself."

Footsteps echoed as they moved away, retreating the way they had come in. They were probably going to leave, but Kent wouldn't risk overstaying their welcome with Cora at risk.

He touched her arm.

She didn't jump, just looked at him with wide, blue eyes.

A pain twinged behind his ribs at the fear in those eyes. He pointed over her shoulder, toward the back door. Cupping her elbow, he gently led her in that direction as he moved around her, staying low.

She went with him, crouching beside him as she waved a beckoning hand at Jana.

The golden popped up, her tags making a slight jingle.

Kent froze, tightened his fingers on Cora's elbow.

She stopped, her quickened breath brushing his ear.

Flickers of the men flashed between crates as they passed them in the next row.

Cora jerked her hand up to cover her mouth, her gaze aimed at where the figures had just passed by. What had she seen?

The footsteps of the men continued to move away, growing fainter as they reached the front of the building.

Kent leaned close to her and whispered. "Are you okay?"

She turned her head, her face inches from his. "I know the boy." Her whisper was soft and careful. "He's the teen Jana caught with drugs at Lofland High."

So the cartel was at the root of the Lofland High School drug problem. They were expanding.

He clenched his jaw. He'd have to put an end to that. Getting kids hooked was not something he'd allow while waiting to move up the cartel's ladder.

The warmth of Cora so close to his side interrupted his thoughts. Drew his attention to her smooth skin, the blond tendrils of loose hair that curled down to tickle her neck.

He dropped his hand away from her elbow and moved in front of her and Jana.

The woman could walk by herself.

And he didn't need any distractions.

Keep the woman safe. Get out. And nail the drug-dealing punk. Then leave this woman and the weakening effect she was having on him as far behind as possible.

Sadness settled with an ache in Cora's chest as she sat in the passenger seat of Kent's car, following Hayden's red Bentley. They'd been trailing him since he had left the warehouse thirty minutes ago.

How could Hayden go from his first arrest for drug possession to visiting a cartel storage facility? Hadn't he learned anything from getting caught at school? He was losing what could be his second chance, perhaps his only opportunity to turn his life around before it was too late.

But Bradley hadn't been any different. Despite her encouragement, lectures, and pleading—everything she had tried had failed to point her brother in a better direction, away from drugs.

"Here we go." The first words Kent had spoken since they'd escaped the warehouse drew her out of the memories.

Hayden's car slowed, then turned into a driveway blocked by a gate. He stopped by the keypad where he would likely enter his password or be buzzed in by someone.

Kent gunned the engine and jerked to a stop, inches behind Hayden's bumper.

Before Cora could react, Kent was out of the car and aiming his gun at the driver's window.

"DEA."

Cora stood behind the passenger door as Kent launched orders at Hayden.

"Slowly get out of the car."

Cora held her breath. *Father, please let Hayden cooperate. Don't let him use a weapon or resist.*

The doorframe popped open.

"That's it. Slowly. Keep your hands where I can see them."

The door opened farther, and Hayden's tall figure straightened, his empty hands lifted in the air.

Cora breathed again. But her heart rate didn't begin to slow until Kent had Hayden in handcuffs. At which point, the teen was still threatening Kent with lawsuits and his father's clout.

Leaving Jana in the backseat of Kent's car, she walked closer. Maybe she could help calm him down.

"You." Hayden sent her a glare lit with an angry fire that almost scared her. It would if she didn't remind herself he was just a hurting boy under his tough exterior.

"Hayden, please. You'll only make things worse for yourself."

"No, that's your job, lady." He snarled at her. "And don't think I won't make you pay for it."

"Hey." Kent grabbed Hayden's upper arm and jerked the teen to face him. "You deal with me, not her. Got it?"

"Kent, it's okay." He was kind to defend her, but Hayden was likely only lashing out because he was scared. And lonely and in pain, just like Bradley.

Kent dangled a bag of pills Cora assumed must be drugs in front of Hayden's face. "These were in your pocket, kid. Daddy can't get you out of this one. So if I were you, I'd wise up and start playing nice, or I'll put you away so long you won't get out till your twenty-five-year reunion."

Cora doubted that kind of prison sentence would be a possibility for Hayden, but Kent's threatening tone and demeanor did the trick in subduing the boy.

Hayden didn't look at either of them as they waited in silence for his ride to the jail to arrive. By the time the officer drove away with Hayden and Cora got into Kent's car, the sun was beginning to set, coloring the sky with deepening orange and pink streaks.

Cora turned to Kent as he pulled away from the driveway they had learned belonged to the mansion of Hayden's father. "May I be there tomorrow when you question him?"

"I don't think that's a good idea." Kent kept his gaze forward, staring through the windshield.

"I realize it's a lot to ask, and I wouldn't get in the way. I just want to make sure..." What she'd planned to say sounded wrong now.

"That I'm not too mean to him?"

"No." Heat flushed Cora's cheeks. Those weren't the words

she had been going to say, but exactly how she'd feared he would interpret them. "I don't think you would harm him." She closed her mouth, drawing in air through her nose. Then she tried again. "I sometimes find that a gentle approach can be more effective in getting people to cooperate."

His gaze turned her way, irritation sparking his green irises. "I'm well-versed in interview techniques." He returned his glare to the road. "Believe it or not, I can be friendly and charming when I want information."

Oops. She'd offended him again.

"I don't like bullies or people who attack innocent parties. He needed to take it down a notch."

"Of course. I'm sorry. I didn't mean to suggest you did anything wrong back there. I appreciate that you were trying to protect me."

His head jerked toward her, then away again. "I wasn't protecting you. Just calming him down so no one would get hurt."

She pressed her lips together. His protest carried a defensive note she doubted he'd meant to convey. But why didn't he want to admit to protecting her? Wasn't that his job, in part, as a federal agent?

Unless…Heat flushed her cheeks, from a different cause this time, as a possibility dawned in her mind. Had he wanted to protect her for a more personal reason?

No. He couldn't possibly think of her in that way.

"Am I taking you back to Phoenix K-9 headquarters?"

"Oh." She looked at the clock on the dashboard. 5:45. "It's so late already. Would you mind dropping me off at my house instead? It shouldn't be any farther for you. Although, I guess I don't know where you live."

"I thought you were staying with your boss."

"I did last night. But I can't trespass on her hospitality any longer."

"She wants you out already?"

"Oh, no, not at all. She would actually like me to stay longer." Phoenix had almost insisted on it, in fact, but not quite. "I also really want to be home in case my brother returns."

"Returns?" Kent's narrowed eyes showed she'd triggered his suspicions again, which seemed easy to do whenever she mentioned Bradley. "I thought he'd already come back to stay with you."

"He had, but he left the night of the break-in."

"You didn't mention that."

"I didn't? Sorry. I was thankful he wasn't there. Especially if the intruder was after him for some reason."

"So you don't know where your brother is now?"

"I do, actually. Phoenix had him followed."

"Really." The word wasn't so much a question as a statement of surprise that matched his raised eyebrows.

"He went to a motel. I think he must still be there, or Phoenix would have told me." Or would she? Cora would have to call her and ask if there were any updates. Phoenix never meant it personally when she left someone out of the loop, yet her need-to-know modus operandi could have that result.

"But you hope he'll come home. Even after the invasion?"

"Of course."

"Right." He clenched and unclenched his fingers around the wheel, looking away. He was probably thinking she was naïve, as many people did.

"Do you have family?"

His posture went rigid as a stone. Then, after a few silent seconds, he relaxed all except the jaw where she still detected a muscle twitching. "Yes."

"Brothers or sisters?"

He stared out the windshield. "Brother."

"If he disappeared or became involved in something terrible, wouldn't you worry about him and want him to come home?"

He finally looked her way, his green eyes glinting. "My brother and I take care of ourselves and leave each other alone." He swung his head back to watch the road.

How terribly sad. Was his brother his only family or did he have parents? Cora kept her curiosity to herself. Asking would only upset him more. But his irritation wasn't personal. She strongly suspected his easily roused anger was a wall for him to hide behind. She'd seen it so often—people hiding their fear or pain behind animosity. Unless she was reading him inaccurately, Kent Thomson was a man in pain. It may be a pain he wasn't yet aware that he was suffering, a burden he didn't realize he carried.

She moistened her lips. "I'm sorry to hear that."

"Don't be. We like it that way."

Did he? The way he twisted his grip on the wheel made her question his sincerity, though he may have fooled himself. She held back her questions, allowing silence—with the exception of Jana's panting from the backseat—to blanket the car.

By the time they reached Cora's street, the waning light tinged the snow blue and gray.

"Right here." She pointed ahead to her small, two-story home on the right. "The blue house."

Kent slowed the car and turned into the driveway. "I don't think you should stay here alone. Or with just your brother." He scanned the house and her yard in the assessment she was used to seeing the PK-9 security specialists make. "I could take you somewhere else. A hotel or your boss's place." He ended his scan by meeting her gaze. If she didn't doubt it so much, she would almost think his eyes held concern now instead of anger.

"That's very kind, but I'll be fine here. Phoenix will make sure I'm well protected."

"What about that car there?" He dipped his head toward a navy-blue SUV, parked on the street beyond Cora's house.

"Oh, that looks like Jazz's SUV. That's what I mean. Phoenix will have set up a schedule of patrols overnight."

"Patrols?"

"Yes. Our security specialists will patrol my yard with their K-9s. I'll be very safe."

"Security specialists." He tapped his fingers on the wheel, staring at her house. "I'll walk you inside."

"Okay, but—"

He pushed open his door and left the car before she could respond. He certainly was abrupt at times.

She got out and went to the back door to release Jana.

"Hey, wondered when you were coming home." Jazz's friendly voice welcomed Cora as the redhead approached the driveway with Flash. She must have been around the far side of the house when Cora and Kent had arrived.

"Hi, Jazz." Cora smiled. "How long have you been here?"

"About fifteen minutes. I get to hang with you until midnight. Then Nevaeh will be up."

"Sounds wonderful. You gals are the best." Cora glanced at Kent, who had stopped on his way to the front door and now stood still, watching her and Jazz. Cora led Jana closer to Kent. "Jazz, I want you to meet Special Agent Kent Thomson. Kent, this is Jazz Lamont and her K-9 Flash, security and tracking specialists."

Kent kept an eye on Flash as he and Jazz closed the gap between them to shake hands. "Security and tracking?"

Jazz nodded, standing straighter without a smile. "Most of the dogs at PK-9 are dual purpose."

"I see. Have you cleared the interior of the house?"

Jazz threw Cora a questioning glance before returning her gaze to Kent. "Yes."

Phoenix must have given Jazz a key as a precaution in case something happened to Cora, and they needed to enter the house quickly. Cora shivered at the possibility of that scenario.

"I guess you're all set then." Kent watched Cora, that blend of softness and intensity that looked like concern tinting his eyes again.

Had he noticed her shiver?

He walked toward her, as if he was going to pass by to his car, but he paused next to her. "Will you be all right?" His voice seemed deeper as his gaze searched her face.

Warmth pumped from her heart into the rest of her body as she met his gaze. She smiled. "Yes, I'll be fine. Thank you."

He looked into her eyes for a moment. Then jerked a nod and brushed past her. He got into his car and drove away without another word or glance. Not that she was looking for one.

"Whew." Jazz let out the word like a puff of air as she reached Cora's side. "He's...intense."

Cora turned away from the road and met Jazz's big eyes, a dark emerald green compared to Kent's, which were more like a gray-green color.

"Though he's super cute in that brooding, dark, and dangerous kind of way."

"I suppose so."

Jazz's mouth curved in an amused smile. "Nevaeh would've loved to meet him. And to see the way you watched him leave just now. She'd tease you for a month."

A flush rushed to Cora's cheeks. "I'm only trying to figure him out. He can be challenging to predict. I'm always saying the wrong thing around him."

"Sure." Jazz grinned as if she didn't believe Cora. "Don't worry, I won't tell Nevaeh. Not even about the way he looked at you."

"What do you mean?" The question came out instinctively —a deflection. But Cora swallowed, hoping Jazz didn't answer.

"Like he wanted to pack you up and take you home so he could protect you himself."

Oh, my. Could Jazz be right?

"You've got an admirer there."

Jazz must be mistaken. He'd made it clear he didn't even want to work with her, and she seemed to offend him every few minutes.

No, any protectiveness he had toward her must be due only to his profession. He was used to keeping people safe. She was grateful God had sent him to protect her along with everyone else he helped.

As she walked with Jazz and the dogs to the house to throw together a quick dinner, she silently prayed for Kent Thomson, that God would show her how to make a difference in his life and that God Himself would heal Kent's pain.

Entering her house for the first time since the home invasion interrupted the prayer.

Fear washed over her, leaving her cold. Her home wasn't safe anymore.

And until they found out for certain who had broken in and why—until they stopped whomever it was—more than her home would be in danger.

EIGHTEEN

Kent sat down across the table from Ramos. A different interview room, but nearly identical to the previous one they'd met in.

Ramos, on the other hand, looked like he'd aged a few additional years since Kent had seen him. Jail must not agree with him.

"You were right." Kent watched the dealer closely.

Ramos looked up from his folded hands that rested on the table in front of him.

"Found your cartel's merchandise at the warehouse."

Ramos's dark eyes widened just a fraction, the only hint the guy might be getting his hopes up.

"Tell me what you know. Why are you here?"

Ramos grunted, slid his hands toward his chest. "I've asked myself that question every day in this place."

"Don't get cute. I can walk."

He lifted his hands, palms out. "Sorry. I'll tell you anything you want to know." He dropped his hands to his lap and let out a sigh. "I came here as a test."

"A test?"

"More of a tryout, I guess. Guajardo is holding auditions to be the next guy in charge of the whole U. S. operation." Ramos paused, as if the news would excite Kent as much as it must have thrilled the cartel members wanting to move up. "He's looking at the regional managers to fill the spot. We're all auditioning, basically."

"So coming here was your audition?"

Ramos shook his head. "Just part of it. Successfully smuggling merchandise on a commercial flight was our first test."

"Did the other regional managers come here, too?"

"No, just me. We were assigned different locations."

"How many managers are doing it?"

"Six, from what I heard."

Kent would need to alert the DEA offices in all states to be on alert for the managers coming individually. Though it was likely already too late to catch them at airports. "What's the next test?"

Ramos's hands appeared on the table again, palms rubbing together. "We're supposed to steal merchandise from JK-16."

The street gang that moved drugs on a smaller scale. Kent smirked. "So he gets to see what you're made of and hurts the competition. Nice. I want the details on that—when and where."

"I don't have them."

Kent frowned. "Thought you were going to cooperate."

"I am. Straight up, I don't know. Díaz was supposed to take me to a hotel where I'd get my next instructions."

It made enough sense that Kent believed him. Guajardo got where he was by being cautious.

"If you let me go, I can complete the other tests."

Kent leaned back in his chair, watching Ramos. The guy was a little too eager to be set free. Then again, who wouldn't be?

"I'll get you to the kingpin."

Kent straightened. "How?"

"I think we might meet him at the end of the tests."

"You *think*?"

"Nobody said for sure, but there's talk he might show up and choose his man in person."

"I need more than talk."

Ramos ran his hand down his long mustache. "I'll get you

to him somehow. I swear. When he makes his pick or after that. I can make it happen."

"Where's this final location?"

"I don't know. Do you think he'd tell us that at the beginning?"

No. He wouldn't. Which made the question a good test to see if Ramos was telling the truth. He could've made up a location for a future meeting if he was only trying to get free.

Kent waited a bit, watching for any tells.

The guy seemed steady, on the level.

"Okay."

"I can go?"

"If you're willing to take the risk the cartel will know you've flipped."

"I have that figured out."

No surprise there. Ramos had probably figured out a way to save his hide from the vengeful cartel before he decided to flip.

"I'll tell them the DA decided she could only charge Díaz with the kidnapping, since I didn't actually take the blonde."

Kent folded his arms across his chest. "And the drug charge?"

"Dropped for insufficient evidence. I claimed I grabbed the wrong suitcase at the baggage claim."

"If you think they'll buy it."

"Yeah, they'll buy it." Ramos would be betting his life on it, even if he hadn't flipped. His buddies were a suspicious crew.

"Okay. I'll give you a private number you'll call to give me updates. I want a check-in every twenty-four hours." Kent leaned across the table and met Ramos's gaze. "No longer, or I will come find you."

"I get it." Ramos was likely far more afraid of the cartel than Kent, with good reason. But the cartel would turn on him if they got a whiff of mole. Kent could alert them to the betrayal pretty easily, and Ramos would know that.

Kent shoved back his chair and stood. "I look forward to hearing from you. I'll let the front desk know you're checking out."

Ramos shot him a look of surprise. Then his mouth angled in a wry grin. "See you on the outside."

Kent went to the door, turned back. "Ramos. I'll write up your deal stipulating my apprehension of Guajardo as a condition. If I don't get him at the end of this, you'll do hard time."

Ramos nodded, grin replaced with a grave set of his lips.

The smile landed on Kent's face instead as he walked into the hallway and shut the door behind him, the sour air suddenly like the smell of victory.

Nineteen years. Nineteen years of blood, sweat, and the memory of the tears that marked the worst evening of his life.

Just a little longer now, and he could finally bring justice to the cartel that destroyed his family.

"Bradley?" Cora sighed, not sure what to say in the tenth voicemail message she'd left at her brother's number that day. He was even less likely to pick up this time, given it was nearly 1:00 a.m. "I know you might be in trouble—" She stopped herself just short of adding, *again.*

"I want to help you this time. Better than I did before." She leaned back against the headboard, shifting her legs stretched out under the bed covers in front of her. "So much of this is my fault, I know that. I must have said something that scared you off. Was it that I asked you to go to church with me?"

She pressed her fingers against her forehead. "I didn't mean to pressure you. I don't know if that's why you left. Or if you left because you're in danger. I want to make up for it if it was my fault. But I can only do that if you come home."

Jana, lying on the bed with Cora, raised up from her side and stretched her head to rest on Cora's calf, watching with her soft, brown eyes.

"Please, Bradley. Will you give me another chance? Please, come home." Her voice faded as emotion cinched her throat. She lowered her cell phone and pressed the button to end the call.

Tears filled her eyes until Jana's face was a blur. "Oh, Father. I'm so sorry I created this mess. Why didn't I pay more attention when he was young? How could I have been so neglectful?"

Digital notes of her "Amazing Grace" ringtone sang from the phone in her hand on the blanket.

The ID, *Bradley*, displayed on the screen.

She jerked the phone up, sliding the icon to answer the call. "Bradley?" She nearly shouted into the phone.

"Yeah." Bradley's voice was like heaven to her ears. But he also sounded cautious and reluctant.

Calm down, Cora. You'll scare him away again.

"I'm so happy to hear your voice. Thank you for calling back." Where the strength came from to sound so calm, she would never know.

"I can't talk long. But you seemed worried, so…"

"Yes, I have been. Someone broke into our house last night." She bit back the urge to ask him if he knew that. He might hang up.

"I have to stay away. I thought they'd forgotten me. I was wrong."

"Maybe it wasn't the cartel. There's a teen I caught with drugs who's very angry. It could have been him or—"

"No." The one word shook with fear. "It's them."

"Then come home, Bradley. I'll help you. We can go to the police or the DEA. The Phoenix K-9 team will prot—"

"No! Don't you get it? They could've hurt you because they were after me. If I go near you, I'll put you in danger. They'll leave you alone if I don't come back."

"Bradley, I don't care about that. I just want to be able to help you."

"You can't help me. No one can. I'll just hide until I figure something out."

"That's not living. I can—"

"What? Pray for them? There's nothing you can do but stay as far away from me as you can get."

"Bradley—"

The background sound on the other end changed.

She pulled the phone from her ear and checked the screen. He'd ended the call.

She pressed his contact icon to call again. Rings repeated in her ear, answered only by the computerized voicemail instructions.

Dropping the phone on the bed, Cora looked to the ceiling, tears dripping down her face onto her neck. "Father, what do I do? How can I help him?"

The cartel. She lowered her head as the idea took shape.

Bradley had miraculously broken free from his addiction, but he still wasn't free to live his life, to come to Jesus and follow Him, so long as the cartel kept Bradley captive with threats and danger.

She could do more than pray about it. She could team with Kent Thomson to do everything she could to help him bring down the cartel.

No more mistakes. She would save Bradley this time, no matter what the cost.

NINETEEN

Kent checked the clock on the wall of the police precinct. Unless he'd lost his ability to read people, Cora would show up earlier than he'd told her.

Sure enough, an elegant blonde made her way up the sidewalk outside the glass doors ten minutes early.

He swung one open for her.

Her bright blue eyes widened with surprise. And a smile lit her face.

His pulse tripped. "Morning."

"Good morning to you." She turned her head toward him, letting her gaze touch his face as she passed through the door he held.

A whiff of delicate, flowery scent that matched her perfectly teased his nose.

Man, he needed to watch himself with this lady. He'd already let her get the better of his judgment when she'd called him that morning, interrupting his shave.

Please let me be there when you talk to Hayden. The pleading in her voice was as vivid now as when he'd heard her say the words two hours ago. *My brother is lost to me right now. Let me help Hayden and try to stop the cartel. I want my brother back, and the only way that will happen is if the cartel is stopped.*

Ending the cartel had been the theme of Kent's life for nearly two decades. He couldn't easily turn away this woman who had the same mission.

But no way was he letting her actually talk to Hayden. He'd agreed to let her watch his interview from a safe distance, and that was all.

"Thank you for letting me come." She slipped her hands into the pockets of the pale blue coat she wore. It had a slim cut and clean design that suited her figure, and the dark blue blouse underneath the open coat made her eyes stand out even more than usual. Instead of wearing her hair up the way he'd seen it every other time in person, it fell loose like in her driver's license photo, framing her face in sculpted waves that curled at the ends to brush against her slim neck. Wow, she was gorgeous.

He dragged his gaze away and started past the desk where Cora would have been required to stop if she hadn't been with him. "Weird to see you without your dog." He cast a glance back at her as she followed. "Thought you never went anywhere without her."

She smiled. "I rarely do. But I think Hayden may resent her even more than me, so it seemed best that she wait in the car. It's a cold day, so she should be fine."

He pressed the buzzer by the door and waited a few seconds.

A tone sounded, along with a click of the door being unlocked.

He pulled on the heavy metal door and held it, looking at Cora.

She stepped through, again allowing him to get a tantalizing taste of her perfume. Or was it a shampoo?

Not that it mattered. He let the door slam hard enough to lock behind them and passed Cora to lead her to the right and up the hall.

What he should be concerned about was what she'd just said—the inference that she left her dog in the car because she expected to meet with Hayden. "You're still not meeting with him, though." He slowed his stride and moved to one side so she would catch up.

As she fell in step beside him, the corner of her lips tucked. "I believe in always being prepared for anything." She sent him a glance that seemed to twinkle. Cora Isaksson could be playful?

His heart skittered as his mouth tried to tug into a grin. He squashed the reaction before it could show.

"I never know what God has in store."

There, that helped. She might as well be carrying a visible crutch around with her and a sign that said: *Hurt me, use me, kill me*. A sign that said she was weak.

And he'd end up the same way if he kept letting her get to him.

Renewed resolve enabled Kent to keep from saying or feeling much as he set Cora up at a computer with headphones to observe his interview with Hayden from the desk of an accommodating police detective.

Kent grabbed Hayden's file and stepped into the interview room, game face in place. The kid likely couldn't give him much on the cartel, not nearly as much as Ramos who was already talking, but he could help end the drug infestation at the school.

Hayden looked as sulky as the last time Kent had seen him, his chin dipped down, tall body slouched low in the chair and arms crossed over his narrow chest.

A dark-haired woman sat next to him wearing a business suit and a confrontational expression she aimed at Kent. The kid's lawyer, no doubt.

He walked to the table where his two opponents sat side-by-side, facing him. "Special Agent Kent Thomson, DEA." He reached his hand across the table to the woman.

She accepted his handshake, her gaze losing some of its sharpness. "Felice Dowerly, Mr. Simpson's attorney."

"Nice to meet you." Kent pulled out the chair facing them

and sat, dropping the file folder on the table in front of him. "Hayden, you and I have already met. Though I'm sorry the circumstances weren't more pleasant."

Hayden's head lifted a fraction, just enough for him to snort and aim a glare at Kent.

"So here's the deal. We both know you don't want to go to prison, right?"

"Scare tactics won't work on my client, Agent Thomson."

Kent lifted a hand. "No scare tactics. Just dealing with the facts." He refocused on Hayden. "We've got you dead-to-rights with illegal narcotics in your pocket. We witnessed you obtain said narcotics from another known drug dealer at a warehouse known to be used by the Guajardo cartel." Kent stared at Hayden, giving a moment for the bad news to sink in. "This is one problem your dad won't be able to buy your way out of."

Hayden's jaw shifted, but he didn't lift his head. Didn't make a sound.

The lawyer smiled. "We won't be giving you any information that could incriminate my client."

And she was right. Fifteen more minutes of trying different tactics yielded nothing. For an immature kid, Hayden was unusually smart about listening to his lawyer and keeping quiet. Nothing seemed to shake his resolve to stay silent.

"Okay." Kent hated this feeling. Needing to give up. "If you don't cooperate with me, Hayden—if you don't give me anything—I can't help you. At eighteen, you're no longer a minor. You will go away to prison for a long time." Kent stood, his chair squeaking on the floor as it slid backward. "How about you and your lawyer discuss that for a few minutes."

Kent left the room, frustration surging through him. Only chance left was that Hayden might let his real feelings out with the lawyer, maybe the panic he'd managed to hide with Kent in the room. And maybe that fear would make him more talkative when Kent returned.

Kent stalked to the computers where a certain beautiful blonde waited. Hopefully.

"Hi." Her soft voice made just that one word feel like a calming splash of water as she removed the headphones from her ears and swiveled in the chair to face him. "I'm sorry." Her eyebrows squeezed closer together in concern.

He shrugged. "Goes that way sometimes. Can't win 'em all." A fact that grated on him every time.

"Would you mind..." She looked up at him, hesitation in her eyes. "I have an idea of how we might be able to get through to Hayden, perhaps encourage him to cooperate."

The insinuation he needed help fanned his irritation into a hotter flame. "And that is?"

She tilted her head, making a silky blond wave fall away from her face. "If I tell you, I'm not sure you'll say yes."

He steeled himself from the mesmerizing affect her hair was having on him, how his fingers itched to feel if it was as soft as it looked. She should always wear her hair down, especially if she wanted men to fawn all over her.

"Could I try it? If it doesn't work, there isn't any harm done, right?" Her mouth quirked with a little smile, an adorable expression he hadn't seen her make before.

And it made a grin conquer his own face before he could stop it. "Fine. But I'll be in there the whole time, and you need to leave when I say so."

Her lips stretched into a full smile as she stood. "Thank you so much. You won't regret it. Just one more thing. Could you promise to let me do all the talking?"

Anyone else would have blown their chance with that request—the demand to essentially run the show and force him to sit on the sidelines.

But all he seemed able to do in response to her was shake his head and chuckle as he cupped her elbow and escorted her to the interview room. Her blend of gentleness and unexpected daring was starting to grow on him.

If he was smart, he'd run the other way. Before it was too late.

———

"Do you know why I asked to talk to you, Hayden?"

"'Cause you're stalking me?" Hayden sneered, his gaze only briefly touching Cora before darting away.

"Don't answer her." Ms. Dowerly gave Hayden a cautionary look, then returned her gaze to Cora. "I'm not sure why you're here, but we are not going to stay for an interview with a civilian."

"Ms. Isaksson is consulting with us on this case." Kent's firm tone and his warm presence in the chair next to Cora's soothed her shaky nerves. "She's authorized to be here and to interview your client."

Cora refrained from giving him a questioning glance. She doubted she'd actually been given consultant status by the DEA, but perhaps Kent intended to do that after this conversation. At any rate, Hayden needed to be her focus right now. "I wanted to speak with you because you remind me of my brother."

"Can't get him to talk to you, huh?" Hayden's shot hit closer to the mark than he likely knew.

Cora didn't try to hide the answering pain that surged in her chest and probably showed on her face. "Something like that. Because he's being hounded by the Guajardo cartel."

Hayden's blue eyes finally found her face, furrows gathering on his brow.

"Yes, my brother was a drug dealer. He started dealing when he was your age, just like you."

Hayden's attention stayed on Cora, so she kept going.

"We had a rich father whom we rarely saw, and he bought Bradley's freedom when he was arrested for drug possession." Cora clasped her hands together on the table and held Hayden's gaze with her own. "But you know what our father couldn't do? He couldn't free Bradley from the cartel. Even now, he has to hide because the cartel is trying to hurt him." She swallowed, not wanting to put the awful possibility into words. "To kill him."

She searched Hayden's face, the conflicted swirl in his eyes as he seemed to process what she said. "You believe you won't go to prison. But do you want to lose your life to the cartel? Because you will, either from their violence or the hold they or drugs will have on you, if you don't cooperate with Agent Thomson. He's offering you a way out."

"Don't respond to that."

Hayden looked away at his lawyer's warning. He shifted in the chair. His arms lowered from their folded position, his hands going to his lap as he looked down at them.

Had she gotten through to him?

He lifted his head. "I don't know what you're talking about. I don't know anything about a cartel."

Cora's hopes plummeted, sinking to her stomach as she drew her hands off the table.

"That's enough, Hayden. Don't answer her in any way."

A touch on Cora's arm drew her gaze away from the protective lawyer to Kent. He didn't look at her, but his fingers lightly brushed her forearm under the table before moving away, leaving warmth through her satin blouse where his touch had been. His gaze stayed on Hayden, sending her a message.

She returned her attention to the teen and saw what she'd missed in her heightened hope, hanging on his answer. The defiant posture was gone, worry and openness on his face instead of anger. She'd broken the shell, his determination to refuse to yield.

What she saw now was a boy who watched her as if he wanted her help but didn't know how to ask for it.

It was up to her to figure out the best way, the route that would help him without requiring him to incriminate himself further. He was obviously smart enough not to do that. Or, perhaps, he truly didn't know the cartel was behind the drug dealing he was doing.

Father, please give me the right words. They came to mind as she finished the prayer. "I met your teammates."

Hayden's eyes widened a small fraction in surprise.

"I hear you're the star of the football team. The Bobcats, right?"

He nodded cautiously.

"What position do you play?"

"Quarterback." His eyebrows dipped as if he was unsure why she was asking. But his defensive posture and expression continued to fall away.

She took a guess. "What would happen to your football scholarship if you were charged with drug possession?"

His peach-toned skin turned white.

She'd hit the mark. He must have received a college scholarship for football.

"I can't speak for Agent Thomson or the DEA, but I'm guessing that if you cooperate, he will work to get you reduced charges. Perhaps enough that you can still play football and go to college."

"Hayden, do not answer her." Ms. Dowerly gave him a sharp look. "You've already said too much."

Hayden's gaze went to Kent for the first time since this interview had begun. Then he brought his focus back to Cora. "It's true what I said about the cartel. I don't know anything about that. I only report to one guy, and he never told me who he works for or where he gets the drugs. He just asked me to sell at the school, and that's all I do."

"That's enough." Ms. Dowerly lurched to her feet, lifting her briefcase with her. "We're leaving, right now."

"No." Hayden snapped out the word with a glare at his attorney. He looked at Kent. "Will you cut me a deal? If I tell you what's going on at the school, will you keep me out of prison?"

Cora's heart raced. Hayden had already admitted some information and guilt. Was he really going to share more?

"I can't make any promises until you give me the information, and I see what you can do for us." Kent's tone was even and calm. "But I might be able to manage that if you're helpful enough."

"Okay."

"Hayden, your father would not want you to do this." Ms. Dowerly leaned toward the seated teen.

"Maybe I don't care what the old man wants." He spewed the answer at her with anger probably aimed at his absent father. He swung his head back to Kent. "What do you want to know?"

"Facts. Not lies, like the one you just fed us."

"What lie?"

"You said your contact never told you where he gets the drugs."

"Yeah. So?" Hayden lifted his hands into the air as if he had no idea what Kent referred to.

"Hayden, we caught you at the warehouse. Remember?"

The teen ran a hand over his mouth. "Okay, yeah. But that was the first time I'd ever been there. And what I meant was I don't know *who* he gets the drugs from."

"Do you believe that?" Kent looked at Cora, startling her with his sudden attention.

A strange warmth filtered through her under his conspiratorial gaze. "It sounds possible."

He shrugged and turned back to Hayden. "Okay, Hayden. One more chance. What's the name of the guy you get your supply from?"

"Trent Netto."

"Why should I believe you?"

"I'm going to meet him." Hayden threw out the words like a last-resort pitch. "Tonight, Lofland High. You could follow me or whatever."

"We could follow you? Good idea. Or maybe we'll drop you off from the prison van." Sarcasm edged Kent's tone. He stood and put his hand on the back of Cora's chair. "Tell you what, Hayden, we're going to go and think about your idea, and we'll get back to you."

Cora took the obvious hint and rose to follow Kent as he went to the door.

"But wait." Desperation squeezed Hayden's voice. "I thought we were going to make a deal. I'll give you this guy on a platter. Trust me."

Kent glanced back as he held the door for Cora. "The trust thing is a no, but I like the platter option. Sit tight, Hayden. You might want to pray, if that's something you do."

She turned toward Kent as he shut the heavy door behind them. "Why did you do that? He was going to cooperate."

"And he still will." Kent folded his arms, his thin green sweater stretching gently to accommodate his expanding muscles. "But he had to know he isn't running the show."

"Oh. So you will let him lead you to the dealer he works for?"

"Maybe."

"And do you think you can release him if he does that?"

Kent lowered his hands to his hips. "I don't know about that. He's a dealer. He belongs in jail, and he needs to do his time."

"But he's also just a teenager. A boy who is lost and hurt and looking for something to fill his empty places." Like Bradley.

"You're something else, Ms. Isaksson."

Was that a twinkle in the green irises that watched her?

Her breath caught.

He took a step toward her, then another. "You took that kid from hating you to eating out of your hand within minutes." One more step, leaving only a foot between them. "I don't know what it is about you."

His eyes darkened, closer to the color of freshly cut grass, as he gazed down at her from his six-foot height.

She hadn't realized he was so tall before. Hadn't known how very handsome he was up close—the strong cut of his jaw, the dark eyebrows, the tanned complexion in the middle of winter.

Her pulse pounded in her ears.

Someone, an officer in a uniform, walked past them in the hallway.

Hayden. She was trying to help Hayden.

She took a step back and angled away, hoping to appear

natural as she turned to leave. "I should get to the high school. Jana and I have our search to do." A thought sparked in her mind. "You know, I used to do random searches at Lofland twice a month. But since the drug problem increased, they've had me do daily searches. It would be so wonderful if we didn't have to do that anymore, if they could end the drug problem and protect all those kids." She returned her gaze to Kent's face.

A shadow seemed to have fallen over his eyes, cloaking the emotion she'd seen there only seconds before.

"I know he can't help you get to the cartel, but perhaps if you go easy on him, Hayden can help you end the drug dealing at the school."

Kent dropped his hands from his hips and stepped to her side. "I'll walk you out." He started forward, and she fell in step beside him.

She didn't attempt more persuasion until he'd escorted her all the way to her car parked outside the station.

As he opened her door and she passed him to get in behind the wheel, he met her gaze. "I'll see you there."

She almost fell into the driver's seat out of surprise. She gripped the steering wheel and looked up at him. "The high school? Does that mean you're going to give him a chance?"

Kent's mouth twitched, as if his rare smile might make an appearance. "You asked me to go easy on him, right?"

She peered up at him as sunlight silhouetted his handsome frame. "I did."

"Then how can I resist the magical persuasive powers of Cora Isaksson?"

A smile stretched her face as her pulse skipped about behind her ribs. "I'll see you there."

As he closed her door and she drove away, she reveled in the hope that God—not she—was working a miracle to give Hayden a second chance.

Another part of her happiness couldn't be so easily defined. The heat that flushed her cheeks at the memory of Kent's smile at the police station, the feel of his touch on her arm when they communicated without words, the intensity in his gaze when he stood so close in the hallway—that fluttery feeling could be explained as relief that he liked her better and had come to respect her.

That had to be all it was, or she could be headed for a different kind of trouble than she'd ever faced.

TWENTY

Kent scanned the parking lot of Lofland high as he turned into it.

Cora's distinctive white Volkswagen Beetle was parked in the third row with an empty stall next to it.

As he pulled into the space, he glanced at her tires. Everything looked unscathed so far, including the new rubber she'd had put on. He smiled, already looking forward to the happy expression on her face when he told her what he'd decided to do for Hayden.

A standard ringtone chimed from his phone in the holder on the dash.

The number that illuminated the screen had no name attached, but the digits were from the burner phone he'd given to his newest CI.

He yanked the device out of the holder and swiped as he brought it to his ear. "Hey, you've got Vince."

A pause. Would the person on the other end use the response he'd told Ramos to give? "Is this Zesty's Pizza?"

The tension that clutched Kent's chest loosened. "What've you got, Ramos?"

"I'm in. I think everything's okay."

"Good."

"Next test is set for tonight. Intercepting a shipment for JK-16."

"Where?"

He rattled off the freeway and exit number. "Around one."

"All right. If things go south or you think they're onto you, call me. Otherwise, check in tomorrow."

"Right."

Kent lowered his phone and ended the call. So far, so good. Going exactly as he planned.

Energy buzzed through his limbs as he got out of the car and headed for the main entrance to the three-story brick building. He finally had a real chance to do what he'd set out to when he joined the DEA. He could almost taste the victory.

But there were a lot of steps to go yet and plenty of unknowns with needing to use Ramos and the drug lord's tests.

Kent pushed through the glass door, instantly spotting the armed security guard who tensed as Kent entered. Good they had some security, and the guy knew how to tell when someone might be carrying.

"Special Agent Kent Thomson, DEA." Kent pulled one side of his coat out of the way to let the guard see the badge clipped on his hip. "I have an appointment to see Principal McFadden."

The guard visibly relaxed. "Sure." He pointed at an angle across the broad hallway. "Just stop by the welcome desk to get a visitor ID. She'll direct you to Principal McFadden's office."

Kent's shoes squeaked on the polished floor as he walked to the desk where a middle-aged woman with short, permed brown hair and glasses welcomed him with a smile. As she documented his name, Kent scanned the huge, empty hallway. The gleaming lockers and floors—all clearly new or extremely well-maintained—and the abundance of wasted space were the polar opposite of the high school he'd attended as a teen. But he wasn't particularly interested in how the privileged lived. He was looking for a certain blonde with a golden retriever.

No such luck. He glanced at his watch. *1:05.* Must've just

missed the mad rush between classes when students had likely filled the hall.

"Here you are." The woman handed him a visitor ID through a slot at the bottom of the window that separated her from Kent. "Just go up this main hallway and take the first right. You'll find Principal McFadden's office, second door on the left."

"Thanks." The principal's office was easy enough to locate, and McFadden made Kent's job simple by agreeing to cooperate fully and allow Kent complete access to and control over the school building and grounds that night. Only wrinkle was the heads-up McFadden gave Kent that Phoenix K-9 handlers would be there with their dogs, patrolling overnight as part of increased security they'd just added.

Kent left the office and took a walk through the building, searching for any of the Phoenix K-9 team. McFadden had said one of the security teams was supposed to be at the school to discourage daytime drug activity or vandalism.

Kent paused at the open doors to the cafeteria and peered inside at the empty chairs and tables.

Movement at the back of the massive room caught his eye.

A lovely woman wearing a purple puffer jacket moved between chairs, a golden retriever sniffing the floor in front of her.

Cora.

A smile stretched Kent's mouth as his heart pumped a little faster. He stepped into the room.

She didn't look up, her focus intent on Jana as they moved away from the row of chairs and tables to search a food rack on wheels. "Good girl."

Her soft voice carried in the empty room, the only other sound some muffled clatters carrying from the kitchen where staff must be cleaning up after the lunch period.

There was something calming about watching Cora and Jana work together. A fluidity and grace in their movements made searching for drugs look more like a dance.

A dance?

Kent shook his head at the crazy direction of his thoughts. He was losing it. He needed to remember why he was here and get on with it. He had work to do.

"Hey." He started toward Cora at a casual pace.

She looked up. A smile brightened her face. She'd put her silky hair into a bun, but she was still gorgeous enough to take his breath away.

If he was the kind of guy that could be so easily affected. He stiffened his spine as he stopped near her. But not too close this time.

"Good to see you here."

He wouldn't let himself be softened by the sweet welcome in her voice or her eyes.

Jana pulled toward him on the leash.

"I guess I'm not the only one who thinks so." Cora laughed, a sound like the trickle of a brook on a hot day.

He shifted his gaze to Jana, who stood at the end of the leash, looking at him as she wagged her tail.

"It seems like you're not comfortable around dogs."

That he was afraid of them, she probably meant. He stepped to Jana and petted her head to prove fear wasn't the problem. "No. I just never had one. Too busy, I guess." And Vince definitely would not have approved, unless it had been a protection dog too prickly to let anyone, including Kent, get close.

Jana leaned her head into his hand and seemed to look right into his eyes. She was surprisingly soft and warm. His muscles relaxed as he ran his thumb over her ear. Did she have the same magical abilities to break through defenses as Cora? "Your dog is nice, though."

"Thank you. She likes you, too."

Kent lowered his hand and looked up.

The approval mixed with happiness in Cora's gaze sent a hot spark zinging through him. Man, that was a feeling he could get used to. "I have some good news."

Her refined eyebrows lifted. "Oh?"

"I'm giving Hayden a deal."

Her mouth fell open in such a charming way he couldn't stop the grin that found his face.

"He agreed to meet with his contact tonight while we watch and ID his source and put a tail on him. He's also told us the names of the students here who have sold or purchased drugs. In exchange, I think I can get him probation with community service instead of jail time."

"Oh!" She pressed her hands together, the leash handle between them. "This is such good news. He'll be able to go to college and have a better future. Thank you so much, Kent." Her smile beamed bright enough to outshine the sunlight streaming through the windows behind her.

He had to admit, with the way she looked at him, going easy on the kid felt pretty good. Maybe there was something to her approach. But it hadn't been an emotional decision. He wasn't going soft.

And he should make sure she knew that. "It makes sense to get his cooperation. I don't think he'll try to pull anything more with your reminder that his football scholarship is on the line. And he should know he'll have to answer to the cartel if he tries to double-cross me. He'd have to tell them he agreed to flip, and they'd never trust him after that. If they let him live."

"I'm just so happy about this. Hopefully, your kindness will set him on the right path in life."

Her phrasing gave him the urge to squirm. *Kindness.* What would Vince say if he heard that?

"Hayden will thank you for this someday." She had to be the most optimistic woman who ever existed.

"I doubt it. But I don't need him to. Right now, I just need to talk to your boss about tonight. I understand Phoenix K-9 people are patrolling here."

Cora nodded. "She's right behind you." Her gaze aimed past Kent's shoulder.

He turned to see a figure standing in the doorway of the cafeteria.

Phoenix and her dog.

He had to hand it to her—the woman knew how to make a dramatic, yet undetected entrance.

"Phoenix, do you have time to talk to Agent Thomson?"

The famous Phoenix Gray, a woman he'd learned was well-known and respected by local law enforcement and the FBI, approached with a confident stride matched by the tan dog at her side.

She stopped about six feet away, her features shadowed under the bill of the black cap she wore low on her forehead. "I heard you wanted to see me." Her deep voice was firm, not friendly.

"You'll have to take the night off of your patrols here tonight. Or at least for a couple of hours between midnight and two."

"Why is that?"

"We're doing surveillance tonight on a narcotics suspect meeting with a distributor."

"Hayden Simpson." Cora angled a look at her boss.

"I see." Phoenix stood silently for a few beats while she watched Kent. At least, that's what he assumed she was doing, but the bill of her cap cast her eyes in shadow, so he couldn't actually see the direction of her gaze. "We'll be here."

Kent glanced at Cora, then back to Phoenix. "Maybe you didn't hear me right. I need you to back off so we can do our job."

"We have a job to do, too." Her tone stayed even and low just like before, no sign of malice or heat in her challenge to his authority. "We'll stay out of sight."

"I can't have civilians here for this operation."

"There won't be." The bill of her cap turned toward Cora. "Ms. Isaksson could be of help to you in coordinating our teams. She's skilled in monitoring coms for such operations."

"I don't think—"

"We'll be here at eleven." She gave the order with more authority than his supervisors had ever conveyed and stalked away before he could strategize the best response.

His gaze drifted to Cora, who lifted her shoulders slightly and gave him a bemused smile.

She looked so cute that the ire rising in his chest fizzled.

"What was that?"

"Phoenix has a very strong personality."

"I can see that."

"You don't have to do everything she said, though. I mean, you don't have to let me help with coms." She glanced away, as if uncertain or nervous.

A sudden desire to put her at ease welled in response. "You have experience?"

She nodded. "Quite a bit. I handled coms for our operation when we captured Libertas."

"The bomber?" Kent had heard Phoenix K-9 was responsible for capturing the environmental terrorist last spring before he could bomb more dams and flood Minneapolis.

"Yes."

"All right." He extended his hand toward her. "You're hired."

She slipped her small hand in his, and for once he didn't judge the person by the strength of their handshake.

He was too busy trying to squelch the spark that singed his fingers and spiraled heat straight to his heart.

Cora shifted her car into drive, her gaze lingering on the man who stood in the parking lot, watching her leave.

Kent had escorted her all the way to the lot, though he excused the gesture by saying he was leaving anyway. Underneath his brusque, grim demeanor, he was quite a gentleman. The brooding cloud that had cloaked him like an extra coat seemed to be lightening, the darkness of his expression now parted by the occasional sunshine of a smile.

Father, I pray this is the start of You working in his life and softening him toward You.

Cora checked both directions before pulling out of the lot onto the street.

She could hardly believe Kent had agreed to help Hayden. It was so difficult for law enforcement professionals to not become jaded by the crimes they saw and the people they had to deal with every day. She didn't blame Kent for being cynical and for initially not wanting to take a risk to give Hayden a second chance.

But perhaps if someone like Kent had gotten Bradley engaged in apprehending and testifying against the people who had used him, he wouldn't have become so lost.

Her stomach clenched at the thought of Bradley, alone, hiding and afraid in a motel. She hadn't heard another word from him since last night. And she'd had no chance to ask Phoenix at Lofland if Remington had given her any news.

Cora scanned the intersection ahead where a navy-blue car waited at the cross-street stop sign. There was no stop for her direction, so she kept her speed steady.

Perhaps she should call Phoenix and ask if she knew how Bradley was, to make sure the cartel hadn't somehow—

The blue car surged in front of her, screeching to a halt at an angle.

She slammed on the brakes. Her tires squealed as she gritted her teeth, watching for her car to stop as if in slow motion. *Father, help me!*

Her car halted within inches of the sedan's back door.

Thank you, Lord. Her heart raced as she remembered to breathe, so grateful there wasn't any ice at this intersection.

Her hand trembled as she shifted into park and turned around to check on Jana in the backseat.

The golden had slipped off the seat to the floor, where she lay looking up at Cora, panting.

"Oh, honey. Are you okay? I'm sorry."

Jana swished her tail against the upholstered seat.

Movement out the rear window caught Cora's eye.

A green car she'd been too busy to notice was parked sideways right behind her Beetle.

A thickly-built man with a dark beard and long, curly hair came from the driver's side, lumbering toward her car.

Was that a gun in his hand?

Cora spun forward, her hand grabbing the gear stick.

But the sedan she had nearly hit was still there, trapping her in the intersection.

Two men who looked just as rough as the one behind her emerged from it and headed her way.

Oh, Father. Please, help.

A squeal, like tires, yanked her gaze to the right where a black four-door zoomed onto the sidewalk, blew past the green car's hood, and screeched to a halt beside Cora's Beetle, about ten feet away.

She knew that car. Amalia?

TWENTY-ONE

Kent wasn't sure who was in the black car that just flew onto the curb and landed by Cora's Volkswagen, but he didn't waste time finding out.

He slammed on the gas and nicked the bumper of the green sedan's back end as he drove past.

The green car jolted, swung at an angle. The two thugs walking beside it had to jump out of the way.

Bought Kent time to tumble to the pavement on the driver's side of his car and whip out his Glock.

They opened fire, bullets spattering the passenger side of his car. Velasquez was going to love his expense report this month.

A bullet pinged the side mirror above his head.

Great. The guys from the navy-blue car blocking Cora's Volkswagen.

Pops answered. From a different gun.

The shots at him stopped while the pops continued.

He moved to the hood of his car and peered over it.

A dark-haired woman drew the aim of all four thugs as she returned fire from a position by the black hood of her car, then the rear bumper, then somewhere he couldn't pinpoint. She moved quickly and frequently, keeping the four shooters busy.

Make that three shooters. The long-haired guy's buddy

yelled as he grabbed his shoulder and made for the front seat of the green car.

Whoever the armed woman was, she apparently wasn't with the cartel.

Kent couldn't see Cora or Jana in the Volkswagen. They must be staying low. Hopefully not hurt.

The guy at the front of the blue car pulled a bigger weapon from inside. An AR-15.

He pointed it at the dark-haired woman and opened fire.

Kent aimed, let off a round.

AR-15 dude squealed and lowered his weapon.

Bullseye.

Kent continued firing, covering the blue sedan while the dark-haired woman pinned down the remaining shooter at the green vehicle.

"Go!" The guy at the blue car let out the shout and ducked into the car, his injured buddy straightening in the driver's seat where he must have gotten ready to drive them off. They gunned it and drove away using the cross-street.

The long-haired thug scrambled into his sedan and tried to swing it around, but the angle and Cora's Volkswagen slowed him.

Kent moved to his rear bumper and started to straighten. Maybe he could stop the green car from leaving.

A round whizzed past him, narrowly missing.

He dropped down.

Tires squealed as they found enough space to turn away and zoom up the road from where they'd come.

Kent jogged around his car to the Volkswagen. He slowed, weapon in hand as the dark-haired woman approached from the other side.

"Stand down, Agent Thomson. I'm Amalia Pérez. Phoenix K-9."

Phoenix K-9 had someone with her skills at the agency?

The driver's door of the Volkswagen popped open.

"Cora?" Kent forgot all about G.I. Jane as he rushed to help Cora from the car.

She trembled as he put his hands on her arms, supporting her if she needed it.

"You all right?" Pérez stood a couple feet away, hands resting on her hips and her weapon gone.

"I—" Cora lifted her gaze to Kent's face, her blue orbs hazy. "Yes. I think we're fine. Thanks to you." Her pale skin tinged with a healthier pink as she turned her head toward Pérez. "Both of you." She braced her hands behind her, leaning against the back door of her car.

Pérez walked around Kent and Cora and leaned into the car through the open driver's door. "Jana looks good. Want me to get her out?"

"I'm not sure. Do you think it's safe? Who were those people?" Cora looked at Kent.

He stopped himself before saying they were cartel. He couldn't prove that. None of them were men he could ID by sight. "Can't say for certain."

"Do you think they were from the cartel?" Her gaze searched his. Then she frowned and her brow furrowed, as if she'd read the answer in his eyes.

"I'm so thankful the Lord had you leave the school at the same time as I did." She turned to Pérez. "But Amalia, why are you here? Phoenix said you couldn't do the high school patrols because you were busy on another assignment."

"Yeah." Pérez grinned. "You."

"I'm your assignment?" Genuine confusion, not offense seemed to color Cora's question.

"Phoenix wanted me to follow you. She suspected you were in danger." Pérez's black eyebrows hiked over dark eyes that flashed with amusement. "Guess she was right, as usual."

"Oh, wow." Cora's eyes rounded. "Praise the Lord He prompted her to do that. I'll have to thank Phoenix for her foresight."

That was it? Kent would have been furious if his boss had secretly put a tail on him.

"When did she ask you to start following me?"

"After the tires." Pérez doled out the information cheerfully, as if there was nothing peculiar about secretly tailing one of her co-workers. And what happened to the intense, aggressive G.I. Jane she'd been only moments ago? This lighthearted woman didn't seem like the same person.

"Well, I'm grateful to you and Phoenix." Cora smiled, but exhaustion seemed to weaken the expression's usual power, tugging the corners of her mouth downward. "I don't know what I'd have done if you two hadn't come at just the right moment." Her shoulders sagged as moisture filled her eyes.

Kent's chest squeezed, and he reached to touch her shoulder.

"You're not going to get all weepy on me now, are you?" Pérez's teasing halted Kent's hand just before his fingers made contact.

He pulled back, didn't think Cora noticed as she sniffed, shaking her head with a gentle breath of a laugh. "No, I wouldn't do that to you, Amalia." She looked at her co-worker. "You didn't have to keep it a secret you were following me. I'd love to have you keep me company."

Amalia shook her head with a grin. "You're something else, Cora."

Kent's thoughts exactly. Anyone else he knew would have been insulted or unnerved by finding out their boss had assigned a co-worker to follow them without their knowledge. But Cora? She was grateful. Would he ever be able to figure her out?

Cora attempted another stronger smile for Pérez. "I'll take that as a yes, that you'll stay with me instead of following me separately, then."

Amalia let out a big laugh. "You got it, girl. As long as the boss is okay with it."

"I think she will be." Cora turned her bright blue eyes on Kent. "And I guess I'll see you tonight."

Tonight? He blinked, his thoughts scrambling through an unfamiliar muddle under her gaze.

"For Hayden's meeting with the dealer."

Oh, that. "Yes. Tonight."

She pushed off the car as if her body could still use the support.

Kent frowned. "Cora."

She looked at him.

"Are you sure you still want to come tonight? I can have one of my DEA people handle coms. You should take some time to recover."

She watched him for a beat. "Would you rather I not come?"

For her sake, yes. She'd be safer and could rest at home. But for his own sake? "No."

"Good. I'd like to be there." She turned to Pérez. "Think we could pull my car out of the way, and Jana and I can ride with you?"

"I was afraid you were going to ask me to drive your Beetle." Pérez laughed again. "Sure, the girls can come get your car."

"I can move it." The sooner Cora got somewhere safe, the better. "Keys in the ignition?"

"I think so." Faint lines crossed her forehead. "I don't remember what I did after...those men came."

"Don't think about it." He did touch her arm this time, giving her a gentle squeeze of comfort he didn't know he could offer.

She looked up at him, the same gratitude in her eyes as the first day he met her. "Thank you."

As he waited for her to get Jana out of the car and grab her other belongings, he didn't see just a lovely, grateful woman. He saw her strength and the steel that seemed to undergird her slight frame.

He saw a woman he'd do anything to protect, even if he had to throw his cartel strategy out the window and personally chase down every thug who'd been at the scene today. Had the cartel sent them to abduct her or kill her?

Her boss was right about one thing—Cora was in serious danger.

TWENTY-TWO

The buzzer signaled Cora to check the van's rear camera.

Her pulse quickened at the sight of the dark-haired man who tried to open the back door of Phoenix's van.

Kent Thomson.

She pressed the button on the console in front of her to unlock the back doors.

One popped open, and Kent's green eyes sparked in the light from the interior of the van where Cora sat. Nighttime darkness served as a fitting backdrop for the tall figure of the brooding man.

Except there was nothing brooding in his expression tonight as he stepped up into the van, a gentle smile curving his closed lips as he kept his gaze on her. "Hey there."

Heat flushed her cheeks, making her glad the interior of the van wasn't so well lit as to expose her blush. Why she blushed, she didn't want to pinpoint. But she was glad to see him look a bit happier than he usually did. She wouldn't ponder what the reason for that change could be.

"We use a lot of vans in my work, but I don't think I've ever seen one quite this...secure." He sat on the chair next to Cora as his gaze pulled away from her to roam the van's interior.

The two front seats were separated from the rest of the van by a floor-to-ceiling barrier made of crisscrossed bars. Behind the barrier, where Cora and Kent sat, the van was windowless and could only be entered through the split back doors.

A large computer monitor stood on the desk in front of Cora, while the console she used to control the cameras and coms system for the PK-9 team was positioned in front of the screen.

She pressed the button to lock the back, and a steel bar lowered to brace the two doors.

Kent turned toward the extra locking mechanism. "Your boss really believes in security."

"Yes, she does." Cora turned back to the screen that was split into four squares showing her the live cameras' views. She gripped the headset that rested around her neck and lifted it onto her head.

"How are you doing?"

Since there wasn't any sound coming from the headphones yet, she could easily hear Kent's deep tone. She turned her head toward him, surprised to find his green eyes on her instead of the screen. Even more surprising was the gentleness that clouded the usual intensity in his gaze. She moistened her lips as her throat went dry. "I'm okay. Thank you for asking."

She moved her attention back to the screen, but she had a hard time focusing. He seemed closer than he had before, the warmth of him filling the small space along with a woodsy, spicy scent that was decidedly masculine. Aftershave or cologne?

She blinked at the monitor, forcing herself to pay attention to something other than the man beside her. She couldn't be attracted to him. He wasn't a Christian, which made him completely off limits.

And she knew she wasn't really interested in him romantically for that very reason. The only man she could ever consider loving and marrying would be a man who belonged to Christ and served Him, first and foremost.

But, apparently, that resolve wasn't quite as powerful a deterrent against developing feelings as she'd thought it was.

Father, help me not to fall into temptation, even though Kent is turning out to be a much kinder and more compassionate man than he had seemed to be. Adding a quick, silent prayer for Kent's salvation, Cora grabbed another headset and handed it to him.

"Thanks." His fingers brushed hers as he took the headset.

She refused to indulge the skip of her heart from the contact. This was likely just an emotional response to him saving her life again today. The third time he'd rescued her. What woman wouldn't feel some warmth toward a man who saved her life more than once?

"So, what are we looking at here?" The voice of the man himself rescued her from her thoughts this time.

"The four views I have up right now are the school's security cameras." At least she didn't sound as flustered as she felt. She pressed a key, and new images replaced the others. "And these are the views from the body cams on the PK-9 team."

"Impressive." Kent peered at the images. "Phoenix said she'd have three K-9 teams on the ground. This looks like four."

"She decided Amalia and Raksa could help, too, since I'm safe in her van."

"Ah."

Cora felt his gaze when he looked at her.

"What's the story with Ms. Pérez? Her combat and tactical skills are at a level I don't see every day, even in my line of work."

Cora kept half her attention on the screen as she switched it back to the school's security cams. "Amalia is amazing. So tough, and yet she's so open and fun all the time. Nothing seems to phase her. I don't know much about her background, but what I do know, I'm afraid I can't tell you." Cora sent Kent a smile to soften her statement. "We have a policy at PK-9. Our stories are our own unless we choose to share them with others. Only Phoenix knows everyone's whole story. And I'm not sure even she knows all of Amalia's."

"Team 1 to Base, we've got eyes on the package." Phoenix's deep and steady voice came through the headphones.

"Oop..." Cora positioned the small microphone of the

headset closer to her mouth. "Roger that." She quickly pulled up Phoenix's body cam image to show on the screen.

A tall figure in a hooded sweatshirt and jeans stalked past foliage that must be partially concealing Phoenix and Dag from his view. The darkness shadowed the color of Hayden's blond hair, but his swagger was unmistakable.

"All teams, look alive, the package is on scene, approaching from the northeast." Cora covered the microphone with her hand and looked at Kent. Her question died at the sight of the small smile on his face, his gaze on her with something that looked like approval. Or was it amusement?

She didn't have time to puzzle it out. Refocusing on the operation, she fished her question from her jumbled thoughts. "Did a DEA agent drop Hayden off as planned?"

"No. We decided it was too much of a risk the dealer could see he didn't come alone and get scared off. We let him drive himself with a tail."

Cora nodded and removed her hand from the microphone. "Team 2, please verify the package's transportation location."

"Team 2, roger." Nevaeh's voice filtered through the headset. "Package's red Bentley is parked by building at the rear, out of view of security cams."

"Roger, Team 2." Cora switched the view to Nevaeh's body cam, and the image of Hayden's luxury car, spattered with shadows, appeared on the screen.

"Base, this is D2." A man's voice Cora didn't recognize came over the coms. D2 would make him the second of the two DEA agents they had looped into the same coms. "We've got suspicious movement. Dark Jeep pulling to the side of the road to the southwest."

Cora rapidly tapped keys until she found the security camera that covered that direction.

The image showed the parking lot, but the darkness prevented any possibility of seeing the road.

Jazz should be in that vicinity. "Team 3, can you get me eyes on this?"

"Team 3, Roger."

"He parked." D2's voice gave the additional information. "Driver is out and approaching on foot. Black male, medium height."

"Team 3 to Base. Go to body cam." Jazz's full voice sounded as confident as the day she'd scared away the football players.

Cora brought Jazz's body cam onto the screen. The image showed a man fitting D2's description in jeans and a leather jacket. He glanced at his surroundings as he walked along the edge of the plowed pavement of the parking lot, apparently just out of view of the school's security camera.

Jazz and the DEA agent must have done a good job hiding themselves from the visitor. Judging from the edge of a wall in Jazz's body cam image, she appeared to be concealed behind a corner except for her shoulder where the body cam was attached.

"All teams, this is the contact." Kent leaned forward, staring at the screen. "Repeat, this is the contact. Stand down and do not interfere."

Cora's breath caught. So this was the dealer they'd been expecting.

"Can you see if he's armed?"

She responded to Kent's question by zooming in the image of Jazz's body cam, close to the waistband area of the contact. A bulge protruded beneath his leather jacket, interrupting the smooth line of his back.

She shared a look with Kent. "All teams," she returned her attention to the dealer as he reached the school building, "be advised: the contact is armed."

"Team 4, are you in position?" The strong, deeper voice that Kent recognized as Phoenix carried over the coms.

Cora switched camera views to one that showed tree trunks and branches—probably the trees that clustered at the east corner of the building. "Roger, Team 1. Team 4 is in position. Be advised, Team 4 is radio silent."

"Roger that. Team 4," Phoenix added, "be ready to disarm if needed."

Movement at the edge of the image caught Kent's eye. "Watch it." He pointed at the screen.

A man came into view. The dealer who matched Hayden's description of his contact. Kent hadn't seen him before tonight. He crossed the camera image, looking around but somehow not seeing Team 4. Was that Pérez?

Kent couldn't believe how advanced and professional the PK-9 Agency was. They were more prepared to protect Hayden and manage this operation than he was. As long as they weren't seen, and their dogs didn't give them away. All it would take was one growl or bark, and they'd be blown. The dealer could become violent, or they could miss their chance to follow him and get more intel on the cartel and the school distribution.

The camera angle from Team 4's body cam shifted slightly to the right as the dealer moved that way and stopped.

Hayden stepped from the trees on the right to stand face to face with the dealer.

They appeared to be talking.

The dealer's hands lifted, gesturing. Was he getting heated about something?

Hayden's body language appeared calm.

But the dealer reached for the weapon behind his back.

Kent tensed, got up from the chair. They'd need backup out there if this went south.

Cora held up a hand, motioning for him to wait. "All teams, standby." She popped another camera view onto the big screen as she spoke into the headset. "Team 4 and Team 3 are in position to subdue contact. Teams 1, 2, and D2, hold positions to cover exit points."

Admiration for Cora's calm confidence loosened some of the tension constricting Kent's muscles as he lowered back to the chair, his gaze on her instead of the screen for a moment. He wouldn't have expected her to be so in control in a potential crisis. And before he'd witnessed Pérez in action on the street today, he'd never have trusted the Phoenix K-9 team to handle an armed suspect. But he'd trust the message Cora had just sent him—that they had things in hand—and let it play out for now.

The new camera view Cora had added showed Hayden and the contact from another perspective—directly behind the dealer. One of the teams must have moved in closer without the dealer noticing.

Hayden gave the dealer's arm a friendly bump with his fist.

The contact moved his hand away from his weapon, bringing his arm to the front of his body. He plunged both hands into his jacket pockets.

Reaching for another weapon?

His hands emerged, gripping plastic bags of narcotics.

Kent watched closely as Hayden took the drugs from the dealer. Kent leaned closer to Cora, covering his headset microphone. "Still recording this?"

She glanced at him, her blue eyes bigger at this proximity. She nodded.

They'd be able to use the recording as evidence when they eventually arrested this guy.

"All teams, exchange has been made." Cora tapped some keys and another camera view appeared next to the meeting coverage.

Looked like the school's security cam overlooking part of the parking lot behind the building. The front bumper of DEA Special Agent Patricia Gilson's car appeared at the corner of the image.

"D1, be prepared for go."

"Roger, Base." Gilson sounded ready and eager.

The views of the meeting showed the dealer turn and walk away, disappearing into the darkness from where he'd come.

"Team 4," Kent spoke into his headset, "keep the package where he is."

"Team 4, Roger." The voice that responded did sound like Pérez.

Good. Hayden wasn't likely to get away with the narcotics if she was watching him.

Cora cycled through camera views until she stopped on a body cam shot of the dealer, rounding the building, then walking out into the parking lot.

He strode away into the darkness where D2 had said the dealer's car was parked.

"D2," Cora switched to the school's security camera of the parking lot and street as she spoke, "confirm contact's status." The street was still too dark and far away to be seen from the camera views. Next time, Kent would put body cams on his agents, too. If there was a next time.

"Roger, Base." DEA Special Agent Billy Shiloh spoke with a hushed tone. "Contact is getting into his vehicle."

"Roger, D2." Cora glanced at Kent and covered her microphone. "Do you want D1 to follow now?"

He nodded and moved the microphone closer to his mouth. "D1, he's all yours."

"Roger, Base." Gilson's microphone picked up the sound of her engine starting.

"Base, this is D2. D1, be advised contact heading north on Velp."

"Roger, D2. Out." Gilson would report to Kent if anything went wrong in tailing the dealer. They'd ID him and keep him under surveillance until they got a bead on his superior in the cartel. Once Kent had enough intel from their connections with the cartel, they'd bring them in and end the cartel's school operation. At least at Lofland High.

"All teams on site," Cora smiled, lighting up the van as well as her voice, "we are clear. Well done." She removed her headset and let out a long sigh capped off with another smile, this one aimed at Kent.

He couldn't help but smile back. "You were pretty incredible."

It was too dark to tell for sure, but her cheeks seemed to redden as she dropped her gaze and set her headset next to the console. "I have an incredible team to work with."

"True. But I mean it. You could have a job at the DEA any time you want it." A strange sensation, like pride or admiration, built up in his chest until he felt he had to say more to release the pressure. "You were calm and in control the whole time, even with the weapon scare."

She kept her gaze at a downward angle, pointing somewhere near the console.

"Cora." He put his hands softly on her upper arms.

She lifted her head, her eyes swinging up to lock on his face.

Whatever he'd been going to say vanished from his mind. She was so beautiful and amazing, but she didn't seem to have any idea how special she was. How could he show her?

His gaze flicked down to her lips.

A clang halted the renegade thought, jerking his gaze to the back of the van where the metal security bar started to lift off the doors.

He looked at Cora. Had she—

"Phoenix." Cora tilted her head toward a small screen attached to the wall of the van that showed a camera view of the back.

In this case, a view of Cora's boss wearing a gray beanie she must have tucked her long hair under.

Kent dropped his hands from Cora's arms just in time for the back door to open.

Phoenix's tan dog jumped into the van first, then she stepped inside. She looked from Cora to Kent and back again.

Did she know? Not that he'd actually kissed Cora. But he had the uncomfortable feeling that Phoenix somehow knew he'd wanted to. It was the same feeling he'd had back in high school when Vince had discovered Kent was emailing a girl, his first crush. His only crush, thanks to Vince's reaction. Romantic feelings and emotions made a person weak and vulnerable. Kent knew that better than anyone.

Irritation for his lapse in judgment clenched Kent's stomach as he rose from the chair but stayed bent over to avoid the low ceiling.

"Amalia's holding Simpson for you with the narcotics."

Phoenix pierced him with a steady gaze. "Still want to let him loose?"

"Once I talk to him. He'll be on probation with community service and a rehab program. He knows he'll lose his football career and college if he missteps again." Kent stuck out his hand to Phoenix. "You have an impressive team."

She returned his handshake with a solid stare and the strongest grip he'd ever encountered from a woman. "Yes, I do."

He left the van without another glance at Cora. Weakness was fatal. He was not going to end up like his parents, no matter how tempting the beautiful, sweet blonde seemed to be to his heart.

TWENTY-THREE

Amalia could always get Cora to laugh, and tonight at Cora's house was no exception.

Until a low growl interrupted the laughter.

Raksa got to his feet next to the sofa where Amalia and Gaston lounged, the big Newfoundland with his head in Amalia's lap.

The German shepherd barked and bolted to the front door where he continued sounding the alarm.

But for what? Cora's overused danger response left her frozen on the sofa. Who was outside?

"What've you got, Raksa?" Amalia popped off the sofa, Gaston perking up his head to watch his canine brother. Amalia stood at Raksa's side within a second, her gun already in hand.

The sight of the weapon jarred Cora into action. She hurried to the kitchen where she'd left her phone. Jana trotted after her.

Cora grabbed the device from the counter. A security alert flashed on the screen. She tapped to see the front door camera view. Her pulse tripped.

A man walked up the sidewalk to the door.

Was that…Bradley?

She practically flew out of the kitchen. "Amalia!" She held

the phone out to Amalia as she came to a stop behind Raksa, Jana bumping into her leg. "It's Bradley."

Amalia grinned. "Just a little excited, huh?" Her gaze dropped to Raksa, still growling at the closed door. "Okay, Raksa. Enough. It's a friend." She shot Cora a glance with an angled smile. "According to some, anyway." She put her hand on Raksa's collar and scooted him away from the door.

He stopped barking, but his muscles were still tense, his head erect and alert in case Amalia was proven wrong.

Cora swung the door open, welcoming a cold blast of air that robbed her of breath for a moment.

Her brother stood with his hand raised, as if he'd been about to knock.

"Bradley." She gulped frigid oxygen into her lungs and opened her arms wide. "Thank the Lord, you're home."

A small smile tucked his lips at the corners, but he didn't move into what she'd hoped might become a hug. "Hey, Sis."

She lowered her arms, swinging one inward to gesture inside. "Come in."

He carried a duffle bag slung over his shoulder, the same bag he'd arrived with only days before.

Jana pranced around his legs, but he didn't pet her.

"I'm so happy to see you."

He gave a short nod, his gaze fastening on Raksa, who met his stare with a challenging one of his own.

"People who look him in the eyes like that can get hurt." Amalia grinned as Bradley gave her a startled glance.

"Don't mind Amalia." Cora smiled at her friend. "Though she is right about Raksa. Or any dog, really. It's never a good idea to stare at dogs you don't know."

Gaston shoved past Raksa, barreling up to Bradley with a massive, wagging body of friendliness. Cora laughed but stopped when she saw Bradley's eyes widen as he backed up.

"Although this guy wouldn't mind. He's always friendly. Gaston, come here, boy." Cora patted her hands and stepped closer to Bradley to draw Gaston's attention away. The

Newfoundland happily leaned his heavy weight against Cora instead as she stroked his head and neck.

She looked at Amalia, whose dark eyes flashed with barely-restrained laughter. "Amalia Pérez, I'd like you to meet my brother. Bradley, this is Amalia, one of my amazing co-workers at Phoenix K-9."

Bradley nodded, looking anywhere but at Amalia. "I didn't see you here the other night. At the party or whatever."

"Yeah. I get that a lot."

Cora chuckled. The idea that the gorgeous woman with stunning bone structure framed in lush waves of raven-black hair could ever be overlooked was laughable. But Amalia was no doubt using that response as a deflection to avoid explaining why she had disappeared so quickly on Friday. She had made her early escape to ensure Bradley hadn't brought any other unexpected visitors with him that night.

"Bradley, Amalia is staying with me for a while."

"Why?" His gaze landed on Cora.

"Because of something that happened today."

Bradley hiked the slipping strap of his bag higher on his shoulder. "What happened?"

"You ask a lot of questions for a drifter who just reappeared." Amalia tilted her head as she watched Bradley, an amused smile curving her full lips.

His gaze shot to Amalia, then bounced away. "Sorry." Pink tinged his otherwise pale cheeks. Did he like Amalia? She certainly was appealing to men, though her beauty seemed to intimidate many, even when they didn't know of her surprising skill set.

"It's okay, Bradley. Amalia's just teasing." Cora wasn't actually sure if Amalia was teasing or using that tactic to get Bradley to stop being inquisitive. But she wasn't going to let Bradley get scared away by her friend the moment he walked in the door. "Here, let me take your bag, and we'll get you settled in your room."

Bradley pulled back from Cora's outstretched hand. "I can carry it. And I was just here. I can find the room."

She blinked at his defensive response. Why had he come home if he was still angry with her? "I just hoped we could talk a bit."

Bradley looked away, but not before she saw him wince. He let out a long sigh. "Sure. Yeah."

"The boys and I are going to make some hot cocoa in the kitchen." Amalia looked at Cora. "You okay alone here?"

"Yes." Cora nodded, gratitude for Amalia's protection and care warming her from the inside. "Thank you."

"Come on, boys." Gaston and Raksa jogged behind her.

Jana looked up at Cora as if asking permission.

Cora smiled at the golden retriever. "You can go, too."

Jana swung away and hurried to catch her friends, her tail swishing as she disappeared into the kitchen.

Bradley lowered the bag from his shoulder and let it drop to the floor. "I suppose you want to know why I came back."

"I'd love to. If you want to tell me."

"It's complicated."

"That's okay. I'm just glad you're here. I don't need to know why." Cora moved toward the edge of the sitting room rug. "Do you want to sit? Maybe visit a while?"

"You said something happened."

Cora turned back to see that he hadn't budged. "What?"

"That's why she's here, you said."

She? "Oh, Amalia. Yes, she's here because, well, I had a bit of a scare today." She didn't want to alarm him. He might worry about her. Or, worse, what if he decided to run away again because of the cartel?

But she wouldn't lie or deceive him by holding back the whole truth. *Father, please don't let this scare him away.*

"Some men stopped me on the road today and tried—well, I'm not actually sure what they were trying to do. They had guns and approached my car. But thankfully, Amalia and Agent Thomson arrived just in time to scare them away."

"Agent?"

Cora paused. That wasn't the response she'd expected. Why

was the agent part the most interesting to him? "Yes. Agent Thomson. He's with the DEA."

"Why was a DEA agent there? Do you know him?"

"Yes. Jana and I have been working with him. We're searching arriving baggage at the airport." Was it her imagination, or was Bradley's skin suddenly even paler than before? And why didn't he seem surprised or worried about the attack?

He couldn't have possibly known about it or been involved. He would never let her be harmed. "So maybe these people who ambushed you—maybe they wanted to stop you from searching the airport."

"Agent Thomson does think they were from the cartel, but I don't think they would do something like that to halt the airport searches." Cora folded her arms in front of her. "They wouldn't be doing any major smuggling through commercial flights. It's too difficult to get the drugs through."

"Yeah. I suppose you might be right."

"I was hoping you could help us determine why the men stopped me. We're not sure what their goal was. Abduction, scaring me, or even trying to kill me. Do you know why they'd want to do something like that?"

He shrugged and looked away, his thumb hooking in the pocket of his jeans. "Why should I know?"

"I just thought you might because you said you worked with them before."

He slid the toe of his tennis shoe in a small circle on the floor, watching the movement. "That was a long time ago."

"Yes, but do you know what they would want now? Do you owe them money? Or might they want to hurt you by harming me, to punish you for leaving?"

His head lifted, irritation sparking in his hazel eyes. "I told you I want to leave all that behind me. I don't know what they want. I'm sorry you think this is all my fault, and I'm putting you in danger." He lifted a hand in the air in a frustrated gesture. "If you want me to leave, I'll leave."

How well she remembered that defiant tilt of his chin. But he wasn't a little boy she could discipline by taking away his video games. He was free to go if he didn't like how she responded.

"I don't think this is your fault, Bradley. I never meant to imply that. I don't blame you at all." She stepped closer to him and looked up to meet his gaze. "I love you, Bradley. I never want you to leave again. I hope you believe that."

His eyes locked with hers for a few moments. Then he turned his head away and picked up his duffle bag. "I'm beat. I'm going to go crash." He gave her a glance, the ire gone from his face. "If you don't mind."

"Of course not. Rest well."

He swung the strap over his shoulder and trudged up the staircase to the second floor.

"Hot cocoa?"

Cora started at the sound of Amalia's voice only a few feet away.

The three dogs surrounded her as she held out one of two mugs gripped in her hands.

The kind gesture calmed the tension curdling in Cora's stomach. "Yes, thank you." She took the offered mug, wrapping her hand around the warmth that permeated the porcelain.

"Do you believe him?" Amalia looked up at the stairs Bradley had just taken.

He had disappeared now, apparently having reached his room.

"You heard?"

Amalia grinned.

Silly question. Of course, she'd heard. Cora took in a deep breath, then let it out. "He's my brother. I believe him."

"Did you always believe what he said when he was on drugs?"

"No." Pain twisted Cora's heart with the memory of the first time she'd caught him in a lie. And the times he'd lied again, right to her face, rather than admit his addiction. "I learned not to."

"But you believe him now." A statement more than a question.

"He's not on drugs now, and he came home." Cora met Amalia's dark gaze. "I know he hated it before when I wouldn't trust him. I have to believe him now. I have to show I trust him, or I'll never win him back."

Cora only hoped that trust wouldn't risk Bradley's life or her own.

TWENTY-FOUR

The one thing Kent didn't like about being a DEA agent stared back at him from his desk. Paperwork. Most of it was digital and on his computer now, but the task wasn't any less tedious than before the paperless push.

Kent had put off the report-writing from last night's operation at Lofland High until this morning. He wasn't supposed to meet Cora at the airport for searching until the afternoon today, so he had time.

Cora. Just the thought of her was enough to tease his lips with a smile. What was it about her that drew him? She made him feel things he never had—the desire to keep her safe, to get to know her better, to find out what made her the way she was. She was sweet and gentle, positive and innocent, yet courageous with instincts and insights about people that were off the charts. The effect she had on everyone she talked to defied logic and science.

And so did her ability to make him lose focus, even when she wasn't with him.

He returned his attention to the computer screen in front of him, re-reading the details he'd recorded. Agent Gilson had followed Hayden's supplier to one of the cartel's suspected drug houses. They'd continue to observe Trent Netto for a few days and, if he consistently visited the drug house and appeared to leave with merchandise, they'd do a search warrant on the house, arrest Netto and the next-level supplier.

Kent's phone vibrated on his desk.

A call coming in. Ramos's number.

He snatched up the device. "You've got Vince."

Ramos responded with the same pre-planned response.

Kent barely waited for him to finish before moving to the new intel he hoped Ramos would have. "How'd it go?"

"I'm still in the running."

Perfect. Swiping the merchandise from the JK-16 gang must have gone well. And Ramos was about to get Kent one step closer to bringing down Guajardo.

"Just one more test."

Kent's gut tensed. This could be it.

"The candidates are each supposed to smuggle a shipment on a charter jet."

"Where are you getting the merchandise?"

"The local boys are helping line it up and supplying me."

Kent picked up a pen on his desk and tapped it against the faux wood surface. "Destination?"

"California. We're flying into San Fran, but we won't know where to take the drugs from there until we land."

"You're supposed to go somewhere other than San Francisco?"

"Think so. We're all going to meet at the same place where Guajardo will make his choice who gets the job."

Kent stopped tapping, his heartbeat seeming to halt at the same time. "He's going to be there?"

"Yeah. He's making the pick in person."

Kent's pulse restarted, taking off at an elated sprint. This was it. The chance he'd been waiting for and planning for so many years. "I'll come with you."

"Uh, I don't think so."

"Don't forget who's running this show, Ramos."

"I just mean the local guy is coming along, and I'm sure the pilot will be on the take. If they see DEA, they'll make a call and blow the whole thing. Maybe blow both of us away, too."

No way was Kent going to let Ramos fly off with a large drug shipment alone or leave him behind when Guajardo would be at the end of the journey. Ramos was Kent's ticket to bringing down the cartel. He wasn't getting out of this state without Kent attached. "Tell the local guy you're bringing one of your people you've worked with before. Vince Muñoz. That's our cover story for these calls anyway. Put me on the flight manifest with that name, and I'll leave my fed clothes at home."

"All right. I guess they'll buy that."

"Oh, and tell them you're bringing two more associates. Your muscle. Make up whatever names you want." Kent wouldn't tell Ramos the muscle would be the slim blonde he'd tried to kidnap and her narcotics K-9. Kent needed the dog to establish the necessary proof of narcotics on board.

Despite Ramos's concerns, it didn't matter if the perps on the plane made him or Cora. The pilot wouldn't want to risk associating with the passengers, so he wouldn't be the one to see them and squeal. And Kent intended to take command of the passengers, including Ramos's new cartel pal, as soon as he boarded the plane. When they landed in California, Ramos could still make a call to meet whoever he needed to alone.

Ramos grunted. "Fine. But let's not push it."

"Take it easy, Ramos. Stay cool, and they won't notice a thing."

"Easy for you to say."

Not at all. Ramos had no idea how much Kent had riding on this. They would finally pay for what they did to his family. And the cartel wouldn't be able to hurt anyone, weak or not, ever again.

"We searched the building but didn't find anything." Bris petted Toby, who stood in front of her where she sat on the sofa in the breakroom of P-K9 headquarters. "Turned out the threat was a hoax."

"Praise the Lord." Cora lowered the coffee mug she'd stopped midway from her mouth as Bris told the story of her bomb search at 5:00 a.m. that morning.

Bris smiled at Cora. "Amen."

"Oh, man, is this gonna turn into a church meeting?" Nevaeh's mirth-filled tone matched her exaggerated eye roll. "'Cause I think I forgot my Bible in the car."

"That's okay. I've got one on my phone I can share." Bris laughed and exchanged grins with Nevaeh.

Cora smiled at their teasing, but she silently sent up a prayer that Nevaeh really would want to read the Bible someday. Only God could heal her from whatever past nightmares haunted her so much that she needed the comfort of her psychiatric service dog, Cannenta. This must be a good day so far, as Nevaeh appeared ready for work with only Alvarez along, lying next to her feet on the floor.

Cora's gaze caught on Phoenix, sitting in her usual armchair with Dagian lying alertly on the floor at her side. Her face beneath her baseball cap was devoid of emotion, but Cora knew talking about God wasn't on their leader's meeting agenda.

Cora cleared her throat, crossing her legs in the armchair she sat in not far from Phoenix. "Bris, Wentworth Packaging called the office this morning after you were done and expressed their gratitude and how impressed they were with your work."

"That's what we like to hear, isn't it, Toby?" She leaned over his black head and rubbed his chest with her hand.

"They'd also like you to make a sweep again tomorrow, just in case the disgruntled employee manages to plant something before the police can find him."

Bris nodded. "Sounds good."

Cora shifted her gaze to Amalia, sitting on the new loveseat Phoenix had added to the breakroom to accommodate the growth in their team size. Raksa had found a place to rest on the floor a few feet away by Jana. "I want to make sure everyone on the team knows how incredible Amalia was when she came to my rescue yesterday with Agent Thomson. She was amazing."

"Ooh, *with* Agent Thomson?" Nevaeh cast Amalia her teasing grin.

Amalia shook her head, her wavy black hair brushing her cheeks as she laughed. "Believe me, girls, that dude didn't even notice I was there. He appears to prefer blondes." Amalia winked at Cora.

The room erupted with exclamations and laughter, even from Jazz, who sat on the other end of the sofa with Flash sitting next to her knees. At least she seemed to be feeling more comfortable with the team.

Despite being able to help that camaraderie along by being the subject of the joke, a hot flush rushed up Cora's neck on the way to her cheeks. "I'm sure you must have been imagining things, Amalia."

"Yeah, because she does that all the time." Nevaeh smirked, letting sarcasm deliver her accurate point. Amalia's observational skills were off the charts, perhaps surpassed only by Phoenix's.

"Well," Cora smiled at the PK-9 women, "I know you all aren't big on thank-yous, so I'll stop being mushy and only say one more thing. Agent Thomson was very impressed last night with how professionally our team handled Hayden's meeting."

"He should be." Phoenix's steady voice headed off the humor Cora saw twinkling in Amalia's eyes. "There were weak spots we'll review in our debrief and address at Saturday's training session. But we got the job done."

Her gaze moved across the group and halted on Cora. "You all know Cora is in danger. I've been in contact with my sources in the local drug scene, and pertinent intel is starting to surface."

Cora's stomach clenched. "About Bradley?"

"My sources confirmed Bradley worked for the cartel seven years ago and had for several years before that."

Cora's heart sank. She'd believed Bradley and Kent when

they'd said he had been involved with the cartel. But, some-how, hearing the confirmation from Phoenix threw the facts into the starkness of reality, and the truth hurt more.

"He wasn't just a low-level pusher. An older manager took a liking to Bradley and wanted to groom him to work at the management level. Bradley was given access to privileged infor-mation and worked with this manager to handle some of the cartel's major operations in the Twin Cities."

Cora's jaw slackened. That couldn't be true. Bradley had just been a boy. Her baby brother.

Phoenix held Cora's gaze firmly with her own, not letting her look away. "He did well, and they gave him solo responsi-bilities. Until he disappeared."

"Did the cartel know where he went when he left?" Amalia asked the question in her easy, casual tone.

Nothing like the strangling sensation that seemed to be gripping Cora's throat. Her Bradley, a cartel leader? Not in the top tiers, perhaps, but on his way to that. How could she have let that happen? How could she not have known? His addiction had seemed to be the only, awful battle she had to fight.

"...lost track of him when he went out of state." Phoenix's voice, strong and steady, drew Cora's attention back.

And awoke her mind to the new worries facing her now. "Do they know Bradley has returned?"

"Yes."

Alarm pinched Cora's ribs.

"But they haven't been able to find him since he arrived in the city. They learned you were his sister and broke into your home, looking for Bradley."

"So that was the cartel." Bris interjected the comment with concern bunching her brow.

"But what do they want with him?" Cora didn't want to know, but she had to. "Does he owe them money? Do they want revenge or to hurt him in some way?" She couldn't voice the worst of possibilities, that, perhaps, they wanted to kill him.

"According to my sources, they want him back."

"To work for them?" Nevaeh tilted her head, her curls dangling in that direction.

Phoenix gave a slight nod.

"With what he'd been doing, he'd have too much dirt on them to let him go." Amalia reached for her coffee mug on the end table next to the sofa. "He's a liability. So he's either in again or he's dead."

Cora flinched involuntarily.

"Sorry, Cora." Bris pressed her lips together to one side.

Cora mustered a smile. "It's okay. Like Phoenix always says," she glanced at her mentor, "better to know the danger so you can prepare to beat it."

"Exactly." Phoenix met her gaze. "The ambush yesterday— it was an attempted kidnapping."

"Oh." Cora's mouth felt pasty as she swallowed. "At least they weren't trying to kill me."

"Maybe not right away, but once they used you to get to your brother…" Nevaeh leaned forward, directing her gaze at Phoenix. "We gotta do something about this, Boss."

"Hey, I'm on it." Amalia shot Nevaeh a look, the exaggerated offense in her tone offset by her grin.

"Yeah, yeah." Nevaeh flashed a smile, but quickly let it drop as urgency filled her dark eyes. "I mean, we gotta go to the source. They can't mess with Cora."

"You're right. We're going to do better than protection." Phoenix watched Nevaeh. "My sources are working to find out who ordered the kidnapping." She swung her gaze over the rest of the team. "We will find the person giving these orders. Even if we have to go all the way to the top."

"To the kingpin?" Cora stared at Phoenix.

She met her gaze with the unshakable confidence that always gave Cora hope. "We're going to end this."

Cora knew Phoenix well enough to add in her mind the words Phoenix wasn't saying.

At any cost.

Cora only hoped that cost wasn't greater than should be paid for her safety. She was already responsible for damage to a loved one she could never undo. If one of these friends were put in danger for her sake, or if Bradley...

She couldn't finish the terrifying thought.

TWENTY-FIVE

Women's laughter echoed in the large room that housed the conveyor belts carrying baggage through to the claim on the other side of the outer wall.

Kent's chest pinched as he watched Cora on the opposite side of the elevated belt, smiling with bright humor at something Pérez had said. His plans to spend more time with Cora during today's search had evaporated when G. I. Jane had shown up with her.

Not that it was a bad idea to have Pérez be Cora's bodyguard until she was out of danger. But it definitely cramped his style. And meant he hadn't gotten to ask her about the flight tomorrow.

He dragged his gaze back to the computer screen at the workstation in front of him. He cycled through a few more passenger ID images, not seeing anyone he recognized as cartel or other known drug offenders.

He glanced at the time on the screen. *11:45 a.m.*

Almost time to leave.

He looked at Cora over the suitcases sliding past. "Let's knock off early. I need to talk to you about something."

"Sure." Her soft voice was barely audible above the noise, but her nod of affirmation was clear enough. She called to Jana, and the dog hopped down from the conveyer belt while Kent walked around it.

The two women and the dog met him at the door at the end of the room.

Cora's eyebrows were drawn downward in concern. "I meant to ask you earlier, but everything has been so chaotic lately. Do you know what happened to Venetia?"

"She's been transferred to the county jail for now until her court date."

"Poor Venetia. I should visit her when I'm there."

He blinked, glancing at Pérez, who stood just past Cora's shoulder with an amused smile on her face. "You're going to the jail?"

"I go twice a month for women's Bible study."

He stared at Cora. "At the jail."

"Yes. It's wonderful." A smile brightened her blue eyes. "Some ladies from my church and I lead a study for inmates who want to come."

Just like something his dad would have done. Cold seeped into Kent's veins, flowing the chill throughout his body. Didn't she know how vulnerable that made her? Caring for criminals and thinking they could change? Weakness like that could only lead to—

He clenched his jaw to keep the words from coming out. He needed her on his side right now. Might as well get it done and get out of here. If he didn't need her K-9 on this flight, he'd forget the whole thing. He didn't need to be around a woman who was practically asking to be a target. Anything could happen to her. Shifting gears, he cut to the point. "How would you like to help bring down the cartel?"

Cora's eyes widened as she glanced from him to Pérez, the two of them exchanging a look that hinted they knew something he didn't. Cora's gaze returned to his face, latching on with a glimmer of enthusiasm. "Of course. I would do anything to help with that."

"Awesome." He scanned the area. Only one employee was in the baggage room, standing where the woman they'd arrested had been last time. "Let's go outside, and I'll give you more details."

He opened the door and held it while Cora passed through.

"After you." Amalia gave him a grin and gestured that he should go ahead of her.

At least that allowed him to walk next to Cora as they went through the baggage claim and stepped outside.

The discomfort of the frigid air would help him keep this short. And hopefully not get distracted by the gorgeous blue eyes Cora trained on him as they stood on the sidewalk.

Pérez came up on his left, so he angled to face them both, though he kept his attention on Cora.

"You remember the older man who kidnapped you, Marco Ramos?"

"Of course." She crossed her arms over her purple puffer jacket, the lines on her forehead implying the memory was one she wouldn't soon forget.

"You know he's one of the regional managers for the Guajardo cartel?"

She nodded.

Kent checked the area around them. The nearest people were fifty feet away, waiting for transportation. "This has to stay absolutely, completely confidential."

"We're very good at keeping confidential information protected at Phoenix K-9. You can trust us." Cora's expression mirrored his seriousness.

He looked at Pérez.

For once, she didn't have a grin on her face. Instead, she gazed back at him with the sharp intensity he'd seen the day of the ambush on Cora.

"Ramos has become a confidential informant for us."

Cora's lips parted. "That's amazing. I hoped he could be reached somehow. He was kind to me when I needed it."

"Thanks to your persuasion."

Pink brushed her cheeks, more from embarrassment than the cold, he guessed. "I didn't persuade him of anything. I just spoke to him and tried to understand."

"Whatever you did, it worked."

Her eyebrows lifted.

"He flipped because of you. He told me you were the reason when he asked to talk to me about becoming a CI. Something you said seemed to bother him."

She slowly shook her head back and forth. "I can't believe it."

"You go, girl." Pérez nudged Cora's shoulder with a grin.

"That was the Lord's doing, not mine. But I'm so grateful he used me for something like that." Cora's gloved hand went to her neck. "Oh, I hope this changes his life and his daughter's." Were those tears collecting in her eyes?

Kent cleared his throat and moved on as quickly as he could. "He's told us the kingpin is having managers do tryouts to become the national leader. He's on the final test, which involves flying a drug shipment via private jet to San Francisco. From there, he's supposed to meet Guajardo in person for the final selection."

"Oh, my." The moisture in Cora's eyes dried as she watched him. "Do you think you'll be able to apprehend him?"

"That's the goal."

"But where do I come in?"

"I want you and Jana to come with me on the flight to San Fran. I need a narcotics K-9 so I can prove drugs are on board to take possession of the plane and the narcotics when we land or soon after. I'll need to have a chain of evidence, and you can help me get that."

She nodded. "Of course, we'll come along. When is the flight?"

"Tomorrow morning, eight o'clock. We'll board five minutes before. No sooner, or we could blow things."

Cora put her hand on Jana, who looked up at Kent as if she knew he was deciding her schedule for tomorrow. "We'll be there, Lord willing."

"Hate to be a wet blanket, Cora," Pérez watched Kent, though she spoke to her co-worker, "but I doubt Phoenix will approve of this."

Cora's mouth tugged into a frown. "You could be right." Her gaze flicked to Kent. "She's very protective of me."

"Glad to hear it." Someone needed to look out for her. She made herself such an easy target. But she was still the most amazing woman he'd—

"I think she'll go along with the plan." Cora halted his thoughts just in time. "She'll understand what a rare opportunity this is to potentially bring down the cartel. And she just said this morning that she wanted to end the threat against me. What better way to do that?"

A smile grew on Pérez's face. "If anybody can get Phoenix to say yes to something, it'd be you."

"You can tell her I won't let anything happen to you." Something powerful came over Kent as he looked down at Cora. A fiery heat that flowed outward from his torso into his whole being. "You'll be safe."

A beautiful smile curved Cora's closed lips as she met his gaze.

"Yes, she will be." Pérez's voice broke the connection between them. "Because I'm going, too."

Kent swung his gaze to her, easily catching the warning in Pérez's dark eyes. Meaning she went along, or Cora didn't. The ultimatum scratched on his nerves like nails on a chalkboard. Usually, he'd say, "No deal," and walk.

But he'd do anything to keep Cora safe. Pérez had proven she was handy in a fight. If things did blow up, Pérez would add another layer of protection for Cora. Looked like he'd be bringing some muscle along, after all.

He gave Pérez a quick nod. "Agreed."

A big smile instantly replaced the grim expression on her face. "You must like our girl a whole lot."

Cora's face flamed red. "I'd better get Jana into the car. We're supposed to do another search at Lofland High this afternoon." She didn't look at Kent as she walked away, Pérez falling in step beside her with a grin tossed over her shoulder at Kent.

They left before he got a chance to answer Pérez, to say the words that had almost found their way to his lips. *You have no idea.*

"You wanted to see me before I leave for the night?" Cora leaned through the doorway of Phoenix's office at PK-9 headquarters.

Phoenix sat behind the desk that was positioned parallel with the right wall of the room, ensuring she couldn't be surprised by anyone at the door or the two windows in the outer wall of the building.

"Come in." Phoenix had removed her cap, but a shadow fell across her face. The one lamp in the corner of the room seemed to be losing the battle against the darkness. Only Phoenix's computer screen offered any assistance by casting a pale, bluish light on the sleeves of the gray knitted sweater she wore.

Jana's tags jingled softly as she followed at Cora's side. Cora sat in the chair opposite Phoenix's desk, and Jana dropped to the floor beside her.

Poor girl was tired after her big day searching both the airport and high school. And the golden knew not to try to greet Dagian, though he sat up at the close end of Phoenix's desk and watched them. Even the friendliest of the Phoenix K-9s, like Toby and Jana, seemed to know they needed to give Dag respect and plenty of space.

"You know why I wanted to see you."

Cora met Phoenix's gaze, more inscrutable than usual thanks to the shadow that darkened her eyes. "I think I might." She moistened her lips. If Phoenix opposed her going, what would she do? She had to do this for Bradley, but could she make Phoenix see that? She swallowed. "Is it about the flight with Agent Thomson tomorrow?"

"I'd like you not to go."

Cora hid a wince. Phoenix didn't even use her usual wording, saying it would be better or safer if Cora didn't go. She made it personal. *She* would like Cora not to go. How could Cora refuse a personal request from Phoenix?

Cora scooted forward in her chair. "I know it seems like it could be dangerous, but Amalia will be with me the whole time. And Agent Thomson promised he will keep me safe, and he's proven he's very skilled and can be counted on."

Phoenix let a pause hang between them. She watched Cora. "You're doing this for Bradley."

"Yes." Cora nodded, grasping at the hope that Phoenix understood. "While the cartel still wants him back, he won't be free to live the better life I want for him." Or to follow God and live a Christian life but voicing that desire wouldn't help her case with Phoenix. "He'll always be looking over his shoulder and living in fear, and if they get to him..." She took in a bolstering breath. "If Jana and I help bring the cartel to justice, he'll be free."

"Are you sure he wants to be?"

Cora blinked. Phoenix didn't ask leading questions like that unless she felt she already knew the answer, and it was in her favor. Cora's mouth grew dry.

Phoenix pulled out the middle desk drawer, reaching inside it. "The day the cartel ambushed you, Jones followed Bradley and saw him meet with this man." She dropped a piece of paper—no, a photograph printout—onto her desk. She rotated the photo so it faced Cora.

Cora stood and leaned over the picture, illuminated by light from Phoenix's computer screen.

The man had dark hair and dark brown skin. About forty years of age. "Who is he?"

"We didn't know initially. But one of my sources ID'd him today. He's cartel."

Cora backed up, sinking into the chair behind her. "I don't believe it."

"Bradley is lying to you again."

Pain surged in Cora's head, an ache that reflected the one pressing on her heart. The look on Bradley's face when he'd told her he was clean had been so genuine, so happy and proud.

That couldn't have been a lie. And he was pleased the cartel had forgotten about him.

I told you I want to leave all that behind me. Had the emotion driving Bradley's statement last night been defensiveness?

Her own response to Amalia after Bradley had gone to bed echoed in her ears. *I have to show I trust him, or I'll never win him back.*

That was exactly what Cora had to do. "I think there has to be some explanation. Perhaps Bradley was trying to reason with the man to get the cartel to leave him alone. I know he was concerned for my safety because of them. He told me so." Hope filled Cora's limbs with the strength that had left them in response to Phoenix's information. "He was probably trying to keep me safe. Perhaps this man is a friend of his in the cartel, and Bradley wanted to ask him to leave me alone."

Another pause added to the silence of the room as Phoenix watched Cora.

Cora had grown comfortable with Phoenix's silences, and now that she had realized the likely reason for Bradley meeting a cartel man, she relaxed as she waited for Phoenix to speak. Usually, the longer the silence, the more profound what she said.

"Don't let your regrets for the past drive you to do something foolish that could destroy your future."

The caution hit Cora hard. Was that what she was doing?

"You believe what happened to Bradley was your fault. That doesn't mean you need to sacrifice your own safety for him now. Especially when he still doesn't want your help."

Cora opened her mouth to respond, then closed her lips as she thought twice. She would take the risk. "Wouldn't you do the same?" Hopefully, she hadn't overstepped by challenging Phoenix.

"Only if I knew the outcome would be worth the risk. Some people will never change."

"But I know God can change my brother. Bradley just needs to be safe and free from the cartel, and then I know I can help him find a better way." Another argument sprang to Cora's mind. "You said you wanted to end the threat against me from the cartel. What better way to do that than helping the DEA catch the kingpin?"

Phoenix looked at Cora for a few seconds while Cora's stomach twisted. She'd never challenged Phoenix this much. Phoenix wouldn't fire her for doing so, but would this damage the special, mentoring relationship Cora had with her boss?

Phoenix stood, her fingertips lingering on the edge of the desk. "You've made your decision. We'll do what we can to back up you and Amalia."

Cora rose, prompting Jana to get up, too. "Thank you, Phoenix. I can't tell you how much I appreciate your support."

Was that one of Phoenix's close-lipped smiles? In the soft, yellow glow from the lamplight that touched her face, it appeared to be so.

Cora left the office with a smile of her own. Phoenix was always encouraging Cora to be tougher and stronger. Perhaps she was finally making some progress that Phoenix approved of. But challenging her employer, even one as intimidating as Phoenix, was a far cry from boarding a plane with cartel members smuggling drugs. Would she have the courage tomorrow morning to resist her instincts that told her to run the other way?

Yes. For Bradley, his safety and future—perhaps his redemption—she would do anything. Even, if necessary, give up her own life.

TWENTY-SIX

"What did you find out about the charter company?" Kent looked up from his notes, glancing across the conference table at Agent Shiloh and Agent Gilson.

"Fleet Air." Gilson's straight brown hair swung forward past her face as she looked down at the notepad in front of her. "The company seems legit and clean. No known cartel associations, no record of smuggling."

Kent nodded. "And the passengers?"

"Here's the passenger manifest." Shiloh shoved a sheet of paper across the table toward Kent. "Safe to assume the other cartel players are using aliases since Ramos is."

Kent scanned the list of names. "Looks like two buddies with him." He leaned back in his chair. "Okay." His phone vibrated on the table. He glanced at the screen to make sure it wasn't Ramos calling.

St. Vincent Community Hospital.

Probably a spoofing scam call.

He darkened the screen. "So once our flight is in the air tomorrow morning, I need you to verify the San Fran agents are ready to meet us at the airport. But emphasize they need to be concealed and quiet. The cartel can't spot them."

"Got it." Gilson's pen moved quickly as she jotted down a note.

"Ramos will call the cartel once we've landed unless they meet him at the airport. But his instructions are to call when he lands, and he'll then receive info for meeting the kingpin. I'll let you—"

His phone vibrated again. Same hospital name. He reached to turn off the screen, but his gaze caught the location.

Tulsa, Oklahoma.

Vince.

He shoved back his chair, bringing the phone to his ear as he pushed through the door to leave the conference room. "Hello?" He paused in the hallway.

"Is this Kent Thomson?" A woman asked the question, knew his name. How did she have his name and this number? It couldn't—

"Are you the brother of Vince Thomson?"

Pain gripped Kent's chest. He braced his hand on the wall. "Yes."

"I'm sorry to inform you, but your brother is in a coma."

Buzzing pulsed in Kent's ears, blocking out what she said next. Vince, hurt? In a coma? Impossible.

He strained to listen to what the woman was saying. "He listed you as his emergency contact."

"Wh—" The word caught in his dry throat. He tried again. "What happened? An accident?"

"No, this is a result of his cancer."

Cancer? He couldn't have cancer. Vince was strong, young.

"I just saw him. He was fine."

"That could be. Most of the cancer's effects would have been internal up until now. His cancer has begun to progress more rapidly. The liver is starting to fail."

"What about treatment?" He reached for the hope like a drowning man reaching for a life preserver. "Chemo?"

"He declined treatment of any kind."

Kent's chest squeezed tighter, as if his ribs were collapsing inward and he had no room left for oxygen.

"Mr. Thomson?"

Must've been silent longer than he thought. "I'm here."

"Would you like to come and be with him?"

"I can't." The response came out fast, automatically. But it was true. He couldn't miss the cartel flight in the morning. This would lead him to the kingpin. He couldn't lose that chance.

"Some decisions will likely have to be made. Your brother may be dying."

Dying. The word pierced him like a knife.

Shadows passed before the eyes of his memory. His mother, the ghostly shape of her body under the white sheet as they wheeled her away on a gurney. The shiny lid of the closed wooden coffin that hid the lifeless form of his dad and the bullet holes Kent didn't want to see.

Vince had identified their dad at the morgue. He'd spared Kent from that. And from a lot of other things afterward. But he couldn't bring their dad back, couldn't keep their mom from doing what she did, couldn't make the cartel pay for what it had done to their family.

But Kent could do that. Now. And if he didn't take this chance, he might never have another one.

Vince wouldn't want Kent there anyway. If he had, he would've told Kent about his cancer when he'd come to the Twin Cities.

The random breakfast meeting made sense now. Vince's way of saying goodbye.

If that's how Vince wanted things, Kent would respect his brother's wishes. Vince wouldn't want Kent to see him weak and frail. Losing a fight. He'd want to be strong to the end and know Kent would stay strong, too.

The best thing Kent could do now was take down the cartel. For Vince and their parents.

"He'll be okay. My brother's strong. He doesn't need me."

———

"I'm so glad you could join me for dinner tonight." Cora smiled across the table at Bradley.

He pushed more potatoes into his mouth and mumbled, "Yeah."

She glanced at Jana who held her down-stay outside the doorway of the small dining room. The golden panted as she watched Cora, a soft look of something Cora could imagine was pity in her brown eyes. Even Jana knew this dinner wasn't going as Cora had hoped.

She'd spread a tablecloth, used their mom's china dishes, and made the steak and potatoes that had been Bradley's favorite comfort food after their mother passed away.

But all the accoutrements, even in the cozy dining room with dark green walls and flowery wallpaper trim, weren't helping Cora and Bradley connect. Not the way they used to, before the drugs.

"I'll be flying somewhere for work tomorrow."

"Oh." Bradley reached for his glass of soda.

"I don't think I'll be gone for more than a day."

He cut off a piece of steak and forked it into his mouth.

"The pantry is stocked and there are veggies and fruit in the refrigerator. Do you think you'll need anything else while I'm gone?"

He finally looked at her, the meat in his mouth protruding his cheek. "I've been on my own for seven years. I think I can manage one day."

A flush traveled to Cora's face. "Of course. I didn't mean to..." Be mothering. As he'd accused her so many times before he'd left home. But how could she show him she cared without wanting to provide for his needs and make sure he was happy?

How could she do what her mother had asked of her when that only seemed to make Bradley push her away or run? Perhaps his defensiveness stemmed from hiding something, like before. Could his meeting with the man from the cartel not have been as innocent as Cora had hoped?

She couldn't ask him directly. He would think she didn't trust him. She picked up her fork, pretending worry hadn't stolen her appetite. "How is the job search coming?"

"Fine." He didn't miss a beat in answering, but he didn't look her in the eye.

"Have you had any offers?"

"Only if you count Zoom-By Burgers."

"There's nothing wrong with working in food service."

His mouth angled in a sneer. "Tell that to Dad."

Cora took a moment to choose her words carefully before she spoke again. "Dad had to start somewhere, too. He wasn't always where he is today."

"And where is he today?" Bradley set down his utensils and leaned back in his chair, crossing his arms over his chest as he switched the meaning of her words. "Does anyone know? Does he ever tell you?"

Cora reached for her glass of water, her fingers settling around it, craving the familiarity of the crystal stemware that was her mother's favorite. Cora rarely used the glasses, saving them for special occasions as her mother had done. "No. He doesn't tell me."

"Then maybe you should work on him more. Get him to go to church and all that." Bradley's jaw shifted, tensing as he looked away at the wall.

"I wish I could. I pray for him every day."

Bradley let out a snort. "Great." He dropped his ivory cloth napkin next to his plate. "I've had enough for tonight. I'm going to bed."

"Bradley, wait."

He paused, midway to standing.

"I wanted to talk to you about something."

He lowered back into the chair but didn't look at her. "Fine."

Her pulse fluttered as she doubted what she was about to ask, but she had to know. "Did you see anyone from the cartel today?"

His gaze shot to her face. "What?"

"I mean, did anyone follow you or try to hurt you?"

"Oh." His shoulders lowered as he shook his head. "No."

The worry swirled in her stomach again. Had he thought she'd been asking him about meeting with the cartel man? Had he something to hide, as Phoenix suspected?

Bradley's eyes narrowed. "They didn't bother you, did they?"

"No."

"Good." He looked down at his plate, staring at it blankly as if his thoughts were far away.

A smile tugged her lips. He was concerned. He did still care about her.

He abruptly stood, his chair scraping across the wooden floor. "I've got to go." He stepped around the chair and turned to leave by the doorway at his end of the room.

Should she try to stop him? To ask if he wasn't telling her something?

He paused before the question reached her lips. "If I ever disappear again, don't worry about it." He angled partway toward her, his body seemingly undecided between the two directions. "It isn't you." He strode quickly from the room, as if afraid she'd argue with him.

She was too busy trying to tamp down the worry his declaration had flamed into something closer to panic. What did he mean? She could run after him and try to make him explain, but she might frighten him away again. Was he planning to leave? Or perhaps he was worried about the cartel getting to him and...Just how far would they go if he refused to work for them?

Oh, Father. Please, keep him safe while I'm away tomorrow.

Her best hope was that Kent's mission to dismantle the cartel worked. Then Bradley would be free, and they could start to build a better life together. One of healing and hope.

All she needed to do first was take a flight with drug dealers on a smuggling operation. Her stomach tensed at the prospect, nervousness making her queasy. But Amalia and Kent would be there. And God would go with her.

Did Bradley have any idea the strength and peace that gave

a person? To have a loving Father Who would always be there and was always in control?

She'd do whatever it took to help Kent successfully complete this operation and bring the cartel to justice so Bradley would have a chance to find out.

TWENTY-SEVEN

The security at the fixed-base operator was basically non-existent. Made the process of flying easy for Kent today, but it was still a problem that needed to be corrected if they were ever going to win the war on drugs in the U. S.

Without even so much as a metal detector to pass through —for himself or his duffle bag—no one noticed he was carrying his Glock in an inside-the-waistband holster or that he had more gear in his bag that wouldn't normally get past TSA. With this setup, he could probably have carried in a visible holster under his wool peacoat instead of the IWB.

He waited with Ramos while Cora checked in at the FBO desk right after him. "So, how often have you taken advantage of the private charter method?" He shot Ramos a glance out the corner of his eye.

"I plead the fifth."

A wry smile lifted Kent's mouth. "Little late for that."

Ramos shrugged, watching Cora at the desk. "She's something special, isn't she?"

Kent's gaze rebounded back to her, as if that's where it had wanted to be all along. She looked beautiful with her hair down, blond tendrils brushing against the light blue scarf that hugged her neck. Her purple puffer jacket flattered her slim figure, stopping at mid-thigh on top of her dark cotton pants that tapered to tuck into blue boots that matched her scarf.

"She should hate me." Ramos's scratchy voice halted Kent's pleasant distraction. "Or at least be scared of me." Ramos stared at her, his hands in the pockets of his leather jacket. "She treats me like an old friend."

Kent had shared Ramos's surprise at the greeting Cora had given him when they met a few minutes ago.

Cora had hugged the man. The drug distributor who had kidnapped her and was going to let her be killed. It didn't make sense.

Ramos sniffed and swiped at his nose.

Was he—

"How can she do that?"

Cora turned toward them and smiled as she started walking their way, Jana at her side as Cora pulled a small suitcase on wheels behind her, a large purse dangling from her shoulder.

"I don't know." But he did know Ramos was right. Cora was special. The way his heart thumped as she drew closer left no doubt about that.

"Well," Cora let out a breath that seemed energized with excitement or nerves, "I think Jana and I are ready."

Kent scanned the area for Pérez. She'd been there just a minute ago. "Where's Pérez?"

"She wouldn't mind if you called her Amalia, you know."

"That's nice, but where is she?"

"She said she forgot something in the car, but that we should go ahead and board."

Suspicion itched the back of Kent's neck. "Does she forget things a lot?"

"She never forgets anything."

Kent's gaze returned to Cora's face, landing on a calm smile that clashed with the warning bells chiming in his head.

"I trust Amalia." Cora seemed to read his thoughts. "Whatever she's doing, it's necessary and for the best."

Terrific. This was why he didn't work with partners or teams. Always someone messing things up or jeopardizing the plan by going rogue. Kent was the only one allowed to make changes on this job. He probably should've just come alone. Just him and Ramos. He worked best alone.

"Who is she, anyway?" Ramos looked from Cora to Kent.

"You don't need to know." Kent stepped between him and Cora and directed the cartel manager toward the exit. "We'd better get going." He glanced back at Cora. "You wait here as planned until I text you. Maybe Pérez will show up again by then."

"Don't worry, she won't hold us up." Cora's reassurance wouldn't have meant a thing, but the way she looked up at him with her beautiful, encouraging smile—that almost made him forget he was getting on a jet with the cartel to smuggle drugs. "Your plan is going to work. I know it."

The adrenaline that always kicked in at the start of a raid or big arrest—any dangerous or crucial moment in a case—wasn't half the buzz of energy and confidence that flowed through him now. He could get used to this. Having her with him. Maybe working alone wasn't always the best.

But now wasn't the time or place to dwell on that thought. "I'll let you know when it's safe to board."

"Okay. Be careful."

Kent nodded and spun away, joining Ramos at the door to the hanger and forcing his mind away from the concern in Cora's eyes and her pretty smile. He had work to do. He'd have to apprehend the two cartel men on the jet and secure them without much fuss or noise. Couldn't appear unusual to anyone from the cartel who might be watching from outside to make sure the flight departed without interference.

Kent and Ramos walked through the large hanger as Kent scanned for any threats and tried to spot the jet waiting for them.

The hanger's large, hydraulic door was open, letting cold air and sunlight flow inside.

As they passed two parked jets, Kent spotted a third with a flight attendant standing at the base of the stairs that led up to the cabin entrance. Ramos had said his cartel contact set up the flight so no attendant would travel with them. The pilot was the only non-cartel person on the jet, and he'd been bought off.

Kent ran through the likely scenario and possible variations he'd be ready for as soon as they entered the aircraft.

Ramos was armed, as his cronies would expect to see, but Kent had made sure before they entered the FBO that Ramos removed the ammo. The cartel manager had proven he was serious about flipping on the cartel and holding up his end of the bargain with the risks he'd taken so far. But Kent wasn't about to chance Ramos turning on him once he was on a jet with drugs and cartel backup.

The other two cartel men would likely be in the first seats closest to the cabin door, thinking they could exit the jet more quickly at their arrival in San Francisco. According to the photos Kent had found of the interior of this aircraft, both sides of the aisle featured pairs of seats that faced each other in the front portion of the plane, right behind the cockpit separated by a door.

The cartel perps could be in either of those two groupings of seats. Or, they could have chosen to sit on each side of the aisle, both taking chairs that faced the cabin door so they could see everyone who entered the jet. Depended on how savvy or paranoid these guys were. And how much they trusted Ramos.

"Welcome, gentleman." The brunette attendant smiled broadly as they reached the stairs. "Your flight to San Francisco is all ready for you to board. Have a wonderful flight."

"Thanks." Ramos paused and looked back at Kent.

He nodded.

Ramos took the short staircase slowly, hopefully out of caution rather than nerves. If the CI looked anything but relaxed when he boarded, the cartel guys could be suspicious of Kent before he got close enough.

"Be cool." Kent delivered the instruction in a low, quiet tone before they entered the plane.

If Ramos could keep it together, handling the two men would be a cinch. Kent wouldn't need the backup agents Velasquez had tried to insist he take along. More agents could've looked suspicious to the cartel. And if Kent reached the point where he needed help with an operation this easy, he should retire.

The adrenaline that would help Kent's reaction time funneled through his veins as he stepped into the jet behind Ramos.

His gaze jumped ahead of Ramos's casual pace, assessing the surroundings. The layout was exactly as pictured.

The cartel cronies had picked the two seats on Kent's left. A wooden table stood between them.

One guy faced away, the top of his light brown hair visible above the headrest, and the other faced the cockpit. Staring at Kent.

Kent's muscles tightened, but he kept his facial features relaxed. Steady. But as unfriendly as the black-haired man looking at him.

Ramos walked past the guy in the first chair and stopped even with the second man, just as Kent had instructed him. "This is Muñoz."

Kent kept his posture casual as he paused by Ramos, positioning himself in the aisle, centered between the two seats.

The first guy moved his disinterested gaze to the window next to him. But suspicion still colored the eyes of the other perp.

No time to waste then.

Kent whipped out his weapon from his holster. "DEA. I'm arresting you both."

"What?" The dark-haired perp reached toward his jacket.

"Don't." Kent aimed his Glock at the guy, shot a glance at his buddy who stared at Kent, face paled to match the snow outside as he pressed against the wall of the jet like it was holding him up.

The troublemaker lowered his hand slowly.

Kent checked on Ramos. He met Kent's gaze, no fear or nerves showing. Or signs of second thoughts.

"Okay," Kent gave the troublemaker a firm stare, "you're

going to take out your gun and set it on the table in front of you, grip first, and *slowly*."

The guy jerked his hand to his jacket.

"Hey." Kent shot the sharp warning, his weapon aimed and ready. "Slowly."

"You're going to pay for this, Ramos." He sent the manager a glare meant to kill as he more cautiously reached inside his jacket. "Guajardo will kill you."

"We can do without the chatter." Kent watched closely as the man lowered his 9mm to the table.

"Doesn't bother me." The same calm expression rested on Ramos's features. "It's his life at stake now." Ramos had to have guts to make it as far as he had in the cartel. And that was serving Kent's purpose well now.

"Go ahead and pick up his weapon." So long as Kent had his own Glock already in hand, letting Ramos take the loaded weapon wasn't much of a risk, and it would eliminate the need for Kent to risk getting too close to the perp.

As Ramos followed the instruction, Kent looked at the quiet guy. Skinny, about twenty-four. Sweat glistened on his white forehead. "Now you. Take out your gun and set it on the table."

"I don't have one."

"And I'm the President. Put it on the table."

"No, seriously." Sweat ran down the side of his face as he lifted his hands, palms out. "I'm not carrying."

That'd be a first for a cartel dealer. Kent glanced at Ramos. "Which one organized this shipment?"

"He did." Ramos nodded toward the nervous guy.

"Stand up."

Kent pulled out one of the two pairs of cuffs he'd brought along as the skinny guy got to his feet. He stood taller than Kent had predicted with such a slim frame. "Hands together in front."

Kent put the cuffs on the man's wrists, then had him stand to the side while he did the same with the other perp. Once he'd frisked them both and secured them on the sofa that ran along one wall of the jet, he texted Cora to board.

Step one, accomplished. Everything was going perfectly. He could be arresting the kingpin this time tomorrow or the next day. Or maybe even today. That long-awaited moment couldn't come soon enough.

Nerves swirled in Cora's stomach as she smiled at the attendant who welcomed her at the base of the stairs that would take her into the private plane. She shouldn't be nervous, but Ramos wouldn't be the only cartel member on this flight. She'd never been on a jet with criminals before. At least, not knowingly.

But Kent could handle the others, especially with Amalia along.

Where was she? Cora looked back at the FBO entrance to the hanger. She breathed a little better at the sight of Amalia and Raksa heading her direction.

"Waiting for someone?"

Cora turned back to the attendant. "A friend. She's coming now. I can go ahead and board, though." Kent might be wondering what was taking her so long.

"Go ahead on up." The lovely woman beamed another professional smile and gestured toward the stairs.

Cora had forgotten how simple it was to fly out of an FBO. She'd only flown on her father's private jet once, and she'd been young, possibly six or seven years old. But she still remembered it well—the plush seats and the television where she had watched cartoons. Mostly, she remembered it being the only time the whole family had been allowed to accompany her dad on a work trip.

"Okay, Jana. Climb." The stairs were too narrow for Cora to walk beside the golden, so she followed Jana up and into the plane. She gently swung the leash to the right so Jana would know to turn that way into the aisle that was slightly wider than on a commercial aircraft.

Cora's gaze skipped past the empty seats at the front of the jet to see Ramos's bulky figure standing at the back of the plane.

Where was—

There. Kent stood just past Ramos, looking at two men who sat on a sofa along the wall of the plane. Her pulse resumed a normal pace as she and Jana made their way to Kent.

The two men must be from the cartel.

Kent had apparently disarmed them without difficulty. It looked like they were zip-tied to each other in the middle and attached to seatbelt buckles on the sofa with cuffs on their outer wrists. At least, that's what she assumed from the closest man being cuffed that way.

Her gaze drifted up to see their faces as she reached them.

She stopped.

Bradley?

TWENTY-EIGHT

It couldn't be Bradley.

Confusion and trepidation tumbled through Cora's body like the freezing, crushing snow of an avalanche.

Her brother's face turned toward her, hazel eyes locked in a widened, horrified state.

But it couldn't be him. He had said he wasn't working for the cartel. She'd believed him.

"Bradley." The word fell from her lips weighted with sorrow, hurt, and dismay. Tears welled in her eyes, blurring her vision.

"You shouldn't be here." His voice was tight, higher pitched than normal. "It's too dangerous." He glanced at someone. "Get her off the plane."

"This is your brother?" Kent's deep voice called to her as if drawing her out of a nightmare.

"Yes." She could only whisper the response as the tears splashed onto her cheeks.

"Cora." Small, but strong, hands gripped her shoulders from behind.

Amalia.

"Let's sit down. We have to get going."

Strength Cora didn't know she had made her resist Amalia's gentle tug. "I want to sit with my brother." She searched for Kent's face through the blur of her moistened vision.

"I'd rather you stay at the front with Amalia." The flickering intensity in Kent's green eyes conveyed his meaning. He was protecting her.

The evidence that he cared so much wrapped around her like a warming, sheltering blanket. "You'll be here, right?"

He held her gaze.

"Then I'll be safe. I need to be with my brother."

He sighed. "All right. You can sit here." He dipped his head to the side to indicate the seat that angled toward Bradley from across the aisle. "For now."

The PA system crackled, and the pilot began to speak, giving flight instructions or information about taking off.

Cora couldn't pay attention as she guided Jana to lie down next to the chair in the aisle and lowered herself into the plush leather, positioning her carry-on suitcase between the seat and the wall. She dropped her purse onto the suitcase and buckled the seatbelt across her waist, her fingers trembling.

Then she braved a look across the short distance at Bradley.

His gaze was pinned to the floor.

It was just as well. Cora didn't know what to say. *Father, how do I reach him? Help me to respond as You would.*

The jet began to move. Cora looked out the window to her right. The hanger wall disappeared, and the sky, more white today than blue, opened up before them as they taxied to the runway.

She felt the warmth of Kent's gaze from the seat facing hers. Turning her head, she didn't know what to expect to see on his face. She had gotten the impression he felt emotions and caring too much were a weakness. She still had tears on her cheeks.

Furrows bunched with vertical lines between his eyebrows as he looked at her, his eyes darkened with compassion, not judgment. Then she noticed he was holding out his hand.

A plastic package of tissues was clutched in his fingers.

Where had he gotten that? It looked like hers, that she'd tucked in the outer pouch of her carry-on. That's probably where he had found the tissues when she was watching Bradley, but she didn't care. The sweet, gallant gesture squeezed her hurting heart and prompted more tears to fall as she reached for the package.

"Thank you." She managed to push out the words as she worked hard to bite back the sob that fought to escape. He was being so kind, but if she didn't pull herself together, he was going to regret bringing her along.

She opened the package and used tissues to wipe her face and blow her nose as decorously as her mother had taught her. Once she had collected her emotions, she became aware of the stares of three men on her—Kent, Bradley, and the man beside him. "I'm sorry." She looked only at Kent, for the moment.

The same expression of concern tightened his features. "You don't have to be."

How had she ever thought this man was harsh and almost unkind? He was sweet, thoughtful, and gentle. And he'd also had to handcuff her brother as a cartel dealer. What must he think of her now, with a criminal brother whom she had defended?

She turned to face Bradley.

He jerked his head away, as if pretending he hadn't been watching her.

"Bradley, I'm not going anywhere." She listened to her own tone to be sure it didn't carry any hint of judgment. "We're going to be on this flight for hours. I want to understand why." She leaned forward and put her hand on his knee. "Why are you here with the cartel? Why did you go back to them?"

Bradley finally looked at her. But his eyes weren't filled with the remorse she'd hoped to see. He glared with anger darkening his hazel irises. "You want to know why? Because of you. I had to do this because of you." His answer couldn't have hurt more if he'd attached it to the end of an arrow and shot it into her soul.

Because of her.

That's how all of this had started, how he'd gotten hooked on drugs in the first place and become entangled with the cartel.

Oh, Mom. I'm so sorry.

Kent's voice rumbled something, an admonishment to Bradley, perhaps. But Cora couldn't hear it clearly as she sank into herself, wrapping her arms around her torso and letting the tears fall again. She pressed her cheek against the cool leather of the chair and closed her eyes as the jet slanted back and left the earth.

When she opened her eyes, she felt the pull of sleep not wanting to release its grip. She hadn't meant to fall asleep. She blinked, clearing her pasty vision and awakening her consciousness.

Kent. Seeing his chiseled features, his presence in the chair opposite hers, was like a balm to her raw nerves.

His mouth curved in a close-lipped smile, warmth softening his eyes as he met her gaze.

"How long have I been sleeping?"

"Just under an hour."

"I'm sorry."

"You say that a lot, don't you?"

Did she?

"Hey." Amalia's voice brought Cora's attention to her left, but her gaze paused on Bradley before reaching her friend.

His face was pale as he avoided eye contact.

"You okay?" Amalia stood in the aisle, leaning her arm on Cora's seatback as she handed her a bottled water.

Cora smiled up at her. "Oh, thank you. That's so kind." Amalia's role on the PK-9 team wasn't offering emotional support, perhaps since she excelled more than most in physical protection. That made her thoughtful gesture all the sweeter. "I'm doing better, thanks." She lifted the bottle in her hand. "Have the men been offered any water or food?"

Amalia grinned. "Still Cora." She tossed Kent a look as if they shared some secret about Cora's character. "Yeah. Agent Thomson's treating them very humanely."

The secret was probably that she was too soft, too trusting. She wasn't naïve. She'd known Bradley could have been deceiving her again. But she had chosen to believe and hope for something better until proven otherwise. She'd wanted him to see she trusted him and loved him, even after all he'd done.

But perhaps Amalia and Kent were right. Being so positive and open—feeling so much—led to the pain that burned like a searing gash inside her right now.

Her brother was going to go to prison because of her mistakes.

A wet touch on her hand drew her gaze down to Jana, still lying by Cora's chair. Jana licked Cora's hand, her brown eyes signaling she knew her partner needed comfort.

Cora stroked the golden's soft head, the motion calming and familiar.

A crackle from the PA system made her jump.

"This is your pilot speaking. We're experiencing an engine malfunction and are losing altitude."

Cora's breath stopped. Had she heard him correctly?

"We're going to have to make an emergency landing."

The jet tilted downward.

TWENTY-NINE

"Cora!" Bradley's anguished call stung Kent's ears as he got to his feet. The plane leaned forward, a slope under Kent's shoes.

The descent was happening too fast for him to get to the pilot and see what was going wrong. But he'd said over the PA system he was landing in a clearing used for air traffic in the Black Hills. If the pilot was skilled, they'd all be fine.

"It's all right, Bradley. Keep calm." Cora was the picture of peace as she leaned across the aisle and put her hand on her brother's knee. "Remember what Mom always told you when you were afraid at night, and you couldn't go to sleep?"

Bradley's shifting attention seemed to latch onto Cora's face. "Jesus loves me."

Kent knelt and reached across Bradley's body to unlock the cuffs from his right wrist and the seatbelt tongue he'd looped the cuffs through.

"That's right. And then she'd tell you the stories of how strong Jesus is. How He commanded the wind and the sea to 'Be still' in the midst of a storm, and made blind men see, and how he walked on water."

Kent brought the freed tongue together with the buckle across Bradley's waist.

The guy nodded, panic still owning his features. "I remember."

"Will you shut up?" The other cartel perp growled next to Bradley. "I need a seatbelt on, too." He glared at Kent.

Kent stood and glared back. "Then I suggest you shut up and behave or I won't put one on you."

"Bradley," Cora continued, undaunted, "Jesus can hold this plane safely as it lands, too. But if He chooses not to, I need to know I'll see you again."

"What do you mean?" Bradley's voice squeaked higher as Kent went to the far end of the sofa to uncuff the other guy and buckle the seatbelt across his waist.

"I mean, you need to be saved by Jesus so you can spend eternity with Him. So I can see you in heaven after this life."

"I don't want to die!" Panic squeezed Bradley's voice as he grabbed his sister's hand.

"Bradley, listen to me." Cora held her brother's hand in both of hers. "If you're sorry for your sins and believe that Jesus died to pay the penalty you deserve, then you'll never die. You'll live forever beyond this life."

The floor angled more steeply under Kent's feet as a rumbling started, like air scraping along the bottom of the jet. A jerk—a pocket of air punching the frame—nearly bounced Kent sideways.

He gripped the high back of the seat he had vacated. "Cora, we need to get Jana secured in case we're in for a rough landing."

"Oh!" Cora's gaze flitted to the golden retriever who had stood up and was balancing on all fours, cheerfully wagging her tail. "Thank you. Let's put her in my seat."

Kent hefted the dog without waiting for Cora to tell her to jump. No time. He adjusted the seatbelt until the strap was long enough to reach the handle on the back of Jana's harness as she sat on the chair. He looped the belt through and buckled it.

"Now you." He looked at Cora. "Take my seat."

"No, you need it."

He shook his head. "I don't. I'll go to the front." Cora

should be safer at the back of the plane if the landing ended badly.

"Is Amalia—"

"She's fine." He glanced to the front of the plane where Pérez had already secured her German shepherd the same way they'd buckled Jana.

"Cora, just sit down and buckle up." Amalia shouted the order in a commanding tone, but the flash of her grin was easy to see.

A light smile curved Cora's mouth as she did what Amalia said, her seatbelt clicking around her waist.

Kent made his way toward the front of the jet, walking downhill.

The floor started to level under his feet.

Another air pocket thudded against the plane, jerking it sideways.

Kent grabbed the edge of the closest chair for balance.

Ramos, buckled into the seat, turned his head next to Kent's hand. He held a magazine, his features relaxed. After the stuff the cartel manager had seen during his career, this probably seemed like a walk in the park.

Kent gave him a nod and went to the seat that faced Ramos's. It provided a view of the back of the plane, of Cora and the men on the sofa.

The plane tilted to the side as it dipped into a turn. They were still descending, but the pilot seemed to have better control than before. Looked like he was setting up a landing approach.

Cora's soft voice carried to Kent in hushed snippets as she talked to Bradley again, trying to calm his panic and probably saying more about the Jesus stuff Cora liked to go on about. Bradley was obviously not very tough. He'd probably grab on to the idea of a God Who could save him just so he didn't have to face his grim reality. If he survived the landing he was so worried about, he was destined for prison. A guy like him wouldn't last long in there either.

The jet shook as it tipped farther downward. Kent looked

out the window as they rapidly descended. Gray, thick clouds blocked his view.

He pressed closer to the glass as the plane rattled. The clouds broke. Snow-covered mountains stood below, coming closer.

The landing gear scraped and vibrated the jet's frame as it lowered.

He clutched the armrests at his sides.

Mountains, trees, forest engulfed the view as the plane reached the ground. Touched down.

A screech.

The jet careened to the side. Gravity yanked Kent's body, tried to rip him from the seat as the plane slid, scraped. Out of control.

This wasn't a landing. It was a crash.

One thought gripped his mind. *Cora.*

THIRTY

Cora opened her eyes and sucked in a trembling breath. "Thank you, Jesus. Thank you." All she'd been able to do in the terror of the crash was say her Savior's name, over and over again. She'd closed her eyes at the end, as the force of the crash rattled and jerked her body so hard she'd thought her bones would crack.

But God preserved her life.

She was still in the cabin of the plane, gripping the armrests of her chair so hard her fingers seemed locked in place. She took in another breath. A shiver quaked through her body.

A whine.

The sound shook her mind free of the shock slowing it down.

Jana.

Cora looked to her left at the seat that held her golden retriever. Hadn't the seats been straight across from each other before? The force of the crash must have slid or angled them somehow.

Jana panted heavily, stress widening her eyes.

"It's okay, girl. We're okay." Cora unclipped her seatbelt and pushed herself out of the chair. Her muscles protested, bruises she hadn't known she had sending jolts of pain through her body. She ignored the soreness and stroked Jana's fur, running her hands over the golden's legs and body to feel for injuries. Thank the Lord, she seemed unharmed.

Bradley. She swung to her right.

He still sat on the sofa, but his left arm, the one tied to the other man, bent in an awkward position. Was it broken?

And his head. His head slumped onto his shoulder. Was he—

Her heart jumped into her throat as she leaned toward him and touched his shoulder.

"Bradley?" She pressed her fingers to his neck, searching for his pulse. The first-aid medical training she'd received for search and rescue certification had equipped her for the basics. She never thought she'd be using that training to tell if her brother was alive.

A slight beat thumped under her fingers. Then more. A steady pulse.

Thank you, Father.

She felt her brother's head. No blood, but there seemed to be a bump starting to swell at the back of his skull.

"Cora?" The deep voice, the wonderous sound of a friend. Of rescue.

Kent.

She straightened and spun toward him in one swift motion. Too swift. Dizziness blurred her vision, and she reached for him, falling against his chest as his arms came around her. She stayed there a moment, resting her head on his shoulder in an embrace the surge of joy within wanted her to share with him anyway.

Kent was alive, standing, and strong enough to hold her safely in his arms. Why that filled her to the brim with relief and happiness, she didn't have the energy to determine right now. She just silently thanked the Lord for saving Kent and mustered her strength to pull back and stand on her own two feet.

She looked up at his face.

Small cuts spattered his jawline, left cheek, and the left portion of his forehead.

She reached toward the largest cut that trickled some blood, but stopped short, her fingertip brushing the warm skin beneath. "Are you all right?"

"Are you?" He captured her hand in his, engulfing her cold fingers with soft heat. His gaze scanned her face, his green eyes filled with emotion so raw and deep, she couldn't look away. Even though it scared her.

"Yes."

"You're sure?" His free hand reached toward her face, his knuckles brushing her cheek as he gently pushed her hair back, smoothing it behind her ear. "You're not hurt anywhere?"

She swallowed, trying to ignore the way his touch sent more shivers down to her toes. "Just some bruises."

"And a cut." His fingers touched her cheek as gently as a feather. "Here."

"Oh." She hadn't noticed pain from that area. "Is it bad?"

"No. Doesn't look deep." He continued to search her face as if he didn't quite believe she was alright. "Okay. I have to check the others."

"Yes, Bradley is hurt." She pulled away, turning back to her brother. "And what about Amalia and Raksa?" She peered toward the front of the plane. And then she saw what her tunnel vision of recovering panic had blinded her to before.

Branches punched through the windows all along the right side of the plane. The whole aircraft listed to the right, pitching the interior at an angle.

Her gaze followed the destruction of the windows back toward the rear of the plane, where she now stood. Dismay squeezed her chest. Windows weren't the only damage. The wall of the jet itself crunched inward just before the sofa where Bradley sat. No wonder Jana's seat had been moved. The front corner of the sofa had jammed into it.

Thank you, Father, for keeping Jana safe somehow.

Cora was standing on broken glass in what used to be the aisle. She hadn't noticed there was now only room for the width of her legs and Bradley's, just barely, between the sofa and her own seat.

At the other end of the sofa—

She gasped, her hands jerking to cover her mouth.

The wall behind the man next to Bradley was crumpled like tin foil, crushing him into the wall in front of him where the bathroom was.

She looked away from the grisly sight.

"How about you go up front with Amalia while I check these guys out?" Kent's gentle voice matched the touch of his hand on her upper arm.

She nodded. "I'll come right back for Bradley. I'll leave Jana clipped in until I get her booties on. The glass isn't safe."

"Sure." Kent stepped back so Cora could pass.

She missed the support of his hand on her arm as soon as he let go.

But Amalia's grin greeted her a few paces away. "What a ride, huh?"

Cora scanned her friend as Raksa walked up to her wearing booties on his paws and swishing his bushy tail. "You two look...wonderful." Like a bit of home. Cora leaned over Raksa and stroked his head as she pressed her face into his fur. It was really true. Nothing rattled Amalia. Or Raksa, apparently. If Phoenix couldn't be here, Amalia was the next best thing.

"I was afraid for a second there I might have to tell Phoenix something happened to you. Pretty sure she'd kill me."

Cora straightened and smiled. "I'm glad you're okay, too."

A groan drew her gaze to the seat a few feet past Amalia on the right.

"Is that Marco? Is he all right?" Glass crunched beneath Cora's feet as she went to the front of the chair.

She gasped. Blood spattered Marco's black sweater, perhaps from the large gash that stretched from his forehead down the side of his face to his chin.

His usually tawny-colored skin was pale and clammy. He groaned again, his eyes closed.

"A tree limb came in the window and broke off, landed on his torso." Amalia looked over Cora's shoulder at Marco.

"Thomson and I lifted it off him. I'm guessing internal injuries."

"He's bleeding internally?"

"Probably."

"Oh, Marco." Cora touched his left arm, where nothing appeared damaged. "Marco, can you hear me?"

"Yeah." The word pushed out with a grimace.

"I'm going to get my first aid kit so we can bandage your cut. I'll be back."

He didn't respond, his eyes still closed.

"Found a kit in there, too." Amalia dipped a thumb back over her shoulder toward the cockpit.

The door that had separated them from the pilot hung open, swinging from one hinge.

"How's the pilot?"

"Dead."

Dead. Two people lost their lives. She should have told them about Christ before it was too late. Regret pinched her heart. "I have to check on Bradley. He's unconscious, and I think his arm is broken. Would you work on Marco's cut?"

"It won't do any good." Amalia turned her dark gaze on Cora. "He has more serious problems we can't fix."

"Would you help him anyway? Please?"

Amalia's lips curved into a bemused smile. "Sure."

"Thank you." Cora returned to the crushed end of the jet, breaking more glass under her feet with each step she took. Had she broken Bradley, too? What if he had internal injuries or didn't wake up? He would never have been on this jet, involved with the cartel, if not for her negligence. If she'd been a better guardian, a better sister, he would be safe right now.

Instead, he lay injured on a crashed plane in a snowy wilderness where they may not be able to get help immediately.

A new realization swept over her and left her cold. Did anyone know where they had gone down? If not, all their lives were still in danger.

Kent paused at the end of the stairs that led outside from the cabin door. Thanks to the tilt of the jet toward the opposite side, the steps stopped short of the ground by several feet. At least Amalia had managed to get the cabin door open while Kent had checked out Bradley's cartel companion, verifying he was dead, and helped Cora tie a sling around her brother's broken arm. She'd made the sling herself somehow from cloth. The pain of the movement had woken Bradley up for a few minutes before he had closed his eyes again. Probably just asleep this time.

The sight that spread before Kent's eyes did little to allay his concerns about the mess they'd landed in. Literally.

Trees, ravines, and tall hills—or were they mountains?—continued for as far as he could see. Except for straight ahead where it looked like the trees ended along a snowy clearing. He dropped the distance to the ground, snow swallowing his shoes and licking his skin with freezing moisture where the snow snuck under his pant legs.

He trudged through a drift that reached his knees and crested a gradual, three-foot rise to where the ground leveled off. A white clearing stretched out in front of him until it hit another wall of trees. It was longer than it was wide, like an airstrip. Probably what the pilot had aimed for. The snow that covered the ground was packed down, as if it had been plowed occasionally, maybe after heavy snowfalls.

But a layer of ice topped off the clearing now. Probably re-frozen snow after the sunlight had melted the top layer. The sun must beat down hard in this open area during warm days.

Right now, the gray cloud cover above hid the sun from view and threatened to drop more snow along with dropping the temperature. Kent stuffed his hands in the pockets of his wool coat and walked farther out into the clearing. He checked the ground as he went.

Tracks showed where the jet's wheels had broken through the ice and snow, then scratched the surface where the jet must have hydroplaned and started to skid. He followed the tracks to where they slipped off, the marks changing as the plane had shifted to the edge of its wheels, then skidded off the clearing into the snow and trees of the forest.

He followed the smashed snow where the plane had slid down the short incline and crashed into trees. Reaching the jet, he turned left to walk along the aircraft toward the plane's nose.

He'd already seen inside the cockpit that the radio and instruments were crushed by the same force and trees that had killed the pilot. But assessing the damage of the entire aircraft from the exterior would tell him if there were any concerning leaks, sparks, or fires.

"Fishy, isn't it?"

He nearly started at Amalia's voice behind him. She knew how to sneak up on people, apparently. He tossed her a glance over his shoulder as he rounded the steps of the cabin door. Even had the German shepherd with her, and he still hadn't heard them. "The crash?"

"The jet was fine when it descended."

How did she know that? "Let me guess, you're a pilot, too?"

"I know how to tell when an engine is having problems. This one wasn't."

He stopped at the nose of the plane, angled in the air and listing to the side where trees seemed to have swallowed half of it. He looked at the dark-haired woman who stood with a widened stance. "Until it crashed."

"Bingo."

"You think he planned to land here?"

She reached in the pocket of her black parka.

He tensed. Going for a weapon?

She pulled out a smartphone.

He let his muscles relax. Cora trusted her, and Pérez was with Phoenix K-9. But he hadn't survived this long by being gullible. And given the situation, he couldn't assume even Pérez was okay.

"Found this on the pilot." She pressed a button to awaken the screen and handed it to him.

He took the warm device in his palm.

A series of text messages trailed down the screen.

DEA just boarded. Call me.

Kent clenched his jaw. Nothing incriminating in the message trail before that text, and it was the last message the pilot had received. But who had known Kent was DEA? He hadn't given that away until he was on the plane and cuffed the cartel dealers.

How did someone on the ground know? And if the person had warned the pilot, why still take off?

He studied the message again. No ID, just a phone number Kent didn't recognize. Twin Cities area code.

"Whoever that is must have told the pilot to land here."

He glanced at Pérez. "Why?'

She turned partially away, scanning the woods. "How big is the shipment of drugs we're carrying?"

He narrowed his eyes as he caught her drift. "Big enough."

The cartel could be coming for it.

And they'd be sitting ducks. Unless backup came first.

He yanked his phone from his pocket. Checked the bars as he had done on the plane. No reception out here either. "You got any service?"

"Nope."

He pocketed the phone and headed back, passing Pérez to get to the rear of the plane. Ramos had said he thought the drugs were going to be stored in the cargo hold, which was why they'd bought off the pilot to be sure he didn't report them if he saw anything.

A dark opening just beyond the jet's wing yawned at Kent. The cargo door was already open.

He glanced back at Pérez, who followed him with her dog.

"Could be the pressure change opened it, or it wasn't properly closed at takeoff."

Or she could've opened it before he left the plane. Had she taken the drugs?

He walked to the hold. Leaned inside.

The daylight behind him provided illumination for Kent to see the shadowy space clearly enough. It was empty.

None of the passengers that Kent knew of had brought luggage to put in the hold. But the drugs should've been there, unless the dealers had changed plans and hid them somewhere else.

He swung to look at Pérez, his hand inching to his waist where he could grab his weapon if needed.

"Aw, don't do that." She grinned. Like she thought this was funny. "I didn't take them. Must've fallen out with the force of the crash." She tilted her head. "Or maybe I opened the hold, and they weren't there. You'll never know. But if you're nice, I'll be happy to help you look."

He lowered his hand. "I can manage." He let his irritation edge the statement.

"Suit yourself."

She turned away and started leading her dog back up to the clearing.

"Hey." He followed her to catch up.

She looked back at him but didn't stop.

"What were you doing at the FBO before you boarded? You didn't forget anything in your car."

"No kidding."

Would she tell him what she was really doing?

She reached the clearing just before Kent did. She stopped, letting him catch up. "Remington Jones texted me he was there and wanted to meet in the parking lot."

"Remington Jones?" Sounded like somebody from a detective novel.

"A P.I. Phoenix hired to tail Bradley."

Ah, yes. "I'm betting she didn't tell Cora about that at first. Does your boss often go behind your backs like that?"

"Only when she needs to. She told Cora about it at the best time."

Meaning, not right away. Kent moved his gaze across the clearing, looking for anything that interrupted the white surface, especially at the edge where the plane had careened off.

"Jones told me he planted a tracking device in Bradley's duffel bag before he boarded."

"You're kidding."

She flashed another grin. "I checked, and the tracker got crushed. But Phoenix will know where we were when we started to land."

Something that looked like a stump next to a tree caught his eye. Could it be the drugs? "Will she call it in or bring rescue crews?" He headed in the direction of the object. It was pretty far from the crash site, but maybe the force of gravity could've flung the drugs that far.

"She'll probably just come herself. With the PK-9 team." Pérez followed just behind with her dog. "She wouldn't assume we crashed. The cartel could've had us land here as part of the test. She'll want to check it out without ruining your operation."

"Velasquez, Minneapolis SAC for the DEA, was going to have our flight tracked on radar, too. But she won't send agents in right away either for the same reason." As he neared the trees, he peered at the object. Just a stump, peeking out from blotches of snow. "I told her not to get trigger happy about it in case Guajardo wanted the destination changed mid-flight or something."

"I need to get going."

He raised his eyebrows at her abrupt announcement. "You're going somewhere?"

"I'll make a sweep of the area. See if there are any cabins or other signs of life. Maybe a radio, if we're lucky."

Smart.

"You should get Cora out here with Jana. They'll find the drugs for you."

Also smart, and something he should've thought of. He wasn't used to having a narcotics K-9 around. Or depending on anyone but himself. That part slid down his throat with a sharp edge. He turned back to head for the plane.

But Pérez blocked his path, her booted feet in a wide stance in the snow. "You'll watch out for her while I'm gone?"

"Cora?"

She just stared straight into his eyes with the most serious expression he'd ever seen on her face.

"Yeah."

"If you don't, I'll take it personally."

Irritation narrowed his eyes. But he held back his instinctive, defensive response. She was watching out for Cora. That was a good thing. "I'll take care of her. You have my word."

"I'll be back tonight. Before the visitors." She jerked a nod and spun away, taking Raksa with her as she cut a brisk pace across the clearing, a brown knapsack on her back strapped tight to her parka.

Visitors. Her tone made it clear she didn't mean Phoenix.

Was she right? If the text message the pilot received had been followed by instructions to land here, then she probably was.

The cartel was coming.

THIRTY-ONE

"Rem did that?" Cora looked ahead at Kent as he led the way through the snow to the cargo hold of the plane.

Jana bridged the distance between them, wagging her tail with glee at getting to be in the snow. Playing in the white fluff was one of her favorite games, even if she had to wear her booties this time.

Kent's eyes narrowed as he paused and glanced back at her. "He's a friend of yours?"

"Yes. He's engaged to Bristol, one of the PK-9 team members."

"Oh." The tension in his features relaxed as he turned back to the plane and walked a few more feet to the square-shaped opening in the side of the plane that had held what little cargo there was. "Yeah, so Amalia thinks your boss will have used the tracking device to see where we are, or at least where we went down, before the device was crushed."

Relief coursed through Cora's limbs that were already growing warmer from her movement. "Praise the Lord. We'll be found." She couldn't help the smile that stretched her mouth.

Kent's lips angled in an answering smile as she reached him by the cargo hold. "Why didn't you mind that your boss had your brother followed without telling you about it?"

Cora swiped tendrils of hair from her face with her gloved hand. "I was thankful she cared enough about me to want to make sure I was safe. And it meant I knew where Bradley was after the home invasion. That was a gift."

He shook his head with a bemused expression. "You put a positive spin on everything."

"I'm blessed to have friends I can depend on. I want to take care of them, too, so I don't begrudge when they want to help me." She tilted her head and pressed her lips together. "Even if they don't always tell me what they're doing."

"You make it sound nice."

"What?" She looked at him, trying to read what he meant. "Having help from friends?"

He put his hands on the edge of the cargo hold and leaned in. "It's empty."

Changing the subject. Not surprising, given how independent he was and how much he disliked having to work with someone else. When he'd returned to the plane to ask her for Jana's help finding the drugs, he hadn't done so directly. He'd asked Bradley where the drugs were. When Bradley said he didn't know and became agitated, Cora had offered Jana's services. But she hadn't missed how Kent had gotten what he'd probably intended—help without needing to ask for it.

She smiled to herself. He likely had no idea how transparent his fear of needing assistance was. But everyone had their fears, so she was in no place to judge. Her own fear over Bradley was allayed for the moment. He was conscious and cognizant and seemed out of immediate danger from a medical standpoint.

"Could Jana smell traces of the drugs so we'd know they were in there at some point?"

"Wouldn't the cargo hold be too obvious a location to hide the drugs?"

"Not if they were confident they wouldn't be searched."

"Sure, Jana can check it."

He looked at Jana. "Should I lift her in?"

"She can jump that high with enough distance."

"Okay." His voice signaled skepticism.

"Jana, with me." Cora led the golden farther from the plane. The ground angled upward there, but that shouldn't interfere with the jump. She positioned Jana so she was facing the cargo hold, then unclipped her leash.

"Jana, in!"

The golden retriever took off, using the extra space to gain some speed before launching herself into the cargo hold, landing safely inside.

Cora hurried to the jet. "Good girl! Search."

"I'm impressed." Kent looked at Cora as she reached his side.

"Something that's hard to achieve, I imagine." She gave him a small smile, then transferred her gaze to Jana.

The golden had her nose to the floor of the cargo hold as she moved rapidly, smelling every inch.

"Will she signal if there's a trace?"

"Yes."

Jana's muzzle swung up to the walls of the hold.

She suddenly stopped, sat, and turned her head to look in Cora's direction. "Yes! Good girl, Jana." Cora glanced at Kent. "That's it. She's found them."

"Just residue probably."

"I don't know. Are you sure there's no hidden compartment? It's hard to see clearly with how dark it is." She reached into her pocket and pulled out the miniature flashlight she'd gotten out of her suitcase to use on the plane when the clouds had covered more of the sunlight.

"You have a flashlight?"

"I always bring one when I travel." She pointed the beam into the cargo hold.

"Even though you were supposed to fly back this afternoon?"

"I packed for an overnight stay, just in case."

"I see." Amusement colored his voice.

"Aren't you glad I did?"

He chuckled, a sound that tripped her pulse. "Yes, I am."

"Can you see anything? It's hard for me to see all the way to the back from here because of the tilt."

"May I?" He held out his gloved hand for the flashlight.

She gladly turned it over.

He aimed the beam at the wall by Jana. "No good from here. Hold this." He returned the flashlight and hefted himself into the hold, making the motion appear easy. "Flashlight." He reached down. "Please." He flashed a smile that nearly took her breath away.

"Sure." She pressed it into his hand as a hot flush traveled up her neck, destined for her face. Good thing he didn't do that very often. Though he seemed to be smiling more and more all the time, heaven help her.

"Got it. It matches the already-existing seam, so it's hard to see. But there's a false wall here, I think."

"Oh, wonderful." He wouldn't need Jana to mark the spot anymore. "Jana, release."

The golden popped up from her sit and rushed over to Cora to get her handful of treats.

"Good girl," Cora repeated as she rubbed Jana's fur.

"I need a pin or something to get it open."

"Would a pocketknife work?"

He sent her a look with his eyebrows lifted. "You have one?"

"Yes." She'd slipped it into her pocket after she had used it to cut a sling for Bradley's arm out of the pajama shirt she had in her suitcase. "Here you go."

He took off his glove to receive the small knife from her hand. "Didn't take you for the pocketknife type."

"Oh?"

He shook his head, a hint of a smile playing at the corners of his mouth as he turned away and opened the knife. As best as she could tell in the shadowy hold, he ran the knife into the seam he'd mentioned.

A panel popped open.

"Another hold." He ducked to look inside. "About half the size of this one."

"Are the drugs there?"

He turned to her. "Yep. Good work."

"Did you hear that, Jana?" Cora scratched the golden's chin with her gloved fingers. "You did it again. Such a good girl."

"Can she jump down?" Kent walked over to Jana at the opening.

"I wouldn't want to risk a drop like that onto the uneven ground. I can lift her down."

"How much does she weigh?" His dark eyebrows lifted again.

"About sixty pounds."

"Uh-huh." Skepticism laced his voice.

"I can lift her, really." Cora smiled up at him. "Though maybe not from this height."

"Thought so." He sat on the edge of the hold, dangled his legs out, and dropped down to the ground. He reached up and pulled the trusting golden into his arms, gently lowering her to the snow.

She shook her whole body as soon as he let her go, then wagged her tail and rubbed against his legs.

Cora laughed. "She's saying 'thank you.'"

"Great." His tone was grudging, but he bent down and petted her with the look of someone who enjoyed it. As he straightened, his eyes held the gravity she was used to seeing there. "I'm going to pull the drugs out and hide them somewhere. Or I might have Amalia do it when she gets back since she'll have scouted the area and will know where the best place might be to hide the merchandise away from here."

"Why would you hide it?"

He stepped closer to her. "Amalia found a text message on the pilot's phone, warning him that I—the DEA—was on board."

Cora's stomach tensed. "Oh, no. Do you know who sent the text?"

"No. The message told the pilot to call the sender. We can assume he did so."

"But why would he still have taken off? Unless…"

Kent nodded. "They planned to do something about it along the way instead. If they'd tried to ground the flight at the airport, they knew I could arrest them. But if they flew us somewhere else…"

"But why here?"

"There's a clearing just over there." Kent angled his head toward the short incline. "Looks like it's used as an airstrip. They must've known about it."

"And the pilot thought it would be usable in winter?"

"Looks like it is maintained. Plowed anyway. But the ice melt created a frozen top-layer he didn't plan on."

"And that's why we crashed. Not because something was wrong with the plane."

"Looks that way."

"Well, it's a good thing Phoenix will know where we are then. We'll get help soon. We just have to wait."

"We might get somebody else coming sooner." Kent's grim tone twisted the jumble of nerves in her stomach.

"What do you mean?"

He glanced past her, and then up the incline. As if someone might be hiding there.

Her breathing shallowed as her mind put the pieces together. "Oh, my. You think the pilot planned on the cartel coming to the plane here? To retrieve the drugs and…deal with us?"

"That's exactly what I think. Your friend Amalia thinks so, too."

"Oh, no." Her knees weakened beneath her.

Kent's hands were instantly on her arms, steadying her, holding her up. His warmth seeped all the way through his gloves and her jacket to provide heat and strength to her muscles. Or perhaps she imagined it so. She found his gaze, the intensity in the green orbs. "If they come now when Bradley is hurt, and poor Marco…" Her hands came up and gripped his forearms as if of their own volition. "They're so vulnerable."

"I'll keep all of you safe."

"What about Amalia?"

"She said she'd return before the cartel came." He looked toward the clearing.

Her gaze followed his, catching on the streaks of color above the trees that turned the sky a brazen orange.

"Sun's setting now. She'll probably come back before dark." His mouth quirked up at the corner as he turned his head back to her. "Then you'll have both of us to protect you."

She met his gaze, the comfort from his words still not enough to loosen the tension knotting her belly. "Thank you."

The hint of a smile disappeared as his lips formed a straight line. "Though the cold tonight could be a worse enemy than the cartel."

She scanned his jeans and wool coat. The coat was better than the leather one Marco wore and Bradley's windbreaker, and at least he'd brought gloves, though they weren't as thick and insulated as she would like. "You should button your coat now and turn up the collar. Is it insulated?"

He looked down at the black wool and lifted one side to check the lining. "I think so?"

"The rest of your clothing is less than ideal. I'll have to see what I can find to help with that or keep you in the warmest area."

His head tilted slightly as he gave her that look that seemed a cross between curious and suspicious.

"But with some preparation, we'll survive the cold."

"We will?"

She nodded with the firmness of Amalia. This was something she could do right. She hoped. *Father, please help me to think of everything I need to keep everyone alive and warm tonight.* She turned around, wanting to exude confidence despite the reality that lives would depend on her knowledge and skill tonight.

She glanced over her shoulder at Kent. "Will you help me?"

That bemused smile shaped his mouth into a curve that surged heat through her bloodstream. "Yes, ma'am."

"So how are we going to attach these once I have them cut?" Kent looked up from the task Cora had given him—cutting the leather from the seats they weren't using into squares they would put over the round openings of the windows that had broken.

"Duct tape." Cora dug through her open suitcase on the floor of the jet. "I'm sure Amalia has some in her knapsack."

"Why would she have duct tape on a short flight?"

"I don't know exactly." Cora's delicate eyebrows drew together as she glanced his direction. "But she says it comes in handy." She pulled a flat, small square of something silver out of her suitcase. "There it is."

"Is that a mylar blanket?"

"Yes. I packed two of them, thankfully." She opened the plastic package and slipped out the blanket. "I'll put this on Marco. He'll have the hardest time staying warm." She passed Kent, who knelt next to the seat opposite the sofa where Bradley slept.

"We'll all have to move to the front part of the plane with Marco tonight to group our body heat in a smaller space." She unfolded the reflective, silver blanket by Ramos and covered his body. "Marco?" She pressed her hand to the man's forehead.

A lump swelled in Kent's throat at her gentleness. How could she care so much about a man who'd once tried to kill her?

Kent returned his attention to cutting more leather to insulate the windows from the cold outside. At least he'd brought his knife with his gear in the duffel bag, so he didn't have to cut all this with Cora's tiny pocketknife.

"He's not doing well." Cora spoke softly as she came back to Kent.

He looked up at her face. Wished he hadn't.

Tears welled in her beautiful blue eyes. "I don't know if I should be keeping him awake or letting him sleep." She wrapped her arms around herself.

Kent pushed to his feet, stood inches from her. He'd never wanted so badly to pull a woman into his arms just to comfort her. But that only made the risk all the more obvious. He could start to need her. He cleared his throat, clenching his fist low at his side. "I'd guess it's best to let him sleep if he has internal injuries."

She nodded. Sniffed, and lowered her arms as if regaining her strength. "Two of us can share the other mylar blanket."

"That will be you and Bradley."

"I agree Bradley should use it, but perhaps you could share with him. I have better winter clothing. I dressed in layers and boots, and I have my warm jacket." She ran her hands down the front of her dark purple jacket.

"I'm going to be outside tonight anyway."

"Outside? No, you can't. It already felt like it was less than twenty degrees out there during the day. It will likely drop to below zero tonight." Seeing the concern bunch in small furrows above her nose made him feel more than warm enough to survive.

"I'll be fine."

"You don't even have a proper jacket or gloves. Believe me, I've seen what happens to people who are ill-equipped to handle the weather they get lost in."

When did she see—Oh. "I forgot you and your dog do search and rescue for Phoenix, don't you?"

"Yes."

"Is that why you know all this outdoor, survival stuff?"

She smiled. "I would guess you don't because you're a city boy, correct?"

"Born and raised about as city as you can get. Figured you for a city girl, too."

"In some ways. But I learned to love nature and how to survive it in SAR training."

"Okay, so tell me how to survive the night outside the plane."

She narrowed her eyes, an exaggerated expression that gave away how rarely she had to look suspicious or irritated. "Fine. We should build a fire anyway. And that will help you stay warm."

"You can build a fire in the snow?"

"If we find the right materials, yes. Thankfully, we crashed into a forest, so that should be easy. There will be kindling under the snow that we can strip down to the dry wood so it will burn."

"And then you rub the sticks together till you get a spark?" He was half-teasing, figuring that wasn't a real thing.

"No, I use a lighter." She crossed her arms over her jacket, this time with the spunk that showed itself too rarely.

"You brought a lighter?"

"I'm quite sure Marco did for his cigarettes. A fire will enable us to melt ice for drinking water, too. I only brought two bottled waters with me."

Kent couldn't stop the grin that crept onto his face. "You're pretty amazing, you know that?"

"It's only basic survival knowledge anyone can learn with a little research or training."

"You're still amazing." Especially like this—confident and take-charge, gentle and caring, skilled and clever with her hidden sense of humor. His hand reached for her before he'd decided to move. He brushed his fingertips along her smooth cheek. Touched her soft hair.

"Kent, I—"

A cough interrupted her whisper. "Cora?" Bradley's voice cracked with dryness.

Her lids lifted as she gave Kent a parting glance.

Then she pulled away and knelt by her brother.

And vulnerable. She was vulnerable. Vince would say she was weak. So would Kent. At least, that's what he would have thought before. Her brother easily took advantage of her, imposing on her and manipulating her into believing whatever he said. All the while exploiting her emotional weakness to give him cover for his drug dealing.

But at the same time, her empathy allowed her to connect with perps better than anyone Kent had seen. She'd gotten Ramos, a regional manager, to flip on the cartel without even trying. That wasn't exactly the result of a weakness. And from what he'd seen her do with Hayden and Venetia, he knew it wasn't dumb luck either.

She was so much like his dad that way. Always caring too much and trying to understand people. Trying to make them change.

And look where that'd gotten him.

Maybe Kent was just getting blinded by emotion like with his first crush as a kid.

No, this was different. So much stronger and deeper somehow.

Look at Mom and Dad. Vince's lecture all those years ago still rang Kent's ears. *You want to end up like them? Always be strong, little man.*

Kent pulled his gaze from Cora as she tended her brother. He turned and went back to cutting window covers.

Did the way his heart pulled to Cora, the way she made him want to smile, the way she made his pulse sprint—did that make him soft?

Maybe so. But at the moment, he had a hard time seeing that as a bad thing.

THIRTY-TWO

A sound behind him made Kent jerk to look.

Cora stood at the top of the stairs, pausing in the cabin doorway of the jet. She gave a cute wave, too far from the light of the fire in front of him to see her expression.

He got up and hurried down to the plane. With all the traffic of their steps up and down the incline during the day, they'd created a few packed trails, which meant no more snow dropped into his shoes this time. Good thing, since Cora had lectured him on how his wet shoes and socks could be life-threatening if he didn't stay by a source of warmth.

He reached the base of the stairs as she stopped on the bottom step, Jana pausing behind her. The stairs still angled upward, reaching the height of his waist from the ground.

He held out his gloved hand, which was much warmer now thanks to the fire Cora had started an hour ago.

Her lips curved into a smile as she put her hand in his. He was tempted to take her by the waist and lift her down, but that would be too obvious. She'd already proven she could make the jump earlier in the day.

He offered support through her hand as she dropped to the ground. She turned back to watch Jana jump. Judging from the grin on the dog's face and the wagging tail, the golden retriever seemed to enjoy it.

"I brought you something." Cora slipped her hand away from Kent's and reached into her pocket. She pulled out a clump of white cloth. "I found these socks in the suitcase of the poor deceased man."

"And you want me to use them?" The idea of wearing the cartel thug's socks, dead or alive, was less than appealing.

"You really need to get out of your wet socks and put these on before your body starts to keep the blood back from your feet. You could lose your toes if it got bad."

"Okay, you've convinced me. But I have my own dry socks I can use in my duffel bag." He'd packed a change of clothes, figuring it might take a day or more for Ramos to meet with Guajardo. If only that had panned out.

"Oh, good." Cora brought his thoughts back to the present with a smile before she stepped away and pocketed the socks she'd brought. "How's the fire going?"

"Strong so far." Kent followed her as she and Jana climbed the incline and moved toward the fire at the edge of the clearing, just past the trees. "I still have a good amount of kindling left from what we found under the snow." He stopped by her side and gestured to the seat cushion he'd pulled from the plane and set on the snow.

"Oh, I don't want to take your seat."

"No problem. I have another one here." He stepped to the pile of kindling and grabbed the short log they'd found. He rolled it closer to the fire, about a foot from the seat cushion. "See?"

She smiled. "All right." She lowered herself to the cushion, and Jana sat by her far side. "My, the fire is warm." She lifted her hands toward the orange flames. Mittens had replaced the purple gloves she'd been wearing before.

"Where'd you get the mittens?"

"I brought them in my suitcase. Just in case I went exploring or something. They're so much warmer than gloves in extreme temperatures." She sent him a glance that almost looked guilty. "I would've loaned them to you since you're outside, but I don't think they'd fit." She turned her head toward the fire. "And I'm sorry I didn't have enough hand warmers to give you some. I thought Bradley and Marco needed them more since they're injured and stationary."

He shook his head as he watched her profile, the fire's shifting light throwing orange highlights on the blond hair beneath her purple beanie. "Do you always think of everyone but yourself?"

She brought her gaze to his face, her eyebrows lifted. "Far from it. I think of myself too much."

"I don't believe that. You're always thinking about others. That's what you do too much of."

"I don't think one can prioritize others too much."

He rotated on the log so that he faced her instead of the fire. "Okay. Take the mittens thing." He pointed at her hand. "You felt guilty because you didn't offer yours to me, even though you knew they wouldn't fit anyway. Don't you think that's a little extreme?"

She looked away, her gaze aimed at the fire. "The guilty part, perhaps. But it wasn't wrong to think of your needs." She tossed him a glance that immediately darted away again. "I mean, to think of anyone's needs."

"But you never focus on yourself. On what you need, what's best for you. I bet when you see a homeless person on the street, you offer him money, right?"

"When it seems appropriate, yes. I'll usually buy the person a meal or give them a restaurant gift card instead."

"I figured. But don't you ever think about how…vulnerable your kindness makes you?"

She turned her head toward him, the firelight flickering on her cheekbones and pink lips. "What do you mean? Physically or emotionally?"

"Physically." He propped his ankle on his knee, resting his hands on the bent leg. "Or both, really."

"I can't let fear of vulnerability stop me from helping people, from showing mercy and kindness."

"Why not? There's nothing wrong with looking out for yourself and your own safety."

"There is if that concern stops me from showing the love of Christ to others."

"Ah." He lowered his leg back to the ground. "The Jesus thing again."

She angled her head as she watched him. No signs of offense tightened her features. Instead, thoughtfulness settled in a gentle purse of her lips. "What is it about following Jesus or showing kindness to others that bothers you?"

"I just think you don't need that crutch of God and religion. I've seen you in action. You can be strong when you need to be."

"Any strength I show is only because I have Christ in me. Any kindness I show comes from the same source."

Kent shook his head in denial. "I don't believe that. You were born this way."

"Were you born independent and strong?"

The question caught him off-guard. He looked at the fire, the way it curled around the sticks at the bottom edge. "No. I learned the hard way."

"What happened, Kent? I can see it must have been difficult."

"I survived."

"Was it something with your brother?"

The flames of the fire seemed to blur as he stared at them. "My dad." He hadn't planned to answer. Didn't want to share. But something compelled him. Maybe her soft tone, her comforting presence.

"Something happened to him?"

"He was shot."

The pounding at the door when the cops had come thudded hard in Kent's memory. His dad had died instantly from a head wound, they'd told his mother. Just before she collapsed into hysteria.

Someone touched his shoulder.

Cora? She must have moved while he was lost in memory. She sat by his side on the short log, close enough to feel her warmth and the brush of her jacket against his arm.

"Oh, Kent. I'm so very sorry." Somehow the way she said it, pain in her voice that seemed to echo his, made the words mean so much more than when he'd heard them from many funeral attendees back then. "How old were you?"

"Ten." Kent clenched his jaw, anger flaring, sparked by the pain. "His cousin killed him. A drug dealer. From the Guajardo cartel."

"Oh, no."

"Yeah."

"How did your mother take it?"

His teeth ground together as he tried to block out the memory of her covered body on the gurney. The sight of her on her bed when he'd found her. "She OD'd within two years."

Cora gasped.

He turned his head to look at her. "My dad kept giving his cousin chance after chance. Kept thinking he'd go straight if he got enough help, caught the right breaks. He met him that night to try to talk him into coming to stay with us again. To stop him from using and working for the cartel."

"You think your dad's kindness made him vulnerable."

"You bet I do." He turned his glare on the fire instead of hitting Cora with it. "He was weak. And so was my mom. She let herself lean on my dad for everything. She couldn't go on without him. Couldn't get over it. Even with two sons she should've—" The fury surging up his throat choked the words.

"You and your brother."

Kent swallowed, clenched and unclenched his fists on his thighs. "Vince was twenty. Old enough to raise me. He taught me to be strong. He wanted to be sure I didn't end up like our parents."

"He must be a good man."

"What?" Kent brought his gaze back to Cora.

"Your brother. To have raised you so well on his own."

"Oh. Yeah." And now he was in a hospital. Weak and vulnerable thanks to a disease.

"I'm so sorry, Kent."

Did she know about Vince? Kent looked into her blue eyes, saw the moisture brimming there.

"You've been through so much. Two parents lost. I can only imagine the pain you went through. And the pain you're carrying now."

"I got over it. I suppose it made me stronger."

She sniffed and nodded. "One of my favorite Bible verses says, 'For when I am weak, then I am strong.'"

The Bible. Kent fought to keep his irritation from reaching his face. "What's that supposed to mean?"

"That God's power shows up most when we are at our weakest. And that sometimes being willing to show and admit weakness, especially to help another person the way your father did, takes the most courage and strength of all." She wiped her cheek with the thumb of her mitten. Was she crying?

Sure enough, the track of a tear glistened on her cheek, catching the firelight.

His chest squeezed, forcing some of his defenses to stand down.

"Jesus did that. He was God Himself, but he came to earth in the form of a baby. He set aside the power and strength of God that we can't even imagine in order to become a weak human. Just so he could live the perfect life we couldn't and pay the penalty for our sins, sacrificing himself like a weak lamb so we wouldn't have to get the punishment we deserve." More tears trailed down her cheeks as she looked into Kent's eyes, earnestness filling her blue irises.

She gripped his upper arms with her mittened hands. "Don't you see, Kent? He became weak for us so that He could do the most courageous thing ever. In choosing weakness, He was being stronger than we could ever dream of."

The authentic emotion in her eyes pressed like a weight on his chest, made him want to agree and give her what she wanted. But he couldn't deny what he knew to be true. "I get this means a lot to you. I can see that." He cupped her elbows in his hands. "But there's nothing strong about throwing away your life, sacrificing yourself for somebody who doesn't deserve it."

Her gaze searched his. "Wouldn't you sacrifice yourself for me, if you had to, in order to keep me safe?"

"Yes." The answer came quickly, easily, truthfully. "But you deserve it more than anyone I've ever known."

She slowly rotated her head back and forth. "I don't deserve it. But that's what mercy is."

Mercy was what led his dad to meet with his cousin that night, to try to take the drugs from him, to interfere with the buy that was going down. Mercy let killers take advantage of the innocent, the naïve, and the weak. But he couldn't say that to Cora. Not now, when she looked at him with such an open, vulnerable expression, as if she'd hung all her hopes on converting him to the way she saw things.

Not when she looked so utterly beautiful, her flawless skin warmed to a golden color from the flickering oranges of the fire, her blue eyes shining up at him. "You do deserve it, Cora. You deserve to be safe and happy and loved. You're the most amazing person I know." He let his gaze skim over her delicate features, touching on each to engrave them in his memory. "I'm starting to think you're just about perfect."

Maybe even perfect for him? In that moment, he forgot about the objections Vince would have. He didn't care about weaknesses and vulnerabilities. The only thing that mattered was this perfect woman and how she made him feel—like he was stronger and more alive with her near.

His gaze drifted down to her perfectly shaped lips.

"I'm far from perfect, Kent. I…" Whatever she was going to say drifted into the cold air as he brought up his hands to cup her face.

He slowly leaned closer.

Her hand covered one of his. "Kent—"

"Glad to see no one was worried about me."

Cora sprang back at the sound of Pérez's voice, catching herself just before she fell off the log. Her face darkened, probably a deep shade of red he couldn't make out in the shadows and flickering orange firelight.

He looked at Pérez, that grin beaming in the darkness where she stood beyond the fire.

"How'd you get so close without making a sound?" And with the German shepherd.

She laughed. "You were pretty busy."

Cora slid off the log and stood, avoiding looking at Kent or her friend. Man, he'd blown that one. Had she even wanted him to kiss her? She was about to say something instead.

"I can take next watch." Pérez glanced at him, then Cora. "Unless you two would rather do something else."

Cora ducked her head and walked away without a word. Jana popped up to follow her, wagging her tail like nothing was wrong as the dog and Cora disappeared down the incline, then came into view again as they climbed the steps into the plane.

"When you're done drooling, how about a report on activities here."

He tightened his jaw as he turned back to Pérez and got up. "We built a fire."

"Funny." She grinned. "Did you find the drugs?"

"Yeah. Hidden compartment in the cargo hold. I left them there, but I want to move them somewhere else."

She nodded. "I saw a good location on my way back."

As annoying as Pérez could be with her ill-timed humor, she seemed in sync with his thinking—at least when it came to tactics and strategy. She knew, without explanation, that he meant to hide the drugs from the cartel if they showed up.

"I'll take the drugs out there now."

He paused. Should he insist on doing it? Cora trusted her. That should mean something to him. And Pérez hadn't tried anything yet, even though she'd had opportunity. "Sure. What'd you find on your search?"

"No signs of human life within miles, other than a road about a mile from here." She pointed across the clearing. "It's been plowed once or twice this winter, but pretty snow-covered right now. I followed it for a few miles, but either I picked the wrong direction or there isn't anything to be found close enough for us to use."

"Turns out Cora's pretty up on survival skills, so it looks like we'll last the night."

Pérez flashed her smile. "Yeah, she's got game. Drugs are in the cargo hold?"

"I left the secret compartment open."

"I'll tell you exactly where I hid them when I get back. Better for two of us to know."

In case one of them was put out of commission. She was savvy enough to prepare for worst-case scenarios, too. Just what was her background? He kept the question to himself.

She walked past the fire and headed for the incline that led to the jet, her German shepherd jogging to keep up with her fast clip. "Thomson." She turned back. "We'll keep the location of the merchandise to ourselves. Don't tell Cora."

Keeping secrets from Cora didn't sit well with him. She didn't deserve to be kept out of the loop. "Why not?"

"We don't want to put her at risk when they come to look for it."

The cartel. She was right. But the image that brought to his mind—Cora, threatened by the cartel—made his muscles clench and heat surge through his veins. He'd do whatever it took to make sure that vision never became a reality.

THIRTY-THREE

Cora lingered in the darkness that shrouded the corner just inside the plane's cabin doorway. It wasn't much warmer here than outside. Colder than by the fire, in fact. She ought to close the cabin door to keep more cold air from getting in. She'd do that after she checked to see if Kent or Amalia wanted to come inside first.

But she wouldn't ask them yet. She couldn't bear to face either of them right now, her face still flaming with embarrassment. How horrifying that Amalia had found them in such a pose. How alarming that it had happened in the first place, that Kent had tried to kiss her.

She still couldn't believe it. She'd suspected he liked her somewhat, from the way he looked at her sometimes and a few of the things he'd said. But she had no idea he liked her *that* much.

She should have talked to him earlier and explained why she couldn't be in a relationship with him. But how could she have made the assumption that was what he wanted? She would never want to presume such a thing, or to stir up conflict and embarrassment where there was no reason for it. What if she had thought he had romantic interest, only to have him say he didn't think of her like that at all?

She pressed her hands to her face, the mittens slippery and

cold against her heated cheeks. *Oh, Father. What should I have done differently?*

She never should have let him get so far as trying to kiss her. She'd been about to stop him, but Amalia still saw them that way, looking as if they were about to kiss.

Cora dropped her hands at her sides, leaning her head back as she stifled a frustrated groan. The worst thing of all was that, for a moment, she'd wanted him to kiss her. She could never love or marry a man who didn't belong to Christ first. She should have that conviction so solidly fixed that she didn't even want Kent to kiss her. *I'm sorry, Lord. Please forgive me.*

A pressure on Cora's hand interrupted the downward spiral of her thoughts.

She looked down at Jana, who nudged Cora's mitten with her nose. Her eyes gleamed in the darkness.

Jana was right, as usual. Nothing good would be accomplished by Cora hiding here as if she could hide from her mistakes. She'd have to talk to Kent the first chance she had and make things clear before this went any farther. Cora released a sigh and stepped into the aisle.

"Cora?" Bradley's tone was tight. With fear?

"What is it?" She hurried the few feet to her brother where he sat in the seat opposite Marco.

"Ramos. I think he's worse."

She turned to Marco.

His breathing had changed. It was raspy and labored. He coughed, heaving forward as if from the force of the cough and no strength in his body. His head collapsed back against the headrest.

"Marco?" She lifted the mylar blanket higher on his shoulders where it had fallen away with his movement.

The larger flashlight Kent had found in the cockpit stood on the floor in the aisle by Bradley and Marco, casting enough light that she could see the man's skin was paler than before. His lips looked to be turning pale, as well—or were they blue in color? It was too difficult to tell in this lighting, especially below his dangling mustache. But he obviously wasn't doing well.

"Cora." He pushed out her name on a weak breath.

Her heart wrenched. Was there nothing she could do for him? "Let me get you some water." She went to her suitcase that she'd brought close earlier and pulled out one of her two bottled waters. They'd melted ice for drinking water earlier, but in his condition, he needed to drink the best and safest water she could offer.

She removed her mittens and returned to Marco, twisting the cap off the bottle. "Here, drink this." She brought the water close.

"No." His lips brushed against the opening of the bottle as he spoke, but he made no effort to drink. Was he too far gone for that already? Should she try to pour some water into his mouth if he couldn't make the effort? Her lack of knowledge was pathetic. She should've studied how to deal with internal injuries and cases like this one. Frustration at her inability to help Marco welled up in her throat with a rush of sadness, nearly choking her.

"Have to," Marco paused, taking in more air before he could go on, "talk to you. God."

Did he mean he wanted to talk about God? She didn't think he'd misuse the Lord's name at a time like this.

"I'm...dying." He opened his eyes, searching for her.

She rested her hand on his shoulder through the mylar blanket. "I'm here."

He pulled in another raspy breath. "Scared. I've done...so bad."

"You're worried about what happens next."

"Yeah." The answer was more of a puff of air than the actual word, but she understood.

"I have good news for you, Marco. The best news in the world." She looked into his eyes, though his lids alternated between closed and open. "You can know where you're going. You can have eternal life in perfect joy with Jesus in Heaven instead of eternal punishment in hell."

"No." His head twitched slightly, as if he was trying to rotate it to deny what she was saying. "Too bad. Deserve hell."

"You're right. You do deserve hell and all the punishment for the bad things you've done. I deserve that, too. But Jesus Christ died for you on the cross, Marco." Tears welled in her eyes, blurring her vision of the dying man's face. "He lived a perfect life and took the punishment He didn't deserve. He took *your* punishment, my punishment, so we wouldn't have to. So we could be forgiven and spend forever with Him when we leave this life."

"Not…possible."

"Oh, but it is, Marco." She smiled, hoping he would at least hear her sincerity and joy if he couldn't see it. "Jesus is our Redeemer. When He died and rose again, He set us free from our slavery to sin. And do you know what else He redeems?"

She paused, but Marco's labored breathing was the only response.

Father, please let him hang on long enough to hear this and come to You.

"He redeems all of the bad things we've ever done, all of our mistakes. He promises He'll use all the bad things for His glory and the good of those who love Him."

She gently smoothed her hand over Marco's forehead, his skin clammy under her palm. "He'll redeem you, Marco. Admitting you've made mistakes, that you've done wrong and that you need Him is the first step. If you're sorry for all the bad you've done, and you believe He died for you and rose again, then you'll be saved, too."

She watched Marco's features, his closed eyes, hoping for a sign that he heard. *Please, Father, save him if it's Your will.*

A long breath trailed into his lungs with a rasp. Then silence.

She stared at the silver blanket where it covered his chest.

It rose when he breathed again.

"Uhhh." A sound of pain pushed out from his lips.

Tears fell down her cheeks. If only she could relieve his suffering. "Marco, it's okay. Try to breathe. I'm here."

"Is...that..." He forced out the words with what seemed to be his last embers of strength, each attempt quieter than the one before.

She leaned close to his head, hoping to catch what he was saying.

"Sunrise?"

The windows were still covered, and the plane was dark, except for the beam of the flashlight.

She opened her mouth to tell him no. But something stopped her. Could he be seeing something she couldn't? If God had just saved him, perhaps the Light of the life to come?

"I hope so, Marco." She whispered the answer, tasting the tears that had fallen down her cheeks to her lips. "I hope so."

Kent didn't move as he stood just inside the cabin doorway. He'd been there for a while without being able to move or speak. Unable to interrupt the most intimate moment he'd ever witnessed.

Whether or not he believed what Cora said didn't matter. What mattered was the way she'd just comforted a dying man. He'd seen the strongest, bravest agents and law enforcement personnel he knew practically turn tail and run when needing to sit with a sick or dying person. The thought even made him squirm, though he luckily hadn't had to do it yet. He usually showed up after the person was already dead. That was easier.

But not for Cora.

"Is he—" Her brother asked the question with fear pinching his voice.

"He's gone." Cora dipped her head forward, resting her hands on Ramos's shoulders, and gave in to weeping.

Something twisted in Kent's chest at the mournful sound, the pain and grief she felt for a man like Ramos. He didn't deserve it, but she gave him that gift anyway.

Jana got to her feet from where she'd been lying next to Ramos's chair and nudged Cora's leg.

Kent walked toward Cora. Jana looked at him, almost as if asking for help.

"Cora." He put his hand on her shoulder.

She turned toward him. In the shadows, her face glistened with tears as plentiful as a waterfall. Her lips were puffy and her eyes watery.

But he'd never seen anyone so beautiful in his life.

Without another thought, he pulled her into his arms.

She pressed her cheek to his chest, wrapping her arms around his back and holding on as if he were her life preserver. "I shouldn't have let him die."

"Shh." He moved his hand in a slow circle on her back, his glove sliding along her jacket. "You didn't, Cora. You couldn't have done anything."

"But if I'd known more, if I'd taken more extensive medical training, perhaps I could have done something to keep him alive longer."

Was she serious? Kent pulled back so he could look into her eyes. Pain shone back at him. Pain and guilt.

He reached behind her back to pull the glove off his right hand. He brought the hand around to cradle her face in his palm, drawing his thumb across her cheek. "You gave him a gift, Cora. You gave him comfort when no one else here could. You made sure he didn't die alone."

A tear welled over and dropped onto his thumb.

She leaned toward him, returning her head to his chest as he took her back into his arms.

He angled a look at her brother.

Bradley stared at his sister, his eyes wide in the dim lighting and his face ghoulishly pale. Did he have any idea how much of this was his fault? Cora was in this position because of Bradley. She never should have had to deal with drug addicts and dealers, with death, lies, and betrayal. She should have the best of everything, not a brother who was nothing but trouble. Who put her life in danger with his messed-up life.

Cora sobbed against Kent's chest, her hands moving to the front of his coat and gripping the lapels tightly.

He held Cora close and tabled his anger toward Bradley. He'd get what he deserved. They all did eventually. Like Ramos. Though Ramos got so much better than he deserved, thanks to Cora. Maybe that was fair since Ramos had tried to do something right at the end. But he'd only done it to save himself. He hadn't really changed. And his come-to-Jesus moment had only been inspired by needing to look death in the eye. That was when a person's true strength or weakness was revealed.

Ramos got lucky. He had Cora to ease his passing and calm his fears.

Who would Vince have? The thought came unbidden to Kent's mind, like a threatening lurker jumping out of the dark.

Vince was strong. He'd do fine on his own, if he really was that sick. Kent had a hard time believing anything could lick his brother.

But Kent knew this much about himself—nothing would ever reduce him to weakness or needing make-believe crutches. For sure not the cartel or anything they might try to do when they showed up.

And not even the woman who was crying in Kent's arms, very near to his heart.

THIRTY-FOUR

Kent awoke with a start. He glanced around.

Across the aisle, Bradley slept under a mylar blanket in the chair opposite Ramos, despite having begged Kent to move him away from the dead man last night.

Ramos's body was covered with the other silver blanket. Kent had told Cora to use it, but she'd said she couldn't take it off him so soon. He'd respected her wishes and made sure she'd covered up with one of the three polyester blankets they'd found on the plane.

She slept in the chair across from Kent, Jana lying on her feet, which probably helped Cora keep warm. Cora's head drooped to one side, her lips parted slightly.

His pulse hitched. She was so beautiful.

And potentially in danger.

He checked his watch. *7:15.* He never slept that late, but they'd stayed up most of the night.

If Pérez was right about the cartel and how soon they'd arrive if they had started out by car, they could show up soon. And he agreed they'd likely wait for enough light to find the clearing on foot.

Looked like that moment was here. Pre-sunrise light managed to penetrate through the coverings, shaping the circular windows with a soft glow that brightened the jet enough to see dimly without the flashlight he'd turned off before going to sleep last night.

Kent pushed aside his blanket and stood. Stiffness and aches greeted the movement. No doubt thanks to the roughness of the seat after he'd stripped it of leather to cover the windows. He reached between the seat and the wall and picked up his backup Glock that he'd brought on board in his duffel bag and had with him outside last night.

He tried to be as silent as possible as he snuck past Cora and went to the cabin door. It was quieter than he expected as he pushed it open, hopefully quiet enough not to wake her. She deserved her rest after everything she'd been through.

A white glow blocked out a portion of the sky to the east, marking the coming of the rising sun.

From the higher position of the cabin, he could see past the incline to the fire at the edge of the clearing. The blaze was gone, snuffed out with snow that covered what had been the center of the fire.

His pulse kicked up a notch. Had Pérez noticed a sign of the cartel or was she just being proactive?

He scanned the area for her.

"Thomson." Her voice came from below him.

She stood next to the steps, a Glock in her hand. Her German shepherd stood a few feet away from her, his leash loose between them as he smelled the snow.

Kent went down the steps and dropped to the ground. "See something?"

"Not yet." She held the Glock out, grip of the weapon facing him. "Need another piece?"

He looked at the weapon. "You've got extra?"

"Gotta love FBOs." She grinned, the black beanie she wore over her hair darkening her eyes. "I can bring as many toys as I want."

He lifted his secondary weapon, the other Glock still secure in his IWB holster. "I've already got backup." He reached under his coat and tucked the weapon behind him into his waistband. If the cartel did show up, there was no predicting how many men they'd bring. Couldn't hurt to have spares. "Got more ammo?"

"Thought you'd never ask." She slapped a box of cartridges into the palm of his glove.

He looked up the incline to the near edge of the clearing. "I'm guessing they'll come from the road you found."

"Yeah, if they expected the plane to land in this clearing, they know how to find it. The closest access via ground is the road."

"They'll have to come on foot and either cross the clearing or go around it through the woods."

"Which gives us the advantage." She slid the Glock behind her back, making it disappear under her parka. "They won't know where the jet is unless we're by it. We can misdirect and keep them away from it if we take up position on the south side of the clearing."

"Good idea. We'd have a clear shot if they try to cross the clearing. And we'll have the trees for cover."

She nodded. "We better get out there now. They'll come today but can't be sure what time."

A sound by the jet made them both spin toward it.

Cora walked down the steps from the cabin door, Jana following behind her. Cora's gaze swept over Pérez and Kent. "What's going on?"

Kent held up his hand. "You should probably stay inside."

"Why?"

"The cartel's coming." Pérez delivered the announcement in a cheerful tone, as if announcing the start of a game.

"What?" Cora wrapped her arms around herself. "Now?"

Pérez shrugged. "Could be. Sometime today."

"What are we going to do?" Fear upturned Cora's voice.

"Hey." Kent walked toward the steps and reached to touch the edge of their frame as he looked up at Cora. "It'll be okay. Amalia and I have got this."

Cora pressed her lips together, worry tightening her features. "I don't want you to get hurt." She lifted her gaze to include Pérez. "Either of you."

"Don't worry." Pérez flashed her grin at Cora. "I'll take care of your man."

Kent's pulse skittered at the idea despite himself. He looked at Cora for her reaction, not surprised to see the telltale flush tint her cheeks.

A low-pitched sound, a growl from Pérez's dog yanked Kent's gaze away.

The German shepherd stared toward the clearing, his body still.

"They're here." Pérez whirled to Cora, her humor gone. "Get inside and stay there. No noise. Hide behind solid objects."

"Be careful." Cora's words were lost on Pérez as the woman sprinted away, her dog keeping pace as they darted into the trees, headed south.

"Do what she said." Kent pulled his weapon from its holster as he backed away. "We'll keep you safe."

"I'll be praying for you."

He didn't care if she did. But the look in her eyes as he whirled away and took off after Pérez—the emotion swirling in her blue irises that said she cared about him—that pumped so much energy into his veins, he felt invincible.

He ran hard, darting between tree trunks, keeping the clearing above him on his right. They shouldn't be able to get a shot at him while he was beneath the incline.

But the ground under his feet leveled with the clearing as he neared the south side. He kept rows of trees between him and the open space for cover. Glanced past the trunks as he sprinted.

Was that movement? A dark figure behind trees on the east side?

A shot cracked through the air. Fired from the south a short distance beyond Kent.

Pérez had begun the battle.

Cora winced as more shots popped. She hugged Jana's neck. The golden sat on the floor by Cora, both of them squished next to Bradley in the aisle between the sofa and the two seats. The crunched section at the back of the plane was just beyond them. It seemed the best location to be protected from stray bullets, which Cora was sure was Amalia's intent when she'd told her to hide behind solid objects.

Father, please protect us. Especially Kent, Amalia, and Bradley. And please bring Phoenix and the rest of the team here soon.

"I told you." Bradley's hazel eyes were only about a foot away, close enough for her to see the fear that belied his angry tone. "You shouldn't have come."

She met his gaze. "I'm glad I did."

He glanced away.

The sound of more gunfire pierced the air.

Bradley flinched. "Do you think we're going to die?" His cracked lips barely moved with the whisper.

"No." She touched his arm through the blanket he'd carried to this spot and wrapped around his body. "The Lord will protect us. He's probably sending Phoenix and the PK-9 team to help us."

"How do you know?"

"I don't know she's coming for sure. But I do know He's already provided Kent and Amalia. I've seen how capable they are. They'll be able to scare the cartel away."

He shook his head. "You don't know the cartel like I do. They won't leave without their drugs." He looked toward the front of the plane. "Probably here for him, too." His gaze seemed to rest on the back of the chair that held Marco's body. "If they know a DEA agent got on the plane with Marco like you said, they'll want him."

Thank the Lord Marco would be spared whatever the cartel had planned for him. Hopefully, he was in heaven now with Jesus.

"It will be okay, Bradley. You'll see."

"That's what you said about Mom." He brought his gaze to her face, his eyes darkening. "Remember?"

Had she? Cora thought back, opening the vault of memories from that time she usually kept closed. She probably had said something like that. Bradley had been hurting, crying every night, unable to sleep while their mother faded away. "I was trying to comfort you." And herself.

"With lies? That God would heal her? That we'd be okay because He loved us?" Bradley's chin puckered as his eyebrows dipped low. "None of that was true."

"God does love us, Bradley. And He loves Mom. He took her to be with Him."

"And left us all alone."

"We had each other."

Bradley snorted and jerked his head away. "Yeah, right." He pulled his hand out from under the blanket and swiped his cheek. "I needed a mom. Why didn't God know that?"

"He knew what was best for all of us, Bradley. It's hard to see it now, and then. But I have faith He's using it for good. And someday, we'll see how."

"That doesn't—"

A scraping sound cut off Bradley's response. Was the noise at the front of the plane?

Cora stared up the aisle, her stomach clenching.

The cabin door creaked as it opened.

Had Amalia or Kent come back?

Shots echoed from the clearing. They were still shooting.

Light fell into the aisle from the open door.

Cora's oxygen froze in her throat.

A man's big fist appeared, then his thick body. Long, curly black hair skimmed the shoulders of his black leather jacket.

It couldn't be.

He was the man from the ambush on the road, the one from the green car who'd almost reached her.

He looked to the left toward the cockpit, then glanced right. "Well, who do we have here?" He grinned as he lumbered toward her. He laughed, a high-pitch sound that was oddly more like a giggle. He paused in the aisle and glanced back, drawing her attention to two more men who had boarded behind him. She didn't recognize them, but she hadn't seen all the men that day on the road.

"Hey, boys. It's Brad, hiding behind a woman."

But Bradley wasn't hiding anymore. He stood, letting the blanket drop to the floor, brushing against Cora's arm as it fell.

The large man moved toward them again, his companions following.

Cora rose, holding Jana back by her leash as the golden tried to great the visitors.

"Ramos." The long-haired man halted next to Marco's chair. He pushed Marco's shoulder. "He's dead." The man cast an evil grin at Cora, or perhaps his aim was Bradley. "That'll make our job easier."

He ambled toward Cora and Bradley. "I know you. You're the chick we were supposed to nab. The sister." His small eyes narrowed further. "You made us look like we don't know what we're doing."

"She didn't do anything." Bradley protectively put his hand on Cora's shoulder. Warmth seeped through her jacket and into her heart, calming its rapid beating. He cared. "It was the DEA agent and the other woman. They're here now, out by the clearing. Why don't you go bother them?"

Oh, Bradley. The hope that had just flickered to life started to dim. Was he trying to put Kent and Amalia in danger to save Cora and himself?

"The other boys got that covered. We came for Ramos and the merchandise." The man made a gun shape with his hand and pretended to drop the hammer, aiming at Marco. "One down, one to go."

Jana sat in front of Cora, giving up on meeting the new arrivals. Perhaps she'd sensed they weren't friendly.

"Where's the stuff?" The man's intimidating glare seemed to aim past Cora at Bradley.

"We loaded them in the cargo hold. In a secret compartment."

"Javier, check it out."

The young man behind the long-haired leader peeled off and jogged back to the door where he disappeared outside.

"Better hope he finds them. Or we might have to have some fun." The man grinned at Cora, revealing a silver-capped tooth at the front of his mouth.

"You don't need to touch her." Bradley's hand gripped her shoulder more tightly. "Guajardo didn't tell you to do that."

"I can make decisions on my own, Brad boy. You get in my way, and I'll take you along with me. Or just finish you here."

"You wouldn't dare. Big Ben just got me back. You know that."

The man stared at Bradley. He smacked his lips, then lifted one bulky shoulder. "I could say you died in the crash like Ramos. Big Ben would never know the difference."

Please, Father, no. Don't let them hurt Bradley.

Shots from the firefight carried to Cora's ears.

"Our boys are having fun out there." His sadistic smile made her knotted stomach twist. "Won't be much longer and they'll finish your friends. The fed shoulda brought more backup than a woman."

Oh, how they underestimated Amalia and Kent. Cora hoped, prayed, that would give them the advantage over the cartel. And, perhaps, Phoenix would come in time to help.

A thump hit the plane just before the younger man who'd been sent to find the drugs popped into the aisle and dashed to his leader. "They aren't there."

"What?" The leader's voice deepened, hardening. "Are you sure?"

"Yeah." The young man, Javier, tried to catch his breath in cloudy puffs of air. "I found the hidden compartment, but it was open, and there's nothing in there. Nothing."

"Bad move, Brad." The third man, standing behind the leader, stepped out of the aisle and leaned his arm on one of the seatbacks Kent had cut up for window coverings. A mustache—shorter and less bushy than Marco's—covered his lip and a sinister gleam marked his dark eyes. "We wouldn't want to have to tell Big Ben you tried going into business for yourself."

"I didn't. I swear, I don't know where they are." Bradley's voice trembled but was no less emphatic. "The fed was messing around back there, looking for the drugs. He must have taken them somewhere."

Jana whined, likely stressed by all the tension. Cora put her mittened hand on the golden's head.

"That's a drug-sniffing dog, isn't it?" The long-haired man looked at Jana.

Cora paused. Should she answer? They likely already knew and refusing to cooperate wouldn't help their mood. "Yes."

"Did you find the drugs with the dog?"

She kept silent, not liking where he was going with his line of questioning.

"You did." He stepped closer to her.

Bradley's fingers nearly bit into her shoulder and probably would have if not for her down-filled jacket.

"Where are they now?"

She forced herself to meet the man's gaze, trying to mask the fear tensing every muscle and nerve in her body. "We found them, but I don't know where they ended up after that. I didn't move them."

The man pressed closer still, stopping only a bit more than a foot from her, thanks to Jana filling the space in front of Cora's legs. "You're lying."

"My sister never lies." Bradley's tone was stronger, as if he was fighting for courage, too.

The leader stared at him, then shifted his hard gaze back to Cora. "Okay. Then you can help us find them now. You and your dog are coming with us." The man grabbed her arm.

Panic gripped her tighter than his big paw. "No, please."

"Let her go!" Bradley's shout stung her ear but shot to her heart like a cry of hope. Her Bradley, fighting for her. "I won't let you take her!" He shoved her to the side, her arm still caught in the man's vise-like grip.

Bradley lunged at her attacker, reaching with his unbroken

arm. He yanked and pulled with enough force that the man let go.

She fell to the side, onto the seat as Bradley swung his fist at the bigger man.

A pop exploded, piercing her ears.

Her gaze jerked to the mustached man, to the gun in his hand, aimed at…Bradley?

She swung her head to see her brother, stark horror framing his open mouth and exposing the whites of his eyes as he slowly looked down at his right arm.

Bradley was shot.

THIRTY-FIVE

Kent had thought he might've imagined it—the glimpse of someone darting past trees by the airplane. Didn't even know that he could see the jet from the south side of the clearing. But he'd told Pérez he had to check it out. She'd given him a "Go" and continued firing at the cartel onslaught. She and Kent had taken out three of them before he left, but at least three more returned fire.

Kent had slowed his jog as he neared the plane.

New tracks ran along the aircraft from the cargo hold. Men's shoes. But not Kent's.

His pulse had hammered in double-time.

Then the shot cracked the air.

From inside the plane.

Kent crouched, moving as quietly as he could on the snow that crunched softly beneath his shoes.

Every fiber of his being screamed at him to enter the jet as quickly as he could.

Cora could be shot, bleeding out.

But he fought the instinct with all the strength he had. He couldn't help her if he got killed.

He hefted himself onto the steps of the cabin entry point. Slowly climbed them. Stopped to listen at the top.

"Bradley!" Cora's anguished cry stabbed like a knife into Kent's chest.

"Come on. You're coming with us."

"No!"

Forget waiting. He couldn't let her be hurt or frightened another second. He swung into the aircraft, aimed his weapon down the aisle.

Three cartel perps stared back at him. The young guy closest to Kent dropped his weapon. But the next one aimed a Colt .45 at Kent.

To his side and slightly behind him stood a big man, the thug from the ambush. Juan Martinez, according to the database results Kent had found when he'd searched for Cora's attackers from the street ambush. Had a warrant out for him, but he'd evaded being spotted again. Until now.

Martinez held Cora by the arm. He yanked her in front of him, making Cora bump into Jana so hard the dog had to catch herself and dart out of the way by one of the seats.

Kent's jaw clenched as he aimed his weapon. "That's enough of that."

"Got a soft spot for the lady, fed?"

"Not at all." Kent kept his voice steady and cool. "But the DEA frowns on agents allowing losers like you to take hostages."

"I bet." The man's sneer made Kent's finger itch to pull the trigger. But he couldn't without risking Cora.

"I'm taking this one and her dog. Unless you want to tell me where you stashed our merchandise."

"Oh, you mean my merchandise." Kent responded with a smirk of his own. "I figured you'd come for it, so I hid it where you'll never find it."

"This chick's dog can."

"Please." Cora tried to twist out of Martinez's hold as she glanced at his face. "Let me stay with my brother." Her voice was calmer, stronger than Kent had expected. That boldness that showed up at surprising moments. "He needs help."

And Cora needed to avoid drawing attention to herself. Kent

had to keep the thug's focus on him. "You always do things the hard way, don't you, Martinez?"

His thick eyebrows drew together. Good. Caught him off guard.

"Yeah, I know your name. And we have a warrant for your arrest for attempted kidnapping and assault. We might be able to tack on attempted murder, too."

"You'd have to catch me first, Fed."

"I'm looking at you right now, and I like the view." Kent lifted his Glock higher in front of his face, emphasizing his point.

"I like where I stand, too." The man's sneer returned as he pulled Cora closer to him.

Kent's skin crawled.

Terror filled Cora's eyes as she wildly looked his way. He had to get the thug away from her. Now.

Only one way he could do that for sure.

Kent kept his weapon up to avoid being instantly shot while he threw himself to the dogs. "You want to do things the easy way, for once? Take me instead."

Martinez snorted, much like the pig he was. "You think I'm stupid?"

Definitely. But Kent ignored the obvious. "Look, I'm the only one who knows where the drugs are stashed, and I'm offering to take you to them."

Martinez stared at Kent for a beat. "Why?"

A moan came from behind the man. Bradley's head rolled against the back of the sofa, just beyond the bulky frame of Martinez. Bradley must be the one who'd been shot.

Kent returned his focus to Martinez. "I told you. The DEA doesn't like hostages on our record."

"Then tell us where you put the merchandise."

"You'd never find it on your own."

"I could just shoot her right now." Martinez lifted his gun and pointed it at Cora's head.

Kent didn't blink. "Then you'd get nothing, plus give me the freedom to blow your head off."

Martinez looked at his armed partner. The guy with the short mustache gave a nod.

"Okay. Always wanted to have a fed to myself."

"Kent, don't." Pleading filled Cora's blue eyes, but not for herself. "Let them take me. You could help Bradley."

His heart swelled in his chest until he thought it might break a rib. He had to look away before too much emotion showed on his face. Before these thugs knew he loved her. He hadn't known it himself until just now. All the more reason to hide how he felt and keep her safe. "It's my job, ma'am." He hoped the platonic statement would eliminate any suspicions on their part.

"Okay, Martinez. I'm going to lower my weapon at the same time you let her go." Kent moved his finger off the trigger. Martinez could go for a double-cross, but he had to take the risk. Had to get Cora away from these thugs.

"Now." Kent lowered his weapon, and Martinez released his grip on Cora's arm.

She stepped to the side, squeezed against the seat by Jana to get away from the man.

"What about your partner outside?" The mustached guy kept his Colt trained on Kent, his voice rough and broken like a chain smoker.

"Yeah, I haven't heard any shots for a while." Martinez narrowed his eyes at Kent as if spying a trick.

"Your boys must have gotten her."

"It's that chick from last time, isn't it? She could be waiting to ambush us outside."

Pérez had sure managed to incite fear in Martinez thanks to her performance in the street attack. And he was probably right. She had mentioned while they were returning fire that she was thinking about getting closer to the cartel shooters and taking them out, one by one, to be done with it. She'd said it with the confidence of someone who believed she could do just that. If she'd succeeded, that would account for the silence. And she would likely be waiting near the plane by now.

"Doesn't matter." The mustached guy held his weapon on

Kent with a gaze that was too assured for Kent's taste. "We're still taking the girl and the dog anyway."

"What happened to our deal, Martinez?" Kent sent him a stare intended to intimidate.

"We can't trust you to show us where the drugs are." Mustached man answered before Martinez could speak. "We need her dog. And your partner won't shoot if we have a civilian hostage."

Kent laughed. "You're kidding. You clearly haven't seen her in action. Tell him, Martinez." He looked at the long-haired thug. "You think she'd have trouble picking you and your boys off without hitting a hostage?" Kent had no idea if Pérez could really do that. There were too many variables, and someone— Cora—could get hurt. But he kept his doubts off his face and waited for the bluff to work.

A glimmer of fear showed in Martinez's eyes as they shifted to his buddy. "He's right."

"Tell you what, boys. I don't like messes, so I'm going to make you one final offer." Kent kept his tone casual. "I'll tell my partner to stand down if you take me, and only me, off this plane. You try to bring anyone else along, the deal's off. And you're all fair game as soon as you leave the aircraft."

The two leaders of this train wreck exchanged glances.

"We can come back if you don't take us to the drugs." The mustached man delivered the threat to Kent.

Martinez found his favorite sneer again. "Yeah. Your lady friend here ain't going nowhere. And we'll make sure you remember that if you get forgetful about our merchandise."

"Fair enough. Let's get this over with." Kent angled toward the front of the jet, trying to hurry them along.

"Hold it." Martinez looked at him. "Got any cuffs?"

Of course. They'd want to secure him somehow. "Used them already. How about a zip tie?"

"Perfect." A silver tooth cap flashed as the man grinned.

Kent pulled the zip tie from his coat pocket and held it out to the approaching thug. Kent immediately put his hands in front of his body and pressed his wrists tightly together.

Martinez expression was positively gleeful as he wrapped the tie around Kent's wrists and cinched it tight enough to hurt.

Behind him, at the back of the jet, Cora bent over Bradley on the sofa. Had she forgotten about Kent already?

"Can we go now?" Kent let exasperation fill his tone as he headed for the cabin door.

"Wait." The mustached man's raspy voice halted them again. "Javier," he pointed to the young guy who looked like he wanted to stay behind, "you go first." The older man gestured to Kent with a dip of his gun. "Call out to your partner. Tell her to stand down, or we'll come back in and shoot the girl."

Kent stepped up to the cabin doorway. Silence, white starkness, met him.

Was Pérez out there?

"Hey, Pérez." He shouted into the emptiness. "I'm coming out with three men. They've agreed to take me instead of Cora and Jana if I show them where I stashed the drugs. The deal is, you stand down and let us go by."

"Or we'll come back and kill the girl." Martinez dug the barrel of his gun into Kent's ribs.

"Or they say they'll come back in and kill the civilians." Would Pérez listen to him? With her skills, she very well might be able to take out the thugs without hitting Kent, but Cora could get hurt in the resulting shootout. Neither of them wanted that. Pérez had said her boss would kill her if she let anything happen to Cora. And he'd gotten the feeling she wasn't exaggerating by very much. He needed to be sure she got the message. "This is for real, Pérez. Don't risk Cora or her brother. He's been shot, and he needs help."

He glanced back at Martinez. "All right. She'll stand down." He hoped.

"Javier." Martinez muttered to the young guy. "Go."

The kid stiffly walked down the stairs, his head on a swivel as he looked for the person who could kill him.

"See anything?" Martinez clapped his big hand on Kent's shoulder from behind.

"No." Javier whispered his response.

"Move it." Martinez gave Kent a shove, and they started down the steps.

They reached the end of the stairs without a shot fired or the slightest sound from anywhere.

They dropped to the ground, Martinez and the mustached guy taking turns to make sure Kent was covered with a weapon at all times.

Kent scanned the area around the aircraft, his ears straining for a sign Pérez was there. He couldn't hear or see a thing that hinted at her or her dog's presence.

But he knew she was there. Or soon would be.

The only sound that followed him as they walked away was from Cora. A sob carried on the cold wind. Cora, crying over her brother. Not for Kent. Maybe she didn't care about him as much as he did for her.

It didn't matter. He'd still sacrifice himself for her any day. He just hoped a sacrifice wasn't what this stunt turned out to be.

The extra Glock he'd put in his waistband rubbed against his back, hidden under his coat.

Once he was far enough away and sure Cora would be safe, he could use it.

If he didn't get killed first.

THIRTY-SIX

"Bradley? Please talk to me." She drew her gaze from the blood oozing down his arm to check his face. His skin was ashen, his eyes closed as his head rested against the sofa back. But he was breathing. His chest moved up and down.

She had to stop the blood. She'd never seen so much. Had the bullet hit an artery?

Panic welled up, surging into her throat and threatening to cut off her oxygen. She could lose Bradley.

She had to keep calm and think. *Stop the bleeding.* She had to stop him from bleeding to death.

Swallowing the cry of fear that tried to escape, she swung away from Bradley. She dashed to her suitcase, behind the seat where Marco still lay. Dead. Would Bradley be next?

No. She shook her head hard, the movement helping to force her brain out of its panicked spiral. *Father, I know you can save him. Please, show me what to do.*

She yanked her suitcase zipper open and flipped the lid back. She fingered the scraps of the thin cotton pajama shirt she'd used for Bradley's sling. She probably needed something thicker and bigger to stop the bleeding. But she was taking too long.

She grabbed the next thing her eyes caught on—her white wool sweater—and ran back to Bradley. She bunched the sweater in her hands and looked at the wound. She winced at the ghastly sight of the hole with blood streaming from it, covering her brother's arm. Would this hurt him? She gritted her teeth and pressed the sweater against the wound.

He groaned.

"I'm sorry." Her lips trembled as tears flooded her eyes. "I'm so sorry."

"Cora, are you okay?" Amalia. Her familiar voice reached through Cora's fear, quelling some of the panic.

"Amalia!" Cora turned her head toward her friend but kept constant pressure on the wound.

Amalia looked the same as ever, her dark waves a little stringier than normal below her black hat, likely wet from the snow. Thank the Lord, she didn't have any signs of injury. And Raksa, standing beside her, looked healthy, too.

"I'm so thankful you're all right. Praise the Lord."

Amalia grinned. "Don't know what He had to do with it, but thanks. Are you injured?"

"No." Cora looked at her brother. "But they shot Bradley."

"I see that."

"And they took Kent." Cora met Amalia's gaze again. "They thought you might be outside the plane waiting for them, but I guess you weren't."

"I was."

"Oh. Did you try to help him get away?"

"No."

That seemed unlike Amalia. She was definitely outnumbered by the cartel in this case, but Cora had never known that to stop her before.

"You're my primary objective here, Cora. Phoenix wanted me to protect you. I couldn't guarantee that if I helped Thomson, too."

Cora nodded. That was exactly what Phoenix would've wanted Amalia to do—prioritize Cora even though she didn't deserve such consideration. "I understand. Thank you." She looked at Bradley, wishing he would open his eyes. But guilt over Kent distracted her from really seeing her brother's face. "Do you think he'll be okay? Will they...?"

"He seems to be able to handle himself."

"Yes. Yes, he does." But thanks to Cora, Kent had made himself vulnerable this time. He'd let them tie him and take his gun. How could he triumph over them when he'd intentionally put himself at a disadvantage? He'd done that for her.

More tears watered her eyes, some trickling down her cheeks as she stared at the sweater beneath her hands, red staining the white wool. She never should have let Kent go in her place.

A murmur, like a muffled moan, yanked her gaze to her brother's face.

"Bradley?"

His eyelids lifted halfway, then fell back down.

Was he too weak from blood loss already?

"Amalia, what can we do? Do you know how to treat a bullet wound?"

"A tourniquet could help stop the bleeding."

"My shirt still has some strips left." Cora nodded toward her suitcase at the other end of the plane, not wanting to release pressure on the wound. "Or grab whatever you think will work."

"Bradley, honey, can you wake up?" It would be a good sign if he could, wouldn't it? Oh, why hadn't she studied more about emergency medicine?

His lids slowly pulled open, revealing those hazel eyes she knew so well. They searched for her, his gaze locking on her face.

"Oh, Bradley."

"What happened?" His voice was hoarse, a rough whisper.

"I'm so sorry, you were shot defending me. But you'll be okay. I know you will." *Father, please let it be so.*

Amalia returned with a sleeve she must have cut from one of Cora's long-sleeved shirts. She started to wrap it around Bradley's arm, just below the shoulder. She pushed him forward slightly to slip it behind his arm.

He yelped.

"It's okay, Bradley." Anguish squeezed Cora's heart, hurting as if she'd been shot, too. "Breathe, honey. Breathe, and we'll get through this."

"Easy for you to say." He expelled air with the words, which perhaps counted as following her instruction.

I had to do this because of you.

The memory of what Bradley had said when they'd boarded the plane came rushing at her like an accusing finger pointed at her soul. Part of her didn't want to know what he had meant. But another part felt she knew already. Didn't she already carry the guilt of the trouble her brother had gotten into? Perhaps he'd also realized his situation was due to her negligence, her mistakes.

Bradley yelled as Amalia finished tightening the tourniquet, twisting a pen she'd wrapped the cloth around.

Asking the question Cora needed answered would distract him from the pain. Though she had the feeling it would only add to her own pain. "Bradley, what did you mean when you said you had to do this because of me?"

His eyes were closed, and for a moment, she thought he'd lost consciousness again. "You won't believe me."

"Of course, I'll believe you. Haven't I always tried to believe you?" To a fault, Phoenix and Kent would say.

"I was clean, like I told you." He paused, his chest rose and fell as he took in air, seeming to gather his strength. "Wasn't going to work for them again. I was only going for a drive that night when I turned off your alarm system. But when I came back and saw the cops...I knew it had to be the cartel, looking for me."

"So you hid."

"I thought...they wouldn't find me."

She wished she could take his hand to comfort him, but she needed both hands as her arms grew weary from applying pressure.

"They found you instead."

"What do you mean?"

"They tried to kidnap you."

Her gaze jumped to Amalia, who didn't look surprised. "I'm going back outside to keep watch. Don't want to get ambushed in here. You can take the pressure off the wound now."

"Thank you." Cora watched Amalia and Raksa briskly exit the plane, then she slowly pulled the sweater away from the wound. Red smeared his arm, but far less blood than before dripped from the bullet hole. She watched it as she tried to make sense of what Bradley had said. "You knew about the ambush? The kidnapping attempt?"

"Heard about it through a buddy from the old days."

Probably the man Bradley had met with in Rem's photos.

"He wouldn't have fingered me to the cartel, but he told me about you. What they did." Bradley twisted his head toward Cora. "They were going to hurt you if I didn't come back. I had to do it to keep us both safe."

"Oh, Bradley." Cora sniffed, trying to hold back the emotion that threatened to choke her. "I'm so sorry. I didn't know." How could she have done this? How could she have put her brother in such a position that he thought he had to work for a drug cartel to keep her safe?

Everyone was getting hurt because of her—because they were trying to protect her. First Bradley and now Kent. If she'd been tougher and skilled like Phoenix wanted, she could've protected herself. No one was sacrificing themselves to protect Amalia. She didn't need that kind of help, and everyone knew it.

"Mom said something…" Bradley grimaced and sucked in a breath as if it was harder to draw than the ones before, "Told me something before she…"

"What, Bradley?" Cora's ribs squeezed inward until she thought they might crack. "What did she say?"

"She made me promise…to always love you." Bradley's eyes slid closed as his words pierced through her flesh into the depth of her soul.

Mom had asked Bradley to love Cora?

"You did it, Bradley. You did it." A sob hijacked her

response as she looked at her brother's pale face. His eyes stayed closed, as if they might never open again.

"Oh, Bradley. Please don't die. I'm sorry I didn't watch over you better. I'm so sorry." Another sob twisted her voice, quaking through her body.

The mistakes she'd made in their past, even not watching him closely enough to prevent his drug addiction, were nothing compared to this. She should have stopped him from returning to the cartel instead of giving him space. She should have mothered and pestered or whatever it took to be sure this didn't happen.

She'd again failed the promise she'd made to her mother to keep her brother safe and to raise him to follow Jesus. That was the worst mistake she was facing right now. Her brother could die without knowing Christ, without having eternal life and salvation.

The horror of that reality made her tremble as she sat back, tears streaming down her face and onto her neck.

The sweater lay in her hands, the once white wool now drenched with her brother's blood. "I'm so sorry."

———

A whirring, buzzing sound hovered overhead.

Kent looked up at the sky, trying to see through the snow-laden branches of massive pine trees that surrounded them.

Martinez shoved him in the shoulder from behind. "Keep moving."

"Hold it." The mustached guy Kent had learned was called Pearson barked the order, holding up his hand from the front of the cartel pack.

Javier was the weakest member, having fallen about fifteen feet behind Kent, Martinez, and Pearson. But he stopped at Pearson's signal anyway, probably glad to get a rest.

"Listen." Pearson looked up as the whirring grew louder.

Turned to more of a chopping roar as Kent glimpsed an object through the tree branches overhead. Had to be a helicopter sweeping past them. Close enough to land. Kent's gut clenched. More cartel?

"The road's just ahead." Pearson looked in that direction. Footprints through the snow, going the opposite way, told the tale of the cartel attackers having come from the road to the clearing. They must have thought to split up before they'd reached the clearing to have some men circle around the airstrip in case of resistance. Smarter than Kent had given them credit for.

Since they had arrived using the road, as Pérez had predicted, that meant they probably had transportation waiting for them there.

The helicopter appeared in bits through the trees as it lowered. Landing.

"Let's check it out." Martinez shoved Kent forward again.

"Careful. Don't shoot unless I say so." Pearson aimed the commands at Martinez as he and Kent passed the leader. Self-appointed, maybe, given the glare Martinez shot him.

"I shoot when I want to, Pearson."

Good. Division among the enemy was always helpful. And so was the information Martinez and Pearson had just given him—they didn't know who the helicopter was carrying. Could mean it was help instead of the cartel. But would it be anyone armed for a fight?

They trudged through the snow that deepened to reach Kent's knees the farther they went. So much for the dry socks he'd put on last night. His toes were starting to turn numb in the frigid snow that had easily penetrated his shoes. His fingers weren't doing much better. He'd taken his gloves off for optimum feel on the trigger during the shootout at the clearing. Never got them back on, which could be a problem if he had to stay outside for a long time yet.

"Hold it."

Martinez clamped his hand on Kent's shoulder to make him stop at Pearson's order. The big thug turned back toward the man who was about two inches shorter.

"Why should we all risk getting caught? Javier." Pearson beckoned the younger guy with his hand.

Javier closed the gap between them, puffing hard.

"Go up to the road and see who came in the helicopter. Don't get caught."

Javier's lips pressed together briefly, as if he wanted to protest. But he pushed forward instead, an obedient soldier for the cartel. Or lamb for the slaughter. Though, in this case, the worst that might happen to him was prison if the helicopter had brought the cavalry.

"Where's the merchandise?" Pearson took a few high steps through the snow to stop in front of Kent. "You said by the road."

"Closer yet." If he'd be able to find the drugs. He wasn't an outdoorsman, but he thought he'd be able to recognize the group of birch trees Pérez had told him about. She'd said the tallest mountain he'd be able to see would look like its right-hand side was sloping down to touch the top of the trees he was looking for. "That way. A little to the south."

"Then move." Pearson looked at Kent with a calm expression that belied the worry Kent was sure motivated him. "We better find it by the time Javier gets back or we might get tired of you."

Especially if the helicopter carried anyone Pearson didn't like. He and Martinez were definitely getting scared, judging from the pace they pushed him to take and the way they tried to keep thick pine trees between themselves and the direction they'd seen the helicopter landing.

Kent hoped their fear was warranted, and whoever had come on that helicopter would be able to help.

He kept the tall mountain in view through the trees as he scanned tree trunks to look for the telltale white of birches. He wouldn't see them until they got closer to the road, though.

Crunching sounded behind them.

Kent turned to look, not as quickly as he would've normally so he didn't startle Martinez into shooting him.

Javier ran up to them, panting double the speed as before.

He stopped in the deep snow in front of them, swaying as he bent to rest his hands on his knees.

"What?" Martinez's gruff tone advertised his impatience and nerves he couldn't hide.

"Four of them." Javier gasped for air. "They came..." He straightened, wincing. "They came pouring out of the copter. Like soldiers or something."

Martinez swore. "Who did?"

"I don't know."

Pearson added a curse of his own. "Never should've sent you." He let out a string of choice labels for Javier.

"There were dogs. A bunch of dogs with each person." Javier rested his reddened hands on his hips. "And they were women."

"Women?" Martinez's voice twisted with his features.

The Phoenix K-9 Agency. The news sparked heat into Kent's cold muscles. If they'd come, Cora would be safe even if the cartel somehow got away from him and returned to her.

"You know who they are?" Pearson watched Kent, his eyes narrowed.

Kent grinned. "Your worst nightmare."

"A bunch of women?" Martinez sneered.

"You know the woman who just took out six of your guys back there at the clearing?" Kent had taken out two himself before going to check on Cora, but the bigger numbers could help him sell the point. "These are her clones. You mess with them, you'll end up like the rest of your boys."

Pearson's jaw shifted as he stared at Kent. He switched his gaze to Javier. "They see you?"

"No way." Javier shook his head. "I dropped down into the snow behind a tree as soon as I saw them jumping out of the copter. I stayed buried until I was sure they were gone."

Martinez grunted. "I believe that."

"All right. We get the package and get out of here." Pearson pointed his finger at Kent. "No more stalling. Show us the merchandise, now."

"We have to get closer to the road."

"Then move."

Kent anticipated Martinez's shove this time and started forward before he took its full force in his already-bruised shoulder. A few more minutes of sludging through the snow brought them to the edge of the road—snow-covered except for a few spots where the sun had burned holes through to the dark gravel beneath.

"Where is it?" Martinez pulled out his gun.

"Let me go back a few feet."

"Sure. I can hit you that far away just as well." Martinez's mouth angled in an overdone sadistic grin he'd probably seen villains use in movies.

Kent walked farther into the trees again, down an incline, then turned around, trying to line up the edge of the mountain with the trees.

He lowered his gaze.

There. The white tree trunks would've disappeared into the snow if not for the black highlights spattering the bark. A cluster of birch trees, different than the pines and other trees he couldn't identify that lined the road as far as he could see.

He paused a moment. Should he give the cartel the drugs? If he didn't, they'd shoot him now. He couldn't evade them yet, not here with the zip ties still on his hands. If he did turn over the drugs, they'd shoot him for that, too. But he had a plan that could work. And if it did, it could buy him time and even a chance to get intel on the kingpin and the goal of this mission that otherwise seemed lost. That was worth a whole lot of risk.

"Over here, boys." He waited while the three jokers slid and waddled down the incline toward him. "See that pine tree in the center of the birches?"

"Birches?"

Wow. Martinez was even less nature savvy than Kent. "The white trees."

"Oh."

"Look under the branches at the bottom of that pine tree in the middle, and you'll find your drugs."

"Cover him." Martinez left Kent under Pearson's supervision and trudged to the big pine tree. "Javier." He waved the young guy over. "Find them."

Kent shook his head at the circus as Martinez pointed Javier to the ground. The thug-in-training dropped to the snow and reached under the bottom branches of the tree. And kept doing the same thing all the way around the base.

Here was hoping Pérez had told Kent the truth about where she'd hidden the drugs. Or he wouldn't live beyond the next few minutes.

"Got it!" Javier sat up, dragging the crate of drugs with him out of the snow.

"Finally. Any last words, Fed?" Pearson backed up a step, his pistol aimed at Kent's chest.

Whoa. That happened a little faster than he'd thought. Kent kept his features still and his voice calm. "Yeah, and I think you'll all want to hear them."

"What's he talking about?" Martinez lumbered back, Javier struggling behind him to carry the large crate.

"I'm talking about why you don't want to kill me. That helicopter just unloaded a bunch of DEA agents." They didn't know who Phoenix was, and he fully intended to use that to his advantage. "How long do you think it'll take them to find out from my partner at the jet that you took me with you to find the drugs?"

Martinez glanced at Pearson, his eyes giving away his concern.

"And how long do you think it'll take them to track you and catch up to you?"

"They won't be able to find us." Pearson met Kent's gaze. "They don't know where we went."

"They have dogs. I saw them." Javier contributed a surprisingly intelligent observation, just when Kent needed it.

"Exactly." Kent met Pearson's suspicion head-on, pushing the bluff. "They're expert trackers."

"Our ride is only like a mile from here up the road. They won't be able to track us then."

A good point. But Kent didn't flinch. "Haven't heard of the

new tracking dogs, have you? They can trail cars by the smell of the treads." He had no idea if that was possible, but all he had to do was sell this story.

"So you want us to let you go." A statement, not a question as Pearson returned Kent's stare. "I suppose you want us to believe you'll make the feds leave us alone."

"Come on, Pearson." Kent let his mouth relax with a hint of friendliness. "I know you're too smart for that. What I'm suggesting is you keep me with you, alive, for leverage."

"Leverage for what?" Martinez stepped closer, as if wanting in on their conversation.

"For when they do catch up with you. If you have me as your hostage, they won't come in shooting. They'll have to play ball to keep me alive." Kent shrugged, an awkward gesture with his hands bound in front of his body. "I can't make any guarantees, of course, but it's the only chance you've got."

"I say we kill him now so we don't have the dead weight." Ironic choice of words that Martinez probably hadn't intended.

"We'll bring him." Pearson looked at Martinez like he expected kickback.

"I don't want to have to keep—"

"We can always shoot him later."

Comforting. But at least Kent had bought himself more time. And maybe a chance at the kingpin. If he survived. At least if he didn't, he could die knowing Cora was safe.

THIRTY-SEVEN

She'd done everything she could. But her everything, her best, wasn't nearly good enough.

Cora sat on the seat opposite her brother, watching him die, and she couldn't save him. She couldn't even tell him more about Christ in his final moments, since he'd lost consciousness again. It was too late.

If her mother were here, her heart would be torn in two. She'd always encouraged Cora, praised her for doing well, for being talented, polite, and smart. She'd been a mother who heaped praise on her children. Cora hoped her mom couldn't see her from heaven right now, because she'd see none of that praise she'd given Cora had been deserved.

Cora tried so hard, especially after her mom died. She'd tried so hard to learn the best way to raise an adolescent boy. Tried to love Bradley as their mother had.

But she just couldn't get it right. She always made mistakes, even when she desperately didn't want to. And some of them were fatal.

A rustling sound at the front of the plane reached her ears. But she was too numb to look, to care even if it was the cartel returning. They couldn't hurt her more now.

Unless they had Kent, and he was still alive. The thought drew her gaze.

A woman and a tan dog marched down the aisle toward her. Phoenix and Dagian.

Cora thought hope would fill her, infuse her with warmth and strength or the peace she usually felt in Phoenix's presence, especially at times of danger.

But her body remained numb and cold.

Bradley was still dying because of her mistakes.

Phoenix stopped a few feet away.

Cora felt her gaze more than she saw it. She knew how she probably appeared to Phoenix—weak and helpless.

But that wasn't fair. Phoenix had never seemed to look down on her. She had only encouraged Cora to be better—stronger and more capable. If only Cora had managed to do that.

"Okay, what've we got?" Nevaeh's voice carried an energy and optimism that Cora couldn't imagine feeling ever again. Nevaeh must have walked around Phoenix somehow because her full head of black curls suddenly blocked Cora's view of Bradley.

"What—" The question caught in Cora's throat that she hadn't known was so dry. She coughed. "What are you doing?"

"Don't worry." Nevaeh tossed a bright smile over her shoulder at Cora. "I did a stint as an EMT."

She did? The fog clouding Cora's brain cleared enough for her to recall Nevaeh's file. Phoenix didn't let even Cora know all the details of the PK-9 members' pasts, but the items they documented in their files were cleared for Cora to see.

That was right, Nevaeh had worked as an EMT for a brief period after she'd worked as a corrections officer. Or was it before?

It didn't matter. The only thing that mattered was Bradley had a qualified professional to help him now.

New life breathed into Cora's body, and she pushed herself out of the chair. "Is there any hope?" She went to Nevaeh's side where she could see her brother, his eyes still closed and his face the color of death. "Is he..."

"He's not dead, if that's what you mean." Nevaeh let go of his wrist, where she must have been checking his pulse.

"But is he...dying?" The word sprang tears to Cora's eyes, already prickly and irritated from the flood of emotion before.

"Give me a sec. Nice job with the tourniquet, by the way." Nevaeh moved to his right shoulder and slowly leaned him forward, peering behind his arm.

"Amalia did that."

"Be better if she'd used bandages from the first aid kit instead of this shirt sleeve, but Mals isn't exactly a healing specialist. More into damage." Nevaeh sent Cora a smile, probably meant to distract. From bad news she was about to communicate?

"I think he'll be okay." She leaned him back against the seat and stepped in front of him.

"What?" Cora didn't dare hope she'd heard Nevaeh correctly.

Nevaeh bent to take his pulse again. "The bullet passed through, which is good. And you girls stopped the bleeding. When did you apply the tourniquet?"

"I'm not sure." Why hadn't she thought to look at the time? She'd been so concerned with stopping the bleeding, with hanging on to Bradley, she hadn't realized the time could be important. "Not long before you came, I think. Amalia might know."

Nevaeh nodded. "I'll ask her."

"There was so much blood." Cora looked at Nevaeh, confusion and disbelief not allowing her to believe her friend's diagnosis. "I thought the bullet had hit an artery."

"Nah, doesn't look like it. The blood would be a different color, and there'd be more of it."

"Why is he unconscious?"

"Could've passed out from the pain. He looks a little shocky, but his vitals are stable. I think you stopped the bleeding in time."

"Amalia did." All Cora had thought to do was press on the wound, and that hadn't helped him at all. He'd kept bleeding.

Thank the Lord Amalia had been there, or Bradley might be dead now.

"Do you really think he'll live?"

"Yeah. I've seen worse who made it. And the boss called in rescue services with a copter. They'll be able to airlift him out of here soon."

Cora shifted her gaze to Phoenix, who stood silently watching them. "Thank you."

Bradley was going to live. Could it be true? The tension twisting her stomach said she still didn't believe it. She couldn't embrace that wonderous outcome only to have it suddenly wrenched away if he took a bad turn.

Bris appeared with Toby at the front of the plane, walking toward Phoenix. "One of the cartel perps Amalia took down is still alive, but unconscious. Want Nevaeh to look at him?"

Phoenix glanced at the former EMT.

"Coming." Nevaeh pressed her fingers against Bradley's neck and looked at her watch.

Phoenix had her back to them as she stepped close to Bris, who leaned in as if to hear something Phoenix was saying too quietly for Cora to hear. Even if she'd had the energy or curiosity to try.

"Don't worry about your brother." Nevaeh paused in front of Cora. "He's gonna be fine. His body is fatigued from all the trauma, but I expect him to wake up soon. You take care of you now. I'll be right back to check on you both."

"Thank you." The numbness that had overtaken Cora's body seemed to make it impossible to feel anything.

Except the gentle, warm pressure of a hand on Cora's where it lay in her lap.

Bris's lovely face appeared in Cora's vision as she squatted down in front of the seat. "Cora, I am *so* thankful you're all right. I've been praying for you nonstop since your plane went down."

Cora put her other hand on top of Bris's and squeezed. "Thank you. I knew you would be. That means so much."

"Are you okay?"

Cora nodded, her gaze drifting to Bradley beyond Bris's shoulder. He still looked pale and weak. What if Amalia hadn't thought to put a tourniquet on his arm in time? Cora should have known to do that right away herself. Why hadn't she thought of it? Could that have spared him the complications that might await as he recovered? If he recovered at all?

"Cora."

She heard Bris speak but couldn't pull her gaze from her brother. She could still lose him. He might have serious complications from the blood loss, the injuries, the trauma.

"Cora, stop." The firmness in Bris's tone snapped Cora's gaze to the gray-blue eyes that stared at her. "You need to stop. You cannot carry the burden of everyone and everything that goes wrong on your own shoulders."

"I'm...not. I'm only recognizing the mistakes I've made. Things I could have done better."

"Are you sure that's all?"

Cora looked at her friend. "Yes. What else would it be?"

"I'm sorry to say this, but it looks an awful lot like you're trying to play God."

Cora drew back as if Bris had slapped her. "I'm not trying to play God." The thought was horrifying. She would never presume to do that.

"Cora, you're taking the blame for everything that happens as if just by doing something differently, you could have changed the outcome."

Cora swallowed, tasting the bitterness of the truth that Bris threw at her.

"You can't control the outcomes. You know that. God is in full control of what happens, always."

"But I make mistakes that keep hurting everyone I care about."

Bris leaned back, sitting in the aisle as Toby pushed his snout past her shoulder. She put her hand on his head without looking away from Cora. "Let me ask you this, are any of those mistakes you're talking about sins?"

"I promised my mother I'd take care of Bradley, that I'd keep him safe and raise him to love and serve God." Tears pricked Cora's aching eyes. How could she have any more tears left to shed?

"Oh, Cora. I'm so sorry." Bris's brow furrowed beneath the blue winter hat that covered the top of her mahogany-high-lighted hair. "That's a tremendous burden to carry."

"It's not a burden. I wanted to do it. For her and for Bradley. But I didn't pay enough attention when he started to change and withdraw. I kept wanting to believe everything was fine and that nothing serious was going on. I never thought of drugs until I found them in his room when I was cleaning. By then, it was too late."

"But Cora, it's never too late."

That's what Cora had told herself for so long. "Maybe if someone else was his sister. If someone else could have helped him."

"Someone else can help him." Bris leaned her head forward as if to emphasize her words.

Cora paused, Bris's point sinking in.

"Leave it to God, Cora. Don't pretend you could have changed the way things went with Bradley. This is God's plan. He planned on your mistake, if that's what you want to call it, and is using that for exactly what He wants. For something good."

Redemption.

A shock of light shattered the numbness as understanding broke through. Why hadn't Cora seen it before?

He redeems all of the bad things we've ever done, all of our mistakes.

The truth she'd shared with Marco, her own words, came rushing back as if carried on a long-lost echo. Christ redeemed not only sins, but the other mistakes, too. Like not monitoring her brother closely enough, not learning more medical emer-gency skills, or not saying the right things to bring her brother to Jesus.

"My grace is sufficient for you…" Bris began the passage from 2 Corinthians that Cora also knew by memory.

"...for my power is made perfect in weakness," Cora finished with her sister in Christ.

Bris smiled. "I've been memorizing those verses. Do you remember what comes after that?"

"Therefore I will boast all the more gladly of my weaknesses, so that the power of Christ may rest upon me." Boast of her weaknesses. Had she ever done that?

"Our imperfections are nothing to be ashamed of, Cora. They just mean we need Christ even more, and He'll get full credit for everything we do."

How had Cora not understood that truth before? But, no—she wouldn't keep lamenting her mistakes. Bris was right about something else, too. She'd been playing God in more ways than one, without consciously meaning to do so. She'd started believing she had to free Bradley from the cartel, or he'd never be able to come to Christ. But that was so far from the truth.

The cartel hadn't prevented Bradley from believing in Jesus and neither had Cora, even with all her mistakes. Only God could bring Bradley to Himself. It was up to God, not Cora, to save Bradley, physically and spiritually.

Cora pressed her hands to her cheeks as stunning clarity opened her eyes to see her soul. She'd put so much weight on her lack of perfection that she'd fallen into thinking she had the power of God without realizing that's what she was doing. But her biggest mistake of all—believing she could somehow be perfect—showed how far she would ever be from perfection in this life. And that was wonderful news. Because it meant she wasn't responsible for what happened to Bradley and everyone else she cared about.

"Only God is perfect." Cora voiced the comforting, freeing truth that unshackled her from years of guilt.

"Exactly." Bris nodded. "We can't be perfect in this life, no matter how hard we try. And, believe me, I've tried."

Laughter, from a well Cora thought would never produce joy again, bubbled up and out. She leaned forward and gave Bris a hug. "Thank you, my friend. He is redeeming my imperfections. I never saw it until now."

She pulled back, taking in Bris's understanding smile. "You know, it's funny because that's the same passage I shared part of with Kent last—" She gasped. "Kent. They took him."

Bris's smile faded as she stood. "Amalia told us."

"We need to find him and free him before…"

"Don't think the worst. From what you've said about him, he's smart and skilled. He might be fine."

"I know, but he went in my place. He sacrificed himself for me. I shouldn't have let him."

"Hey." Bris lifted her finger to point at Cora with a gentle smile. "No more of that."

"You're right."

"Why don't you go outside and talk to Phoenix? I think she was planning to go after your agent once we were sure you and Bradley were okay."

"He's not my agent." Heat flushed Cora's cold cheeks.

"But you want to go after him anyway."

Cora looked at Bradley, his eyes still closed. "I don't know that I can leave Bradley."

"I'll watch him until Nevaeh comes back in. I'm guessing Phoenix will want her to stay with Bradley and the other injured cartel perp."

"Thank you." Cora put her hand on Bradley's forehead, his skin warmer than she'd expected. *Father, if it's Your will, please heal him and bring him to know you.*

She took a deep breath, called Jana to her side, and for the first time, left Bradley completely in God's perfect care.

THIRTY-EIGHT

Kent squinted as he dropped from the SUV to the unplowed snow of the driveway that reflected bright sun into his eyes.

He peered ahead.

A small cabin sat in the middle of snowdrifts, framed with pine trees in a setting out of an idyllic painting. Not a hideout for a drug cartel.

But that's apparently what it was today.

"Move it." Martinez assumed his role as cattle herder and shoved Kent toward the cabin.

He followed behind Pearson, Javier bringing up the rear with the narcotics. The fifteen-minute drive here had helped him bond with his captors to the point where they'd stopped threatening to kill him every five minutes.

An indoor captivity would be good. He'd avoid freezing, and he'd have more options for weapons. Maybe they'd finally let him out of their sight, too, and he could gain the element of surprise by doing what they didn't know he could—break out of the zip tie.

Movement by the cabin drew his gaze. A guy in dark clothing and holding an AR-15 rounded the corner to the front. He'd worn a path in the snow along the cabin walls, probably patrolling as a lookout.

How many more were inside? Looked like Kent was about to find out.

Pearson knocked at the door while the guard gave Kent his best intimidating stare. Real cute.

The wooden door swung inward, and a man stood to the side as he held it open.

Big Ben Greer. With average height and build, there was nothing big about him other than his reputation. He was one of the high-level dealers in Minneapolis who had occasional personal contact with the kingpin. This was getting more interesting by the second.

"Why'd you bring him here?" A kid's whiney tone hit Kent's ears, recognition a second behind.

He knew that voice. He jerked to look at the tall guy who approached.

Hayden Simpson.

The kid stomped over to Pearson. "You were supposed to kill him, not bring him to our hideout."

"Hideout?" Annoyance crossed Pearson's features. "It's your dad's cabin. And nobody tells me what to do."

Pearson wasn't half as irritated as Kent. "You were supposed to be at home, Hayden, keeping your nose clean."

"Oh, yeah." Hayden's mouth angled in one of his familiar sneers. "So I wouldn't lose my football scholarship, right?"

Kent fought to keep surprise from showing on his face. Had the kid faked caving in to Cora in the interview? Had he played her? Played Kent? No way.

"You and that chick were so easy to fool. Who cares about football when I can make millions this way." Hayden stepped toe-to-toe with Kent, so much closer than he'd dare if Kent's hands weren't tied. "Thanks to you, I'm making a name for myself. Guajardo might make me one of the regional managers to replace whoever he picks for the top when he hears what I organized here."

Kent gritted his teeth, fighting to keep from slugging the grin off the punk's face, hands tied or not. Better to keep the kid talking. Kent would need that info when he arrested him. "And just what is that?"

Hayden laughed and spun away, stretching his hands out at his sides. "All of this. I saw you get on the flight I'd gone to so much effort to set up. My clueless father doesn't care what I do with his planes or his pilots." He planted his hands on his jeans-clad hips. "But you tried to mess it up. So I had a chat with Tim, that's your pilot, and told him to emergency land out here."

This little brat was responsible for the landing, the crash, and everything? Kent leveled his breathing, trying to hold back his anger a little longer. "How'd you know about this location?"

"We used to take hunting trips here. Can you believe it? But now I guess you're the prey."

"All right, this ain't a movie, kid." Pearson wore the exasperated look of an uncle who hated his nephew. "Cut the blabbing and show us a room where we can stash him."

"Why? Just shoot him."

"He's leverage if the DEA catches up with us before we get out of here."

Hayden looked at Big Ben.

"Couldn't hurt. For now."

"Fine." Hayden glared at Kent. "I'll get to tell Guajardo I captured the DEA agent who tried to trick him."

Hayden was in direct contact with the kingpin? Seemed unlikely. "What are you talking about?"

"I figured out what you were doing as soon as I saw you get on the jet. You were using Ramos to get to Guajardo. You flipped him."

"That's why you landed us here." Kent's blood boiled inside him, but he kept his voice even. "So you could get Ramos and the drugs for Guajardo." Smart plan for a kid who apparently wanted to climb up quickly through the ranks. "Only you failed to get Ramos." Would that jeopardize Hayden's bargain with the devil?

The kid shifted his attention to Pearson and Martinez. "You didn't get him?"

"He was already dead." Martinez rubbed his hand under his nose.

"You didn't shoot him, did you?"

"The crash killed him."

Hayden swore. "What about Brad and García? Did you bring them back with you?"

Martinez and Pearson exchanged a look. "Brad's dead. García died in the crash, too."

"You killed Brad?" Big Ben's eyes filled with intensity as he stared at Martinez.

"He did." Martinez pointed at Pearson.

Big Ben launched himself at Pearson, clutched the man's throat as he slammed him against the wall. "I said to bring him back, not kill him. He was special."

Pearson grabbed at Big Ben's hands. "He flipped." Pearson forced out the words in a raspy tone, panic in his widened eyes. "Tried to stop us. Had to shoot him."

"That true?" Big Ben shot his glare at Martinez.

"Yeah, man."

Big Ben released Pearson and whirled toward Hayden. "Show them where to lock him up and radio Alonso. We got the merchandise, took care of Ramos, and have the agent who thought he could capture Guajardo. Make it look good, and we'll be going to California."

"Hear that, Agent Thomson, sir?" Hayden emphasized the words like a taunt. "Wonder what your girlfriend will say when she hears she helped me make a name for myself in the cartel."

Man, Kent couldn't wait till he got free and could give this kid what was coming to him.

Hayden grinned. "Maybe I'll tell her myself after we get rid of you. I don't mind older women."

Kent's blood boiled over and exploded. He swung his hands upward, smashed them into Hayden's jaw.

The kid fell backward.

Something slammed into Kent's head. Sparks lit his vision. The cabin swung upside down. The lights went out.

———

What was happening to Kent? The frightening question was almost all Cora could think about as she tried to persuade Phoenix to let her join the SAR mission to find him.

"You're not in any shape to go." Phoenix folded her arms across her gray parka as she stood opposite Cora in the snow outside the tilted jet.

"I can see why you think that. I was just very emotional. But Bristol helped me through it." God had, really, but Cora wasn't sure if that would support or undermine her case in Phoenix's eyes. "I'm energized and focused now. And you can see Jana is ready."

Cora put her hand on the golden's head as Jana smiled up at Phoenix. Perfect timing.

Phoenix shifted her gaze from Jana back to Cora. "It's too risky. If we meet with the cartel, you'd be in danger again."

The subtext to Phoenix's statement was clear. She didn't want to put Cora in danger. Perhaps she regretted that Cora had been in jeopardy already. Did she blame herself? No, Phoenix didn't really do that, did she? Questions for another time when Kent's life wasn't hanging in the balance.

"I won't be because you're here now. And the whole team is here. I always have confidence in you." Cora smiled, a genuine expression of the security and safety she felt thanks to the PK-9 women taking charge of the situation. Though her pulse did jump about a little as she waited for Phoenix to break her thoughtful silence.

"All right."

"I can come?"

"Jana is a terrific SAR K-9. You'll both be an asset in finding Thomson more quickly." Nice of Phoenix to include Cora in her assessment.

Nevaeh and Amalia approached through the snow, Alvarez

and Raksa leading the way in front of their handlers. Nevaeh's rottweiler mix must have stayed with Amalia earlier when Nevaeh had treated Bradley on the plane.

Phoenix turned to face the K-9 teams as they approached.

Nevaeh shook her head in answer to the unspoken question. "Didn't make it."

Cora's heart fell for a moment. Another death. Thank the Lord that He'd placed Amalia and Kent here with her to defend against the cartel. But it was so tragic that men had lost their lives so pointlessly, all over drugs.

"Amalia, you and Bristol are coming along for the SAR. I've brought snowshoes for each of you. Jazz can show you where they are. She and Flash are patrolling the other side of the jet."

Amalia nodded and went to the nose of the plane, disappearing behind it.

Phoenix looked at Nevaeh. "You and Jazz will stay here to take care of Bradley and wait for the rescue team and DEA agents. Be on the alert for more cartel to show up in the meantime."

"DEA agents are coming?"

Phoenix nodded in answer to Cora's question. "I contacted them via the satellite phone I brought. They hadn't been able to locate you after your jet went off the radar. They're on their way by helicopter."

"Praise the Lord." But would the agents be too late to help Kent?

"Okay." Amalia and Raksa jogged to them, Amalia carrying multiple pairs of snowshoes. "Sunglasses and snowshoes. And Jazz is grabbing everyone's gear."

"You brought our SAR backpacks?" Cora smiled at Phoenix. "Thank you."

"Do you have something of Thomson's for Dagian?" The tan dog looked up at Cora with his striking blue eyes, as if seconding his handler's question.

"Oh." Had Kent left something behind they could use? Socks.

"Yes, he changed out of his wet socks and used another pair

he had in his duffle bag. He left the socks on the plane, I think. He might have other clothes in his bag, too. I can check."

"Nevaeh, duffel bag and Bristol." Phoenix thumbed toward the jet, and Nevaeh hurried to board with Alvarez and retrieve the clothes.

"It's the black one!" Cora called after Nevaeh's retreating figure.

Phoenix grabbed a pair of snowshoes from where Amalia had dropped them in the snow and handed them to Cora.

She hoped Nevaeh or Bris could find a piece of clothing so Dag would have a scent to home in on. He'd be able to track Kent through the snow while the other dogs air-scented for general human odor. Flash could track, too, but Cora appreciated Phoenix's decision to leave him and Jazz here. If the cartel did return for some reason, Bradley would need Jazz, Nevaeh, and their protection K-9s.

"I can take us to where I hid the drugs." Amalia straightened from securing her snowshoes, which Raksa bent to smell thoroughly. "That's likely where he took them first. Unless he decided not to let them have the drugs. In which case, they wouldn't keep him alive."

Cora's stomach clenched. She looked at Phoenix, wishing she could read her inscrutable expression to see if Phoenix thought Kent had been killed.

"But he's smart, Amalia." Bris walked up beside Cora and placed a reassuring hand on Cora's shoulder blades. "He'll know how to buy time." She gave Cora a small, encouraging smile, then grabbed a pair of snowshoes.

Yes, he was clever and skilled. He would be okay, wouldn't he?

Cora strapped her boots into the snowshoes. *Hang on, Kent. We're coming.*

She prayed they would be soon enough.

THIRTY-NINE

Kent opened his eyes. A ceiling made of dark brown logs hung above him. At least, he thought it was a ceiling.

Splitting pain seared his skull as he sat up, using his ab muscles since his hands were bound. The end of a bed with a quilt blocked his view to the left. To his right, a closed wooden door cut into the wall. Framed photos of deer and one garish mirror decorated the walls he could see.

The cartel thugs had apparently dumped him on the floor in this bedroom of the cabin after somebody had clunked him over the head.

At least indulging his desire to silence Hayden got Kent what he wanted. Isolation.

He leaned forward over his knees.

He swayed, a sudden bout of dizziness whirling the room. He closed his eyes, waited it out. Opened his eyes again. The room still swayed.

But he'd have to push through. No time to waste. Maybe he'd be better if he stood up.

He tried to pull one foot under him to stand, but something tugged on his ankle through his jeans.

Handcuffs. Binding his ankles together.

Terrific.

He brought his legs toward him, planting his feet flat on the floor.

Swinging his weight forward, he balanced his upper body over his feet in a squat. He stood.

Whoa.

The pictures on the wall shifted sideways, threatening his balance. He shut his eyes. Didn't help. He just swayed now instead of the room.

His stomach lurched. He could not get sick.

And he couldn't manage all the thugs in the next room if his head didn't stop spinning. He opened his eyes, found the bed. Needed to lie down. Just for a minute.

But with his lack of balance right now, he'd fall over if he tried to hop over there. The thugs could come in any second. Needed his hands free. He'd break out of the zip tie first, then deal with righting his head.

Wait. If his head hadn't been such a mess, he would've realized it earlier. His wrists weren't in front of him anymore. They were behind his back. In handcuffs, judging from the metal feel.

He looked behind his shoulder, a motion that made his vision spin all the more. But he stuck it out and stretched his arms away from his back so he could see. Handcuffs.

Terrific. There went his plan to snap the zip tie and take them by surprise.

Somebody out there was smarter than Martinez and Pearson. And had managed to get some cuffs.

His Glock.

He lifted his bound hands higher behind him, feeling for the weapon the first three goons had never noticed.

Gone.

Kent's legs weakened beneath him as the room tilted. *Keep it together.* He hopped forward. If he went fast enough, maybe he wouldn't fall. The room shook, pounding his head with each jump, but he was almost there.

His body tilted this time. He swung his shoulder toward the bed, fell onto the patchwork quilt that covered the mattress.

He willed his stomach not to empty its contents as he lay on his side, eyes shut. He breathed hard, just from hopping to a bed. Pathetic.

Just like this situation. He was handicapped by a head injury, cuffed, and weaponless with at least six cartel members ready to kill him at the slightest provocation.

And one of them was Hayden Simpson.

The first mistake Kent had ever made as a DEA agent.

How could he have let him out of jail? If he'd been behind bars where he belonged, none of this would've happened. Kent would be on his way to nailing the kingpin of the cartel right now. Cora would be safe and happy because her brother wouldn't be dying on a jet in the middle of frozen nowhere.

What had Kent been thinking? All his life, he'd worked and planned for the moment when he'd defeat the cartel that stole his parents and his childhood.

Now his plan had exploded in his face.

Because he'd become like his parents.

The stark truth smashed into him like someone had slammed that mirror over his head, shattering the glass into a million pieces. He'd become his dad.

He'd let Hayden go, took it easy on him, given him another chance. Exactly like his dad with his cousin. Kent's jaw clenched as he ticked off the evidence that convicted him.

But Kent knew better. Should've known better. Why had he fallen for Hayden's act the way his dad had fallen for Charlie's? It was so unlike Kent to take pity on anybody.

Cora.

Her name didn't make him want to smile this time. She was the reason he'd gone easy on Hayden. The only reason. She'd asked him to, and he hadn't been able to tell her no.

She'd made him soft, convinced him to show the leniency he knew had no place in his business. Or in his life.

How could she have undone a lifetime of Vince's guardianship and training so quickly? How could Kent have let her do that? Vince wasn't the only one who knew being nice meant being vulnerable. He had only emphasized and reminded Kent of what he'd known already, from the moment the cops had shown up at their door and told them their dad had been murdered.

He'd known it when his mother broke down and killed herself.

Weakness like theirs led to death and pain. The same kind of weakness Cora had.

And the same Kent had now, thanks to her.

He never should have let her in. Never should've started to dream and to care for a woman like her.

He wouldn't be in this mess now if not for her. Not only because of Hayden, either.

But Kent just had to volunteer to go in her place. Because he couldn't take watching her get hurt, couldn't let her die. He couldn't have handled that.

Which made him like his mom, too. Easily broken, cut down because he'd let himself love.

Yeah, he loved Cora. The stupid ache in his chest told him he still did, even now when he knew that love had reduced him to this.

Cora had become his greatest weakness—the weakness he promised himself he would never have. Her influence on him allowed Hayden to accomplish what looked like it would be the end of Kent and victory for the cartel.

But he could've salvaged things at the jet when the cartel showed up. Arrested them and made them lead him here or to the kingpin with all the aces in his hand.

Instead, he'd had to save Cora. Because he would've been destroyed if he hadn't gotten her out of danger. And now he was about to be destroyed because he had.

Good thing Vince couldn't see him now, following in their dad's footsteps. Right to the grave.

***

Cora thanked the Lord for the sunglasses and snowshoes Phoenix had brought. Walking on top of the deep snow on the trek to the road was so much easier and faster with snowshoes, and she didn't have to risk snow blindness from the sun's bright reflection.

Jana still sunk into the snow with only booties on her feet, but her energy had increased the moment she sensed they were going on a SAR mission, and she had no problem bounding through the drifts. Search and Rescue was Jana's favorite task since it carried a double reward—finding humans and getting treats.

Phoenix stopped when they crested the road, and Cora, Bris, and Amalia grouped around her. A momentary break for their dogs, though all the K-9s looked ready for much more.

"Dag's trail stops here." Phoenix glanced at Dagian, who stared sharply at something in the distance as he stood by her side.

Dag had been able to track Kent's scent through the snow so far, while Toby, Raksa, and Jana searched for airborne human scent.

"Tracks and tire treads indicate they put him in a vehicle. Probably an SUV or the car also parked here."

"This is where I hid the drugs, right over there." Amalia pointed toward a stand of birch trees. "They probably loaded up and left after Thomson led them here. I wonder if they kept him alive."

Cora's stomach twisted. *Please, Father, let Kent still be alive.*

"No signs of violence." Bris looked at Cora with sympathy in her eyes. "He probably talked them into keeping him as a hostage. That's what I'd do."

"It's not too late for you to go back." Phoenix directed her statement at Cora.

She must look terrible. She was exhausted, physically and emotionally from the past several days. But her greater understanding of God's promise to redeem even her mistakes emboldened her like never before. God wouldn't let her mess this up, even if she was weak where the other team members were strong. She wasn't a liability. She was a vehicle for showing how amazing God was and how He could use the weakest vessels for His plan.

"I'm doing well, Phoenix. Really." Cora smiled at her caring mentor. "Kent went with them for my sake, to save me. I need to try to help him now."

Phoenix stared at Cora a few more seconds. Then she nodded. "The satellite view of this area wasn't recent, but it showed three cabins within sixty miles of here. Two are closer, fifteen or twenty minutes away by car." Her gaze moved past the women toward the trees on the opposite side of the road. "The road curves. Not a direct route. We'll shorten the distance if we cut across instead."

"If they're using a cabin at all." Amalia made the statement as her gaze followed Phoenix's across the road.

"True. Why would they stop?" Bris petted Toby's head with her gloved hand as she looked at Phoenix.

"Intel from my sources says someone's trying to move up in the cartel by sabotaging Thomson's operation." Phoenix glanced at Cora. "From Amalia's description, that person didn't come to the jet with the others. He'd be waiting somewhere close. Somewhere with a radio."

"Makes sense." Amalia shifted her weight on her snowshoes, apparently as eager to get moving again as Raksa, who entertained himself with smelling the ground. "How are we dividing up? He could be anywhere along the way, too."

Dead or injured, Amalia probably meant. Cora usually appreciated Amalia's pragmatic realism, but every suggestion Kent was dead stung like a dart tossed at her hope.

"Grids. Three of them." Phoenix's answer to Amalia's question drew Cora back from her worry tangent.

They usually divided the search area into grids when doing SAR as a group, but why only three? She looked at Phoenix. "Why not four?"

"You'll come with me."

Cora held back the objection she wanted to voice. Phoenix was only trying to keep her safe. And she would be much safer with Phoenix. But Kent's life could depend on a more thorough, faster search. They needed all four of them to split up.

She took a breath and aimed for a firm tone. "We need to

divide it up four ways. We'll be more likely to find him or the correct cabin faster." She met Phoenix's unreadable gaze. "I can do this, Phoenix. You know I can, don't you?"

A flicker of something sparked for a split second in Phoenix's dark blue eyes. But she still didn't speak.

"Please, Phoenix." Cora let her voice return to its normal softness, even if that made her sound weaker. It was real. And real emotion was probably all that would make Phoenix change her mind and risk Cora's safety right now. "I can't bear to think of failing to find Kent in time. He's…special. To me."

There. She'd said it out loud, an effort at naming and not denying the strong emotions his presence—and now the thought of his life being in danger—conjured within her. No, she couldn't act on any of them when she saw him. He wasn't someone she could hope to love and marry, since he didn't belong to Christ. But her heart had apparently decided to care for him deeply anyway. And God had a purpose in that, too, she was sure.

"You'd have to carry a gun." Phoenix's statement in her deep tone surged hope through Cora's veins. And trepidation. She'd only held a gun one other time, when Phoenix had taken her to the shooting range shortly after hiring Cora. The day Cora had discovered she loathed guns and never wanted to hold one in her hand again, let alone fire it. Guns carried far too much power and risk that one mistake on her part could get someone killed.

But this would be Phoenix's final offer. Her non-negotiable terms. She didn't barter.

Cora straightened. "I can do that."

Phoenix pulled her gun out of the holster on her hip. She held it out to Cora, flat in her hand.

"That's yours." Cora stared at the weapon, not quite able to reach for it yet. "Don't you need it?"

"I have spares."

Probably in a hidden waistband holster and maybe in her boot or in her pack. Cora's thoughts weren't enough to distract her from the gun staring up at her from Phoenix's hand.

"Safety's here." Phoenix tapped a small switch on the side. "Aim, put your finger on the trigger, and squeeze."

Cora's mouth went dry, but she forced her hand to extend, and Phoenix placed the gun in her palm. It looked strange lying on the purple glove she'd replaced her mittens with before they'd left the jet, so she'd have a better grip on the leash and gear. She hadn't known she'd need a better grip on a gun, too.

"A good weapon makes for a good bluff."

Cora's gaze flitted to Phoenix's face. Gratitude rushed to calm the quivering of her nerves. She gave her kind mentor a shaky smile. "I'll remember that."

"No time to lose, ladies." Phoenix stepped back and scanned the group. "Let's move."

Cora stared at the gun in her hand. What if she had to use it? What if she shot someone?

"Cora, you still want to do this?" Phoenix's voice reached through Cora's mounting panic.

Kent was in trouble. Remembering that pumped courage through her body. "Yes. Absolutely." She stuffed the gun into the generous pocket of her long coat, pushing her mind ahead to the search. She looked across the road, envisioning the four grids they were using to divide the search area.

The last time they'd covered a large space like this, they were searching along the Mississippi River after the flood caused by a bomber. They'd found twenty-one survivors then. They could certainly find only one now, couldn't they?

They would find Kent. And he would be well. *Oh, Father, let it be so.*

A hand touched her shoulder. Bris leaned close with a smile as the others started across the road. "God's got this, Cora." She handed Cora a radio and pointed at the tree-spotted snowscape that awaited them. "And you've got the northernmost section."

Cora must have missed Phoenix's assignments. She'd given Cora the most unlikely section to find Kent, since the vehicles had driven south from here. Cora appreciated Phoenix's protection. She always watched out for her.

But who was watching out for Kent?

God was. And as long as someone found him and gave him any help he may need, that would be enough.

Then why did a shiver pass through her, a sense of foreboding that left her colder than before? Was something bad happening to Kent right now?

"Come on, Jana. We have to find Kent." She unclipped Jana's leash, and the golden dashed ahead of her, staying within sight as she moved back and forth, smelling the air. Cora followed at a quick clip, her pulse rushing twice as fast as her unease increased.

Please, Father. Be with Kent and give him strength.

Somehow, she knew he needed it now more than ever.

FORTY

So this was what weakness felt like. What defeat tasted like.

Kent lay on his side, on a quilt of all things. The contents of his stomach were on the floor below—a consequence of his last attempt to sit up. The putrid scent wafted to his nostrils, sickening him more.

And the world continued to spin. Even with his eyes shut.

Muffled voices filtered through the wall from the main part of the cabin, but Kent couldn't make out the words. Didn't have energy to try.

Had his dad had time like this, to know he was going to die and lament his actions? Probably. The multiple gunshots to his chest likely wouldn't have killed him instantly.

Had his dad regretted giving Charlie another chance after that same cousin had already turned his back on the family so many other times? Had he thought about Kent and Vince, how he was leaving them alone to survive this world on their own?

Vince. He was all Kent would leave behind. To survive. On his own. Kent's condemning thought about his dad came back to him in pieces, pointed at himself instead.

But it wasn't the same thing. Vince was strong. He could take care of himself.

From a hospital bed? Alone?

Kent swallowed, an awkward attempt around the lump in his throat while lying sideways. He coughed instead.

He hadn't left Vince to fight alone, even if he did have cancer. Vince had chosen that path. He didn't want Kent's help. He wanted to handle everything by himself, no matter how hard. If that left him alone now, that was Vince's choice.

Just like this was Kent's choice.

Being trapped by a malfunctioning body must lead to insanity. What a ridiculous thought. But Kent couldn't talk himself out of thinking it again.

He was here alone because he'd chosen to be alone. He hadn't brought backup on the jet when he could have. Sure, more agents could've blown the operation sooner, but his presence alone, boarding the jet, had accomplished that anyway. In reality, he hadn't brought them because he'd wanted to handle this on his own. He wanted to handle everything alone.

And he'd always been able to. Until now. Until he'd found out he was as weak as his parents. Until he'd met a beautiful woman who made him want to give a break to a punk who didn't deserve it.

But, maybe, that had been his choice, too. What had Cora said?

...sometimes being willing to show and admit weakness, especially to help another person the way your father did, takes the most courage and strength of all.

He could still see her beautiful blue eyes, glistening with tears as she'd told him in the sweetest way possible that she disagreed with him. That his dad hadn't been weak. That he'd been courageous and strong.

Could she be right?

...when I am weak, then I am strong.

The Bible quote Cora had shared blazed in his mind. It wasn't possible. Didn't make sense. Weakness made a person weak, not strong.

The memory of Cora later that night filled the blackness behind Kent's closed lids. The way she'd looked when she leaned over Ramos as he took his last breaths. Her voice had been powerful, filled with an unshakable certainty he'd never heard before from people talking about God and death.

She cared so much about a criminal—her kidnapper—that she'd wept over him and poured out her heart and soul to offer him comfort in his last moments. She was unafraid in the presence of death. Unafraid of the pain her emotions brought on her. Unafraid to make herself vulnerable to help someone else.

She'd looked so...strong.

Was that what Cora had wanted Kent to understand? He could still feel the pressure of her small hands on his arms as she'd looked him in the eyes last night by the fire.

Don't you see, Kent? He became weak for us so that He could do the most courageous thing ever. In choosing weakness, He was being stronger than we could ever dream of.

Was that true? That God had made Himself weak to help people out of love?

Had his dad been right, been strong, when he'd done that, too?

A memory long-forgotten, blurry as if in an old photo yellowed at the edges, filtered through Kent's mind. He'd fallen off the bike his dad was teaching him to ride. His dad hadn't scolded or told him to man up or get back on by himself. He'd gotten down on the ground behind Kent and held him in his strong arms until Kent's tears had dried.

And in that moment, Kent had known his dad was the greatest man alive.

A wet drop fell from the corner of Kent's eye to the quilt beneath his head. "Okay, God. Cora said something about you showing up when we're at our weakest." He paused as another wave of dizziness swirled the darkness at the back of his closed eyelids. "I admit it. I'm there. Maybe I was never as strong as I thought. I don't know. But I know I can't get out of this mess on my own. And if I end up dying here, I'd like to go where Cora's going to in the end."

An oddly-timed smile quirked his mouth. He thought back to what Cora had told Ramos before he died. What he needed to do to make things right with God. "I'm sorry for how I've messed things up. Not just now, but with Cora and Vince. And how I've thought I don't need anyone, including You. I guess I was wrong. And I guess that made me think of You as weak if You really did sacrifice Yourself the way the story goes. But that's what we do for the people we love, isn't it?"

Even Kent had let the cartel tie him up and take him hostage in Cora's place. And he'd do it again if he had to. "I guess there's nothing weak about that. So if You did that for a guy like Ramos and saved him, maybe You can save me?"

Kent waited. Idiot. Not like he'd hear a voice from heaven. "If You can do it, God. If You want to do it—redeem me like Cora said—I'll do my best to learn how to be okay with being weak sometimes. Because Cora says that's when we're strongest. With You, I guess."

The tension that had stiffened his muscles since the dizziness came on began to loosen, flowing out of his body as some sense of an answer flowed in. Peace? Is that what it was?

He took a deep breath and tightened his abs to slowly sit up, sliding his legs around to hang off the bed in front of him.

The room whirled, and his stomach lurched.

Okay, so maybe God's power showing up didn't mean Kent could function any better or have instant healing. At least on the outside.

Inside, it was as if cracks were being filled in and broken pieces were being put back together, because the pain he'd carried since he was ten years old suddenly wasn't so intense anymore. And that made him feel stronger than ever.

A smack drew his gaze to the door, now open against the wall, Hayden Simpson standing in the doorway with a sneer. And a Glock in his hand.

His image swirled before Kent's eyes as the punk spewed out a threat. "We're leaving now. And I get to say goodbye first."

God, if You want to show up with more of that power, now would be the perfect time. If He didn't, Kent wouldn't make it out of here alive.

A droplet of sweat trickled from beneath Cora's hat and dripped down the side of her face. She pressed ahead to keep up with Jana, the golden darting back and forth through snow and between trees as she searched for human scent off-leash.

The combination of physical exertion and sunlight that broke through the trees resulted in enough warmth to make Cora's clothes damp from her sweat. She should take off her jacket but stopping to stuff it into her backpack would slow them down.

She didn't want to delay a moment in finding Kent. They'd already been searching for thirty minutes. Radio check-ins with the rest of the team confirmed no one else had found a cabin or Kent yet.

Father, please help us find him. And please keep him safe until we do. I don't know what You have planned for him and for me. But I know You are at work in both our lives.

The nearly constant prayers that had been filling her mind as she followed Jana comforted her and infused her with strength she knew didn't come from herself. The anxiety twisting her stomach had lessened as her faith grew—her trust that God had control of Kent's fate, too. He would do what was best.

But she desperately hoped and prayed that included sparing Kent's life. And that she would get to see him again. Talk to him once more.

The memory of his chiseled features and intense green eyes appeared in her vision. And that rare smile that was so worth earning.

Jana veered in front of Cora, catching her attention.

Cora wouldn't do anyone any good if she didn't stay focused.

She clapped her eyes on Jana and sped up her stride so she didn't fall behind. Their pace had varied as they searched, sometimes running, sometimes quick walking. Cora left the speed up to Jana.

The golden retriever paused, halting for the first time since they'd started out.

She lifted her black nose high into the air. Her tail wagged, and she took off.

Cora's heart surged as she sprinted after Jana. Thank the Lord for the snowshoes that prevented her from sinking into the deep snow so she could keep up with the golden.

As she ran, Cora reached into her left pocket for the radio. "Cora to Phoenix." She breathed hard as she pushed her legs fast enough to keep Jana in sight.

The radio crackled. "Go for Phoenix."

"We have a scent." Cora would've shouted the words with the excitement pumping through her if she hadn't been so short on air. "Jana's on the trail."

"Roger that. What's your location?"

Cora relayed the coordinates as best she could from her last check.

"On our way. Bristol, close in. Amalia, continue search for subject in your grid."

Phoenix was right. Jana had definitely found human scent, but it didn't have to be Kent. Hunters or someone else could be staying at a cabin.

But, oh, how she hoped it was Kent. That hope fueled her feet to fly over the snow faster than she thought possible to keep in view the SAR K-9 who was streaking ahead to save a life.

The life of the man who'd become far more important to Cora than she'd realized. The man she didn't want to lose.

FORTY-ONE

Kent couldn't believe it. Trying to do Cora's thing actually worked. He'd stayed alive for at least five more minutes, keeping Hayden from pulling the trigger by getting him to talk.

Kent had kept still and listened, seated on the side of the bed while Hayden drifted farther into the room.

The Glock was gripped in the kid's hand but lowered to his side as he walked back and forth at a slow pace. "I don't really care if he gets mad or not. You saw how he sent the lawyer to the jail instead of coming himself." Hayden rattled on about his dad, like he'd been doing for the past several minutes.

Cora had been right. This kid had daddy issues. She'd said he reminded her of her brother, who also had an absent, rich dad.

Add to that the intel Kent had picked up from Hayden—his dad owned the charter company and planes, and Hayden was desperate to attain success in a different kind of business—and Kent had the keys to getting Hayden to open up. And direct the conversation to a helpful end, hopefully.

"Yeah, I saw." Sympathy and understanding had been the name of this game. Trying to think like Cora, be an empathetic listener, was a whole lot harder than it looked. Half the time, Kent gritted his teeth with the frustration that he couldn't just haul himself up and disarm the perp.

"When I meet Guajardo, he's going to make me a name in this business. I'll have more power than my dad ever dreamed of. Then he'll see I'm more than just a football player or the kid who has to be bailed out of jail."

"Yeah, he'll have to see you're better than he is." Kent injected his voice with sincerity he didn't feel. Man, this kid was messed up. But so were thousands of other kids, and not all of them chose the path Hayden had picked for himself.

"When will you tell him about your success?"

Hayden smiled, not the sneer from before, but a genuine smile as if sharing a fun moment with a pal.

Cora would feel bad for him, this pitiful, resentful kid who thought his dad and the rest of the world owed him everything he wanted. And if this was going to work, Kent had to try to get to that same empathetic place.

"When I've made more money than he has. Then I'll invite him to one of my mansions, and I'll send a chauffeur to pick him up in *my* limo." Hayden stopped walking, his smile broadening to a grin. "And when he gets to my place, I won't be there. I'll be too busy to see him." He laughed.

"Good plan." Kent forced himself to see things from Hayden's point of view. Kent's dad wasn't there because he'd died. But what would it have been like to grow up with a dad who was never around because he didn't want to be? A dad who abandoned his kid by choice? Had to hurt. A lot. And lead to even more anger than Kent had been carrying around for his dad. "So what are you going to do about your dad in the meantime?"

Hayden shrugged. "Nothing. I'm going to meet the kingpin. I won't need him anymore."

"Impressive. You're going to give it all up. The cars, the money you've got now."

Hayden paused a beat before answering this time. "I'll make my own money."

"I bet you've already figured out where you're going to live in California or somewhere."

Another pause. "Sure." Hesitancy entered his voice and eyes.

"You probably have a plan about the charter company, too."

"What?" Hayden's forehead wrinkled.

"Your dad already lost the jet the pilot crashed, of course. And the DEA will probably take possession of all his planes since we know they're being used for smuggling." More likely, they could only take possession of the one aircraft used if his dad wasn't aware of the smuggling, but Hayden didn't know that. "At the very least, his whole charter business will be shut down during the investigation to see if he's involved in other narcotics trafficking."

Hayden stood still, staring at Kent. Just how much did he hate his dad? Enough to be glad his dad would be ruined?

"That's good." Hayden's reply lacked conviction. "He deserves it."

"What are you doing in here?" Big Ben stood in the doorway, anger punching his words. "What is this, a counseling session? You're supposed to shoot him. Everyone else is already loaded up outside."

Hayden hiked his broad shoulders and drew himself up to his full height. "I can take as long as I want. I'm the one who set up this whole operation. And I'm the one Guajardo wants to see."

"Don't get too big, kid. I backed you, and my guy ended up dead."

Did he mean Bradley?

"You're lucky we waited for you at all." Big Ben pulled out his Glock. "Now finish him, or I will."

Kent stared at the blurred weapon, pointed at him. He'd run out of time.

<hr>

Cora slowed when they reached the clearing.

A log cabin stood in the snow with sparkling, marshmallow

drifts cushioning its walls like a sweet image from a children's fairytale.

But this was real life. And if this cabin held the cartel right now, it was far from sweet.

Jana ran ahead to the cabin.

Cora should've called her back, but she hadn't been able to see the cabin or the clearing until they were upon them. Now, shouting wasn't an option.

Thankfully, Jana wasn't a barker, even when excited. She wouldn't make a sound, though she would try her best to reach the humans she had found.

Cora turned the receiving volume low on her radio and held it to her mouth. "Cora to team." She spoke as quietly as she could while still hoping to be heard. "Found cabin. Black SUV and black sedan parked outside. Appears to be our subjects." She didn't want to mention the cartel specifically over the radio in case someone was listening to the frequency. But Phoenix and the others would know what she meant.

"Proceed with caution." Phoenix's voice came through quietly, thanks to the reduced volume setting. "Help on the way."

Phoenix hadn't told Cora to wait or stand down. And somehow, the absence of a cautious warning empowered Cora to move forward despite the fear gripping her chest.

She tried to stay in the trees as she moved around the edge of the clearing where the cabin stood at the center. Was anyone in the parked vehicles at the front? They could have seen her.

Father, please give me protection and courage. Enable me to help Kent.

Oh, how she hoped he was still alive and unharmed.

Her pulse pounded in her ears.

Jana had immediately rushed to the back of the cabin instead of the front. Did that mean Kent was at the rear of the cabin? Or it could be any person, really. She wasn't necessarily focused on Kent's scent alone.

Cora bent to loosen her snowshoes, unstrapping them from her feet as quickly as she could. Aligned with the back wall of the cabin, Cora stepped out from concealment and walked through the two-foot snow that shallowed down to a foot and then mere inches toward the center of the clearing, thanks to wind and sun melt. Next to the cabin, the snow drifted, slanting against the log walls as if helping prop them up.

Jana pranced in place near a window as Cora reached her. Large footprints imprinted the snow along the wall. Was whoever had made those still here?

Muffled voices caught her attention, filtering out from the cabin.

Cora squatted down and handed Jana treats from her pocket. She petted the golden's head, hoping the rewards would be enough to signal Jana had completed her search and didn't need to find the people inside anymore. She didn't dare even whisper to Jana.

A deep, strong voice with an edge contrasted with a slightly higher, younger one.

Wait, was that first voice Kent?

She held her breath as she moved closer to the window. She inched her head to the edge, just enough for one eye to see inside.

Kent. Her heart leaped into her throat. *He's alive! Oh, Father, thank you.*

He sat on the edge of a king-sized bed, his arms pulled behind him like he was bound. They'd tied his hands in front with zip ties when he'd left, so something had happened since then to account for the change. Why was he sitting? She couldn't imagine he'd be so relaxed when someone from the cartel was talking to him. Unless he was hurt.

She angled her head so she could see more of the room to the left.

Oh, my.

Two cartel men stood facing Kent's direction. And they both held guns.

She had to act fast.

Cora yanked Phoenix's gun from her pocket and flipped the handle of it toward the window. She smashed the handle into the glass as hard as she could. The old window shattered, mostly inward, as she'd hoped it would.

She spun the gun around and stuck it through the window opening, gripping the weapon in both hands as she aimed at the men who thought they could kill Kent.

FORTY-TWO

Kent had never been more impressed with anyone in his life.

Cora was a vision, standing behind the shattered remnants of the window she'd broken, her blond hair blowing in the breeze beneath her hat. Her blue eyes were bright, the set of her jaw as determined as the steady way she aimed her Glock at the cartel thugs.

Kent hadn't thought Cora even carried a weapon. He'd seen she could be courageous, but not like this. His heart swelled at the sight of her, even though he had to twist awkwardly to see where she was, eight feet behind his right shoulder. Why had he ever thought it would be a bad thing to need rescuing?

He turned his head back to the perps.

Hayden's eyes were huge, the weapon in his hand tilted downward as furrows bunched above his nose.

Big Ben had switched his target. His weapon pointed at Cora.

"Hayden?" Cora's sweet voice was like music to Kent's ears. But the softness in her tone, unlike the confidence she'd shown moments ago, tensed his muscles. Was she going to lose her determination and leverage because of Hayden? "You're behind this?"

Hayden looked at Kent instead of Cora. "Yeah." Seeming to rally his bravado, the kid glanced Cora's way. "Yeah," his voice was louder this time, "I did the whole operation. You were easy to fool. And now I've got your boyfriend." He sneered.

"I'm sorry, Hayden."

Kent clenched his fists at Cora's words. She wouldn't back down out of pity, would she?

"I hadn't wanted to see you get hurt."

Hayden stiffened. "What do you mean?"

"I'll have to shoot you or your friend if you try to harm Kent." Cora's statement was matter of fact.

Kent smiled. Couldn't help himself.

"I'll just shoot you first, lady." Big Ben's growl said he'd had enough of the games.

"I wouldn't try it." Cora's tone was firm. "I'm aiming at you. Even if you hit me, I'll hit you, too. You don't want to take that risk, do you?"

Wow. If this was a bluff, it was the best one Kent had ever heard.

"But I'll shoot your boyfriend."

Hayden's word choice struck Kent's awareness this time. Her boyfriend? He couldn't be more wrong. But, man, Kent liked the sound of that.

"Do you expect me to believe that, Hayden?"

"You can see I've got my gun on him right now." The kid tightened his jaw and regripped his weapon as if his palms were sweaty.

"You wouldn't dare shoot him there and get blood all over your mother's quilt."

Kent barely held back the laugh that wanted to burst from his mouth. How had she known the quilt was his mom's? The same way she always read people and sized up the situation.

But they were still in a standoff. Cora's bluff was stalling them, but she was outnumbered. They'd figure a way out or take a risk and call her bluff, maybe in a matter of seconds.

If only he wasn't so useless right now.

He twisted to see Cora again.

And the room didn't spin. The dizziness was gone.

Cora must have hit the nail on the head with her guess about the quilt belonging to Hayden's mother.

Alarm widened his gaze as he looked at the lovely patchwork bedcovering. "We should move him." The muttered comment seemed to be intended for the older man he leaned toward.

"Shut up." The man with a rough smattering of silvery whiskers on his chin and jaw kept his glare steady on Cora. "We can wait. We have others here. They'll take care of you any second."

The vehicles out front. They must have had people in them, or the older man would have called his henchmen from within the cabin, and she would have been overtaken.

Were the men in the cars creeping up on Cora even now? Would they shoot?

She didn't dare take her eyes off the man to check.

A good weapon makes for a good bluff.

Cora had been riding on Phoenix's words for the last half hour, it felt like, though the standoff had probably only lasted a few minutes so far. She had to keep the bluff going long enough for Phoenix or the DEA to arrive. She was sure Phoenix would have called them from the satellite phone as soon as Cora identified the cabin, and they would fly here in their helicopter.

That's what she should say. And it wasn't even a bluff. She looked at Kent, who had twisted his head to see her. He smiled.

Strength filled her again and flowed out to her limbs. She lifted the gun a little higher, correcting the drooping of her weakening arms. "I have backup, too. They're on their way right now and are almost here."

"What backup?" The older man's mouth contorted in a disbelieving scowl.

"Oof!" A deep exclamation came from her right, outside the cabin.

She jerked her head to see a man land with a thud. Looked like the young man who had boarded the plane when Bradley was shot. And Jana stood on top of him, her paws planted on his chest.

Cora's mouth dropped open. Jana must have knocked him over. Had she found some fighting spirit, too?

His eyes were closed, his head propped against the wall of the cabin. Praise the Lord, Jana had managed to knock him out.

Cora swung her attention back to the interior of the cabin.

Hayden was by Kent, grabbing his arm and pulling him up.

Where was the older man?

A big hand clamped around the gun in her hands from the side. The older man had snuck up to the wall when she wasn't looking. He pulled the gun, trying to loosen it from her grip.

She held on.

He yanked one of her hands away.

She pulled it back, felt in her jacket pocket as she fought to hold her grip on the gun with the other hand. Her fingers closed around her pocketknife.

She snapped it open using her teeth on the inset edge of the blade.

She reached through the window and slashed the man's hand.

He yelled and released his grip.

Cora pulled the gun outside the window as she caught sight of Kent.

He was standing now, Hayden lying on the floor at his feet. He looked unconscious.

And Kent looked incredible. Like the handsomest man she'd ever seen.

He held a gun in his hand, likely taken from Hayden, and aimed it at the older man from behind his back.

"Good work, Cora." The sound of Kent's strong voice filled her with warmth.

"You can't actually hit me with your hands cuffed behind you." The older man's voice didn't sound as confident as his statement.

"Try me." Either Kent was bluffing now, too, or he could indeed shoot well with his hands bound behind his back. It seemed to work to keep the older man from reaching for the gun he must have dropped when Cora cut him.

But what about the other men outside?

A shot rang out. Then another. Her answer.

She'd never liked the sound of guns very much. This time, they signaled help had arrived.

She jogged around the cabin, Jana happily bounding through the snow with her.

Phoenix and Bris held their weapons on the cartel men as they filed out of the vehicles, hands lifted in the air. Dag crouched in a low, protective stance, barking and growling more for intimidation than anything else. He was more effective in that department than the guns.

A chopping sound drew Cora's gaze heavenward.

A helicopter hovered overhead, descending toward them. DEA reinforcements.

Thank you, Father.

She swung to the door and pushed inside, hurrying to find the room where Kent was. Her breath hitched as she spotted the open doorway and moved toward it, Jana slowing with her by her side. What if the older man or Hayden, if he'd awoken, had overpowered Kent since he was in handcuffs?

Cora still held Phoenix's gun in her hands. Would she have to use it yet?

She cautiously stepped through the doorway.

There he stood, tall and strong. "Kent."

He glanced at her. He'd moved to the side of the room where he could watch both the entrance in which she stood and the older man he needed to keep covered. The intensity, the emotion in his quick look nearly drew her to him.

She wanted nothing more than to go to him and be held in his embrace.

But such a thought was beyond foolish. They couldn't have a relationship, and she would be wrong to indicate otherwise. He still wasn't a Christian, so he couldn't be the man God wanted her to marry.

And, secondly, he was cuffed and holding a criminal at

gunpoint. Her gaze dropped to see for the first time that even his feet were cuffed. Her face heated at her complete lack of practical thinking. How the PK-9 ladies would tease her if they knew how her heart had been captured by this handsome man. They couldn't ever know, and neither could Kent.

But, oh, how good it was to see him alive and well. She silently praised her heavenly Father as she moved farther into the room and addressed the older man who glared at Kent. "Do you have the keys for those handcuffs? I'd like to free my friend."

FORTY-THREE

My friend.

Kent barely heard Agent Gilson's wrap-up of how Phoenix had reached them on the satellite phone after the DEA copter had landed by the crashed jet and told them to come here to the cabin instead.

Cora had called him her friend. Of course, she had been talking to a known criminal at the time. But Cora also tended to only say what was exactly, completely true. Did she think of Kent as just a friend? He should probably be grateful he ranked that highly, given what he'd put her through. His unfriendliness with her when they'd first worked together had been nothing compared to the trauma she had to go through when he invited her on a flight to San Francisco.

Either way, as a friend or something more, he had to talk to her. Had to tell her what had happened in the cabin. Had to tell her the difference she made and how amazing she was and—

"Looking for someone?" A woman's voice halted the scan of his searching gaze and racing thoughts.

A brunette wearing a dark blue beanie stood in the driveway in front of the cabin, ignoring the chaos of personnel around them to stare at him instead.

"Bachmann, isn't it?" One of the Phoenix K-9 women who'd worked surveillance at Lofland High.

"Yeah. But you're looking for Isaksson, right?" She smiled.

Annoyance would be his normal response. But if she knew where Cora was right now, he'd rather kiss the ground this woman walked on.

"She's in the cabin."

"Great. Thanks." His remnant of pride kept his feet from moving. Didn't need the world to know he'd fallen for Cora. He searched for something casual to say. "Did you know she could be like that?"

"Like what?"

"So...fierce. She threatened to shoot those perps. Knifed one of them."

A closed-mouth smile hovered at the corners of Bachmann's lips. "Cora's courage always shows up when someone she cares about is threatened."

Someone she cares about. Did Bachmann mean...?

"Before you go letting that grin grow any bigger..."

He was grinning? Sure enough, his mouth stretched wide with the hope rising in his chest.

"I want to warn you of something. If you hurt Cora in any way—"

"Let me guess, you'll come after me?"

"No." Her lips pressed together, an amused glint appearing in her eyes. "But Phoenix will. Believe me, you don't want that to happen."

He glanced behind Bachmann to the woman who stood with a commanding stance, talking to Valesquez as if Phoenix held the superior rank. "Got it."

His thoughts quickly turned to the woman he'd rather be looking at. Forget trying to seem detached.

He spun on his heels in the snow-topped gravel and walked as fast as he could to the cabin without alarming anyone.

The same urge he'd had when she'd stood close to him in the cabin, unlocking the cuffs from his wrists, fueled his quick pace. But he'd been holding a drug dealer at gunpoint at the time.

The next thing he'd known, Phoenix and Amalia had burst

in, followed by DEA agents, and the place swarmed with more help than he needed. He'd lost track of Cora in the fray, as agents started asking if he needed medical attention and other questions about the situation here and at the downed plane. He'd had to go outside to ID the cartel members the Phoenix team had apprehended. And then there'd been the paramedics who arrived and insisted on checking his head. He'd need stitches, they said, but he talked them into a temporary patch until he could wrap things up here.

The only thing he really wanted to wrap up wasn't a thing at all—it was the woman who had changed his life, changed him, in more ways than he'd dreamed possible.

He entered the front room of the cabin. DEA personnel and Pérez with her German shepherd cluttered the space. No Cora. Was she still in the bedroom?

He paused at the doorway, his pulse pounding while he had to wait for a couple agents to come out of the room. As soon as they passed, he stepped into the bedroom.

Cora. She hovered over the paramedic treating Big Ben's hand, her body tense, arms wrapped around herself. That was his Cora. Always caring for everyone, even her enemies.

His Cora? He caught his own mental slip. Could she be?

He walked closer behind her, stopping a few feet away. "Cora."

She turned quickly toward him, as if startled. But the smile on her face said the surprise wasn't unwelcome.

Everything he'd thought he would say when he saw her evaporated as he looked into her amazing blue eyes. He cleared his throat. "Not blaming yourself for that cut, are you?"

"I was, for a bit. But I would do it again to protect you." Pink tinged her cheeks as she glanced away. "Not that you need protection. I know you—"

"Cora, it's okay." He chuckled and took a step closer. "I did need help. Your help." He glanced at the paramedic and the criminal behind her. No way was he going to say all this in front of Big Ben. "Would you take a walk with me?"

"I think the helicopter is going to fly us to the jet to get our things."

"It'll only take a few minutes. They'll wait for us."

A smile curved her closed lips. "Okay." She looked at the golden retriever who had settled on the floor a few feet away. "Jana."

The dog's head perked up and her ears lifted.

"Let's go."

Jana popped to her feet and trotted over.

"Lead the way."

He held out his arm instead. Ridiculously formal, and he had no idea why he did it. If Gilson or any of his other colleagues saw him, they'd rib him for months. But when Cora beamed a smile at him and slipped her arm through his, resting her hand in the crook of his elbow, he didn't give a whit what anyone thought.

He escorted the lady out of the cabin and past the agents, ignoring glances from the feds and the Phoenix team. He took her out a little distance off the driveway, where the blown snow wasn't deep, and a stand of snow-covered pine trees blocked the wind.

He stopped and turned to face her, capturing her gloved hand in his before she could pull it away.

"Cora."

She looked down at his hand holding hers. When her gaze flitted back up, her eyes were filled with uncertainty.

"I just want to say thank you."

Little furrows gathered between her eyebrows.

"Thank you for...rescuing me." It wasn't as hard to say as he'd thought it would be. To admit he'd needed to be rescued. Maybe because she was the one who had done the rescuing. Or, maybe, because God had done it first.

He swallowed, shifted his feet in the snow, looked at her small hand in the purple glove. "I don't just mean showing up to help the way you did here." He glanced at the cabin, then brought his gaze back to her face where it belonged. "You were awesome, by the way." A smile stretched his mouth. "I've never seen anyone more magnificent."

"Oh, my. I know that's not true." Hot pink flushed her cheeks, making her look more adorable than ever. "I don't have the skills you do, or the rest of the PK-9 team."

"Then you don't see yourself and your capabilities clearly. Your courage and understanding of people make you unstoppable."

She avoided looking at him, a smile shaping her mouth when she turned her head away, but not before he saw her face flame with a deeper shade of pink.

He reached for her other hand hanging by her side and held both her hands in his. "I intend to make sure you know how special you are, no matter how long it takes."

That brought her gaze back to him with her eyes widened.

His heart thudded against his ribcage. He'd gotten ahead of himself. Hadn't meant to make that kind of declaration quite yet. Would she shoot him down?

"Kent, I—"

"I also—"

They started and stopped at the same time. Smiled.

"You go first." Cora, of course, deferred to the other person.

Normally, he'd let her continue before him, but this was too important to wait another second to tell her. "I need to thank you for something else, too." Emotion swelled in his throat. How could he say this? He didn't even know the right words. He thought of the explanation Cora had used when she'd talked to Ramos. "You know how you told Ramos about God before he died?"

She nodded, her eyebrows bunching together as she watched Kent intently.

"Well...I did that. What you wanted him to do."

"You..." Her hands tensed in his.

"I thought of that Bible quote you told me about. Being strong when we're weak. Because of God." He cleared his throat. "And I remembered what you told Ramos, about being sorry for what he'd done and asking God for help. And I did that."

"Oh, Kent." Her eyes filled with moisture as a smile lit her whole face. "Praise the Lord. That is the best news I've ever heard in my life." She tugged her hands from his, but he didn't have more than a second to wonder why before she threw her arms around him.

He laughed as he hugged her back, cherishing the feel of her in his arms and the joyful laughter that gently shook her body.

Too soon, she lifted her head and leaned back. Her cheeks glistened in the sunlight, wet with tears.

He frowned. "You're crying."

She shook her head, her smile big. "Happy tears. Such happy tears." She put her hand on his arm. "You know, we're in the same family now. The family of God."

"That's...cool." How he'd love to make the family thing official in another way, too. But would she ever consider that with him? The lone wolf?

"Speaking of family." His mind grabbed for the easier question, the one he'd decided to ask her as soon as he got the chance. "My brother, Vince." Kent glanced away, trying to swallow back the sudden wave of sadness. "He has cancer."

Her eyes seemed to reflect everything he felt as concern filled her voice. "Oh, no."

"Yeah. He's not doing well. Last I heard, he was in a coma."

"Are you going to see him?"

"I wasn't. But," he forced his gaze to stay on hers, even though his vision blurred with emotion he would never let anyone else see, "I don't want to leave him alone. Maybe..." His voice pinched. He swallowed again. "Maybe it's time we started helping each other be strong."

She gave his arm a gentle squeeze. "That sounds like a wonderful idea."

"Would you..." His breath paused, but he pressed on. "Would you come with me? I need your...help."

"Of course, I will. I'd be honored to go with you." She didn't miss a beat. This wonderful woman who was ready to help everyone.

"Thank you." The words came out as a whisper. His gaze lowered from her mesmerizing eyes to her lips.

He closed the gap between them, slipping his arms around her again, and slowly lowered his head toward hers.

"Kent." She put her gloved finger to his lips. But she didn't pull away. "I made a promise."

A promise? He blinked. To someone else?

"To God and myself that I wouldn't kiss a man until we were married. I want to save all of myself for the man God has for me and no one else." A smile curved those lips he badly wanted to feel on his. "I have a feeling you could be that man."

Hope surged through his body, warming him from head to toe with a blend of love and passion that was as heady as if he'd actually kissed her.

"Will you wait with me?"

He'd have to be the biggest fool in the world to say no. He grabbed her gloved hand that had just been on his lips and brought it back up to his mouth. Would he wait with the woman who'd rescued him? He met her gaze as he bent his head to kiss her fingers, right through the glove, and promised, "Forever."

EPILOGUE

"Have I told you how beautiful you look?" Kent's murmur by her ear sent a tingle up Cora's spine as she smiled and turned toward the man who held her heart.

They sat at a round reception table with Bris's mother, stepfather, Grandma Jessica, and Bradley, but the rest of the occupants had their attention captured by the groom, Rem. He stood on the far side of the table, regaling everyone with behind-the-scene mishaps that had occurred before the wedding ceremony a few hours earlier.

"Bristol must have picked that dress just for you." Kent's gaze skimmed her maid-of-honor garb—a royal blue dress with an empire waist and spaghetti straps. He captured her hand from the table, holding it in his. "The color makes your eyes more stunning than usual."

Cora laughed. "Who would have thought you could be such a charmer? Thank you."

"I meant every word." He lifted her fingers and brushed his lips against them, the gesture that had become his favorite during their four months of courtship. It never got old, thrilling her down to her toes every time.

"And I agree."

Cora looked over her shoulder, spotting Bris standing behind her and Kent with a grin on her face.

Warmth flushed Cora's cheeks. "How long were you standing there?"

"Long enough." Bris laughed.

Cora couldn't stay embarrassed long or begrudge her friend any joy on her wedding day.

Bris was a gorgeous bride in her cream gown with modern lines and her hair swept to one side in a low bun, threaded with ribbons of blue. But her greatest beauty was the joy that beamed from her smile and reflected in Rem's. Cora couldn't remember when she'd seen two people quite so blissfully happy on their wedding day. It was beautiful.

Cora extended her hand to her friend, and Bris took it in hers. "I'm so happy for you and Rem."

"Thank you." Bris beamed the smile that didn't seem like it would ever dim. She looked over the table at Rem.

The handsome groom gave her a smile that split his beard wide, so much love in his gaze it brought tears to Cora's eyes.

"We're so thankful the Lord brought us together again." Bris returned her attention to Cora. "And I'm happy for you, too." She included Kent in her pointed look. "We're going to do the first dance now, and then I expect you two to join us on the dance floor." Her mock stern expression fell away when her husband swept in and wrapped his arm around her waist.

"Care to dance, beautiful?"

Bris giggled, a sound Cora had never heard from her before. "If you think you can keep up."

The happy couple floated onto the dance floor, and the music started.

Motion at the corner of Cora's eye caught her attention. She turned her head in time to spot Bris's Grandma Jessica giving Toby a taste of the wedding cake. The black lab, at the reception as Bris's K-9 partner, licked his chops as he sat politely next to Grandma Jessica, staring adoringly at her face.

She seemed to sense Cora's amused gaze, and she looked Cora's way, sending her a wink along with a mischievous smile.

Cora shook her head and laughed.

"I'm starting to see how that woman survived being kidnapped by a terrorist." Kent leaned close to Cora.

"She's really something, isn't she?"

He gave her sidelong look. "Just like someone else I know."

"And someone I know." Cora squeezed his hand that still held hers under the table.

"Okay, we're up."

"What?"

"The dance floor." Kent tilted his head toward the open area.

"We don't have to dance if you'd rather not." Cora had gotten the impression from his reaction before the wedding, when dancing was mentioned, that he wasn't thrilled with the idea.

"And miss the excuse to hold you?" He winked. "Not a chance."

She laughed as he sailed her out to the dance floor on his arm, his eagerness palpable. "You know," she met his gaze as he took her in his arms and held her close, "I don't mind this part myself."

He grinned and started to sway with the music. His steps were slightly stiff, but not clumsy or unsure.

"So you do know how to dance."

He shrugged the strong shoulder under her hand.

She lifted her eyebrows.

"Okay." His mouth spread into a grin. "You got me. You'd be very proud, actually. I asked for help."

"Ah. That's very good. I am proud of you. Did you take lessons?"

"Do online videos count?" The cautious tuck of his lips was so adorable, she had to laugh.

"Well, they apparently did the trick. You're dancing very well." Not that she'd care if he stepped on her toes. She'd still want to spend forever in his arms. "I'm also proud of you for letting other agents take over the effort to apprehend Guajardo. I know how hard that was."

The drug lord had managed to evade federal agents in California, apparently fleeing the country again when he heard of Kent's attempt to find him through Ramos.

"I was too close to the case. Time I admitted it and left it in other agents' hands."

Cora swelled with gratitude for the work God had been doing in Kent these past months. He was a new creature, a man not afraid to admit weaknesses and let others come around him to help. He was softening toward people in need, too. He'd even found Sydney, Marco's daughter, and told her mother how Marco had died trying to do the right thing. Sydney's mom had accepted Kent's offer to be Sydney's godfather and to be on call if she needed assistance or financial support. Perhaps best of all, Kent was letting Cora into more and more of his life and his heart. And that was a marvelous journey.

"Besides," Kent's voice drew Cora's attention back to the present, "I wanted more time to spend with Vince right now."

"It's so wonderful you were able to convince him to start treatment."

"That's what family does, right?" Kent smiled, leading Cora into a turn. "Help each other?"

"Exactly right." And Vince was on the path to beating his cancer, or at least surviving it longer thanks to Kent's support and the treatment he'd decided to undergo.

"Speaking of family," Kent nodded toward the tables. "Glad to see you managed to talk Bradley into coming to the wedding after all."

She looked across the floor to where Bradley sat at the table, engaged in conversation with Grandma Jessica while petting Toby's head. "I didn't. He actually announced this morning that he'd changed his mind and wanted to come."

"Oh. He's doing that kind of thing more lately."

"Yes, thank the Lord." Bradley had even started to attend church with Cora and Kent the past month. Because Bradley had only helped the cartel under threat to him and Cora, and due to his efforts to stop the cartel from kidnapping her, he had been released without charges. Kent had helped Cora set up boundaries and guidelines for Bradley while he lived at her home, and the routine and accountability that resulted seemed to have created a climate where Bradley could thrive. Either that, or his change was evidence God was taking hold of his life and slowly bringing Bradley to Himself. She hoped and prayed that was the case.

Meanwhile, Bradley's story had at least been an opening she was able to use with Hayden and Venetia when she visited them at the jail as they waited for the long process of jurisprudence to decide their sentences. They also seemed to be softening toward her and God.

"I see Phoenix brought her dog, too." Kent angled his head toward Phoenix as they danced along the edge of the floor.

She stood by the wall near the exit door with Dagian sitting alertly at her side.

"I don't think she ever goes anywhere without Dag."

"Does she think we'll need a protection, tracking, whatever-else-he-does dog at a wedding?" Humor twinkled in Kent's eyes.

"Knowing Phoenix, I don't doubt she does."

"She's kind of an enigma, isn't she?"

"Definitely." After six years of working for Phoenix, Cora sometimes felt as though she still didn't know her at all. Just before the wedding, Cora had approached Phoenix about the surprising information Bris had just shared. "Bristol said you told her to talk to me about God on the plane, when I was so lost and hurting over Bradley."

Phoenix had simply met Cora's inquisitive gaze with an impassive one. "It was what you needed."

Cora had wanted to ask what Phoenix needed—this strong woman who helped so many without asking anything in return. But Cora left Phoenix's privacy intact and only voiced her gratitude. "Yes. It really was. Thank you." What a gift that God had given Cora a boss and mentor like Phoenix.

"So why does Nevaeh have a dog here, too?" Kent's question drew Cora's thoughts away from Phoenix.

She glanced around the room and caught sight of Nevaeh's easily recognizable thick, black curls. Cannenta leaned against her leg as Nevaeh sat at one of the tables with Amalia, Jazz, and some of Bris's former bomb squad partners.

"She has a special job she does for Nevaeh." Cora didn't think it was her place, at least not right now, to share that Cannenta was a PTSD service dog. But soon, perhaps, she and Kent might have their own wedding and be united in a relationship so close that she could share that and more with him. He hadn't asked yet, but they'd talked about the possibility, and he'd made it obvious he didn't want to wait longer if she didn't need the time to be sure. And she'd told him she didn't.

The music changed, from a slow ballad to a dramatic orchestral fanfare, like an introduction before something was about to happen.

Kent lowered his arms and stepped back. What was going on?

He bent down on one knee.

Cora's hands went to her mouth as her heart leaped into her throat. Was he about to...?

He pulled something small from the pocket of his suit jacket and held it out to her.

Light caught the diamond in the center of a ring.

But here, at Bris's wedding reception? Cora wildly looked around, catching Bris's huge smile and nod of approval. Clearly, she'd been part of this plan. Cora couldn't have dreamt of a better time or setting than this special celebration where the people she loved most were gathered to witness what it seemed Kent was about to do.

"Cora Isaksson." Kent's voice drew her gaze back to his. "You have changed my world and changed my life. You introduced me to the God Who saved me." Intensity sharpened his beautiful green eyes. "I love you, Cora. Will you be my wife, my helpmate, and partner for the rest of our lives?"

"Yes." The answer welled up with the tears that surged to her eyes and spilled onto her cheeks, running down to touch her smile. She glanced at her Phoenix K-9 family, grouped along the dance floor to watch the proposal. Kent was so sweet to know she'd want them there. "Oh, yes."

She reached for Kent as he stood and swept her up into his arms, lifting her so her feet no longer touched the floor.

Applause and whistles filled the banquet hall.

As Cora clutched Kent's shoulders, joy filled her being, and she wasn't afraid of messing this up. Because this moment and the prospect of the future were already perfect.

Turn the Page for a Special Sneak Peek of:

GUARDIANS UNLEASHED, BOOK 2

AVAILABLE NOW

EXCERPT OF COVERT DANGER

Michael swung back to face her. "I don't know why you lied to them and why you're lying now, but you know better than anyone I won't lie. For you or anyone else."

An odd sensation pinged Amalia's chest. As if he'd shot an arrow that bounced off the rock of her heart. She mentally brushed away the ridiculous image and returned to her objective—persuading an uncooperative protected witness not to blow her cover.

"There's a lot at stake in your cooperation, though I can't tell you what it is." The words, *You'll have to trust me*, died before they came out. She wouldn't go that far. Not with Michael. She didn't even trust herself, and she was certainly the last person he would trust.

"I understand you don't want to lie." She held the breath she wanted to exhale, knowing it would be a tell that revealed she was compromising, giving up ground. "You don't need to lie about knowing me or keep our history a secret if you're asked directly. All I'm asking is that you call me by my right name and don't reveal my former identity to anyone. I am Amalia Pérez now, so you won't be lying. The person you knew no longer exists."

He walked farther away from her and stopped at the end of

the king-sized bed, looking out the glass patio doors ten feet in front of him. "Okay."

Amalia relaxed her grip on Raksa's leash. Another successful negotiation.

"But on one condition." He turned toward her, sunlight from the window behind him backlighting his strong frame. "That you tell me what happened to Sofia."

Relieved she couldn't see his blue eyes well or the emotion that might be in them, she nodded. A non-binding gesture. "I could do that."

Why hadn't she just straight-out lied and said she would? Some strange instinct made her pick the evasive phrasing that kept her from having to actually lie. She'd been able to abandon that avoidance tactic years ago, when she'd reached the point where any identity she chose to assume became real and allowed her to lie with authenticity in a way most people couldn't. Lying to Michael shouldn't be any different than—

A vibration in her back pocket saved her from having to answer her own question. She pulled out the phone.

Ramone.

Calling her? She hadn't planned to contact Ramone when she came to Minneapolis, where she knew her former asset from the Colombian rebel group had planned to retire with family members who had immigrated before him. But working for Phoenix K-9 meant she could use a source with a pulse on criminal and underground activities in the city. She'd opened up communications with him, and he'd proved useful again. Especially with the intel he'd provided that helped them catch the bomber terrorizing the Twin Cities.

But though he had Amalia's number, he'd only texted. A phone call had to mean this was something he wanted to guarantee she, and no one else, received.

"I have to take this." She turned toward the oversized armoire in the corner. "Hello?"

"*Quien es este?*"

She'd hoped to avoid saying another of her names with Michael in the room, but Ramone was being cautious, wanting to verify who she was. "Marita." Speaking only the name shouldn't make Michael assume she was saying that she was Marita.

"Verdugo is here."

Amalia's grip tightened on the phone. "Are you sure?"

"*Si*. I verify with more than one of my people. Someone hire him for job in the Cities."

"What job?"

"I don't know."

The possibilities sprinted through Amalia's mind. Would the arms trafficker have brought in an assassin as high-caliber and expensive as Verdugo? It would be a smart move. Then again, there could be any number of criminals in the Twin Cities area who might have brought him in for a different job. "Who hired him?"

"This I don't know, also. But I want to tell you he is here."

"Thanks. Keep me posted if you hear anything else."

"*Si*. Be careful, Marita."

"Trouble?" Michael's voice, different but familiar at the same time, beckoned her to turn around.

She could leave now. She'd accomplished what she needed to. Activating her radio earpiece, she moved toward the door. "I need to get to work."

Raksa emitted a low rumble.

She jerked to see what he was looking at.

He faced the patio doors, his erect ears trained forward.

"Is he growling at me?" Michael watched the dog with raised eyebrows.

"What is it, boy?"

A bark burst from Raksa's deep chest, and he lunged toward the doors, hitting the end of the leash. He barked and snarled as he pulled hard.

"Get down!" She released the leash as she ran for Michael and threw herself into his torso.

A suppressed gunshot sounded.

Glass splintered as they hit the floor.

A K-9 protection team. An assassin. Only one can survive.

An assassin is on the loose in the Twin Cities, aiming to kill FBI witnesses the Phoenix K-9 Security and Detection Agency is hired to protect. Rogue CIA agent Amalia Pérez and her protection K-9 must get the edge on this deadly opponent before he kills her childhood best friend—the only man who knows her true identity.

Investigative journalist Michael Barrett can't believe his eyes when the woman he's spent years searching for walks back into his life. But he soon fears the woman he loved is lost forever beneath the secrets Amalia wears like armor.

As the assassin closes in, Amalia will risk anything to keep Michael safe—anything except believing in the God he trusts. When the layers of deception become as dangerous as bullets, can Amalia and Michael uncover the truth in time to stop the assassin from completing his lethal mission?

Shop *Covert Danger* at
CovertDanger.com

She never invites visitors. But visitors sometimes invite themselves.

When a winter storm brings more than snow, May Denver is forced to flee from her home and fight for her life. Can she trust an unwanted neighbor and risk her greatest fear in order to survive?

GRAB THIS ROMANTIC SUSPENSE STORY FOR FREE
WHEN YOU SIGN UP FOR JERUSHA'S NEWSLETTER
www.FearWarriorSuspense.com

Shop the *Guardians Unleashed Series*
at
JerushaStore.com

ABOUT JERUSHA

Jerusha Agen imagines danger around every corner, but knows God is there, too. So naturally, she writes romantic suspense infused with the hope of salvation in Jesus Christ.

Jerusha loves to hang out with her big furry dogs and little furry cats, often while reading or watching movies.

Find more of Jerusha's thrilling, fear-fighting stories at www.JerushaAgen.com.

f facebook.com/JerushaAgenAuthor

instagram.com/jerushaagen